"Kincaid . . .   to me," Jessica pleaded, laying her hand on his forearm. "I . . . I admit there is some kind of mild attraction between us, but . . ."

"Mild attraction! Good God, woman!" He grabbed her arms and pulled her against him. "I think you're just afraid. Of this." His lips moved quickly and firmly to hers. His hands ran over her shoulders and down her back, pressing her nearer.

She gasped and tried to push him away. But he grabbed her hand and placed it on his chest.

"Put your arms around my neck," he urged. "Look at me."

Against her better judgment, she responded and stared into his eyes.

"God, Jess," he murmured roughly, "I'm in agony with wanting you."

Scoundrel's Captive

JoAnn De Lazzari

AVON BOOKS ◆ NEW YORK

SCOUNDREL'S CAPTIVE is an original publication of Avon Books. This work has never before appeared in book form. This work is a novel. Any similarity to actual persons or events is purely coincidental.

AVON BOOKS
A division of
The Hearst Corporation
1350 Avenue of the Americas
New York, New York 10019

To Thomas—my husband, my lover, my friend—
You really are the wind beneath my wings.

Chapter 1

"You just can't go!" Bonnie insisted as her cousin continued to pack. "Mama said it's a terrible place!"

"I've decided to go and I will!" Jessica stated emphatically.

Her decision had been reached a week before as she'd sorted through her mother's personal things. Jennifer Langley had been a good mother and her friend, but she'd never talked about Jessica's father. He had been just a vague image in Jessica's mind that had faded with the years and she probably would have been content to leave it at that, but that was before she found her mother's diary. With it Jeffrey Morgan came to life. Her mother had died with all her secrets, even the fact she had taken her maiden name when she fled the wilderness, yet she had set it all down on finely written pages for her daughter to read upon her death.

Jeffrey Morgan had left his wilderness home in '63 to join the Union army. He'd come from the Wyoming Territory with plans to catch an eastbound train, but he never ventured farther than St. Louis, and a beautiful young girl. When fate brought together the high-spirited banker's daughter and the handsome mountain man, there was only one possible ending. Her quest for adventure set her imagination in high gear as Jeff Morgan spun his tales of wild mountains, untamed wilderness, and enticing excitement; her beauty and grace trapped and claimed his heart. She could not resist him when he asked her to share his life. Against her parents' will, she married him and journeyed with him to his homeland.

Their life was idyllic until she discovered she was with child. They had traveled together, explored and discovered the majesty of the land and a passionate love, but the arrival of a son dimmed their passions and restricted their freedom. Not wanting to let Jennifer return home, Morgan settled a small patch of land with hopes of building an empire for his family, but the fates were not with him. The death of their son and the birth of a daughter took their toll. Hardships pressed them as their ranch was slow to materialize. With the end of the war, supplies were scarce and merely surviving became a struggle. The dreams of adventure had become the reality of living.

Jennifer began to press her husband to abandon the wilderness for civilization. She played on his love for his three-year-old daughter, pleading with him to return to St. Louis, but he refused. His child would be better off in Wyoming. He was a man of the wilderness and she was destined to be, too. They would not leave, but leave she did.

Bonnie continued to try and persuade Jessica to stay. "Father will stop you! I'll beg him to!"

Tired of arguing the same point, Jessica threw one last item into her suitcase and spun around. "Listen, Bonnie, and listen well, for I shall not discuss it again. I am eighteen years old and responsible for myself. Uncle Walter understands why I must go and has offered his blessings. I love all of you, but I can't stay here anymore. I'm going to Wyoming! I leave tomorrow and that's final. Don't interfere!"

As Bonnie's lips began to tremble Jessica was sorry for her outburst. Sitting beside her dear cousin she softened her words. "I'm sorry, Bonnie. It's not that

I'm angry with you, I'm just anxious. I'm facing something I don't know and it has me a little nervous, but I have to find my father. I have to go to Windy Creek and see him. I know he's there, waiting. Mama wrote that he swore he'd never leave the ranch until she returned. With Mama dead—'' She swallowed to hold back the tears. ''—it has to be me. Don't you understand? I want to know him.''

Bonnie saw the pain on Jessica's face, thinking that, despite her grief, her cousin was the most beautiful girl she had ever seen. Her chestnut hair was drawn into a thick braid that was wound into a coil at her neck. With her hair drawn back, her green eyes took on an exotic appearance. The smile that would light her face in happier times revealed straight white teeth and set dimples deep in her cheeks. Even in her black crepe gown her complexion was one of cream. Being of a plumper form like her father, Bonnie thought she should be jealous of the long, lithe limbs of her cousin, but the genuine affection between them eradicated any envy.

''I know, Jessica, and I do understand.'' Bonnie threw her arms about her. ''It's just that I'll miss you so much!''

''It won't be forever, Bonnie.'' Jessica sniffed sadly, hating to give up the past but needing to face the future. ''We'll see each other again. I know we will!''

March had certainly come in like a lion, Jessica thought as she stood with the three people who were the only family she knew. She had chosen a black gabardine suit for her journey and would not have worn a coat but for Aunt Clara's insistence. As she stood in the dusty station, she was glad she had. Outside the wind blew a mixture of rain and snow, and inside, the coal-burning stove gave off little warmth.

Uncle Walter checked his pocket watch and proclaimed the train to be on time as its whistle sounded. As the stationmaster announced its arrival, Aunt Clara began to fuss over Jessica. She touched the upward curve of her black hat and set it slightly to one side, adjusting the sweeping white feather. Mumbling about how Jessica looked so like her dear sister, she handed her extra handkerchiefs and used one to daub the tears from her own eyes. Aunt Clara always fidgeted when she was under pressure. Uncle Walter ignored his wife's nervous behavior and made sure Jessica had her bank draft and cash supply pinned in her clothing, and that her ticket was ready.

All in all, it was only Bonnie who revealed her true feelings. She openly cried and hugged her cousin. She would deeply miss her best friend. "Take care, Jess. Write me all about your trip and the ranch and everything!"

Uncle Walter went off to ensure that her luggage was aboard; Aunt Clara remained for hugs and kisses, and final instructions.

"Don't speak to strangers and watch where you stay in . . . in . . . oh—" She waved a hand forgetfully. "—that town you're going to."

"Yes, dear." Jessica smiled.

"And remember, those cowboys aren't used to being around a proper lady." She leaned close for effect. "They're used to a . . . a looser female," she whispered.

"I'll be careful, Aunt Clara. I promise." She hugged her aunt and exchanged a tolerant smile with Bonnie.

They moved to the platform at Uncle Walter's signal. Steam rolled from beneath the wheels into the cold air and Jessica trembled, feeling a combination of excitement and fear. The final farewells were shared, Uncle Walter handed Jessica her small traveling bag, and she began to step aboard.

"Be careful of savages!" Aunt Clara called in a final warning.

Jessica laughed, nodded her head, and waved as

the porter escorted her to a seat, stowing her satchel under the one beside hers. She looked out the steamy window and wondered if this was how her mother had felt when she left St. Louis all those years before. The anticipation, the hopes coupled with fear welled up in her. Yes, it would have been the same, but Jessica was not a St. Louis debutante looking for adventure. She was part that and part child of the wilderness. Her father's blood flowed through her veins and she was determined to join him, to learn about him and his dreams. It was her heritage, but there was also that hidden side of herself she had to discover. Somehow she knew she would find it at Windy Creek, beside the icy springs, beneath the sky-high mountains.

Taking a deep breath, she realized she was no longer frightened. This was her destiny, and she smiled to herself as she felt the wheels begin to turn on their westward journey.

Chapter 2

Civilization, as Jessica knew it, slipped away in a matter of hours. The paved roads and street-lights became suburbs, then rural farms, but the real changes began as the train left Missouri and edged its way through the fertile plains of Kansas and Nebraska. As far as she could see the land undulated in pale, snow-dusted grasses. Occasionally a chimney in the distance would spew smoke, filling her with a sense of isolation.

It seemed colder on these wintry-colored plains. Snow drifted across the land like a sheer curtain blowing in the wind. Despite the shelter of the car and the small stove kept burning for the comfort of the passengers, Jessica found herself bundled in her shawl and still chilled. Oh, what she would give for a soft, warm bed away from the whistling wind.

The train began to reduce its speed in the middle of nowhere. When it had inched to a stop, Jessica looked about from her seat and tried to determine why. The snow was falling lightly, a mere dusting, and without a tree in sight, she could think of no cause for the delay.

A call from the conductor for men to help remove a drift from the train's path relieved her. They were in no peril. It was simply an inconvenience. Four of the five other people sharing her car rose and donned heavy coats to follow the trainman to the obstacle. The remaining passenger, a woman of indeterminable age, moved to the end of the car to peek out and estimate the duration of their stop.

"Shouldn't take long," she offered as she returned to her seat. "It's a small one."

Stranger or not, after two days of silence, Jessica needed someone to talk to. "Have you traveled this route before?"

"Lordy, yes. I'm almost a regular." She laughed. "My daughter lives in Kansas City and I visit her at least once a year. Least now I do. Before the train got to Cheyenne in '67 I could only make it every couple of years, but it was a harder trip then, even if I was younger."

"Is Cheyenne in the Wyoming Territory?" Jessica's interest perked at the affirmative nod she received. "I'm going there, too! Is it much further?"

"No . . ." She looked about outside and Jessica marveled that she could tell from a terrain that looked the same to her mile after mile. "About eight hours, I'd say. By the way, my name's Mary Smithers." She offered a strong, firm hand.

"Jessica Langley," Jess responded.

Mary settled into the seat beside Jessica, uninvited, but her natural friendliness was more than welcome. "So, you're headin' to Cheyenne, huh?"

"Not exactly," Jessica replied. "I'm going to Lander and I'm certainly glad this trip is almost over."

"Lander!" Mary laughed. "Honey, you got over three hundred miles to go after Cheyenne to get that far."

"Three hundred miles! But—"

"Wyoming ain't like the East," Mary sympathetically educated her young companion. "It's a big sprawling land, growing in all directions. Ain't nothin' to ride a whole day and never see another human bein', and towns can easily be a day or more apart." She watched the awe settle on Jessica's face. "You got somebody waitin' for ya?" At a shake of her head, Mary went on. "Look, maybe you ought ta get off in Cheyenne and buy a return ticket."

"I can't do that," Jessica said softly. "I have to find my father, and his ranch is near Lander." Taking a deep breath, she straightened her shoulders and spoke more firmly. "I'm going to Lander. It's where I belong."

Mary smiled. "Well, you're a bit skinny and you ain't got no wilderness learnin', but ya sure got spunk." Slapping a knee, she laughed. "Damned if I don't think you'll do it!"

Mary predicted their arrival in Cheyenne to within half an hour. Saying good-bye was harder than Jessica would have thought for such a short acquaintance, but the fleeting hours they had spent together were both enjoyable and educational. She now had a better picture of what was to come, and an itinerary. She would leave the train at Green River, and coach to Farson then Lander. From there she could hire a guide to find her father. She had planned it all so well. Nothing could stop her now, she thought as she clutched her notes.

The snow stopped as dawn broke. Jessica used the primitive facilities on the train for washing and straightening her clothing as well as she could. Her suit was badly wrinkled but the dark color hid most of the damage from the casual gaze. As she returned to her seat, she gasped at the unexpected vista. Mountains! The Laramie Mountains spread north of the track and, in her ignorance, she didn't realize that these snowy hills were the infant children of those ahead.

A small herd of large furry cattle caught her eye and offered the only break in the landscape of rolling hills and prairies from the time she departed Laramie until dark. The cattle turned out to be buffalo and she would have felt foolish indeed if she had spoken to anyone before overhearing two other passengers discussing their dwindling state.

Aunt Clara need not have worried about strangers though. Her cool facade held everyone but Mary at bay. Attempts at conversation were met with chilly, curt answers that let intruders know she was not interested in making small talk *or* new acquaintances.

Jessica felt as if she had ridden the train all her life. Her back ached and attempts at finding a comfortable position to sit were fruitless. She was exhausted, dirty, lonely, and nearly ready to leave the train at its next stop for a night's sleep when she heard the call for Green River and knew she was finished with the first part of her journey.

The sizes of the towns reduced proportionately with the miles traveled west, but Green River broke the pattern and was larger than she had anticipated. Arriving in the middle of the night, Jessica could make out little of what it had to offer but the stationmaster informed her of a reasonably priced hotel and had her bags, along with herself, delivered there. She had to cross a dirt street of frozen ruts and puddles to a wooden sidewalk alongside the buildings. The clatter of her heels didn't cover the din of a well-lit building on the opposite side of the street. A large, weathered sign was placed above the doors and in the faint light she could just make out that it was a saloon. It was obvious to Jessica, even in her exhausted state, that much of the town's male population was enjoying whatever it had to offer.

The lad who guided her opened a door and motioned for her to enter the hotel. The lobby was small and neat. It was just past two in the morning but the sign on the wall said ring any time, so Jessica went over to the bell on the desk and did so without hesitation. A broken night's sleep for the proprietor meant little compared to the five nights of restless discomfort she had endured to come this far.

It was a matter of minutes before a man came from behind a curtained door, pulling suspenders over

his shoulders and grumbling. He assigned her a
room and told her it would cost three times the regular rate for a bath if she wanted one at this hour.
Hoping to deter her, the manager sighed as she
gladly paid the price. There was no way she was
going to climb into a clean bed with five days' soot
and grime clinging to her.

She was shown to a room that unfortunately over-
looked the street. Raucous laughter and loud piano
music drifted through the thin walls, but Jessica
knew she was tired enough to ignore it. Besides, she
dared not press the manager again. He was not too
happy about lugging in a tub and enough water to
fill it. Any other problems or complaints might make
him change his mind.

Opening a suitcase, Jessica located a soft, clean
nightgown and robe, and laid them on the bed. She
found sufficient towels near a basin and a small bar
of scented soap. As the tub and water arrived, she
began to prepare her weary body for a soaking.

Leaning back against the door she had just closed,
she stared at the scant steam rising from the dented
brass tub. The water wasn't very hot but it would
be wonderful nonetheless. Moving to the bed, she
removed her hat and jacket, tossing them on a chair.
She sat on the soft mattress and lifted her skirt to
slip off her dusty shoes, garters, and hose. Standing
and looking at the water, she unfastened her skirt
and blouse, piling them with her jacket for future
laundering. She pulled the pins from her hair and
uncoiled it, shaking it free and running her fingers
through the mass.

Taking a deep breath, she removed her camisole,
bloomers, and underslip, and stepped into the warm
water. Sighing, she leaned back and spent a moment enjoying the muscle-easing warmth. It was
well worth the extra money it had cost her to pur-
chase such luxury. Relaxed, she began to lather her
hair. Ducking to rinse it, she came up, squeezed the
excess water from it, and started to bathe. As she

straightened a slender leg to lather, she could hear an argument in the hallway. Someone was shouting. The sound of a slap, followed by a thud, made her stiffen. There was indeed a fight going on and the melee was moving toward her door.

A resounding crack brought her door slamming back against the wall, the molding torn from its frame. She was too stunned to scream as a large blur flew past her, hit the bed, and brought it crashing to the floor. In an instant, another, larger figure appeared, laughing, in the doorway.

"Jack, you bastard! You're gonna cost me plenty in damages this time," he roared as he entered the room, grabbed the collar of the undoubtedly unconscious man on the bed, and pulled him to ride over his shoulder. He left as he entered, laughing and without saying a word to Jessica.

Anger began to replace shock as Jessica shivered from the draft entering her room. Disregarding the opened portal, she raised herself out of the tub and grabbed her robe. She was wrapping a towel about her wet head as the tall, dark stranger returned. He surveyed the damage with a whistle, raked his fingers through his hair, and began to chuckle.

"Made a hell of a mess, didn't we?"

"Mess? *Mess!* Why, you swaggering drunk!" Finding her tongue she began to rail at the intruder. "How dare you? You . . . you oaf!"

As he turned his eyes from the broken door to the screaming, scantily clad woman, his grin widened. Using her robe to cover her wet body had been a mistake. The moisture gripped the thin material of the wrapper, outlining not only the shape of her body, but the details as well. The cool air hardened her nipples and her deep, angry breaths strained her breasts against the already clinging fabric.

In her fury Jessica didn't notice the man's perusal. "What kind of a town is this where men brawl like animals in a decent establishment? Who's going to

clean up this mess? Oh, just get out!'' she yelled.
''I'll take care of it myself!''

Now that she had his full attention, she was sorry.
His eyes began to move over her slowly, assessing
and clearly liking what he saw. ''I'd apologize,
ma'am, but I'm not sorry. Nope—'' He looked at her
through long, dark lashes. ''—I'm not one bit sorry.''

Her seething rage gave way to a growing sense of
uneasiness. This man towered over her as he stood
with his hands on his hips and his legs spread in a
wide stance. She knew that part of the height difference was the result of her bare feet and his booted
ones but she knew at least eight inches was natural.
He had to be almost four inches over six feet. Coal-
black hair fell across his deeply tanned brow and the
eyes of a cat held her immobile. They had been hazel a moment ago, she knew it, but now they were
a deep brown and a warning went off inside of her.

He began to move slowly toward her as though
stalking prey, his smile fading. She backed up until
her ankle struck the fallen bed frame and she would
have tumbled to the floor if he hadn't caught her.
He drew her quickly into his arms, pushing the
towel from her head. Her chestnut hair was wet but
he held one long tress between his fingers.

''Don't touch me! Keep you hands to yourself, you
. . . you animal!'' She spoke between clenched
teeth.

''Don't be so fast to judge a man by the way he
lets off steam,'' he said gently. ''This is a hard land.
We work hard, we play hard, and . . .'' His hands
began to slide up and down her back, ''. . . we love
hard.''

His lips began to descend toward hers but she
mustn't let him kiss her! She had to pull away before it was too late. She tried to push at his chest,
but it merely seemed to heighten his desires as her
fumbling managed to part the fabric of his silken
shirt.

A picture she'd seen once of a fancy gambler

flashed in her mind as his hand slid over her shoulder to her throat. He caressed the soft, sensitive skin beneath her ear as his mouth gently touched the corners of hers.

"Don't do that!" she cried.

"Why?" He pressed another kiss to the side of her mouth.

"I don't know who you think you are, but—" The stranger didn't allow her to finish. He stopped teasing her with little kisses and brought his lips firmly down on hers. Her lips parted in a horrified gasp as his tongue ran back and forth across their moist surface, and she held her breath indignantly as its warmth penetrated her mouth. She hesitated, stunned for a moment that this could be happening. But then she began to push with all of her strength at the wide shoulders that seemed to dominate her.

"Damn! Did I do this?" a deep voice asked.

Startled from their embrace by the return of the other man, Jessica tried to wrench herself free—her dignity ruffled—but the stranger tightened his arms to hold her a moment longer.

"Gee, I'm sorry, Steve," the other man said, seeing his friend had lost his advantage with the indignant lady. "I didn't know—"

"You have a hell of a knack for showing up at the wrong time, Jack." Frustration edged his voice as the woman stepped clear of him.

"Yeah, well, if everything's okay here, I'll . . . I'll be goin' back downstairs. I'll see you down there," he said, backing out quickly.

"You just better go with him!" Jess snapped. The man she knew only as Steve turned to see that a determined resolve filled the green-eyed temptress before him.

"Perhaps you're right." He smiled, creases etching his cheeks. His hand came up to cup her chin. "We'll finish this another time, when we won't be interrupted."

Before she could hurl a denial, he turned, gave

her a wink and a crooked grin, and pulled the battered door closed behind him. It would need something to keep it braced shut, she thought logically, and slid a chair beneath the knob. Relieved to be rid of the arrogant oaf she walked to the bed and removed her robe. Her image was reflected in the mirror across the room, catching her attention. She looked different, her face was flushed and her lips looked slightly bruised. The nerve of that man! she thought angrily as she touched her lips. What if his friend hadn't returned? What would he have done to her if she hadn't been able to fight him off?

Trying to calm herself down, she donned her warm gown, pushed the headboard off the mattress, and blew out the lamp. She lay down on the bed and stared at the ceiling. She wouldn't think about the stranger, the strange exciting way he had made her feel or his parting words to her. She was leaving tomorrow and she'd never see him again. But the image of him—big and muscular with coal-black hair—stayed with her until she fell into the oblivion of sleep.

There was little to hold her attention as the coach jostled along its dusty path. Jessica leaned her head back and wondered how she could have been so fortunate as to arrive in Green River in time to catch a coach the next morning. She was so afraid of meeting the stranger again, she would have been tempted to hire a carriage and try it alone rather than come face-to-face with the man who had invaded her room last night.

Thoughts of the stark white of his ruffled shirt spanning his wide chest and broad shoulders filled her mind. Black trousers had ridden low on his slender hips and tapered down his long legs, but it was his eyes she would remember forever, even if she never saw them again. They had darkened with his thoughts and she was frightened by the strange sensations his gaze and his bold caresses had stirred in

her. It annoyed her too that she had noticed so much
about him in so little time.

Shaking away thoughts of the previous night, Jessica began to take a forced interest in the other four
occupants within the confines of the small vehicle.
Since the outset of the coach ride her body had been
suffering bruises, thanks to the bumpy road and the
very slender lady on her right. With each rut, a bony
elbow found its mark in her ribs. There would have
been enough room for everyone to sit comfortably
had the woman's rotund husband not taken more
than his share of the seat. Jessica smothered a
chuckle when she thought how appropriately the
two were matched.

Opposite her sat a tall, rangy cowboy. His hat was
pulled over his eyes and he appeared to have slept
through the whole journey. The sight of a pistol
strapped to his thigh unnerved her at first, but perhaps it was wise to carry a gun in this savage land.
If she had had one the night before, she would have
taught that stranger a thing or two, she thought.

The last passenger was a middle-aged woman
dressed in a satin gown of yellow and green stripes.
From her bustle hung bright pink ribbons. Her full
figure did not complement the gathering of a bustle,
and the layers of ruffles over her large breasts only
emphasized the roundness of her shape. A small
green hat sat forward on her strawberry-blonde hair
and a deep pink ostrich plume swept back past the
crown. Her face was heavily rouged and her nails
and lips sported a bright red coloring. Jessica had
heard her referred to as "Roxy" at the stage depot
and the familiar way she bantered with the men led
Jess to suspect she might be one of the women her
aunt had warned her about.

Not one to sit in judgment on another, Jessica
smiled warmly when their eyes met. Roxy seemed
to relax a bit then and even began to chat after her
first endeavor met with a friendly response. When
she discovered Jessica was from St. Louis, she

wanted to know all about the latest fashions. Not
being particularly fascinated with clothing, Jess drew
on all her social experiences to enhance her descrip-
tions and please her listener.

"Where ya headin,' honey?" Roxy finally asked
when silence threatened to end their conversation.

"Lander," Jessica replied.

"Why, ain't that a coincidence! That's where my
place is."

"Then . . . then perhaps you know Jeffrey Morgan? He has a ranch near there." Jessica held her
breath in hope.

"Yeah, sure, I know Jeff. He comes to my place
every now and then, but I wouldn't call Windy
Creek a ranch." She laughed. "What ya lookin' for
him for, if ya don't mind my askin'?"

"He's my father. I'm Jessica Lang . . . Langley
Morgan." Jess liked the sound of it. Jessica Morgan.
Jess Morgan. Yes, she'd go by that from now on.

"So, you're his kid. Small world." Roxy turned
to look out the window.

"Miss." Jessica tried to get her attention again.
"Miss Roxy." When the woman looked at her in
surprise Jessica explained how she knew her name.
"I heard the driver talking to you in Green River. I
hope you don't mind." A shrug gave Jessica the
courage to go on. "You said Windy Creek isn't much
of a ranch. Have you been there?"

"No, but I rode past it once on the way to a bar-
becue at Kincaid's," Roxy said. "He's your pa's
nearest neighbor. Anyway, I wouldn't have even
known it was Jeff's place except for a broken sign
hanging off the gate. I could see a weathered old
shack of a house with weeds growin' right to the
door. If smoke wasn't comin' out the chimney, I'd
have sworn it was deserted." Seeing the anguish on
Jessica's face, Roxy apologized. "Sorry, honey, but
you asked me."

"Thank you, Miss Roxy." Jess grew quiet. Perhaps it was better to know in advance. Had she

driven up to Windy Creek expecting a ranch, she
might have run back to St. Louis without even both-
ering to see her father. This way, she was prepared.
There would be no surprises.

It was two days before they reached South Pass
City, where they spent the night in a way station.
The three women shared a small room filled with
cots and bedrolls. While Roxy snored blissfully, Jess
found it difficult to sleep. Thoughts of her father and
Windy Creek spun through her head. She began to
drift off with visions of her youth fading into a heavy
mist. She jerked herself awake when a tall, dark
stranger moved out of the mist, a crooked grin on
his lips as he said, "Another time." After struggling
for hours to keep her mind blank, she finally slept
until a heavy knock at the door brought her awake.

"Fifteen minutes to breakfast, ladies!"

Jessica moaned and stirred from her cot. She felt
as if she had had no sleep at all. Roxy led her to a
private place outside where they could wash up.
Yawning, she followed, not too anxious to start the
day. The cold water in the basin helped clear her
groggy head and she stretched her aching muscles
in the damp, chill of the morning. Wrapping her
arms around herself for warmth, she turned to watch
the sun rising on the prairie and gasped at the pan-
orama that her eyes beheld.

Soft pink clouds covered the northwestern horizon. No, not clouds. Mountains! Giant sentinels of
the West had risen up from the plains. There had
been no warning. The rocky, barren landscape had
given no hint of the majestic cathedrals of time that
would appear.

"I've never seen anything so beautiful," she
whispered. It seemed sacrilegious to speak of them
in a normal voice.

"Yeah, I know how you feel." Roxy joined her to
marvel at the magnificent mountains. "I never tire
of lookin' at them." She finished drying her hands

and face. "Come on, they don't wait for slow-pokes."

The Wind River Range remained on her left all the way to Lander. The journey had been worth any inconvenience just to see the vista that held her spellbound for hours. Occasionally, her attention was drawn to a small herd of animals she was told were antelope. They were close enough to the coach to raise their heads and watch with cautious interest. A flash of a white tail would signal their departure and they would spring off in search of a more private dining room.

Heaven must surely be in this land, she thought. How could her mother, having lived here, chosen the noisy, cold life of a city over the panoramic magnificence that held her breathless.

Chapter 3

I t was again night when Jessica entered the town of Lander. Roxy pointed out a small hotel and told her she could get a room—but no bath until morning. Seeing Jessica's despair, she hesitated before offering an alternative.

"Look, honey, now don't go gettin' me wrong, but you could stay with me at my place. You can get some food, a bath, and a bed in my private place." She saw the young woman's doubt. "Nobody would bother you, I promise. It's just that, well, you've been real nice to me. Not many ladies even bother to look my way and . . . and you make me feel kind of good."

Jessica liked Roxy. There was a friendly warmth about her, and an air of honesty. It was late and she was in a strange place where the only familiar face belonged to the older woman. "Thank you, Roxy. I truly appreciate your offer."

With a relieved sigh, Roxy led Jessica to her place of business and residence. Instead of marching through the double swinging doors, they entered an alley on the side of the building. A set of stairs led up to a door that was guarded by a giant of a man. He tipped his hat to Roxy; she smiled and waved.

"Business area," Roxy cast over her shoulder.

Jessica was glad of the dark as the warmth of her face told her she was blushing. Not knowing what she expected, she was pleasantly surprised as Roxy lit a lamp in the small parlor. She could be standing in a small, neat house in St. Louis. Tasteful furniture graced the room. Dimity curtains hung at the small windows and a frail china service filled a cabinet at one end of the room.

"It's lovely!"

"Thank you, Jess. Look around, " she said as she removed her hat. "I'll go see to a couple of baths and order us a meal. I'll show you your room when I get back."

Fingering the china and admiring the silver service on a buffet in a corner, Jessica thought Roxy was an enigma, indeed. She returned in a few minutes and announced their baths and their dinner would be ready soon.

"Come on, I'll show you where you can sleep. Sam's gone to get your cases. He'll be right back."

Jessica's room was behind one of the doors lining the hallway off the parlor. Roxy pointed out the locked door at the end as the entrance to the saloon, and assured her she had the only key. A third door was Roxy's room and the last, a kitchen, laundry, and storage room, were both similarly locked.

"Oh, Roxy! It's simply beautiful," Jessica told her. Several shades of yellow reflected back from the glow of the lamp Roxy carried. The furnishings were small, as if for a child. The curtains and quilt were all ruffles and lace. A rich luster shone from the dark wood furniture and it was easy to see that loving hands tended it. Jessica noticed a trembling smile on Roxy's face. "Roxy, what is it? What's wrong?"

"Nothing's wrong. It's just . . . this is my daughter's room." Roxy lovingly touched a small figurine. "She lives in Boston with my sister. She's s-sixteen and a pretty little thing." Tears began to streak her cheeks.

"Don't." Jessica gently touched the arm holding the lamp and transferred the lamp to a small table. "Don't talk about it if it hurts."

Roxy sighed and sat on the bed, her eyes filled with a plea for Jessica to listen. "I . . . I want you to know. You may not want to stay after you hear." Jessica stood quietly near the door and nodded. Taking a deep breath, Roxy told her story. "I was fifteen when I met Phillip Santini. He was a gambler passing through the small town in Virginia where I was born. Oh, he was handsome and dashing, and I looked older than I was. Pa's store was suddenly very dull and . . . and when Phillip asked me to go with him, promising me the world, I went. Silly, huh?"

Jessica sat beside her. "Not so silly, Roxy. My mother ran away with my father against the wishes of her parents. What you did was no different."

Roxy smiled sadly. "But she married her man, I never did. Anyway . . ." She sighed. ". . . five years later, after winning and losing several fortunes, he brought me here and bought this place. It was just gamblin' and drinkin' then. I was a dealer, least till I got with child and it was noticeable. After that he found excuses for me not to be around the place." Brightening a bit, she smiled slightly. "He did fix this place up for me though, I'll give him that, but he started chasing other skirts as my time came near. I didn't mind by then. I had my baby to get ready for." She stopped talking and looked pensive for a moment. "Well, Phillip managed to get a nice girl in trouble and her brothers came gunnin' for him. It was a fair fight but he was killed. That night Becky was born. Kind of like God was taking away a mistake and givin' a clean new life a chance."

She rose and paced the room, caressing a trinket here and there. "I raised her myself until she was five. I'd . . . I'd had to expand what was offered here to make enough money to save for her future. I wanted her raised like a lady, like you."

Sensing Roxy's story had come to an end for the moment, Jessica's eyes shone with unshed tears.

"Thank you for telling me, Roxy, but I'm not judging you."

"I know, honey, but I want us to be friends and that means you have to know."

Jessica's bags arrived at that moment and Sam turned out to be an old, silver-haired black man. He smiled and nodded his head when Jessica thanked him.

"No trouble, miss. Water's ready, Miss Roxy, if'n ya want a bath now."

"Thanks, Sam. We'll be right along." Turning to Jessica she added, "Get your things ready, honey. I've got the only bathhouse in town and it's closed at night for my use." She headed out the door.

"Roxy!"

She turned back.

"That's how you knew I couldn't get a bath tonight, isn't it?" Jessica smiled. At the shake of a head she added, "Roxy, you're quite a lady."

"Thanks, Jess," she returned with a smile.

Sam stood beside the buckboard and waited for Jessica.

"I can't thank you enough, Roxy. You've shared your home and hospitality with a stranger." She held the other woman's hands. "What better way to start a friendship?"

In the cold light of day, with the makeup washed away, Roxy looked older than her thirty-six years. Her years of sadness and hard living had left their mark, but she was standing there smiling happily.

"I should be thankin' you. You're some kind of special lady, Jess Morgan. Your pa's gonna be right proud of you."

Embracing quickly, they promised to see each other soon and Jessica climbed into the wagon. As she headed for Windy Creek, she waved over her shoulder at Roxy.

She paid close attention to the town of Lander. The empty dirt streets were a mass of miniature dust storms as horse and wagons found its length. The buildings had high, square fronts designating their purpose—hardware, hotel, saloon, general store, and the like. What struck her as amusing was the true roof of each building was considerably lower in most cases than the facade. A covered walkway stretched from end to end of each building only to open in the alleyways and begin again at the start of the next.

It was a busy town. Ladies in homespun bustled about doing their shopping while cowboys either rode in and out or lounged about at pillar and post.

The one thing that Jessica didn't notice was the curious and appreciative glances cast her way. Sitting perched upon the wagon seat, she was like a portrait of an unknown beauty, one that could be admired, but not touched. Her very stylish suit was a deep mauve. The bustle was unadorned and the short jacket well-fitted. A pale lavender blouse rose high on her throat and a cameo was set in the center. Her hat offered no protection from the weak winter sun and covered little of the chestnut coil at her neck.

Conjectures would begin the moment she was out of sight. She'd come out of Roxy's place. Maybe she was a new girl. The wagon had gone northwest, she might be going out to the K-D, a friend of Kincaid's. At any rate, they could agree on one thing: she was right good to look at.

The early morning sun felt good on her back. She asked Sam if her father's ranch was in the mountains. They seemed so close, but he assured her they were some thirty miles from the taller peaks. There was a feeling of solitude within her as she gazed at the rugged, snow-packed range, and a sense of freedom, too, but there was also a humbling of the spirit. She was so small, so insignificant in nature's design. Looking at the magnificent land around her, she felt as if she were confronting her heritage, the half she had come looking for. No matter what happened at Windy Creek, her intuition told her she would remain. It had been ordained eighteen years before by the father she didn't even know.

"See that smoke yonder?" Sam pointed out a rising column of thin gray. She nodded. "That's yer pa's place. We'll be there in a few minutes."

Breathlessly she watched as the patch of smoke became a chimney then the outline of a house. Roxy had been all too right. It did look deserted. The once-strong fence leading across the front of the property had fallen in some places and leaned so badly in others it could fall any time. The gate was propped against several remaining sections and a sign reading WINDY CREEK was just visible on a slanting post.

Wild grasses had reclaimed most of the lane leading to the house; only wheel marks designated where it was in parts. Jessica couldn't imagine her quiet, sophisticated mother ever having set foot there. The house was in worse condition. That it could stand at all surprised her. The windows were bare of covering. Two were broken in the one frame that graced the front of the house. The door was so weathered and warped, she couldn't see how it kept out the smallest of breezes. Weeds pushed their way through the missing boards of the small porch and one of the posts used to hold the roof above it was missing.

"Ya sure ya wants ta stay here, miss?" Sam asked.

For a fraction of time Jess was undecided, but she wanted to meet her father and get to know him. If this was where he lived, it was her home also. "Yes, Sam. I'm sure." She climbed down and stood looking about. The door was hanging open and she called out. "Jeffrey Morgan! Are you there?" There was no answer. "Sam, would you please put my cases on the . . . on the porch."

Hearing his affirmative reply, she went up to the shaky porch. Testing it with her foot, she stepped onto it and peeked inside the house. It wasn't dirty, it was filthy! The light that managed to get through the window reflected off dust motes and cobwebs. Trash and food scraps were scattered about a cooking area and laundry littered the few pieces of furniture the room contained. That any kin of hers could live like this disgusted her.

Sam poked his head through the doorway to tell her he was leaving. He paused to give her time to change her mind but she insisted she would stay and asked him to tell Roxy that she would be okay.

After Sam left she ventured farther into the hovel. A rodent scurried into a pile of wood and she squelched an impulse to scream. Smoke escaped from a loose pipe on a wood-burning stove and a blackened coffeepot was shoved to the back of it. The floorboards creaked as she crossed the room to a closed door. Its hinges were rusty and she had to press her shoulder to it to get it to squeak open.

"My God!" she cried, held motionless by the contents of the room. Furniture, crates, and trunks filled it. She had to brush cobwebs aside as she inched forward. Boards had been nailed across the window and very little light penetrated. She bent down beside one of the trunks and slowly opened it. Flatware! China! Linens yellowed with age! Falling to her knees she caressed the items lovingly. These were her mother's things, she knew without a doubt. Her father must have—

"What the hell's goin' on here? Who are you? What do you—"

Jessica gasped and spun about. The outline of a man filled the door and she drew her hand to her mouth.

"Jennifer!" He started toward her and stopped. "You're . . . you're not my Jenny!"

"No, I . . . I'm not." She stood and stepped toward him. "It's me, Papa, J-Jessica." She watched him begin to tremble. He reached out his hand to touch her face and pulled back, afraid she was not real.

"Jess," he breathed. "My . . . dearest . . . Jessica." He extended his hand again and she placed hers in it this time. He backed out of the dark room, pulling her gently with him.

They stood immobile, looking at each other. Her green eyes stared at the tall, thin man she had come to meet. His face was drawn and leathery, and long hair hung shaggily at his neck. Several days' stubble roughened his chin. His plaid shirt and patched pants were badly faded and his boots were scuffed and dusty. The hand she held was calloused but strong.

"How . . . ? Why . . . ? Oh, God, Jessica!" He opened his arms and embraced her.

"Papa!"

They didn't speak, they just held one another. So much time, so many questions, but for the time being it didn't matter.

Nervously her father pulled away. "I . . . I bet you're hungry." She said no and he offered her coffee. Needing something to occupy her hands she accepted the beverage. As he set about making it she cleared a spot at the table and found a second chair to accommodate them. There was an awkward silence. Jeff kept looking at his daughter. She was a mirage, a dream in his mind, and he would have forgotten to speak at all if she hadn't begun.

"Papa, I've come to stay with you." She had to tell him about her mother but she needed an opening.

Jeff smiled for a moment then grew serious. "You can't, honey. It would break Jennifer's heart to lose you, and I don't think she could ever be happy here." He turned away and began to putter over the coffeepot.

"Papa, sit down, please. I . . . I need to talk to you. I know having me just appear with no warning is a surprise but . . . please, let's talk."

He hesitated, then nodded and sat beside her. "You're right. I . . . I just can't believe you're here and you're all grown up." He placed his hand over hers. "You've grown to be very beautiful, honey. Why, if it wasn't for your eyes you could be your ma." She did indeed have his eyes, though his had paled with time and tears. "What brought you out here after all this time? Not that I'm not happy about it. God knows, it's been my dream since you left!" He smiled and Jessica saw a trace of the handsome young man her mother had fallen in love with.

"It's . . . it's Mother." There was no easy way to tell him. "Papa, she died two months ago."

His smile froze, then faded. "Dead," he whispered. He got up and walked to the door. Bracing his hands on the overhead frame, he leaned his head against his arm. Jessica didn't go to him. She let him come to grips with his wife's death. Rising, she poured out two cups of coffee and drank half of hers before he issued a deep sigh and spoke.

"How? How did she die?" he asked without turning around.

"Her heart. She d-died in her sleep. She hadn't been ill nor did she linger." Jessica began to cry softly.

"So young," she heard him say. "So very young. I . . . I thought she'd be well and happy in St. Louis. That's why I let her go." He turned back to the table, and sat down. He began to drink his coffee. "Did she . . . did she tell you about us?"

Jessica told him no. "I found her diary after she died. I remembered bits and her writing filled in the rest."

"She should have never come west. She never really got used to the hard way of life here. She tried, but it wasn't in her to be a pioneer. She wanted adventure but she paid a dear price for it. Did she tell you you had a brother?"

Jessica shook her head sadly, drying her tears with a lacy handkerchief. "No, but I read about him."

"He died his first winter. He would have been

two years older than you. I think that's why she was afraid to stay here after you were born."

"I wondered why she never talked about Windy Creek and why she left here. It must have hurt her very deeply."

"It did. She almost died from grief. She blamed the land. What was beautiful once became a cruel reminder of her loss. I couldn't convince her that David would have died even in St. Louis. He was born early and so small. I think his lungs must of been bad. He had trouble breathing right from the start."

Jessica could feel a bond forming with her father. They were talking as if they had shared the past years instead of having been apart. "Papa." She spoke to break the sorrowful mood. "Why do you still have all of Mother's things? You must have known she wouldn't come back."

"I knew. I just couldn't give them to anyone else, nor could I destroy them. The only thing I could do was store them away." He smiled warmly at her. "Maybe I hoped you'd come west someday and want to stay and use them to make a home here."

"That's exactly what I'm going to do." She squeezed his hand lovingly. "I'm here to stay, I swear it."

"Well, then." He cleared his throat. "I guess I better get your bags and," he looked about the house, suddenly realizing the decay the years of neglect had wrought. "I better see to cleaning up this place."

Jessica leaned toward him and threw her arms about his neck. "We'll do it together!"

Chapter 4

J essica pushed the gingham curtains back from the window. She laughed as her father pulled a face from the opposite side. "Lunch is almost ready," she called with a smile.

"I'll be just a few more minutes." He smiled in return.

She went to the stove and checked the beans and cornbread. Everything was done perfectly and she set the coffee on to perk. Her father was applying the last few feet of whitewash and she reviewed what they had accomplished in the last week.

With her father's help, she had pulled everything she could from the front room out the door. Her father had found a broom and a bucket, and between them they'd scrubbed and swept every inch of the house. As she cleaned and returned the items, she set her father the chores of repairing the porch and building a small lean-to for wood, declaring that the nesting rodents could nest outdoors!

For two days they labored to bring the house to a tolerable state. Jessica made a list of things they would need. A ride to town for paint and glass, along with supplies for the larder, gave her a chance to see Roxy. She excitedly told her of the treasures her father had saved and what they planned to do. Seed was being ordered and new roofing would be delivered by the end of the week.

Jess chuckled as she finished setting the table. Yes, it had been a busy week. She would begin to sort the furniture left by her mother the next day, and soon the storage room would be hers.

Her father came in shaking water from his hair. He'd fixed the well and set up a washstand beside the house. Things were looking better every day and, as the house was transformed from hovel to home, his appearance changed as well. He shaved daily and Jess trimmed his hair. They'd both bought new clothes during the trip to Lander. His wardrobe needed replenishing and hers needed Westernizing. Her fancy suits and blouses were packed away, to be replaced with serviceable skirts and plain shirts. A pair of boots and a riding culotte completed her needs, or so she thought until her father had laughingly placed a Stetson on her head. It hung beside the door on a hook, waiting for her to venture outside.

"I think I'll start a vegetable garden tomorrow," he said as he sat at the table. "We shouldn't be getting any more frosts."

"Okay, Papa, but don't forget about helping me empty the other room."

"You're a slave driver," he said, laughing, "and I love it. No, I won't forget."

They ate, quietly talking about what they were going to do with the rest of the ranch. Jess grew pensive. She chewed her lower lip as she stirred her coffee.

"What's troublin' you, Jessie?" he asked, taking the last bite of his lunch.

"I was wondering where we're going to get the money to fix up the rest of the ranch. Don't we need horses and cattle? I have some money left, but not much. Probably enough for supplies and immediate needs."

"I've been thinkin' about that, too. I don't want your money, Jess," he stated.

"It's not my money. It's our money for our home!" she said firmly.

"Okay, okay, but we need a lot more. A couple of hundred won't get us far." He rose for more coffee. "I have a friend who lives near here. I think he'll lend us what we need."

"You mean Kincaid?" she asked.

"Yeah, but how do you know about Kincaid?"

"I don't really, but Roxy said he was your nearest neighbor and a . . . a cattle baron she called him, so I guessed he'd be the one you meant."

"Well, you guessed right." He sat back down. "I knew his father and watched him grow up. He's a good man, fair and hardworking. He's built the K-D to what it is today from a place not much bigger than Windy Creek."

"When do you think we can see him?" She began to clear away the dishes.

"He's away now, but I left word with Chad to have him get in touch with me when he gets back."

"Who's Chad?"

"He's Kincaid's partner. Well, not really a full partner but a good friend who bought in early when Kincaid needed money. He's his foreman, and he and his wife live on the K-D so when Kincaid has to go to Cheyenne for the Cattlemen's Association, his ranch is in good hands. Besides, Kincaid likes to take off into the mountains sometimes for months at a time. He doesn't have to worry with Chad there."

"The K-D—do the initials stand for 'Kincaid'?"

"Kincaid and Duncan, that's Chad's last name."

Jessica nodded her head in understanding and took the dishes outside for washing. The sun was shining and the warmth felt good. She had linens on the line and they gleamed white in the sunlight. She was thankful to her mother for teaching her household chores. Maybe she knew her daughter was destined to need that knowledge.

* * *

Steve Kincaid stepped from the tub and wrapped a towel around his lean hips.

"It's not like you to go traipsing all over the countryside looking for a woman. Jesus, Steve, they flock to you in droves!" Chad laughed. "What's so damned special about this one?"

"Hell, I don't know!" Steve growled, applying lathered soap to his face. "I just need to find her." He began to shave.

"Sounds like you might be taken with her," Chad teased, lounging on the bed with his feet crossed and his head balanced on folded arms.

"Taken with her! I don't even know her whole name! She signed the damned register 'J. Langley'! I followed her to South Pass after losing two days trying to find her around Green River. The stationmaster remembered her but couldn't recall if she'd gone north to Lander or west to Boulder. Then I got held up in that damned pass with a spring slide." He finished shaving and wiped his face.

"So now you're off to Lander to see if she's there, right?" Chad rose and stretched as Steve pulled on his pants.

"Yeah." He slipped his shirt over his wide shoulders and began to button it. "Somebody must know her. I can't see someone forgetting her, not when I tell them about those eyes." His mind shifted as he finished dressing. Green eyes flashing anger, soft lips quivering beneath his. She'd started a fire in him, one that wouldn't be quenched until he found her again.

Chad laughed and pulled gently on his blond mustache. "I think I'd like to hear this whole story when you have a mind to tell me. There's more here than you're lettin' on. A chance meeting doesn't set a man's blood boiling, and yours is as hot as I've ever seen it."

A towel flew through the air and Chad ducked a fraction of a second too late as it slapped against his head. "Get out of here. Go see your poor wife and take out your evil thoughts on her, poor girl." Steve laughed and Chad grinned rakishly as he opened the door.

"Not a bad idea, but one last thing. Check with Roxy. She was in Green River about that time and, come to think of it, one of the hands mentioned some looker coming out of her place a few weeks back."

"Roxy's!" Steve was surprised. He would have sworn the girl had been genuinely frightened that night. "Thanks, Chad," he yelled as Chad closed the door with a wave.

"Kincaid! You rascal, how are you?" Roxy called, throwing her arms about Steve's neck and planting a big kiss on his cheek. "Sam said you'd come in. Why didn't you go see one of the girls 'stead of sittin' here like you was mad at the world! Or better yet, you could have come to see me!" She winked.

"I did want to see you, Roxy, and it might concern one of your girls."

He was serious, she thought. Usually he came in to drink a little, gamble some, and, occasionally, call on one of the girls. But not this time. He looked as if he had something on his mind and nothing would help until he cleared it. "What's wrong, love? I haven't seen you like this before."

"Is there someplace we can talk?" he asked.

"Sure." She nodded. "We can go back to my place." He followed her to the locked door and watched her produce a key from her pocket. Settling into a chair in her parlor a moment later, he accepted a whiskey, tossing his hat to a nearby chair.

"I'm looking for someone, Roxy, and you might know where she is."

Roxy lifted a brow. "Sounds serious, Steve. What do you want her for?"

"I don't really know." He laughed at her patent disbelief. "It's true! I met her a few weeks ago in Green River and to tell the truth, she's haunting me.

I thought if I could see her again, I could forget about her."

Roxy hid a smile. So, the mighty Kincaid wasn't immune after all, she thought. "What's her name?" she asked, sitting on the sofa.

"J. Langley."

"Jay! What kind of name is Jay for a girl?"

"Her name's not Jay, that's her initial. I don't know her name." He tossed off his whiskey and rose to get another. He related the story for the second time that day. "So if she didn't go to Boulder, she must have come here."

A picture of Jessica flashed in Roxy's mind. "What's this gal look like? Might be I've seen her."

"She's taller than most and her hair is dark brown with red shining through it. It looks kind of fiery in the lamplight." His thoughts drifted and he spoke more to himself than to her. "You would remember her if you've seen her. Her eyes . . ." He gazed off into his mental image of her.

"What about her eyes, Steve?" Roxy asked, sure now that he was talking about Jessica.

"What? Oh, yes. Her eyes are the color of new grass."

That cinched it—he was looking for Jess Morgan, all right, but the name . . . oh, yes! She remembered now. Jessica Langley Morgan.

"Well, do you know her or where she might be?" His stance seemed rigid and tense.

"I don't know a J. Langley," Roxy told him seriously. He sighed heavily, not knowing where to go now. "But I know the girl you're lookin' for." She smiled.

Steve scowled. "What the hell are you talking about, Roxy? Either you know her or you don't!"

"Take it easy, Steve. I know a girl who fits your description but her name isn't Langley. It's Morgan, Jessica Morgan."

"Morgan!" Steve couldn't believe his luck. "Is she related to Jeff?"

"Yes." She laughed. "She's his daughter. I suppose she used her ma's name until she saw Jeff." She related the part of the story she knew and watched Steve absorb every word. "They've been workin' real hard out at Windy Creek."

He'd heard Jeff Morgan wanted to see him about a loan for his ranch. It could be real interesting to see how desperately his daughter wanted him to have the money. Perhaps a private business deal, he thought, and smiled.

"You're up to somethin', Steve, and I warrant it's no good. She's a good girl and you better remember that!" Roxy warned. "He's your neighbor and she's my friend. Don't do anything to make me regret leadin' you to her," Roxy warned.

"Don't go getting motherly on me, Roxy. I won't hurt her, and I promise I'll never do anything to her she doesn't want me to do."

Not sure if that was a promise or a threat, Roxy had to be content that he wouldn't harm Jessie. She couldn't run the girl's life but she could keep an eye on the situation. She accompanied Steve to the bar and joined him in one drink before he left.

His mind was lighter and he whistled as he mounted his horse, turning it toward the K-D. As he passed Windy Creek, he tipped his hat and smiled. "Another time, Jessica Langley Morgan."

"I thought you'd be sleeping late this morning, Steve," Sarah said as she poured more coffee. "Chad told me you went to Roxy's last night."

"Jealous?" Steve winked at Chad.

"Oh, you!" She slapped his shoulder and sat back down to finish her breakfast. Steve joined them occasionally, usually when he wanted to talk to Chad in private. "At least you decided to get back to the ranch in time for your party. Wouldn't have surprised me if you didn't show up after asking everyone. It's just like you to throw a party and leave all the work to me," she teased.

"Now, Sarah, you know I love you and only you. Would I miss a chance to dance with you? Where else can I hold you in my arms right under your husband's nose and have no one the wiser?" He twisted an invisible mustache, enjoying his role as villain.

"You joke, Steve, but one of these days you're gonna find someone you really love, and I hope she leads you a merry chase."

"Chad, how did you get such a shrew for a wife?" Steve turned to his partner.

"Lucky, I guess." Chad smiled at Sarah. She was a small woman, short in stature and frail-looking, but she wasn't frail. She had worked beside him for six years without a complaint. Her long brown hair was pulled back and tied at her neck. Gentle brown eyes looked adoringly at him. She was all he could ask for. Yes, he had the right woman for him.

A light blush colored Sarah's cheeks and she lowered her lashes as Steve broke the loving exchange between his friends.

"What do you know about Jeff Morgan and his . . . his place? You mentioned he wants to see me."

"Yeah, he came over a few days ago to talk to you. Seems he's fixin' his place up. Looks good, too. I rode by there and it's all cleaned up." Chad chuckled. "Looks like he might have a woman there, by the laundry and stuff."

"I think the woman is his daughter," Steve informed them, not sure if he recalled a resemblance between her and Jeff. "She's supposed to be from back East."

"Well," Chad continued, "he wants to get his herd started up again and he needs capital. I think he wants to talk to you about a loan, Steve."

"Yeah, that's what I figured."

"Ya gonna lend it to him?"

Thinking about Jessica, he thought he just might. "Don't know. Send a rider to his place and tell him

I'll see him this morning." He rose to leave. "Thanks for breakfast, Sarah."

"Anytime, Steve."

He took his hat from a peg near the door and twisted it in his hands, pausing. "Might be nice if you called on Morgan's girl, Sarah. Maybe invite her to the party if you want." Without waiting for a reply, he left.

Sarah moved to stand behind Chad's chair. She caressed his shoulders absently. "Something seem strange to you, Chad?"

"Yeah, I have a feeling you've just been made Cupid, hon." At her perplexed look he patted her hand. "I think Steve's found his mystery woman and I'd bet a month of sleepin' in the barn that she's Morgan's daughter." He laughed and rose. He took his wife in his arms and she laid her head on his chest. "Well, neighbor, you gonna go callin'?"

She looked up into his sparkling eyes. "Um, in a little while." She snuggled against him and he smiled lovingly.

"Yeah, there's no hurry."

Jessica brushed the loose strands of her hair that had escaped her bun and tucked them behind her ear. A rider was approaching from the northwest and she was uneasy. She'd dreamt of the stranger again the night before. He had called to her in the dream and she was nervous. He couldn't know her name, she thought, but it didn't help to dream he did.

The dust cloud came closer and she could see it was a young woman. Since she was coming from the same direction her father had taken to see Kincaid, she might be his wife or daughter.

Picking up the laundry basket, Jessica went inside to remove her apron and recomb her hair. Finishing the task, she heard a knock at the door. She opened it to see a small, pretty woman in her early twenties.

"Hello! I'm Sarah Duncan from the K-D."

"Oh, hello! You must be Chad's wife!" Jess smiled. She made a beautiful picture standing in the door, the sun reflecting on her hair and in her eyes. Her white shirt was partially undone and a white lacy shift was just visible. Sarah felt a pang of jealousy toward the lovely woman she was looking at.

"Do . . . do you know Chad?" she asked, wondering why he hadn't mentioned one so beautiful.

"No, but Papa said he was Kincaid's partner and that he had a beautiful wife, so I assumed she had to be you."

Breathing easier, Sarah smiled. "Passable maybe, but not beautiful, not compared to you." She laughed.

When Jessica invited her in she was amazed at the transformation the house had undergone. "You've done quite a job on this place. I didn't think it could be salvaged."

"Papa had a lot of my mother's things stored here so it was not really too hard. A good scrubbing and some whitewash was the cure for most of it."

They chatted amiably for over an hour, sharing coffee and talking about what was left to do.

"So, if Mr. Kincaid lends Papa the money, we'll add a room to the cabin and make the ranch operational again."

"You like it here, don't you?" Sarah asked after watching the animation on Jessica's face as she spoke about Windy Creek.

"Oh, yes! Who wouldn't? It's beautiful! Every time I go outside and see those mountains, I'm drawn more deeply to them. It's like I've found paradise."

"Excuse me for saying so, but . . . your mother might have made a mistake in leaving Wyoming and her man, but she did okay by you."

Another half hour passed before Sarah said she had to go. She would have to get some lunch on the table soon since Chad was always starving. "There'll be a party at the K-D Saturday. Some of the associa-

tion's men and their wives are coming over. Why
don't you and your father join us? It'll give you a
chance to meet some more of your neighbors," she
explained, more tempted than ever to play Cupid
between Steve and her new friend.

"We'd love to. I'll check with my father when he
gets back," Jessica promised.

Waving good-bye, she went inside to start pulling
the remaining crates from the spare room. If she
worked hard, she could be in it by nightfall.

It was nearly dinnertime before Jeff returned from
the K-D. He came in smiling, kissed her cheek, and
handed her a still-warm loaf of bread. "From Sarah.
She said she enjoyed meeting you and talking to
you. There ain't many womenfolk about so don't be
surprised if you see a lot of her."

Anxiously awaiting to hear of her father's success
or failure with the loan, Jessica began to serve dinner. Jeff asked her about her visit with Sarah and if
she liked the way things were coming along. He
went from that topic to Jessica's room and whether
it was usable yet.

"Yes, Papa. I can use it tonight but it needs some
final touches." She sipped her coffee. "How'd you
do at the K-D today?" she asked.

"Fine, just fine," he replied, wiping stew gravy
with a piece of Sarah's bread.

"Papa!" Jessica cried, unable to wait any longer.
"What happened? Did Mr. Kincaid lend us the
money or not?"

Jeff frowned at her. "I'm sorry to say he did."

She sighed deeply then realized what her father
had said. "Oh, Pa!" She jumped up to hug him.
"That's wonderful! When can we get our cattle?
When should we order the lumber for the barn and
the addition?"

"Easy, girl!" He laughed. "Take it easy or we'll
be needin' that money for a doctor!"

"I'm just so excited! I can't believe it, Windy

Creek is going to be a real ranch!'' She spun about the room happily.

''Sit down! and I'll tell you all about it.'' Breathlessly she sat and listened attentively. He told her about Kincaid selling them a small starter herd at a fair price and carrying the loan until the herd was large enough to drive to Laramie for sale. The money for building would be available in a few days.

''The party! I forgot in my excitement!'' he exclaimed, changing the subject. ''Kincaid asked me to come by for the money Saturday. I told him about you and he insisted we both attend his shindig.'' Jeff smiled. ''And I told him we'd be delighted.''

''I'm so happy, Papa. Now we can really get down to work!''

''Get down to work! My God, girl! What do you think we've been doin'?'' They laughed together. The future looked bright. Windy Creek would be reborn and a dream would be coming true.

Chapter 5

On Friday, Chad, Duncan, and several hands from the K-D drove a herd of one hundred twenty head to the range of Windy Creek at first light. Sarah joined Jessica later in the morning to watch the wavy W of the Windy Creek brand set to their rumps. They prepared lunch for the tired cowboys and talked about the next day's party. Excitement reigned until mid-afternoon when the K-D crew returned home and Jessica stood with her father watching the cattle graze on their land. It was good to see and a deep feeling of accomplishment left them both content despite their exhaustion.

"I think I'll ride over to Lander for a while," Jeff told his daughter as he stood with his arm draped over her shoulder. "Want to go?"

She grimaced. "No, I think I'll go down to the creek and wash some of the dust from my hair, but," she called as she went toward the house to gather her bath items, "tell Roxy I said hello!"

"How'd you know I was going to Roxy's?" he called after her, grinning and mounting his horse without waiting for a reply.

Jess wasn't a very good rider yet. She never ventured too far in case she had to walk back. She had ridden for the first time only a week before and hadn't been able to sit for two days afterward. Her father had made her mount again, despite the pain,

41

and soon she could handle short trips alone. She liked riding. A feeling of freedom suffused her when she was astride a horse.

Her father had shown her a quiet spot not far from the house where a bubbling stream passed through an outcropping of large rocks. Several cottonwoods, which had rooted at its edge, offered additional cover. It was an ideal bathing hole and she knew as the summer approached she would use it often.

The nervousness she had felt disrobing the first time she had bathed outdoors was no longer with her as she shed her blouse. She knelt on the bank and lowered her head into the water. She began humming as she lathered her long tresses and didn't hear the steady clopping of a horse as it slowly neared her. She rinsed her head and twisted the mass into a towel. Sitting back on her heels, she dried her hair, enjoying the feeling of the sun on her shoulders as it shimmered through the leaves. Pulling a brush through the damp tangles, she thought she might as well bathe as long as she was there. She'd been going to make do with a hot-water basin bath but relished the idea of submerging her whole body. Reaching behind her, she unfastened her skirt and pushed it over her hips to the ground. She stepped from it, stretched languidly, and gazed at the mountain scene before her while pulling the top ribbons open on her camisole.

"Don't stop now," a deep voice ordered as she paused.

Jessica turned and gasped. Stretched catlike on the grass behind her was the stranger from Green River. "You!" she cried. He remained totally at ease, perched on an elbow. Lying on his side with one leg bent for balance, he held a long blade of grass and chewed at it. His hat shaded his eyes and she couldn't see their color. "What . . . what are you doing here?"

He remained silent as he watched her. Her long hair hung to her waist and several strands blew in the strong breeze. Her white camisole covered her but enough ribbons were untied to make him want to see the rest undone. The wind gusted a bit and her petticoat outlined one side of her. Deciding it was better to answer her than put himself through the agony of watching her, he said, "I live here."

"Liar! This is my father's place and he has no one working for him!" She clenched her fists and looked about for help. Of course there was none, and her own bravado would have to prevail. "Go! Get off my land!" she yelled.

He rose lithely to his feet and pushed his hat back. He leisurely stepped closer as he spoke. "You better get your facts straight, honey. This is K-D land and that's where I live."

"Oh! But . . . I . . . how could you . . ." Suddenly all too aware of the man standing so casually before her, Jessica realized the impact of having him living so near. "I wouldn't have trespassed if I had known," she said angrily, bending to retrieve her skirt, unaware of the appreciative gleam in his eyes.

"I'll get my things and—" Before she could finish, his easy manner vanished and he grabbed her arms, pulling her into his. The shock wore off in an instant and she began to struggle. "Let me go! You have no right!" She kicked at him unmercifully and tried to sink her teeth into his hand at her shoulder, her fears becoming unreasonable.

He chuckled at her wasted efforts and brought his leg around hers, lowering her to the ground effortlessly. She screamed and clutched his shirt to stop her fall but he lowered her so gently she felt nothing but the cool grass to confirm she was no longer standing. He followed her down and she could feel the outline of his hip pressing into her stomach as their legs entwined. He tossed his hat aside and drew her arms above her head, his face only inches from hers. She wiggled and squirmed to free herself.

"You better hold still," he breathed against her

cheek, ''unless you're prepared for me to make love to you here and now.''

''You wouldn't dare!'' she challenged.

''Oh, I'd dare.'' He smiled wickedly. ''And who could blame me when I tell them how prettily you undressed for me?''

Jessica was filled with panic. He wanted her and there was no way she could stop him. ''Steve! Please, don't do this!''

''What's the matter?'' He kissed her neck, pleased she remembered his name. ''You liked my kisses the last time.'' He tried to seek her lips but she kept turning her head from side to side. Pulling both her hands into one of his, he gripped her chin. ''Maybe that's what's wrong. Maybe you liked it too much. Are you merely disappointed that I didn't return that night? Is this your way of getting even?'' He lowered his head until his lips brushed the corners of her mouth.

''Of course not!'' she gasped, as he outlined her lips with the tip of his tongue. She felt the warmth of him covering her and she stiffened. What did this savage think he was doing? His mouth stopped tracing and claimed a kiss that seemed to drive him to oblivion. He released her hands and pulled her with him to his side, stroking her hip and thigh with one hand while cradling her head with the other. She felt impotent. He was manipulating her every move masterfully even as she struggled to block his intimate caresses.

His hand slipped between hers, pressing against his chest, to the remaining ribbons of her camisole. She was totally unaware of her partial nakedness until his hand pushed a strap from her shoulder and his mouth trailed to her breast.

''No! Don't!'' she cried, when the shock waves of his action rippled through her. She resumed her struggles with greater determination, pushing her fingers into his hair to try to pull him away.

Releasing her, he rolled to a seated position. His

breathing was deep and rapid as he raked his thick black hair with a trembling hand. "You're right. This isn't the time either." Kneeling, he watched her clutch her scant clothing across her breasts. "But have no doubt, we will finish this." He grabbed her shoulders and drew her close. "I promise you that." He spoke in a husky whisper.

Feeling she was safe for the moment, her anger flared. "And I promise you that Mr. Kincaid—" His head shot up. "—will hear about this! I'll see you're fired! He . . . He's a friend of my father's and he won't like one of his men attacking a friend's daughter!"

Standing, he hid his smile and let his eyes rake over her as she knelt by him trying to tie her camisole with trembling fingers. He bent and drew her to her feet, brushing aside her hands to help her. "And will you tell him I helped you dress afterwards? I'm sure he'd appreciate how gallant I'm being."

His smile infuriated her. He wasn't afraid of her but he'd give her more credence when she met his boss! She slapped at his hands as his fingers tried to brush the fullness below the lacy edging.

"Or will you tell him that only fear kept you from giving in. Or is it bigger and richer prey you are after?"

In response to his question Jessica slapped his grinning face.

"Feel better?" he asked, still grinning.

"Damn you!" she screamed and pushed him out of her way. She grabbed her shirt and pulled it on. Stuffing her soap, towel, and brush into her saddlebag, she threw it over her horse's saddle. She struggled to climb into it and gasped when a hand landed firmly on her bottom to give her a boost. Her petticoat rode high on her thigh as she straddled the mount and she pulled the reins hard when he caressed her bare knee.

"You won't be so smug when I tell Mr. Kincaid!"

she yelled at his crooked grin just before galloping off.

God, but she was one hell of a woman! He hadn't planned to see her until the party but when he did, and at the very spot he'd decided to visit for a bath, he couldn't resist. He knew that if he had continued his assault on her senses, she would have surrendered, but he wanted to see her face when she discovered that the magnanimous Kincaid and the man that threatened her peace of mind were one and the same.

In dire need of the cold water, he stripped and followed through with his reason for coming there in the first place. He smiled to himself as he thought of her struggles and ultimate surrender. Yes, she would be worth waiting for. He flexed his shoulder, remembering her hands kneading that flesh, and smiled. She played the innocent role well, yet at his merest touch the passionate woman within tore through the facade. She might have fooled Sarah, and even Roxy, but she didn't fool him.

As he dried and dressed, he spied her forgotten skirt. Scooping it up, an idea came to him. Her threats had been made, impotent as they were, but his would bring her willingly to him if he played his cards right. His shoulders began to shake as a deep, rumbling laughter broke the silent air.

Jessica slid from her horse and stomped across the porch, slamming the door behind her. She ran to her room and threw herself across the bed. ''Damn him!'' she yelled as she pounded her pillow. ''Damn! Damn! Damn!'' She stood and began to pace the small room, catching a glimpse of herself in the mirror. Again she had had a disturbing encounter with this man and again she noticed a difference in her appearance.

No evidence remained of the cool, sophisticated belle of St. Louis. Gone, too, was the naive, blushing girl who had looked back at her in Green River.

It wasn't just the clothing that barely covered her or the disheveled hair with bits of grass still clinging to it. It was something else that made her look different.

Tentative fingers traced her lips. She could still feel the fiery passion of his kisses. Closing her eyes she recalled the agony of an unknown desire when his hands held her breasts. She knew what the difference was between what she was and what she had become. She had discovered desire—raw, hot passion, and it frightened her even as it beckoned her.

Groaning and shaking off the effect of those memories, she boiled water and returned to her room. Stripping down to nothing, she scrubbed herself clean. Donning a fresh set of clothing, she brushed her hair until it crackled, then secured it at her neck. Still needing to keep herself fully occupied, she decided to vent some of her fury with physical labor. When her father returned he found her scrubbing an already clean floor.

"Why's the horse saddled? You goin' somewhere?"

"Oh! I forgot the poor thing!" she cried. "I'll take care of it right away!" She made to rise but he waved her off, saying he would see to it.

Somehow she managed to get through the evening without crying out her anger to her father, but she decided the only one who could punish Steve was indeed Mr. Kincaid. And she'd make sure he did just that!

The night had been long and too little of it had been spent sleeping. Jeff had eaten and was out with his chores when Jess woke and went looking for some breakfast. The coffee smelled good and she settled for a cup with a leftover biscuit. She needed to generate some enthusiasm for the party. She should be plotting the downfall of one very arrogant cowboy but somehow vengeance had lost its flavor in the cool light of morning.

She could no longer deny the attraction she felt for him. Was it so hard to believe he felt the same? Could she condemn him for the same feelings she herself experienced when they were together? No, she wouldn't cause him any trouble, she'd just be more careful in the future. She wouldn't set herself up for an intimate encounter. Pleased with her decision, she set about selecting a dress and preparing her father's clothing.

"You look lovely, dear." Her father smiled as she turned a pirouette before him. She wore a rich cream-colored gown of satin and it shimmered with the reflected light from the small lamp. The fashionable bustle was gathered with deep green ribbons and a matching pair of green slippers peeked out from her hem. Jess felt the gown might be a bit provocative for a party in the wilderness but her father assured her the cattlemen's wives vied for the most updated wardrobes and many would envy her choice.

She pulled a wrap over her bare shoulders and checked to see if the green velvet ribbon about her throat was in order. A pat to her hair confirmed it was neatly twisted atop her head. Roxy had lent them a carriage for the occasion and Jeff helped his daughter climb into it.

The night was cool but Jessica hardly noticed as she examined the diamond-studded black sky. There was no moon but the million tiny lanterns above her seemed to light their trail. A falling star briefly lit the heavens and she gasped at its beauty.

"Make a wish," her father urged, playing on the superstition.

A picture of the stranger's face descending over hers flashed in her mind. She shivered and said aloud, "I wish Windy Creek success," to quickly negate the wish her body had made. They rode in silence after that and Jessica thought she should have wished the stranger not be present this evening, but it was too late for that.

She could see the main house way before they were upon it. A circle of light was cast from the many windows of the two-story structure. It was magnificent! She had been to Mobile once as a child and this house could rival any of the plantation estates she had seen there. A huge porch skirted three sides of the ground floor. The brick-red coloring contrasted with white shutters and posts. Intricately leaded glass windows were set in the double entry doors and a massive chimney rose beyond both stories to sit above the roof.

"You should have told me Mr. Kincaid lived in a palace." She laughed. "It's breathtaking and seems so in tune with the land."

"Old Kincaid and his wife started the house thirty years ago but Steve did most of the work in the last ten." He didn't notice Jessica's tensing.

"S-Steve?"

"Yeah, Steve Kincaid. What's wrong?" he queried as he thought he saw her tremble.

It had to be a coincidence. Lots of men were named Steve! "Nothing. I . . . I just didn't know his first name, that's all." She would have asked what their benefactor looked like but they pulled up near the door at that moment.

She waited for her father to help her down and stood on the drive until he pulled the carriage aside and returned to her.

"Well, my lovely daughter, let's go to a party." He offered his arm and, smiling for his benefit, she placed hers in it and went up the front stairs.

Chapter 6

Bits of conversation drifted through the open windows as Sarah responded to their knock.

"Jessica! Mr. Morgan! I'm so glad you've come." She ushered them in and took Jessica's wrap. "You look beautiful!" Sarah sighed.

"So do you!" Jess offered honestly. Sarah had chosen a sun-yellow gown and she shone like its namesake. Her hair had been braided and looped behind her ears. Lightly tanned shoulders sat above the low sweeping neckline and a full skirt swirled about her hips.

"Chad had a fit when I bought it but now that I'm wearing it, he can't keep his hands off it," she confided with a giggle.

"What are you two conspiring about?" Chad asked as he joined the trio. He shook hands with Jeff and turned his attention to the lovely ladies, putting his arm around his wife's waist.

"We're going to see how many of these old cattlemen in there Jessica can bring to their knees," Sarah teased.

"I can think of one who'll be quaking in his boots." Chad scanned Jessica's bodice and winked at Sarah. He received an elbow to his stomach in response.

"Don't let this lecherous peacock make you nervous. You look enchanting.'' Sarah cast an angry glance at her red-faced husband.

"Th-thank you, Sarah.'' Jess looked around the foyer and tried to change the subject. "Your home is beautiful.''

Sarah laughed. "We don't live here! Our place is about half a mile from here. It's not much bigger than your place. I just act as hostess when Steve entertains.'' Before Jess could find an excuse to slip away, Sarah took her hand. "But I'm being a poor one now by keeping you standing here. Come on, I'll introduce you to everyone.''

Chad ushered Jeff to a bar and offered him a drink. They turned and watched Jessica and Sarah move about the room. They talked about cattle and ranching but Chad kept a watchful eye on Steve, who was engaged in conversation with Bill Harrison and his daughter, Margo. She was clinging to Steve's arm. It was obvious she had set her sights on the most eligible bachelor in the territory, and Chad shuddered as he thought of the simpering brat at the K-D. Margo was attractive, he thought, but Steve needed a woman like his Sarah or like . . . like Jessica.

Steve had been in fine spirits all day. He was assured that Jessica was going to attend and had gone off whistling. Maybe he had plans for Miss Morgan after all. Maybe he wasn't the fool Chad accused him of being. Perhaps he was using Margo as a catalyst to stimulate Jessica's interest. This could be the best party of the year! Something was going on between those two and he could feel the crackling in the air as they moved closer to seeing each other.

Jess had noticed the tall man by the fireplace the moment she entered the room. He had his back to her but something about the thick black hair and wide shoulders caused her to stammer through her first introduction. Sarah led her about the room. Her confidence grew and she calmed down as one couple after another greeted her warmly. She was being absurd! Surely even the kind Mr. Kincaid didn't allow his hands to mix with Wyoming's finest.

"Now, I'd like you to meet your host." Sarah drew her to the three people by the fire. "Steve," she called, "I'd like you to meet Miss Morgan, Jeff's daughter."

The room began to spin as the man in the finely fitted black suit turned toward her. She knew she was as white as his shirt as he took her hand and raised it to his lips, never taking his eyes from her astonished face. Steve! Kincaid! The same man!

"So glad you could come . . . Jessica." He smiled and held her hand tightly in his own. She tried to pull away without causing a scene, but had to concede to his superior strength. "Would you care for champagne?" He pulled her hand under his arm and led her, spellbound, to the bar, ignoring a furious Margo and a bewildered Sarah. Jess stood speechless and stunned as he picked up a glass of the bubbly wine before escorting her from the room.

Jeff made to follow. His daughter wasn't herself tonight. Something was wrong; he'd sensed it all day.

Holding his arm, Chad spoke. "Let them go, Jeff. They know each other, they just didn't know they did." As Jeff tried to make some sense of Chad's words, he laughed. "It's a long story. I don't know all of it but I can guess what I'm not sure of, and I think I'd better fill you in."

The noise of conversation had vanished. Jess stood in the library grasping the stem of a cool glass. The numbness of surprise was wearing off and she felt her limbs start to tremble. Someone reached from behind her to take the still-full glass of champagne and she stood doll-like staring at the fire. Large warm hands began to move up and down her arms and she snapped out of her stupor. Pulling from the embrace she spun to face her nemesis.

"You . . . you louse! You've played me for a fool! All the time I was yelling threats at you and y-you stood there grinning, you were planning this! I hate you!" She pulled her hand back to slap him but he grabbed it in midair, halting her attack. He pushed her arm behind her back and pulled her hard against him.

"Then we're even. I was the fool who chased all over the countryside looking for a J. Langley and I find her under a different name right under my nose!" He brought his free hand up to trace her neck and shoulder. "But now that I have you here, here you'll stay."

She tried to break the grip he held her in. "Like hell I will!" She struggled. "Let me go!" He released her and she stumbled backward to hit the edge of the table. He was relaxed and undisturbed by her outburst. "If you ever come near me again, I'll . . . I'll kill you!"

She started to leave and he casually asked, "What about the mortgage your father signed?"

She froze in mid-stride. "What . . . what mortgage?"

He walked silently to stand behind her. She could feel his breath against her hair. "I'm a businessman. You don't think I'd give Jeff a loan without collateral?"

"You can keep your money! We'll make do somehow without you!"

His fingers played with the sleeve of her gown. "What about the cattle?"

She stiffened. Without the cattle they'd have nothing, but she wouldn't bargain with this man. "You . . . you can have the cattle back." She started toward the door.

"I don't want them back. Besides, they already have the Windy Creek brand. I want the money they're worth."

Jess spun to face him. "You know that's impossible!"

Steve smiled, walked away from her, and stretched out in a large chair near the fire. "Yes, I do know. You see, my beautiful vixen, I don't enter games I can't win."

Jessica felt beaten at every turn. How could she have misjudged this man so? How could she have thought him an ordinary cowboy? As she looked into his eyes and saw the hazel there, she knew she was dealing with a cool-thinking, hard-driving man and that she had little chance of besting him. She walked slowly to a chair opposite him. She sat on the edge and balanced an elbow on the arm. She felt defeated as she slumped forward with a deep sigh.

He watched her struggling with the problems at hand. Though he looked at ease, she wasn't aware of the terrible strain he was under. He was bluffing about calling in the mortgage. It was merely a trap to see if he could determine what she was after. She was too beautiful to hide away at Windy Creek for the rest of her life, even if her father was there. After all, she'd done without him all these years. He'd speculated that she might be a fortune hunter yet here she was willing to give back everything! Maybe she was gambling on more. Perhaps she had planned to seduce the wealthy man she knew only as Kincaid and was now caught in her own trap.

While he tried to figure out her secrets, her mind was racing for solutions to her dilemma. If she could secure enough time, she might be able to wire her Uncle Walter for a loan. "How . . . how much time will you give me to raise the m-money?"

After a span of tension-building silence, he replied. "I'll give you twenty-four hours."

"I can't do it in so short a time! Nobody could!" she cried. Chewing her lip, she knew it would kill her to beg this man for anything. "Give me a week." When he remained silent she left her chair and stood in front of him, her gaze locking with his. "Please!" she added in an urgent whisper.

Steve shook his head. "No, Jessie." Leaning forward, he cupped her chin in his hand. "Give it up, you can't win."

"N-no." Her lips trembled. "No!" She slapped his hand away. "T-take it all! Papa and I will settle somewhere else and we won't need your help!" She started to turn away and was immediately pulled into his lap. She pounded at his chest until he secured her arms, squeezing until she was breathless.

Damn, he thought, he still wanted her despite his doubts, and he knew he had one more way to force her hand.

"Sit still, Jessie!" he ordered. She gritted her teeth as she settled on his lap and stared at the wall. "That's a good girl." He settled his hand on her thigh and felt her wince. "I didn't want to use my ace in the hole, but you've turned out to be a noteworthy opponent. You don't scare easy, do you?" She remained silent, trying to focus on anything but the feel of his fingers as they slid about her waist. "When you ran away yesterday, you left something behind." He felt her stiffen. "I have your skirt."

"Y-you can't prove it's mine!" she flared.

"Can't I? Perhaps not if that was all there was, but I also found a letter from your loving cousin, Bonnie, in the pocket."

She looked at him in panic. "You can't mean to . . . to blackmail me?"

"Your father's very proud of you. How do you think he'd feel if I went out there right now and presented him with his daughter's belongings?"

"He . . . he wouldn't believe you! You could have . . . have taken them from the house!" she gasped, grasping at straws.

"And if I tell him about the mole you have on your breast, do you think he'll believe me?"

Jessica's hand quickly covered the telltale blemish now covered by her bodice. "You can't! You wouldn't dare!"

"I told you before, I'd dare anything to get what

I want, and I want you." He watched as tears welled up in her magnificent green eyes.

"Why? Why me?" she asked angrily.

His hand rose to her breast and he gently brushed his palm over it, not really sure himself why he was pursuing her so recklessly. There was only one thing he knew. "I want you," he repeated.

After a moment's silence, Jessica sighed. "And what happens a-after you . . . we . . . ?"

"That depends on how well we get along." He smiled, kissing her neck. When she remained silent and stiff, he whispered, "Can I assume you agree to our little arrangement, you for your father's dream?"

Jessica tried to stand. "No. I won't be black-mailed."

He pulled her head to his shoulder and held her gently, almost lovingly. "I won't let you go until I have your word. Either you come to me on my terms, or I ruin your father's hopes for the future." He placed a finger beneath her chin and pulled her head up to look at him. "Your word."

A knock sounded at the door and before they could rise it opened. Margo burst into the room with her father in tow. "Steve! Darling! Whatever are you doing?"

Jess tried to get up but he held her firmly, seemingly at ease. "I don't believe you were invited in, Margo, but since you're here, I guess you'll be the first to know. Miss Morgan and I are going to be married." He quickly kissed Jessica's astonished mouth. "Aren't we, darling?"

"No . . . Y-yes," she stuttered, appearing to be a nervous bride-to-be.

"Well, congratulations!" Bill Harrison offered. "Come on, Margo. I think this couple would like some privacy."

"But Father! I won't allow it! I . . ." she seethed.

"Keep quiet, Margo!" He grabbed her arm and pulled her from the room. "I said they want to be alone!'' The door closed and Jessica pushed away from Steve, standing before him.

"How could you say such a thing? They'll go out there and tell everyone, including my father, that we're . . . we're going to be married! I hate you! I'd never marry you!''

He rose and poured a whiskey from a nearby decanter. "Don't worry. Being engaged and getting married are not the same thing. It will give us a good reason to spend a lot of time together.'' His eyes raked her slowly. "And you may yet come out of this with your reputation intact.''

"You've thought of everything, haven't you? It won't bother you one bit to ruin me, will it? The mighty cattle baron! The Lord God Kincaid!''

Driven by her stubborn refusal to bend to his will, Steve said roughly, "Yes! Yes, I have thought of everything! And if you'd like to cease this farce, then come upstairs with me right now and do what your body admits to even if you don't!''

She had faced his humor and his passion but his anger could be more than she could handle. He towered over her and the tension from his body exuded an almost tangible force. She shook her head.

"All right then.'' He sighed, brushing his fingers against her cheek. "We'll both play our roles and I promise it won't be so bad.'' He pulled her close, kissing her lips gently, still not sure why he had to have her at all costs.

He knew she would follow his lead, at least for the time being. Drawing her hand through his bent arm, he led her to the door. She was pale and shaken. No one would believe she was a happy bride-to-be. He'd have to do something to put some color in her cheeks.

Jess was numb. She still could not fathom the depths he'd gone to to force her hand. In her state she was unprepared for his hand on her breast and his lips claiming hers. Breathlessly, she tried to pull away but the kiss was over before she could fight it.

"That's better." Steve grinned, noting her high color.

It was an incredible nightmare. The room silenced as they entered and she wished she would awaken, but her father's beaming face made her realize it was all too real. She was trapped.

"Jess! Why didn't you tell me? Chad hinted there was something afoot but I never guessed you two were . . . well, seeing one another." He hugged her and shook Steve's hand. "I'm happy for you."

"Th-thank you, Papa," she whispered, seeing Sarah moving closer. "Sarah, I . . ." Before she could finish, Sarah hugged her.

"I knew he was up to something," she whispered for Jessica alone, and they held each other while Chad stepped forward to congratulate his friend.

"You work fast, my friend. Why, I'd have sworn—"

"Thanks, Chad," Steve interrupted. He placed his arm about Jessica's shoulder and pulled her to his side. "It was fast, but we both knew it was right." While brushing a kiss to her ear, he whispered, "Smile and put your arms around me. I'm going to kiss you."

Reluctantly she responded to his command. His lips pressed hers and cheers went up for the handsome couple. She felt detached, as if she were watching the whole thing but not participating. She managed to cooperate with his subtle instructions and an hour passed. Dinner was served and she barely touched her food or knew what she was eating, despite the warning glares from Steve. She had noticed, however, that Margo and Bill Harrison were not among the diners. She had wanted to cry to the petite blonde Margo that she would gladly trade places with her!

Shortly after they finished eating, people began to leave. It wasn't long before only the five remained. Sarah and Chad wanted to know when the wedding would take place and Steve maneuvered the conversation in such a way as to imply it would be in early autumn. He sat on the arm of her chair and insisted on lovingly stroking Jessica's neck. When she thought she could stand no more, Steve suggested they call it a night.

Sarah gave a sign to Chad and Jeff and suddenly Jessica and Steve were alone. They'd been given time to say good night away from prying eyes. Jess would have followed the others but Steve held her back.

"There's no need to keep up the charade! We're quite alone!" she snapped.

"So why not take advantage of it?" His eyes were dark as he circled her waist with his hands and pulled her to him. Her arms hung at her side. She would give him nothing, no response, no encouragement. He knew her game and began to nuzzle her ear while whispering love words to her.

"We'll be good together, Jess. I'll discover all your secret places and teach you how to please me as well." Her breathing quickened. "I'll make you want me as much as I want you." His hands caressed her hips and pulled her hard against the essence of him. "And I do want you. If there was some way I could take you right now, I would." Steve lowered his lips to hers, and although she tried to turn her face away from him, he wouldn't let her. Slowly and sensuously, he caressed her, tempted her, and she gasped as a sharp pang of desire shot through her.

Jeff came in to find them in each other's arms and he cleared his throat. "Jess, we . . . ah . . . better go." His embarrassed smile let Jess know he believed they were lovers or soon would be. She refused to look at Steve as she followed her father to the door. She knew Steve would see the confusion in her eyes, and though she hated him, she couldn't deny his power over her.

Steve held her shawl and wrapped it, along with his arms, about her shoulders. "I'll see you tomorrow," he whispered. She refused to answer and walked out into the night. Jeff helped her into the carriage and she turned to see the dark outline of the man who had played so many roles in the six weeks she'd been in Wyoming. Now, he was destined to play one more—her lover.

Chapter 7

J ess rose with the sun. There was no sense lying
in bed, she couldn't sleep. Every time she closed
her eyes, visions of Steve Kincaid beckoned her, first
furious and demanding, next passionate and still demanding. He wanted all of her. Her mind, body,
and soul would be the least he would settle for.

She pulled her robe more tightly about herself and
took a cup of coffee out the front door, glad her father still slept. The sky was blooming in the fiery
colors of sunrise as she sat on the porch step. She
held her mug in both hands to help keep the chilled
air at bay. For the beauty nature was displaying, Jessica could concentrate on none of it. Her thoughts
were on Kincaid and what she was going to do. He
was as powerful as the land he ruled.

She had come to love this wild new place. It was
a land that made her think of roots. She could imagine children growing strong on its fertile plains. They
would be straight and tall as the magnificent peaks,
like Kincaid. Was it possible he was predestined to
be a part of her life? She could not deny the physical
attraction she felt for him, yet his arrogant challenges
didn't seem to lend themselves to anything more
than a game.

Jess sat up straight, her eyes wide and her mind
racing. A game! He was bluffing! She had been too
close to it all last night, she thought. He wouldn't

risk his position in the town or the territory for a woman or a brief affair! He had more to lose than she did!

She had been led through the first act by a professional. She had responded to his every cue and been maneuvered through the dialogue so smoothly, no one doubted her performance. But now she knew and understood, and the roles would be reversed. She would lead and there was nothing he could do about it!

Oh, it was going to be a beautiful spring day! Jess got up and returned to the house. Her father was stirring and she began to hum to herself as she whipped up hotcakes and sliced some cured ham. The aromas filled the room.

Jeff yawned and watched his daughter. She was happy this morning. He had been worried the night before. When they left Steve's she was quiet and restless. At first he thought she was thinking of the man she loved, then he thought she might have a problem she wasn't ready to talk about, but this morning he felt more at ease.

"Smells good!" he announced as he rolled up his bedroll.

"Morning, Papa." She smiled and took a nibble of ham. "It is good." The coffee was still fresh and she poured him a cup.

"You seem chipper this morning. I got the feeling last night there might be something wrong."

"Wrong! What could be wrong?" She laughed. "No, Papa, everything is very right."

"Good!" He kissed her cheek and sat down to breakfast. She joined him and they talked about the ranch. Steve had given Jeff the money at the party and he was heading into town to order what they needed.

"Don't you think you should wait a bit before spending it?" She tried to appear calm but she kept thinking she might need the leverage of throwing the money back in Kincaid's face.

"No, we need the barn built to store for winter and I don't think we should wait. Besides—" He grinned. "—you'll be goin' off to live with your husband and I'd like to have it done while you're still here. Kind of like a weddin' present, seein' as how it was because of you my dreams are comin' true."

"Y-yes, of course." She sighed. She couldn't ruin the joy her father was experiencing. All his dreams were coming true, but at what expense? "So . . ." She brightened. "Finish up here so I can clean up and you can get to town." She got up, kissed his brow, and went to her room to dress.

Having donned a soft brown skirt and a white shirt, she pulled her hair back at the nape and tied it with a ribbon. She rolled up her sleeves and walked barefoot to get more coffee. Her father was slipping on his vest and getting ready to leave.

"Stay out of trouble and don't worry about dinner. I'll be staying in town till late. I might even ride to Riverton if Zeke doesn't have all the supplies I need. If I'm not back by sundown, I'll see you tomorrow night sometime." He hugged her to him. "I'm happy for you, honey. You're gettin' a good man in Kincaid, but he's gettin' the best!"

She didn't want to stay alone but she couldn't disillusion her father. Without saying a word, she returned his hug and watched him walk out the door. She followed him to the porch and stayed to watch him ride out. He turned and waved before breaking into a gallop.

Jessica sighed. No matter what happened, she'd have to face it alone. A movement caught her eye to the north and her heart rose to her throat. She watched, mesmerized, until she could make out a rider. It was a young boy, maybe twelve or thirteen. He rode up to the porch and yanked off his hat. The tension eased in her neck as she realized she was holding her breath. This boy was certainly no threat.

"Ma'am, I got a message for you from Mr. Kincaid," he beamed, proud to be serving his boss. "He wants ya ta come ta the K-D."

The smile froze on her face. So, he thought she'd come running. He was so sure he had sent a boy to beckon her! Well, she'd send a message of her own.

"I . . . I'm not feeling too well this morning." Her smile faded as she brushed a hand against her brow in mock anguish. "I fear I drank too much champagne last night. If you'll wait a moment, I'll send a message back for Mr. . . . for Steve." He nodded and she slowly entered the house. The moment she was out of sight she ran to her room and grabbed pen and paper. Her note was brief and she hurried back to the rider, returning a pained expression to her face just before stepping outside. She handed him a sealed envelope and stepped back. "Thank you for all your trouble, ah . . . ?"

"Willy, ma'am, and it weren't no trouble." He tipped his hat, a blush of appreciation staining his cheeks.

"Thank you, Willy." Her smile widened and she flashed her dimples at him. "Now, you make sure you give that to Steve personally."

"Oh, I will, ma'am! You can bet on it!" He pulled the reins about and spurred his horse to a gallop.

"Yes." Her smile disappeared. "I bet you will." Jess went back inside the moment he was out of sight. She felt like she had shed the weight of her burden at last. Her note was clear and to the point. Steve Kincaid would have no doubt what she meant.

Willy rode up to the K-D whistling a tune. Mr. Kincaid's woman was special, all right, and he felt a twinge of envy. Someday he would have a woman like Miss Morgan and a ranch like the K-D, he thought.

Steve walked out to the yard at the sound of a rider. He didn't expect Jess right away; she'd have to get ready and come later. After all, the invitation was guised for a luncheon. He smiled as he saw Willy and thought over his reason for sending him.

The night had been long for him. Wrestling with his conscience, he'd realized he couldn't go through with what he had planned. He wasn't a savage. No civilized man would force a woman to his bed, no matter how much he desired her. No, he'd set her free of the bargain and let nature take its course. If they were destined to come together, they would.

Willy jumped from his horse and ran to Steve. "I got a note for ya from Miss Morgan." He pulled the envelope from his shirt pocket and handed it to Steve.

A small smile tugged at the corner of his mouth as he opened it. He read the single sentence and his eyes flashed with anger for a brief moment, then humor replaced it. She was calling his bluff! She was giving no credence to his threats. She obviously underestimated him! Gone was his conviction to free her from the arrangement, forgotten was his regret. She was more woman than he imagined and this time she was the one throwing down the gauntlet. The hunt was back on, and she was making the challenge.

Willy watched the fleeting exchange of emotions on Steve's face, his own mimicking them in concern. He finally broke into a smile as Steve began to chuckle. Suddenly the yard was filled with deep, rumbling laughter.

"Saddle my horse, Willy," Steve managed to get out. "I have a debt to collect." He turned and strode to the house. Taking the stairs two at a time, he crossed the porch. Walking into his den he looked at the note again.

"Jessica Morgan, you are one spirited filly, but there has not been one yet I haven't broken and ridden!" He laughed, tossing the note on his desk, and grabbed his hat.

He went to the corral and told Chad he'd be gone for a while. Willy was holding his horse in the yard and he mounted in one lithe movement. "Thanks, Willy," he tossed over his shoulder as he headed for Windy Creek and his woman.

A picture of the note flashed in his mind and he smiled. *Go to hell!* it said, and he might, but he would damn well take her with him!

Steve dismounted a short distance from the ranch house. He couldn't see any movement but he knew she was nearby if not inside. Her horse was still in the corral and smoke rose from the stovepipe. Walking carefully, he inched forward, avoiding going near the front until the last minute. He tested the porch edge for squeaks and climbed up, slinking low beneath the window and hugging the wall until he reached the open door. He hoped to catch her unaware and add to the surprise.

Peeking inside, he found the main room empty and noticed the door to the back room was ajar. Slowly he entered the house and moved forward quietly. The door behind him slammed shut and he felt a blow to his head just before he hit the floor.

Jessica wasn't sure if she had hit him hard enough with the pitcher to knock him out. She bent and lifted a hand. When she released it, it thumped to the floor. He certainly fell hard, she thought, but he was breathing so she hadn't done too much damage.

Steve moaned and Jessie knew her only possible means of escape was to flee, and right away. He moaned again. Stepping gingerly over his sprawled body, she took one last look at him and ran out the door. She looked about frantically and decided the safest place to go was to Sarah. Grabbing a handful of skirt, she began to run as fast as she could. The horse! Maybe she could use it to make her escape. She reached him and wondered how she could mount. The huge steed stood too high for her and she couldn't risk leading him back to the house in

case Kincaid woke. Sighing, she left the mount and
started out on foot.

Steve rose to his knees and rubbed the back of his
neck. He looked at the shattered china and shook
his head. He'd underestimated her. He got to his
feet and staggered to the basin by the door. Dousing
his head with cool water, he straightened and
grabbed a towel. Drying off, he saw a flash of white
through the side window. Jessica!

Swooping his hat from the floor, he ran out the
door to his horse. Wincing when he pushed his hat
on his head, he mounted. Spinning the horse about,
Steve set off after his prize.

Jess stopped, gasping for breath. She pushed the
strands of hair that had come loose behind her ear.
She looked back to check her progress and was
pleased to see the ranch house was just a small outline. If Steve remained unconscious another half
hour, she would make it. She rubbed her right leg
which felt sore. Looking back one more time, she
froze. He'd revived and was riding toward her, but
he was still at some distance. With no place to hide
she started running as fast as she could toward a
stand of trees.

She knew she had no chance of outrunning his
horse, but she was determined to try and get somewhere Steve couldn't follow on horseback. Suddenly, Steve rode past her and she halted. He turned
his horse and she took off, retracing the path just
covered. Again he rode past and caused her to di-
vert her course. She felt trapped, like a wild animal
being toyed with before the kill, but her sense of
reasoning might make a difference.

Picking up a rock she made to run to her left and
he turned in that direction. Then, just as he passed
her, she hurled the stone as hard as she could at the
horse's flanks. The steed, not used to such abuse,
reared and nearly dumped his rider. Jess darted
away, panting and desperate.

By the time Steve was back in control of his mount Jess had gained several hundred yards. He pushed his hat low over his eyes and smiled. He was tired of the chase. It was time to move in. Watching her skirts billow out behind her, he started forward at a lope. As the gap closed, he increased his speed. Moving along beside her, he reached down and circled her waist, drawing her up to his side.

"Let go of me!" she panted, struggling for release. Her back was pressed to his chest and she wasn't able to push away from him. "Damn you, Kincaid!" she screamed. "You can't do this!"

"We made a bargain and it didn't include chasing you all over the countryside." He pulled her about until she was on the horse instead of hanging from it and halted their ride. "Did you really think your little show of bravado was going to make me quake in my boots? Or did you think I was bluffing?" He smiled a crooked grin as she gasped at his correct assumption. "Ah! So you thought I would merely set you free if you dared me to. One of the rules of survival here is know your man before dealing with him. Remember that, my love."

Jessica chewed at her lip and tried to decide what her next move should be. Perhaps he could shed some light. "Now what?" she demanded.

Determined to break her defiant will before he released her from their pact, he grinned devilishly. "Now I teach you a lesson, one I think you'll enjoy." He moved his arm and brought his hand up to cup her breast. She tried to push it away but lost her balance and had to grab the saddle horn. Steve spurred the horse forward and she saw the swimming hole they were approaching.

The stand of trees she thought to run to didn't look the same on foot, but atop the horse she knew it. They rode up beside the crystal-clear water and he lowered her to the ground. Jessica immediately took flight.

"Jessie!" he called and watched her stop. "Come

here!'' She didn't move as he threw his leg over the horse and slid down. He tied the horse near good grazing and walked to lean against a large boulder. "I said, come here. You know I can catch you if you try to run, don't you? So be a good girl and come here.''

Defeated, tired and angry, she spun around. ''No! Damn you, Kincaid! No!''

Using his thumb he raised his hat off his brow. ''Now, honey, we've spent enough time playing this morning, at least on horseback.'' He seemed at ease, relaxed and expecting her to obey.

Jessica let out a frustrated scream and started to run. Before she could get but a few feet she was grabbed about the legs from behind and fell to the ground. Steve wrapped his hand in her skirt and began to pull her closer as she kicked at him. When she was in reach, he straddled her legs and gripped her wrists, pulling them over her head. Jessie bucked and twisted until she exhausted herself. At last, she stilled, breathing heavily and furious at the ease with which he held her.

Leaning down until the brim of his hat shaded her face, he gave her a one-sided grin. His eyes were dark and threatening. ''Give it up, Jess.'' He leaned and tried to kiss her. She kept turning her head and he lowered his lips to just below her ear, getting caught up in the feel of her beneath him. The veneer cracked, then shattered completely. The savage was free and wanted her. He paused to try and rein his passions one last time but the silent dare in her eyes as she defied him destroyed the last of his good intentions. He drew her hands beneath his knees, trapping hers and leaving his own free.

''No!'' Jess screamed as his long fingers moved to the buttons of her shirt. Slowly he released each one.

He spread the two sides to reveal the heaving chest barely covered by the lace of her camisole. ''Stop it! You . . . you've got too much to lose! No! Damn you!'' she screamed as he rolled her to her stomach and undid her skirt. While he pulled her shirt from her shoulders she continued her tirade. "I'll tell everyone you raped me! I'll . . . I'll have you arrested!" He knelt and drew her skirt down over her hips. "I'll ruin you, you bastard!"

"Jessie, Jessie," he sighed in mock distress as she rolled to her back, seething. He tossed his hat aside and removed his vest. "What am I going to do with you?" He started to remove his shirt. "Here you are, professing to be a lady yet you're kicking and swearing like a common whore." As he stripped off his shirt, the muscles across his chest and down his arms flexed and gleamed bronze in the sunlight.

Steve moved to his knees at her side and Jessica sat up, pleading. "Kincaid . . . Steve, listen to me." She laid her hand on his forearm and felt the strong warmth travel up her arm. She pulled away as if burned and looked at the ground. "I . . . I admit there is some kind of mild attraction between us, but—" Before she could finish, Steve grabbed her arms and pulled her against him.

"Mild attraction! Good God, woman! Either you're lying to yourself or you're the most cold-blooded bitch I've ever known!" Her hands pushed at his chest as he drew her closer. "I think you're just afraid of this." His lips moved quickly and firmly to hers. The touching of their lips turned to a melting as his hands ran over her shoulders and down her back to press her nearer still. Sensing her desire to respond, he released her and sat back on his heels, watching her sway slightly. Jessica's eyes were closed and her lips parted. He reached across the space between them and pulled the ribbons fastening her camisole. He did it so carefully she gasped when his palm stroked her bare flesh.

Jess looked down to watch his tanned fingers trace her pale breast, and she uttered a whimper when his thumb brushed a peak. She attempted to push him away when he took her hand and placed it on his chest. Holding her wrist, he moved it over the coarse dark hairs that tapered down his chest to disappear beneath his belt. When he let go of her hand, she kept it there of her own accord.

"Put your arms around my neck, Jess," he urged, and exhaled deeply as her hands slid up his torso and over his shoulders. His hands went to her waist and moved beneath the loosely hanging camisole, drawing her hardening peaks to press against him. "Look at me," he ordered.

Held within his seductive power, and feeling too tired to fight him anymore, she responded. With passion-glazed eyes she looked into his nearly black ones. She gasped at the hot sensations that were running through her body. Their matched breathing was rapid and shallow as her eyes half closed and her lips parted in silent invitation. Steve held back, watching her until her hand slid up into his hair and she pulled his mouth to hers. All her fears evaporated. All his pent-up frustration and passion broke in a savage embrace. His hands stroked her back, pulling her tightly to him. Her nails raked his back and the pain only added to his desire.

Slowly he lowered her to the grass and lay with her, never breaking the kiss. As his lips traveled down to her neck, he whispered her name; as they sought and found her breast, she called out his. Rolling to his side, he drew her into the circle of his strong arms and worked the fastenings of the last of her clothing. As his hand slipped beneath the fabric about her hips, she gasped. She knew she should protest yet she allowed his words to lull her.

"Easy, honey," he said gently. "I won't hurt you. I'll go slowly, though God knows I'm in agony with wanting you." His lips began to nibble at hers. When she responded, he moved to her shoulder, then her breast. All the time, he inched her petticoat lower and lower until she lay naked beside him. "My God! You're so beautiful!" he groaned as he pulled back to look at her. She tried to cover herself with her hands but he stopped her. "Don't! Please don't, honey. I want to look at you, to touch you."

Jess couldn't tell if the warmth she felt coursing through her was from the sensuous melody he played on her body or the high April sun. Closing her eyes, she knew that she was spiraling higher and higher, and a great ache blossomed in her. She needed release. She didn't know how it would come, but she knew he did. Opening her eyes, she reached for him.

"Steve, please," she sobbed quietly.

"Not yet, my love," he breathed huskily. "You must explore me now."

Jessica started to roll away. "I can't!" she cried when he clamped an arm about her middle to hold her.

"Yes, yes, you can. I'll help you." He released his belt buckle and began to unfasten his pants. He sat up and removed his boots, quickly returning to her side. He pulled her hand to his waist. "Help me, Jess." She nodded, closed her eyes, and began to pull away the last barrier between them. She kept them closed as he lay back and gripped her hand.

"Touch me," he begged, but she couldn't. Steve forced her hand lower until she brushed the hardness of him. "God, Jess! Please!" he moaned, needing her consent to their lovemaking, even if it came begrudgingly.

Trembling, Jess took a deep breath and wrapped her fingers around him, suddenly filled with the need to know him. He drew his breath between clenched teeth and she started to pull away in fear that he mistook for coy teasing.

"No! No, don't!" he said harshly. "Not . . . not yet." Jess lay very still and lifted her eyes to watch his face. He'd thrown an arm across his brow and it shaded his eyes. A nerve twitched in his cheek and she could see the rapid pulsing in his throat. Perspiration glistened on his top lip and his nostrils flared. Jess felt a surge of feminine power as she realized she was responsible for his ecstasy. With this power came daring and she began to move her hand against him, with an instinct that he thought came from experience.

"Enough!" he ordered, angered by the image that filled his mind of her with other men. Turning, he pushed her to her back. He moved with a catlike grace to kneel between her thighs and leaned forward, braced on his hands. "Open your eyes, Jess. I want you to watch me as I make love to you. I want you to remember me and only me as your lover!"

Jessie opened her eyes, anticipating the pleasure he promised. She saw the triumph in his eyes. She could feel him touching, seeking, until he found the haven he sought. Her hands went to his shoulders, wanting to explain there had never been another, but she was too enrapt in the sight and feel of him.

"The other time I promised has come, Jess." He pushed into her and froze as she let out a pained cry. It wasn't possible! he thought. Her every move, her response to his touch—she couldn't be a virgin!

Jess tried to pull out from beneath him but he clamped his hands about her waist and held her pinned to him. Tears ran down her cheeks.

"Jessie." He sighed. "My beautiful innocent, it is done and cannot be undone. The pain will quickly pass, I promise you." He began to move in her slowly and her hurt eased, to be replaced with the building need she had felt before.

"Steve! I . . . I need . . . I want . . ." she groaned. He moved faster and pushed deeper until she called out to him again in released passion. Wave after wave of delight radiated outward, drawing her very soul from her. She was at once one with the elements, drifting and blending with paradise. Her return to earth came in the way of a deep shudder above her. Holding him to her she felt the fiery heat of him pulse into her.

As his breathing returned to normal he rolled to

her side and drew her into his arms. He brushed back her hair from her face and gently kissed her. Reaching for his shirt, he wrapped it about her shoulders. They lay together in the warm sun and were silent. The savage was sated and the civilized man reflected on the wonder of the woman he held.

Physically exhausted and emotionally spent, Jessie was beyond thought. Steve felt her relax into a quiet slumber, trusting him to watch over her. How could he have been so wrong about her? When he thought of his furious pursuit and his threats, he cringed inwardly.

"I'm sorry, Jessie," he whispered and kissed her brow. She snuggled against him, content in her slumber. He smiled softly. "I'll tell you again, some other time."

Chapter 8

Perched on an elbow, Steve watched the sleeping beauty beside him. She was a proud, beautiful woman, one he admired as well as desired, and he thought of the future. He needed to marry soon if the K-D was to have an heir. He had thought he would probably marry Margo. Not that he loved her but because she was used to his way of life and would represent him well. Having no need for love, it would have been a mutually satisfying union. Despite her airs, Margo was well-acquainted with a man's bed, and they had shared some pleasant moments. It seemed inevitable that he would choose her. That is, until he stumbled upon a stranger, one who invaded his thoughts and appeared in his dreams, one that he was finally holding in his arms.

Jessica, a passionate virgin woman. Jessica, a green-eyed enchantress. It seemed fated that they should meet and love. Love? No, make love, he thought, but not be in love. He was too old for schoolboy romances but it made no difference. He had been the first with her and he would be the last. He would marry Jessica Morgan. She would give him sons and keep his home. Having decided her future his thoughts went to her awakening. Would she be frightened? Would she cry and lament what he had taken or be woman enough to admit that what they shared was wonderful?

Suddenly he needed to wake her. He needed to know her mettle. He wanted to face her in the light of day and see if she was all she seemed.

Not wanting to wake up, Jess brushed away whatever was tickling her cheek, but it returned to her neck and she turned, annoyed, toward the warmth at her side. The persistent pest moved to her hip and ran down her thigh. Jess sat up to swat it away and came fully awake with a gasp. Lounging beside her, totally at ease with his nakedness, was Steve, a piece of grass dangling from his hand. Averting her eyes from the golden body stretched beside her, she thrust her arms into his shirt and started to button it.

"Don't." He smiled, taking her hand in his. "I like looking at you."

"I . . . I can't sit around with nothing on!" She blushed.

"Why not? I am." Steve pulled her to him. "Besides, I can think of nothing nicer." He seemed to be thinking. "Why, I can even imagine you cooking my breakfast in nothing more than an apron," he teased.

Seeing the humor of his fantasy, Jess grinned. "You're a rogue!" she sighed, realizing it felt so right to be in his arms. "I'd catch my death of cold in no time!"

Running his hand under the shirt, he nuzzled her neck. "Want to bet you would never get cold?"

Playfully, she tossed her head. "Ha! Why you would be out running your ranch and I'd be trying to explain my new style of dress to callers."

He growled at her, "No chance." She giggled and tried to pull away. "Oh, no, you don't." He grabbed her waist and began to tickle her. She had accepted him and what they had done together as natural. The future looked infinitely brighter.

"No! Steve, don't!" she begged, laughing and squirming. He rolled with her in the grass and enjoyed her frantic efforts to escape the sweet torture.

Tears of laughter slid down her cheeks and she begged again. "Please, stop!"

Suddenly his fingers went from tickling to more passionate play. Panting from her laughter, Jess watched the grin fade from his face and she sobered. "Why don't I feel shame for wanting this?" Her fingers kneaded his upper arm. "I should hate you for what . . . what you did, but . . ." She sighed as his hand slid to her breast.

"But what?" he urged. She turned her head, refusing to answer him. He ran his tongue across the tip of her breast and inched toward her waist. "But what, Jess?"

"Ow! Damn you, Kincaid!" she yelled as he gently bit her hip.

"Are you going to answer me?" He looked up through his thick lashes and the corner of his mouth quirked in a grin.

She was afraid to speak of what was in her heart, afraid he would turn away. "No!"

"Okay, then I guess I'll have to go to extremes." He stood quickly and pulled her to her feet. Scooping her up into his arms, he started toward the stream.

"Steve, no!" she cried, squirming to gain her freedom. "That water is cold!"

"Yes, it is, and you're going in if you don't answer me."

Jessie wrapped her arms securely about his neck. "If you throw me in, you'll go too!" she pointed out, determined not to answer his question.

"Very well." He began to wade into the stream as she begged him to stop, but he was going to get his answer. With luck it would be what he wanted to hear. As the cold water touched her feet, she squealed.

"You won't really do this to me, will you?" she dared. Jess screamed when Steve sat in the water. "Oh! Oh, God! You beast! You—"

Steve pressed his lips to hers and suddenly the

temperature of the water made no difference. His lips traveled her face and she laced her fingers through his hair.

"Why don't you hate me, Jess?" he breathed against her cheek.

It had started as a seed in Green River. He'd nurtured it with kisses and caresses, and beside a sparkling stream in a land called paradise, it had blossomed before her. "Because . . . because you're the first man I ever wanted, Steve, and I think . . . I think I . . . I love you," she whispered. Holding his face in her hands, she looked at him. "Are you angry with me for loving you?" she asked. "I know it isn't part of the bargain, and it won't matter, I'll see it through." His silence made her nervous and she rattled on to ease her fears. "I . . . I won't make any trouble, I promise. I—"

"Shut up, Jess!" He grinned at her shocked expression. "Shut up and listen. I'm not angry. In fact, I couldn't be happier. You see, honey, I fell into my own trap." Jess looked at him in confusion. "I want you, Jess. Not for a quick affair, but forever. I think I have from the moment I first saw you standing there in that hotel room, all damp and furious."

"Oh, Steve!" She kissed him with all her limited experience, but left no doubt that she was his woman. "I can't believe it." She kissed him again until he drew back.

"Don't you think we should get out of this cold water and let me prove it to you?" He lifted her clear of the water, his eyes twinkling.

"Um," she purred.

"You know, Chad told me you might be the one I needed." He stepped to the bank. "I'll have to tell him he was right."

He lowered her to the grass and she pulled off his wet shirt, throwing it at him. She was miffed he would discuss her with Chad, but she had to laugh when the sopping shirt hit him.

"What am I supposed to do with this?" he asked

and she shrugged, reaching for her own shirt. Before she could grasp it, he tossed her to the ground, pinning her. "Well, at least I know what to do with you," he groaned, feeling the passion between them leap to life.

"And I want to learn the things I can do for you," she said seductively, sliding her arms about his neck. He hadn't mentioned love, but he must love her, she thought, he must!

The sun was near to setting when they rode up to Windy Creek. Steve's chest was bare and Jess pressed her face to his warm skin. Her fingers played with the dark hairs and he slapped her hand when it crept lower.

"Unless you want to be made love to on the back of a horse, you better restrain yourself a few minutes longer."

"I'm sorry." She pouted playfully. "But this is all so new to me. I find I can't resist you, especially when your hands are making promises."

Steve laughed. "Good! Then you'll be calling for mercy before this day is over since I always keep my promises." When she wiggled her hip against his thigh, his husky voice sighed in mock dismay. "I fear I've taken on more than I can handle. I'll be old before my time if I'm forced to meet your lusty demands."

A low, sultry growl was his answer. Teasing, she said, "If you would rather I find someone else to—"

He pulled her tightly to his chest, all humor gone. "Don't ever try. You're mine and what's mine I keep. I've never fought over a woman before, but I think I could kill anyone who tried anything with you."

Jessie was thrilled by the possessive quality in his voice, and a little frightened. She was, indeed, Kincaid's woman. What that would entail was yet to be seen.

They arrived at the ranch and he lowered her to the porch. "I'm glad your father's not home," he whispered. Leaning over, he swatted her bottom, his lighter mood returning. "So you can fix me something to eat!" He laughed.

Jess stuck out her tongue and sashayed into the house, his laughter following her.

Coffee was brewing and some leftover stew was heating. Jess was thinking about the afternoon and blushed as she recalled her wild abandon. She had employed every means known to her to tempt and please Steve. She still didn't know where she stood with him, but she knew it didn't matter. If she could be with him, it would be enough.

Deep in her thoughts, she didn't hear him enter and was startled when he slid his arms about her waist. Sighing, she leaned back and enjoyed the warmth and strength of him.

"I could eat a horse." He nibbled at her ear.

Jessie slapped his arm and pulled from his embrace. "Well, I'm not a horse, Steve Kincaid, so sit down and I'll dish you up some stew!"

Steve straddled a chair as Jess set a plate in front of him. He wrapped an arm about her hips and rubbed his chin at her waist. "You're just what I need, Jess. Bossy in the kitchen and a veritable vixen in my bed."

"How would you know?" she bantered. "The nearest we've been to a bed was the shattered one in Green River."

"I'll remedy that," he promised with his eyes and his hands, "right after I eat. I'll need my strength."

"Am I going to spend all my time worrying about your stomach?" She smiled, serving him coffee before joining him at the table.

"What do you think?" he responded with a wide grin. They finished eating and sat quietly content, contemplating the evening ahead. Steve thought about the beautiful woman sharing the table. She had been magnificent! Her fiery hair curtained them when she straddled him in playful teasing and her hands were quick to learn how to please. The best was, it wasn't only her body that he found delightful. Her wit and reason were enchanting. She would captivate him in and out of bed, but his thoughts were rapidly turning to the former.

"Honey, before my thoughts carry me and you to your bed, I want to talk a minute, about the bargain."

Jess stood and moved to his side. He pulled her to his knee and she hugged him. "Please, Steve, I don't want to talk about it. It's enough to be with you and I'll do whatever you want, not because of our agreement but because I . . . I want to."

"Good girl." He began to open the buttons of her shirt. "Then we'll be married a week from Saturday."

"Mmm hmm." She moaned as he pushed her shirt from her shoulder. Realizing what he had said at last, she gasped. "Oh, Steve! You mean—"

"I mean that I really want you as my wife. Will you marry me, Miss Morgan?"

"But the bargain . . ." she mumbled, stunned by his question.

"The bargain be damned! I've been a fool for trying to trap you, but I'm not sorry, not if you'll be my wife." He waited for her to decide his fate. Standing alone had suddenly lost its appeal. He wanted Jessica Morgan for his wife.

Her answer was swift and undeniable. Her kisses rained on his face. "Yes! Oh, yes!"

Steve lounged propped against the headboard of her bed. He'd rolled a cigarette and was taking a puff, blowing the blue-gray smoke into the air. Jess reached up and swirled the smoke with her fingers. Her head rested on his chest and his arm lay across her rib cage. He hadn't said much since waking near midnight.

"Why so quiet?" she asked as she rolled to her stomach. Her fingers traced about his chest and she watched his eyes half close as he pulled again on the cigarette.

"I was thinking about us, about you." He doused his smoke in a nearby dish and drew her across his lap. "Today, yesterday, at the creek . . . well, I . . . I was . . . I didn't hurt you, did I? I mean, Jess . . . you screamed and . . ." Jess placed a finger against his lips.

"Why the concern now?" She smiled lovingly. "It didn't stop you then, nor have you thought of it until this minute."

Steve nibbled at her fingers playfully. "I didn't know I wanted to marry you then. Now I do. You were just a woman I wanted badly, needed to have, now you're the woman who will bear my sons and share my life. I won't hurt you again, Jess. Not ever."

Snuggling against his chest, she said, "Whether done in love or lust, it would be the same and the pain is swiftly gone and forgotten. I love you, Steve. I can no longer deny that. The only way you could hurt me is if you stopped wanting me. I can bear anything else, but knowing you loved or wanted another could destroy me."

His arms held her protectively and his lips brushed her hair. "Then you'll never be hurt again."

Jess nestled in his arms and enjoyed the lazy warmth and security of being his. She had never thought of belonging to anyone before, but she found the idea of being his woman intoxicating. Loving and sharing was a responsibility she was looking forward to. She would give all he ever needed if only he'd love her and keep loving her. In time he would tell her. She knew he would.

She felt the gentle cadence of his breathing and knew he slept. Smiling to herself, she thought of their lovemaking, at times fierce and demanding, at others gentle and giving. She knew life with Steve

Kincaid would never be dull—and that thought she carried to her dreams.

A hearty slap to her bottom brought Jess upright in bed. "Are you going to spend the rest of your life in that thing?" Steve grinned down at her.

She lay back down and stretched like a kitten. "Um, maybe," she teased. Steve leaned over her and she waited for his embrace, but instead she squealed as he grabbed the blanket covering her and ripped it back. In the light of day, she blushed at his perusal. He drew her up into his arms and rubbed his stubbled chin against her neck.

"Ouch! Steve, stop!" She giggled. "Put me down!" He let her legs go and she slid down his body while holding on to him. "You need a shave and I need to get dressed and make you something to eat."

"I'll shave later." His deep voice was husky. "And you can get dressed later." He paused and began to bite at her shoulder and added, "But I'll eat now." They tumbled back across the bed in laughter.

"You're insatiable!" she exclaimed as she ran her hands up and down his back.

"Who woke who in the middle of the night?" he said, resting his head on her breast.

"Well, I . . . that's different." She flushed pink. "I'm just not used to sharing a bed and it caused me to wake."

"You'd better get used to it." He kissed the fleshy rise of her breast. "And I'd love to lie here and argue the difference," he said, sitting up and beginning to pull on his pants, "but I have to be in Riverton by dinner for a Cattlemen's meeting and I'll have to report in at the K-D before I go. If I start tumbling with you, I'll never get there."

"Steve! Your back!" she cried, running a finger across the red welts that ran the length of it.

He glanced over his shoulder and laughed. "And you call me insatiable."

Jess brought a hand to her mouth in dismay. "You . . . you mean I did that?"

"Mmm hmm, you certainly did, my little savage." He turned and pulled her warm naked body into his lap. "But you don't hear me complaining, do you?" he murmured against her tousled hair.

"No, but . . . I'm so sorry." She felt dreadful at having done such damage.

"I'm not. you've merely branded me as yours." He kissed her quivering lips gently. "Now, be a good girl and get up." He ran a hand softly down her side to her hip. "Or I'll never have the strength to leave you."

Jess watched, still breathless, as Steve rode toward the K-D. Sitting down on the porch, she pressed her trembling hands to her warm cheeks. Steve's good-bye kiss had set her senses whirling and she was aching to be back in his arms already.

He had told her he would be away for two or three days and she should start preparing for their wedding in his absence, but right now all she could do was sit and remember. If she closed her eyes, she could feel his hands, his lips as they traveled her body. As her breathing grew more rapid, her eyes flew open.

"Oh! My goodness! I'm terrible!" She started to laugh. "He's not yet gone ten minutes and I'm dreaming of him." Standing and stretching, Jess decided she had better ride into Lander and see Roxy. With her father due back in late evening, she knew she couldn't stand to spend the day alone. Her heart was bursting and she just had to talk to someone about becoming Mrs. Steve Kincaid. In just twelve days she was getting married and she had to get someone to help her back to earth and get her started with the plans.

Anxious to see her friend, Jess ran into the house.

She paused long enough to straighten her very rumpled bed and change. Smiling to herself as she saddled her horse, she looked about her.

"Thank you, Wyoming! Thank you for molding and shaping the man I love. He is a man of your womb and I am a daughter of the wilderness. To share our love in your beauty is all I can ask." A cool breeze rustled her skirt and caressed her hair. She felt as though the land was answering a gentle and consenting reply.

"Well, if you don't look like the cat that ate the canary!" Roxy smiled as she opened the door for a glowing Jessica. "Come in and tell me what's on your mind before you burst."

The normal hello forgotten, Jess entered in a flurry and turned a pirouette. "Do I look different, Roxy?"

"Um, yes." Roxy stood with one hand on her hip and the other at her chin. "But I can't put my finger on it," she teased. It was obvious that Jessica was blooming like a perfect rose. Her eyes sparkled and her cheeks were aglow. There could be but one reason. Jess was in love.

"Oh, Roxy! I'm getting married!" Jess cried as she ran to embrace her friend.

"Aw, honey, I'm so happy for you." Roxy held Jess at arm's length. "And who's the lucky man? Someone from St. Louis who found he couldn't live without you after you left?"

Jess shook her head and grinned. "No, it's Steve Kincaid."

"Kincaid!" Roxy stepped back until her legs met the sofa and she sat down. "Our Kincaid?" she asked.

"Y-yes." Jess fell to her knees at Roxy's side. "Roxy, what's the matter? Aren't you happy for me?" Chewing at her lower lip, Jess watched Roxy's face with intensity. Her friend looked worried.

"Of . . . of course I'm happy for you, honey. It's just that I . . . I figured you two might know each other by now, but married! Well, I never thought of Kincaid as the marryin' kind." Smiling and patting Jessica's hand, she added, "It will take a bit of gettin' used to."

"Why? Why do you say that about him, Roxy?" Jess wasn't sure she wanted an answer but it was her future and she needed to know.

"Kincaid is . . . well, he has quite a reputation. I wouldn't have told you but I'll not see you hurt. I don't know how much of it is true, of course. Cowboys are notorious for spinnin' yarns." Roxy watched a frown form on Jessica's brow. "But I've never known him to ask anyone to marry him." To soften her disclosure she added warmly, "He must truly love you, honey, if he wants to make you his wife."

"I love him, Roxy. With all my heart, I love him." A tear glistened on her lashes as she looked to her friend.

Sighing deeply, and sorry for telling Jess about Kincaid, Roxy placed her arm about Jess and hugged her tightly. "And when is the wonderful day?"

"A . . . a week from Saturday."

"Well, that won't give you much time, will it? You had better start movin' and stop wastin' time with a foolish old woman."

They both rose and the excitement of a wedding began to fill them. Questions on what to wear, where it would be held, and who was to attend became the topics of the hour. Roxy sent Sam to bring lunch and they enjoyed a pleasant repast.

"Where is the prospective bridegroom, anyway?" Roxy sipped at her coffee.

"He's in Riverton. He had to meet with the association."

"Why didn't you go with him?" Roxy's defenses reared up.

"It wouldn't be proper and he couldn't ask me. Besides, he . . . he said I had to start getting ready for the wedding."

"Of course," Roxy agreed, "but if Kincaid was my man, I'd never let him out of my sight, even if it wasn't proper!" She winked and chuckled at the blush that rushed up Jessica's neck. "But I have a better idea! Why don't you go stay at the K-D while he's gone?"

"Oh! I . . . I couldn't! It wouldn't be right." Jess stammered. "What would people think?"

Roxy laughed. "What's to think? He's in River-ton, honey. You'll be in his house gettin' ready to marry him, not in a hotel room sharin' a bed! Good grief, child! People don't look down on an anxious bride, especially if she's to be Kincaid's bride."

"Do you really think that it would be okay?" Jess asked. Her eyes twinkled in anticipation. Steve's home—her home.

Roxy slid an arm about her shoulder. "I think it would be just fine, honey. Just fine."

Jess flashed a brilliant smile at her friend as Sam brought more coffee. They both set to laughing as they sat and began to outline one of the loveliest weddings Lander would ever see.

Chapter 9

The meeting had gone on for hours. Prices were discussed and arguments ensued over the ever-present threat of barbed wire and closed pastures. Steve contributed much to the conversations, but his thoughts kept drifting back to the woman who would soon be his wife.

At thirty-one, he had pictured himself a loner. He hadn't met a woman with whom he felt he could share the many facets of his life, but perhaps Jess was such a woman. Hadn't she ventured into the wilderness alone to seek a man she'd never really known and made a home for him and herself? Hadn't she thrown off the rules of the East to become nature's child in a few short weeks? And hadn't she gone from child to woman as naturally as Eve?

Maybe Jessica could be the one he had searched for in his youth. He had dreamed of a woman who would ride at his side in the high country and share a fur-piled bed throughout the long nights in a mountain cabin, a woman who would swim naked with him in the icy swift rivers and walk beside him through the lush, thick forests. His youth had passed, but the dream still surfaced from time to time.

A break to replenish the coffee and liquor gave Steve a few minutes longer to reflect on his future bride and his life. There were women in his past, but none he loved. He never gave his heart and didn't plan to start now. Oh, he was tempted to love her, but after some thought, he declined. He was too old for romance. He needed a woman to grace his home, bear his sons, and share his name, but his heart— that was another matter.

Walking to the window overlooking the street, he drew back the curtains and remembered. He thought of the many complexities that were the essence of her. Jess, warm and trusting in his arms. Jess, laughing and teasing. Jess, seductive and tempting. Even her fury was titillating. Life with her would not be dull. No, he chuckled, never that.

Reluctantly, as his associates reassembled, he cleared his head and rejoined them.

The days were lengthening, Jess thought as she headed toward Windy Creek. It was late afternoon and the sun was still warm, but the chill of early April nights would soon creep across the land with the setting sun.

A rustling in the grass ahead caused Jess to rein in with curiosity. A smile played at her lips as a rabbit ventured out into the road and looked about nervously. Her nervousness was soon justified as three small young ventured forth. Jess sat astride her mount and watched the tiny family move cautiously across her path to the safety of the high grass once again.

Spring, a time of birth and rebirth. The bright green of new growth could be seen in the fields and decking the scattered trees. Each of nature's creatures was setting forth new generations. The world felt young and clean. It was the only time the plains could rival the beauty of the rugged mountains. Wildflowers were in abundance and a fresh scent filled the air. Jess thought about her cousin, Bonnie, as she resumed her homeward journey. She would love all these flowers.

Nearing the ranch, Jess noticed smoke curling skyward from the house. Her father was back and she could tell him of her plans. She hoped he was of the same mind as Roxy. It would be a lot easier for her to accept it as suitable if he did.

Jeff came out onto the porch at the sound of an approaching rider. He smiled as he saw his daughter wave and ride to the corral. He joined her at the gate and helped her to unsaddle her horse and see to its needs for the night. Draping an arm about her shoulders, they walked to the house.

"I thought you'd be with Steve. What were you doin' in town?" He smiled.

"I had to tell Roxy about Steve and me! He's in Riverton at the Cattlemen's Association meeting and I was just busting to tell someone. I wanted Roxy to hear it from me firsthand anyway."

They mounted the steps and entered the now-cozy home. Bacon was frying on the stove and beans were boiling gently. The coffee brewed earlier still left a lovely aroma drifting through the room. Jess poured out two cups, humming as she stirred the pots before sitting a bit before dinner.

After a span of silence as chores were seen to, Jeff sat across from his daughter. He fidgeted with his cup, trying to build up the courage to speak to his girl. He finally just spoke out.

"Jess, you can tell me to mind my own business if you want but . . . well . . . do you love Steve Kincaid?"

Jessica looked at her father and noted a worried brow. She searched his face to determine the cause and he mistook her silence for not wanting to answer.

"I know, I know. It's none of my business. I'm not prying, I'm just wanting you to be happy. Life here ain't easy. It's a lot of hard work. There'll be hard times when cattle die or grazing is bad. Grass fires can burn you out as well as a blazing sun with no rain in sight. The rains can come but be too late or too early or too hard or not enough. If you don't love him enough, child, the land can beat you. You've done well here since your comin' but things have gone well, too."

A tear rolled down her cheek as Jess reached across the table and took his hand.

"Papa, I love him and I love Wyoming." She swallowed back a lump in her throat. "And Papa, I'm . . . I'm not Mama. She was born and raised in the East. Her heritage was always there and part of that is in me, but part of me is here from you. Yes, Papa, I love him enough."

Jeff didn't answer, he merely nodded his head and gave her a smile before rising and going to wash. Jess knew she had said the right things.

Jessie was nervous as she packed a few of her belongings in a saddlebag. She wondered if Sarah and Chad would think it strange that she wanted to spend a few days at the K-D. Her father thought it a great idea as she could better see to the plans for the barbeque that would be expected on their wedding day for all the neighbors, hands, and friends. He felt it to be a sound idea, but the Duncans were like family to Steve. Maybe they would think she was being too possessive. She didn't want to cause any animosity between herself and the people of the K-D.

"No! It's not like that!" she said aloud and startled herself. She shook her head and continued to think more silently. It would be her home and she had every right to see it and be there. It would be easier to make a guest list with Sarah's help and she knew she would be able to count on her for other assistance as well. Anyone else working there would be working for her, too, when she and Steve married.

All her excuses were valid, but the real reason for her doubts and discomforts finally surfaced, and she acknowledged it. She was afraid, afraid they would know of the bargain and think she had been willing to sell herself for her father and his land. She knew it wasn't true and Steve damned it as foolishness. That's what was important, she decided. People would see she loved him. They'd know in short order that she was his choice.

Feeling better and a bit more confident, Jess picked up her bag and went out to her horse. Her father stood holding the reins until she mounted.

"I don't know why I'm so happy you're marryin' Kincaid." He smiled. "I just get my daughter back and he takes her away."

Patting his weathered hand and leaning to kiss his brow, Jess replied, "I won't be in St. Louis, Pa. I'll be just a few short miles away. Miles I expect will get shorter as we travel back and forth often."

He nodded in agreement. "See you in a couple of days, honey."

"Come have lunch with me tomorrow, Pa. It would be fun and good for you. You've been working too hard."

"I should be gettin' started on the barn," he hedged.

"Pa, I won't take no for an answer. As lady of the manor—" She struck a regal pose. "—I demand it!"

They shared the jest and he promised he would come. Jessie pulled the reins about and headed on her short journey.

As Jess headed for the K-D, Steve was getting ready to enter his second day of meetings. If all went well, two more days of talks should wrap it up. The contract for the army might get sticky but he was hopeful that the negotiations would go well. He was just about finished shaving when someone knocked at the door. Expecting coffee to be sent up, he shouted for whomever was delivering his morning fare to enter. Toweling off the last of the lather, Steve turned to find Margo Harrison slipping into his room.

"What do you want, Margo?" he asked coldly. He had seen her in town the day before but managed to avoid meeting her. "I don't think your father would be pleased to know you're here."

"Steve, darling. Is that any way to talk to an old friend?" Margo advanced toward him. She was dressed as seductively as daytime would permit and she was obviously ready to do anything to get Steve to make love to her.

"Old friends can meet in the lobby or the restaurant." Steve walked past her to get his shirt and she chuckled.

"My, my. Someone has been playing with a wildcat, I see. If those scratches are from that new whore you picked up, they should be seen to, darling," she purred viciously.

Steve swung about, a black rage flowing through him. Margo backed up against the dresser and cowered at the fury in his eyes.

"If you know what's good for you, Margo, you'll get out of here right now and never come near me again."

Sure she could convince him otherwise, Margo smiled. "You don't mean that, Steve, not after what we've shared." She slowly stepped close to him and set her hand on his chest. Her fingers gently caressed him as he pulled on his shirt. Steve moved away from her in disgust and sat in a chair to don his boots.

Seeing a chance to keep him in one place long enough to reach her objective, Margo knelt at his side and ran a hand up and down his thigh, inching closer to his manhood with each sweep.

"You always wanted me before, Steve. Why not now? Your meeting can go on without you for a while." She pressed her full breasts up against his upper leg. "If you're worried about word getting back to your fiancée, don't. No one really believes you're going to marry her. They know she's just your latest toy and that when you tire of her you'll come back to me." Steve's silence encouraged her to boldly go on. "I don't care if you play with her for a while, but spare me the joke of marrying the slut!" With her blonde head on his lap she could not see the anger burning in him.

Margo had gone too far. Her slander of Jessica had only reinforced his choice. Her father was his friend and he didn't want to cause him any trouble or embarrassment but he couldn't let Margo go on. His fingers entwined in her curls as he spoke.

"So, you think you have it all figured out." His restrained fury barely audible, his fingers began to tighten and she winced.

"Steve darling, you're hurting me!"

He pulled her head back and pressed his face near to hers to emphasize his words. "Listen to me, Margo, and listen good. I don't want you! You came after me from the start. I'm going to marry Jessica and if I ever hear you call her anything but Mrs. Kincaid, I'll expose you for the conniving little bitch you are! I never made you any promises. Any ideas you have about us you contrived yourself. If you try anything that hurts my woman, you'll be hurting me and you know I'd be hell to reckon with. Do you understand?"

"Yes . . . yes, I understand!" she cried.

"Good." He released her and rose, picking up his coat and heading for the door. "Good-bye, Margo. For your own good, remember what I said." He didn't even turn back to look at her before closing the door.

"I'll remember, Steve. I'll remember and so help me you'll regret the day you ever met that whore." She clenched her fists at her sides. "You're mine and the K-D is mine. No gutless city bitch is going to take my place. You need me. You'll see, Steve. Me and only me! You'll come back!" she cried to the empty room. "I know you will."

* * *

Coming to the K-D had been the right thing to do, Jess thought as she climbed into bed. The day had been more than she could have hoped for. Sarah proved to be a wealth of knowledge and a bond of friendship was fast forming. Another delightful surprise of the day had been Red.

Upon entering the yard at the K-D, Jess encountered the young lad who had brought her the note from Steve, the reply to which had changed her life. He doffed his hat and took her horse. She had smiled and thanked him after instructing him to see to stabling the animal for a few days. With her saddlebag over her arm, Jess walked to the front door, drew a deep breath, and knocked firmly. Within moments the door opened and a stunning woman greeted her.

"Ay, an' what can I do for ya, lass?" A lilting brogue rolled from the tongue of the red-haired woman on the threshold.

"I'm Jessica Morgan. Mr. Kincaid and I . . ."

"Come in, come in, lass! Saints be praised but he can pick 'em."

Without a moment to think, Jess was ushered into the foyer and her bag taken from her arm and set aside. Before she could explain, she found herself the object of scrutiny. With hands on her hips, the Irishwoman walked around Jess, shaking her head and smiling.

"I just knew that lad would come to his senses sooner or later. You're a real beauty, lass."

"Thank you, but . . ."

"Och, here I am rattlin' on when you don't even know who I am. Constance Stuart." Her hand was extended for a shake and as Jess responded, she continued, "But everyone calls me Red." She pointed to her rust-colored hair. " 'Tis my good Irish heritage which blessed me with this fiery top and a temper ta match!" Laughter rang through the room and Jessie was again impressed with the loveliness of this woman.

After explaining why she was there and being ushered to the kitchen for tea, Jess learned that Red was Steve's housekeeper and cook, but she avoided his social functions.

"Don't like those uppity folks," she confided, "but I'm right sorry I missed this last one!" Jess smiled shyly and Red went on, telling how she'd worked for the Kincaid family for fifteen years, since she was widowed at twenty. Her brown eyes sparkled as she related some tales from her past and questioned Jess alternately. It wasn't until Chad came in for coffee that Red resumed her chores and let Jess catch her breath.

"She talk your ear off yet?" Chad teased, and was slapped on the arm for his efforts.

"Listen, me lad, if she's to be mistress of this house she needs ta be knowin' the likes of you and that great oaf she's marryin'!"

"If I know you—" Chad straddled a chair at the table with Jess. "—she knew everything within twenty minutes after she came!" Red left in a mock huff to see to a room for Jess. The kitchen grew quiet in her absence.

"She's a fine-looking woman," Jess broke the silence, after considering what to say.

"Yeah, she is that. Sometimes I think she thinks she's Steve's mother the way she runs this house. Bossy and stubborn, and always after him to find a wife, at the same time yelling that nobody in their right mind would have him. I had a crush on her when she first came here." Chad chuckled at the memory. "That's until she boxed my ears and gave me the worst tongue-lashing of my life for following her to the creek once to watch her."

Jessie relaxed and laughed after hearing the story. "How's Sarah? I hope to see a lot of her while I'm here. I'm afraid I need her help if this wedding is to come off right."

Chad smacked his forehead. "Lord! That's why I

came in! Sarah wants me to invite you to dinner tonight. As soon as she heard from Willy that you were here, she started baking and fussing. Will you come? Don't say no or I'll have hell to pay.''

"I'd love to, Chad.''

And so her first day was filled with touring the house with Red and dining with Chad and Sarah. As Jessie snuggled beneath the down comforter and laid her head on the plump, soft pillow, she smiled. The image of a bustling, frightening regime was dissolving and the reality of friendly, hardworking folk filled the void. She had been accepted. No one suspected the approaching wedding had begun as a farce. No longer a stranger, she felt as though she was truly home.

It was late morning and the three women sat in the kitchen sharing coffee and freshly baked cookies.

"I can't believe we're expected to feed all these people!'' Jess laughed, pointing to a two-page list.

"Aye, and they'll be expectin' the best,'' Red offered. "You can't expect them to ride miles for a weddin' and not fill 'em up. 'Sides, this ain't a regular weddin'. Everything Kincaid does is on a grand scale.'' Smiling, she added, "Didn't he pick the prettiest gal in the territory to wed?''

"This is one time you aren't full of blarney, Red.'' Sarah grinned and squeezed Jessie's hand.

"Aye, but gettin' back ta the weddin' guests—''

"Guests! My goodness, I forgot!'' Jess cried. "I invited my father for lunch today! Will it be all right, Red?''

"Aye, lass, 'twill be fine and if he's as goodlookin' as his daughter, who knows?'' She threw up her hands in a fatalistic gesture and smiled, looking at the grins on the faces of the two younger women. "Well, seein' as how I've no man o' me own, I should think ya'd be pleased ta see me showin' an interest!''

"I think you'll both be in for a pleasant surprise." Jess laughed.

Her father came for lunch as instructed. Slipping her arm through his, she led him to the parlor and offered him a drink before lunch. She told him about how helpful Sarah was and the lovely time she'd spent with Chad and her at dinner the night before. As Jess was telling him about what they'd planned for the barbeque, she realized he was staring past her and not hearing a word. Jess turned to see what the distraction was and saw Red standing in the doorway. She grinned as she watched them sizing each other up and liking what they saw.

"Pa, I'd like you to meet Constance Stuart. She's Steve's housekeeper." Jess laughed as he kept staring. "Pa!"

"Oh! What?" he stammered. "Yes . . . house-keeper." He advanced quickly and extended a hand. "I'm pleased to meet you, Miss Stuart." He grinned boyishly. "I've heard about you, but . . . well, somehow I figured you were . . . well, older."

"It's Mrs. Stuart," Red replied, a bit more softly than usual. Noticing his grin fading she quickly added, "I'm widowed, and me friends call me Red." She smiled warmly, shaking his hand longer than was necessary. After a lengthy silence, she pulled her hand back. "If you'll not be mindin', I'll serve lunch in the kitchen."

"Fine!" Jeff said. "I don't want you going to any trouble on my account."

Red tapped his shoulder playfully. "Och! Won't be no trouble at all havin' ya ta lunch wherever ya want ta be eatin'."

Jessica held her hand over her mouth to suppress the giggle that threatened as these two grown people acted like nervous teenagers. She'd hoped they would like each other but as she looked on, she felt sure it would soon be more than that. Her father would need someone now that she was leaving. All the years he'd tended himself were forgotten as the natural female instinct to matchmake reared itself.

Still smiling, Jess eased past the two. "If you'll excuse me," she said, "I'll go freshen up."

Within minutes she entered the kitchen to find them acting like old friends. Jess didn't bother to question why they had never met, she just accepted the fact they knew each other now.

"I hope you enjoyed lunch, Papa." Jess watched him mount.

"Yup, I sure did." He smiled. "Connie's a right good cook."

Jess had noticed his use of a shortened version of Red's Christian name during lunch and how quickly she responded to it. It was like a private message between them, something special. Jess knew she would be seeing a lot of her father after the wedding and who could tell, perhaps another would be occurring shortly.

"Remember, Pa, Steve took me from you and turnabout is only fair." Before he could answer she ran up the steps to the porch, turned to wave, and entered the house laughing.

"Children!" he grumbled as he rode out. A broad grin slowly crossed his face. "They're pretty smart sometimes."

That evening Chad and Sarah joined her for dinner. Chad finished and went out to see to some unfinished chores. The sun was close to setting and the kitchen was being put to order for the next day's use. Bread was rising on the back of the stove and fresh-ground coffee blended with the aroma of warm yeast.

Wiping her hands on her apron, Red turned to Jess. "You know, lass, I wondered what you'd be like, bein' from the East. I never doubted you'd be a looker but I figured you'd be all fluff and soft.

Watchin' ya workin' with me today . . . well, lass, you're what the lad needs.''

It was a simple statement but it was just what Jessie needed to hear. ''Thank you, Red.'' Tears glistened in her eyes as she hugged the older woman.

''Well, isn't this a cozy scene.''

Sarah dropped the apple she was peeling as she recognized the sugary voice of Margo Harrison. Jess spun about and tried to gain some composure at the shock of seeing this woman.

''Miss . . . Miss Harrison, isn't it?'' She walked to the intruder and offered her hand politely.

Margo looked at the offered hand and ignored it. ''Prepare a room for me, Red,'' she ordered.

''The name's Mrs. Stuart to you and I had no word from me boss that you'd be callin' or stayin' here.'' Red's cool disapproval would have deterred a less desperate person.

''Steve sent me here to wait for him. Do as I say!'' Margo demanded. It was sweet enough making her mark on the K-D, but finding Jessica there was sweeter still.

Red's Irish temper flared and she moved to argue that statement, when Jess placed a hand on her arm in restraint.

''Prepare a room, Red.'' Though softly spoken, a quiver could be detected. ''P-please.''

''Aye, lass. As you wish.'' Red smiled gently, casting an eye toward Margo to see if she got the message.

Margo had indeed, but she followed Red without another word. Sarah silently watched Jess move toward the sink and grip the counter in anguish. She rose quickly and placed an arm about Jessie.

''H-how could he s-send her here?'' she stammered.

''Listen to me! I know Steve and he wouldn't do anything like this!'' Sarah insisted.

''But she's here and she was engaged to him before I came along. She has a right to hate me.''

Sarah grabbed her shoulders and pulled Jess to face her. "Never! He was never engaged to Margo. Jess! He wants you! He loves you!"

"He's never told me," Jess said in a trembling voice.

Sarah gathered her into her arms. "Isn't that just like a man. The big ox! He can take on the whole government, Indians, and all forms of pestilence, but handle a woman right—never!" Sarah sat Jess down and joined her, still holding her hand. "I don't know what Margo is up to, but I'll bet Steve throws her out when he gets home."

"Do you really think so?" Jessie's eyes pleaded for an affirmative answer.

"You're damned right!" Sarah swore, then blushed. "Oh! I'm sorry but that creature makes me furious!"

Chad entered and, blissfully unaware of the current events, he moved to kiss his wife. The look of surprise on his face when she pushed him away with an indignant "Men!" was laughable.

"What'd I do?" he queried.

Sarah and Jess looked at each other and burst into laughter.

Chapter 10

T he night was long for Jess but she clung to Sarah's words and they gave her some peace. That peace, however, was shattered the moment she left her room and found Margo beginning to descend the stairs.

"Are you still here?" Margo's disdain was all too obvious. "I'd have thought you were smart enough to get the message." Her smile was shallow and never touched her eyes. Clad in a light peach silk wrapper with ecru lace escaping at her cuffs and about her throat, Margo looked ethereal. Her pale blonde curls hung loosely at her shoulders and her equally pale skin lent no depth to her features. She was like a painting, with the only color that of her light blue eyes.

Jessica's green eyes spit fire but she refused to rise to the bait. She could hear Red in the kitchen, rattling pans and talking to someone, and she was drawn to the familiar sounds. Holding her skirt aside, she eased past the new guest. Jess was sure she had moved far enough to the wall to avoid contact when she heard a faint whispered warning. "Watch out" echoed in her ear just before she felt something trip her up.

A scream tore from her throat as she fell forward, grasping at air to save herself. Her shoulder came up hard against the wall and it changed the angle of her descent. Instead of falling head-first to a certain death, Jess began to roll over and over until she hit the floor at the base of the stairway.

It was getting dark, she thought, and cold. She hurt but she wasn't sure where. It felt like all over and she thought that if she closed her eyes, the pain would go away.

"What the hell's going on out here?" Chad yelled as he ran from the kitchen. Spying the crumpled form at the foot of the stairs, he ran forward with Red in his wake.

The first thing Red saw was long strands of auburn hair spread out across the floor and wrapped about a slender outstretched arm. "Jess!"

They reached her at the same time and Chad carefully checked to see if she was breathing. "She's alive!" He gently felt her arms and legs for breaks and, finding none, turned her to her back.

Red looked from the dark bruise forming on Jessica's cheek to Chad. Before she could speak, she spotted a movement on the stairs. Red clutched Chad's arm and motioned toward it. He turned to watch Margo holding the rail like a lifeline. She looked into their accusing eyes and began to stammer.

"I . . . I called a warning. She pushed past me. She must have have tripped." Chad and Red continued to stare at her accusingly. "Don't look at me like that!" Margo screamed. She had hoped to kill Jessica, she knew that, but they mustn't. They'd tell Steve and it would ruin everything. "It . . . it was an accident!"

Chad turned back to see to Jess, and Red ran into the kitchen for water and cloths. Ignoring Margo as she stood and watched them administer to Jess, neither saw the hatred in her eyes. Her mouth was drawn to a tightly pinched line and her nostrils flared. If they had turned to her at that moment, they would have thought her mad.

"Careful," Red warned unnecessarily as Chad gently lifted Jess and began to carry her to her room. Passing Margo without even a glance, Chad moved swiftly as Red led the way in preparation.

Left standing alone in the empty hall, Margo mumbled, "You're all against me, but I'll get you. I swear it. When I'm mistress of the K-D I'll get even with you all. You'll come crawling to me on your hands and knees, you'll see!" She slowly returned to her room, pausing outside Jessica's door. "This is all your fault," she thought as tears formed and slid over to splash on her cheeks, "and you'll pay dearest of all."

There were voices, no, whispers, Jess thought. They seemed so far away. Where could they be? She tried to open her eyes but it was still dark and she was afraid of something. Who could help her? Steve! He had said she'd never be hurt again. He'd protect her. "Steve," she moaned again and again. Something cool was pressed to her brow and gentle hands stroked her hair. She relaxed and it all began to come back. Margo, the stairs, falling! She threw out her hands and screamed.

"It's okay! Jess! It's all right now." Firm hands clasped her own and her eyes fluttered open.

"Chad? W-what are you doing here? What h-happened?"

"In a minute, honey. Just take it easy. You've had a bad fall. Nothing's broken but you'll have some nasty bruises for a while." He released her hands and sat on the edge of the bed. Red came in at that moment and sighed deeply in relief.

"Saints be praised!" She moved in a flurry as she set aside a tray she carried and hurried to the other side of the bed. "How are ya, darlin'?"

"A bit sore." Jess smiled faintly. "But I'll be okay. Dr. Duncan has given me a clean bill of health."

Chad laughed. "Humor's a good sign."

Jess tried to push herself up. She winced and

grabbed a throbbing shoulder. "H-help me up, Chad," Jess gasped.

"You better stay—"

"Please, Chad. I need to sit up. I'm just sore, that's all."

He looked at Red, and when she nodded, he slipped an arm beneath Jessica's knees and carefully about her waist. The short journey from prone to sitting brought tears to her eyes.

"Are you sure I'm all in one piece?" she asked. Before Chad could reply, Sarah came bursting into the room.

"Oh, Jess!" she cried. "Thank God you're all right!" Chad went to his wife and placed an arm about her shoulder. "When I think of what could have . . ." Covering her face with her hands, she turned to her husband for comfort.

"Don't cry, Sarah," Jess pleaded. "I'm fine. Why, in a few hours I expect to be coming down to dinner."

Although she could stand for a few minutes in the late afternoon, she couldn't keep her dinner date. A tray was brought up by Red, and Sarah joined them. There was little to talk about as each woman was busily investigating her own thoughts. No one mentioned Margo or the accident, but it was there, in the air, and Jess needed it cleared.

"Where's Margo?" she quietly asked when Red took her tray away. After no answer, she looked at each. "Sarah? Red? Where is she?"

Sarah sighed deeply. "In her room, I guess. She . . . she came down to dinner as though nothing had happened, ate, and retired. None of us spoke to her but that didn't stop her from playing the honored guest."

Red was straightening the bed and fidgeting as Sarah replied, but she couldn't keep silent any longer. "Jess, darlin', did Margo . . . did she push ya down those stairs?"

Jess looked down at her lap. Her hands were clasped and she pulled them apart to trace a blackening spot on the top of one. "I . . . I don't know," she whispered. "I could hear you in the kitchen. I remember wanting to be there. I moved past her and . . . and I heard a whisper, a warning, I think." She leaned her head back against the headboard and closed her eyes. "The next thing I knew, I was falling. Something had . . . had tripped me."

"That bitch!" Red seethed.

"Red!" Jessica's head jerked up. "I can't prove that she did it on purpose! It could have been an accident. I couldn't accuse her, Red, not without proof." Steve might think the whole thing was a figment of her imagination. It would be Margo's word against hers and she wasn't sure where Steve's sympathy would lie.

"She's right, Red," Sarah added. "There is none, and Jess said she might have heard a warning."

"Or perhaps a threat," Red corrected.

"No! Don't say that!" Jess began to cry. "Please, Red, let it go. I'm going to be okay. Just let it go."

Red sat beside her and brushed some strands of hair from her cheek. "Okay, lass," she assured Jess, "I'll not speak of it again." But I'll remember, she thought, and I'll watch. Margo would make a slip and Red would be ready.

Jess winced as she slid her arm into her shirtsleeve. Red thought she could spend another day in bed but Jess was adamant.

"Wasn't it bad enough you slept in here last night? I feel like a five-year-old with croup and my nanny close at hand." Jess caught a grin on Red's face at the comparison. "I'm fine, Red. Really! And I don't need a watchdog."

Jess understood Red's motives. She was afraid the "accident" was no accident. The thought had lain on the fringes of Jessica's mind as well, but she refused to have someone at her elbow each time she moved.

"I'm no watchdog," Red hedged. "I just thought you might be wantin' company while ya mend."

"All right, I'll accept that for now." Jess smiled. "We'll start the morning over. Good morning, Red! I'm feeling much better this morning." Her smile grew as wide as her sore cheek would allow. "What's for breakfast? I'm famished."

"Point taken, Jess." Red grinned. "I'll go down an' start somethin'." She reached the door and mumbled, "You'd try a saint."

"And you're no saint, Red!" Jess called after her. "But keep trying!"

Jessie's call informed Margo that she was finally alone. She had spent the night formulating a plan that would get Jess off the K-D in short order. When Steve returned and found her, Margo, there, he'd forget all about the bitch, she'd see to it.

Easing the door open, Margo checked the hall. Finding it empty and hearing the clangs in the kitchen, she moved into the hall and across to the open door of Jessica's room. Looking in, she watched as Jess wound her long thick hair into a knot at her nape, catching escaping strands with pins.

"I'm glad to see you've recovered." Margo startled Jess with her bold announcement.

Jessica's pale face lost more color as she spun from the mirror to see her uninvited guest. Her hands were shaking so badly she had to grab the folds of her skirt to still them. Her shoulder throbbed badly from the sudden movement but she was unable to trust her hands to move to it.

"Yes, I'm much better. Thank you."

"You really must be more careful." Margo was lightly examining the furnishings. Jess wondered why Margo had come to her room. Idle chatter wasn't part of Margo's personality, and Jess decided to take the offensive.

"I'll be very careful from now on, I assure you, and I don't think anything like that will happen again." With her words she had firmly thrown down the gauntlet.

"No, I don't suppose an opportunity for such a thing will occur again," Margo parried. The duel began. "I don't think there will be a need when Steve returns." Margo's smile was secretive and drew the first blood.

"I don't believe he sent you here, Margo. I think you are grasping at straws. I understand your desperation. You thought you'd be mistress of the K-D, and you hate me because he chose me over you." A thrust and a point for Jess, for Margo paled and fought hard to keep her temper in check. It wasn't in the plan.

Glancing into the mirror to fix hair that needed no repair, Margo took a deep breath and clearly prepared for the final thrust, the kill!

"I suppose you think because he rode between your thighs and promised marriage that he meant it." Margo watched Jessica blush and her eyes widen. "Oh, don't be embarrassed. It happens to all of them sooner or later. Although you were easier than most and, I must say, a little savage. Of course, he likes that."

Jess half-stumbled to the bed and sat. She gripped the spindle at the foot. "What are you talking about?"

"Why, the scratches, my dear!" Margo felt victory was near. "You really must try to restrain yourself a bit." Jess was staring across the room, transfixed. It had been played out, and well, Margo thought, as she silently left the room. The seeds of doubt were deeply planted. It wouldn't be long now.

"No tears," Jess murmured. "My world has been torn apart and I can't cry." She went over what

Margo had said. The scratches! His back! They must have met, and talked, and . . . God! What a fool she'd been! "Not the marrying kind," Roxy had said.

A bargain! Windy Creek for her body! Kincaid's woman! Kincaid's mistress! Kincaid's whore! Jess put her hands over her ears to close out the words in her mind.

"I've been such a fool!" She sobbed and then straightened up. "But no more!" Thoughts of Steve naked in Margo's arms, his dark body in contrast to her milky-white one, and them laughing together at her caused a deep ache in her chest. She could hardly breathe with the agony of it.

What could she do? She couldn't stay. The thought of seeing Steve and Margo together would kill her. Where should she go? St. Louis? Windy Creek? Yes! Her father would know what was to be done. She'd go to him with everything. They'd work it out together, just like they'd fixed up the ranch together.

"Papa," Jess whispered as she left the room and walked slowly down the stairs. She could hear Red and Chad talking as she moved quietly across the foyer and carefully opened the front door. The click of its closing was like a gunshot through her heart.

Filled with resolve, Jess walked quickly toward the barn. She spotted a horse tied near the corral, all saddled. Without any hesitation, she hiked up her skirt and mounted. Pain shot through her hip and down her thigh, and a buzzing started in her head.

"Don't faint!" she ordered her screaming brain. With a deep breath her head cleared, and she started her painful journey to Windy Creek. A few short miles, she called it, but it felt like the longest journey she had ever traveled.

The first thing Jess noticed was the lack of smoke coming from the chimney, and she knew that her father must not be there. "Oh, Papa!" she cried aloud. Her body was aching terribly. Every muscle was pleading for rest but she had to find her father before she could. Looking about the yard, she knew for sure he was not there, and sat still upon the horse's back to think it out.

He must have gone to town, she reasoned. She would have to go farther to find him, but she wasn't sure if she could make it. She wanted to get off her horse and stumble to her bed, yet she knew she couldn't. If she gave in to her fatigue, she might not have the strength to remount later.

Her decision was finally made with a single thought. Steve was due home any time. He might even now be at the K-D. He could be angry with her for upsetting his plans. She had to move on. She couldn't bear to face him. A chill wracked her body and she thought self-disgust the cause.

"I can't find her anywhere," Sarah lamented as she drew her apron corner to wipe her eyes. "Where could she have gone?"

Worry made Sarah nervous and upset, but it gave Red a cool, clear head. She watched Margo sitting on the sofa, as demure as she was disinterested. The only sign that she wasn't as collected as her image suggested was the way her teacup rattled when she picked it up. Red knew that she had something to do with Jessie's disappearance.

"What do you know about our Jessie goin'?" Red addressed Margo.

"Me! Why should I know anything?" Margo played with the folds of her gown. "Maybe she just decided it would be smarter to go on her own instead of waiting for Steve to throw her out."

"Why, you—"

"She took a horse!" Chad yelled, interrupting Red's retort.

"She must have gone home," Sarah offered. "We better go after her."

"Let her go!" Margo stood and shouted. "You're

supposed to be her friends. Why do you want her here to be humiliated? Just let the bitch go!"

Red would have hit Margo if Chad hadn't sensed the violence building in her at Margo's words and restrained her arm. Ignoring Margo's slur, he attempted to soothe Red. "Get the buggy ready and go to Windy Creek. You and Sarah will be more useful than I would be." Red pulled to free herself and Chad stepped between her and Margo. "Red, it won't help Jess."

Red sighed and shook her head more calmly. "Aye, I'll . . . I'll go."

"Good." Chad went to Sarah. "Honey, I'll wait here in case she returns. You take Willy and if you need anything, send him back with a message."

"I will." Sarah's lips quivered. "I hope she's all right."

Chad wrapped his arms about his wife and pressed his lips to the top of her head. "She will be. Don't worry, honey." He cupped her face with his large, browned hands and drew her lips to his. "She's a survivor, Sarah, like you." He smiled gently. "You better get goin'."

Steve could see the roof and chimneys of the K-D. He had left Riverton early and made good time getting home. First he would check on things at the ranch and then go to see Jessica. He had actually missed the chit, he mused, and he was suddenly anxious to hold her in his arms. He realized he wasn't thinking about bedding her. He knew he wanted to, yet it was seeing her, hearing her voice, that was filling his mind.

Riding into the yard, he was surprised by the quiet. Where was everyone? Why wasn't there the usual activity about the house and yard? Something was wrong. He could feel it in his gut. He could taste it like bile rising in his throat. Urgently he jumped from his horse, tied the reins, and took the stairs two at a time.

Margo was the first to see Steve standing in the doorway. She pretended otherwise and felt fortune was smiling on her as she began a conversation with Chad, one that was meant to damn Jess for good.

"You're very fond of Jessica, aren't you?" she asked as Chad stood at the bar and poured a whiskey.

"That's a stupid question. Who wouldn't be?" Margo saw Steve out of the corner of her eye standing back from the threshold, listening. Perfect! she thought.

"You spent an awfully long time in her room yesterday." Margo gracefully moved to stand beside Chad.

"Look, Margo, I don't want to talk about it! I feel rotten enough about all this. When Steve finds out—" Before he could finish his sentence about the fall, he was spun about. "Steve! Am I glad to . . . ugh!" A blow to his chin sent Chad sprawling across the floor. "Christ, Steve! What the hell's wrong with you?" he said, rubbing his jaw.

"You son of a bitch! I should kill you!" Steve's rage was explosive and Margo seized the moment to intervene. She couldn't allow Chad to talk to Steve, not yet.

"Steve! Stop it! You're acting crazy!" She flung herself against him and held his arm. Looking over her shoulder, she spoke to Chad. "Get out of here, Chad. I'll find out what's wrong."

"But he . . ." Chad was unsteadily rising to his feet.

"Get out!" Steve shouted.

Chad nodded and left the room, casting a glance at Steve in passing. He had disengaged Margo's hands and grabbed a glass for a tall whiskey. His friend had had black moods before and Chad agreed that he needed a cooling-off period.

Silence reigned for long moments. Margo needed to fuel the fire she had kindled, yet it must be done slowly.

"How was the meeting, Steve?" she asked coolly.

Tossing off his drink, he poured another. "What the hell are you doing here, Margo?"

"I came to apologize for my disgusting behavior the other day." She set her hand on his arm. "I'm so ashamed. Believe me, Steve, it won't happen again."

He wasn't really interested in what she was saying, she knew, yet her next words would interest him. With a deep sigh she walked across the room toward the window. "I'm glad you're home. Poor Sarah, she was so upset when she . . ." She let her voice fade purposefully.

Steve slammed down his glass and spun about. "When she what?" he demanded.

"Steve, darling. You're tired now. You mustn't get involved in someone else's affairs, even if they are your friends. Why don't you go upstairs and—"

"Margo! I'm in no mood for games! What the hell are you talking about? What upset Sarah?"

"I . . . she ran into Jessica's room." Hanging her head, she appeared upset. "Chad was there and . . . and I . . . I heard her crying."

Steve hadn't moved. His breathing was deep and rapid. His hands were tightly fisted at his sides. Margo ran to him and slid her arms about his neck.

"I'm sorry, darling, that I had to be the one to tell you." She laid her head upon his chest. "I told you she was no good. You should have—Steve! Where are you going?"

Like a crashing bull, Steve pushed her away and ran from the room. The front door smashed against the wall with the force of his pull. Margo stood in the parlor and smiled. He'd be back, she thought. It was part of the plan that he'd come back.

Chapter 11

Steve came around the back of the house to find Chad splashing water over his head in the horse trough. The first Chad knew of his presence was when he spied Steve's dusty boots planted near him. Chad shook the excess water from his hair and stood to face his friend. Barely restrained black rage filled Steve's face and his stance was battle-ready. Chad thought it best to let Steve initiate any conversation.

They stood facing each other like two titans of old, one dark and one fair. Both untamed giants who had managed a veneer of civilization. How long would it take to crack that veneer?

Not being one to mince words, Steve spoke boldly. "Did you sleep with her, Chad?"

Too stunned to answer quickly, Chad stared in total disbelief. He finally replied in disgust at the accusation. "You fool! I won't even embarrass you or myself by answering that." He started to move away.

Grabbing his shirtfront, Steve yanked Chad back. "Answer me, damn it! Did you make love to Jess?"

Steve was jealous, Chad thought, insanely jealous! His lifelong friend, who swore he'd never fall in love, had taken the plunge, and he didn't even know it! Chad's eyes sparkled and a wide grin crossed his face.

"What the hell's so funny?" Steve roared. Chad

114

broke into laughter as Steve shook him and it enraged him further. Blinded with fury, Steve drew back an arm and smashed his fist into Chad's stomach. Losing his desire to laugh with the blow, Chad began to defend himself. He landed a blow to Steve's cheek, and it began.

Sarah and Red were shocked to see what was going on as they entered the yard at the K-D. Two grown men, blood oozing from split lips and running from their noses, grappled on the ground.

"Chad! Steve!" Sarah stood in the buggy and yelled. Neither man responded. They were too deeply involved in the battle, one hell-bent to kill and one fighting to survive.

Red could see it would be impossible for her and Sarah to separate them. No amount of shouting would help, nor could they physically intervene. Their combined strengths would not hold one of them.

Jumping from the wagon, Red ran for the kitchen door, her skirts flying and her hair tearing loose of its pins. Just inside the back door was perched a shotgun. Red never had to use it, but she knew how. Throwing her shawl to the floor, she gripped the double barrel and swung the gun across her arm. Standing on the back steps, Red aimed the shotgun skyward and let both barrels discharge.

The roar was enough to bring the combatants to their senses. They raised themselves to their knees, breathing heavily. Red ejected the spent shells and slid two more in before she walked angrily to the men.

"If I live to be a hundred, I hope I ne'er see such foolishness ag'in," Red scolded. " 'Tis the very divil ye've been playin' and I want to know why." Her brogue was heavy when angered. "Be speakin' yer piece, an' now!"

Like two small, guilty boys they answered at the

same time, each blaming the other, each trying to outtalk the other.

"Steve made crazy accusations about Jess and . . ."

"I won't be cuckolded by my woman and my best . . ."

"Enough! I don't know what's going on here—" Sarah joined the fracas. "—but I'm going to find out." Chad attempted to interrupt and was firmly told to shut up. "Red, the next one to talk is to be shot!" She looked at her gun-toting friend and gave one firm nod. It was greeted with a satisfied smile. "Chad, get up off that ground and wash up." Stiff and filthy, he complied, followed by Steve who was given the same order.

After they had washed off most of the dust and blood, Sarah ordered them to the kitchen for some tending. They were still not allowed to talk as Red took great satisfaction in applying an excess of salve to the open cuts and an extra prod or two to the bruises. Sarah stood like an ancient guardian, waiting until the men were put to repair and coffee was set to brew. She looked from one to the other in disgust as they avoided eye contact with her or each other and sat sulking.

"You should both be ashamed of yourselves! I reckon it's time to find out what made two grown men behave like children." Sarah waited, but this time neither would speak. She stood with her arms crossed and her foot tapping. "Well, Chad?"

"I don't want to talk about it, honey."

"Don't 'honey' me! You two have been friends for twenty years. Now you're at each other's throats!" She paced the room and clutched at her shawl. "Hasn't there been enough trouble in this house the last few days?"

Steve slammed an already bruised fist to the table. "That's what we were fighting about!" he roared. He looked ready to resume the fisticuffs.

Sarah was confused and Red, totally baffled.

"Why would you an' Chad fight about the fall? It was no doin' o' his," she stated.

"Don't put the blame on Jessica, Red!" Steve spouted as he fell back into his chair.

"What are you talking about, Steve?" Sarah suspected there were two different lines of thought here. "There's no evidence and we can't prove it, but we all feel Margo caused it."

"Christ! Margo! What's she got to do with all this?"

Chad placed his elbows on the table and rested his head in his hands. "Wait a minute," he broke in. "Somehow I think Margo is still up to mischief. Steve, what did she tell you after I left?"

Steve looked at Sarah with pity and embarrassment. "I'm sorry, Sarah, she told me about finding Chad in Jessica's room. She said she heard you crying and . . ."

A deep rumbling could be heard coming from Chad's chest. He had put the pieces together, and despite the gravity of it, he could see the humor and understand Steve's actions. He burst into laughter before the astonished faces of his wife and friends. Red caught on next, then Sarah.

Steve looked from one to the other. Had they all gone mad? "Would somebody let me in on the joke!" His anger was surfacing again.

Chad settled and began to shed light on the entire mess. "There is, in fact, no humor in our laughter, Steve. Only irony and a well-phrased word placed in a worried ear."

Twenty minutes later Steve knew the whole story. "And she wasn't at Windy Creek?"

"No. We think she must have gone on into town, though how in her condition, I'll never know," Sarah replied.

Shaking his head, the puzzle fit together for Steve, at last. "Chad, can you forgive me for being such a fool?" He extended a hand.

Chad looked at the offered hand and then to the battered face of his friend. He rubbed a swollen jaw and grimaced. "I guess if I have to . . ." He hesitated. "Hell, everyone's entitled to go crazy at least once!" He clasped Steve's hand.

"What'll we be doin' about Margo?" Red asked.

"I'll handle her, Red." Steve rose. He felt he could kill her for what she had done to Jess and nearly done to himself and Chad.

"I don't think that's wise, Steve," Chad offered, gingerly touching his split cheek. "You're a bit sensitive where Jess is concerned."

"I suppose you're right, but I want her out of my house and right now!"

Red pulled off her apron and stuffed it on a chair. "If ya don't mind, Steve, I'd like ta be seein' Miss Margo out."

"And I'd like to help." Sarah moved to stand beside Red. "I owe her a few things and I'd like to personally settle them."

"I can't let you do it. It's my responsibility," Steve said. Moving about the table, he was held back by Chad's hand.

"Let them, Steve. I think she'll get the message."

Steve and Chad couldn't resist investigating the banshee-like screams coming from upstairs. As they reached the landing, they witnessed an incredible sight. An hysterical Margo was screeching and grasping at Red's hand. It was wound tightly in her blonde hair as she pushed Margo ahead of her.

"Come on, Miss Harrison," Red coolly commented, "this ain't no way for a lady ta be actin'."

Sarah came up behind, dragging Margo's trunk with garments hanging from beneath the lid. "She packed quite hurriedly. Seems she's anxious to leave."

"Steve! Please! Stop them!" Margo shouted.

Steve moved to stand before Margo. He placed his large hand tightly about her throat. "Would you have listened if Jess had begged you? Did you give her a chance to plead? Get out, Margo. If I ever see you again, I may break your neck.''

Too stunned to argue, Margo gasped for breath and realized it was all going wrong! She had thought it out so well. How could it be?

Steve released her neck and watched Red propel her out the door. With a mighty heave, she pushed her toward the waiting carriage. She fell to her knees in the dust and pushed Willy's hand away when he offered to help her. Without a word, she rose and climbed aboard the carriage. She watched Sarah shove her trunk down the stairs. Willy set it in the back and barely had enough time to settle it when she applied the whip and made a hasty departure.

Self-satisfied grins played on the women's faces. Chad moved between them and slid an arm about each one. ''You look proud of yourselves and your work.''

''Aye,'' said Red as she turned and entered the house.

''Indeed,'' Sarah said as she followed.

Steve, who had not come out to witness the departure, did so now. ''They seem awfully pleased with their efforts,'' he noted.

''Yeah.'' Chad smiled. ''And I better be careful in the future or that two-woman crew might just turn on me. Come on, I need a drink.''

''I don't have time. I have to go track down Jess.''

''Looking like that?'' Chad asked, pointing to Steve in a sweeping gesture. ''You'll scare her to death!''

Looking down at his filthy clothes and battered body, he agreed with Chad. He'd take a bath and clean up before leaving, though he was mighty anxious to be off.

Jess drew stares again as she rode into Lander, but this time they were not admiring her beauty. There was concern and fear for the girl who could barely stay atop the horse she rode. A long, coppery curl hung down her back and several others outlined her pale, bruised face. Whispers of conjecture began to fly as she stopped in front of Roxy's. "Wasn't that Jeff Morgan's girl?" "I think so." "Wasn't she supposed to marry Kincaid?" "Yeah, or so I've heard." "You don't think he beat her, do you?" "No, not him!" "What could have happened?" Curiosity ruled over common sense as they talked instead of helping her.

As Jess swayed in the saddle, she had no idea of the thoughts of the people she had just passed. She thought only of rest as she used the last of her strength to dismount and climb the one stair to Roxy's place. She knew she couldn't make the trip to the side entrance and she half-stumbled through the swinging doors. Looking about the empty place in the light of day all that registered was wood. So much wood! The floor, the tables, the bar, the stage. They kept passing her eyes as if she were on a carousel.

A frightened voice called her name. It came from far off. No, she'd been wrong, the voice called for Sam. Sam? What was he doing in St. Louis? Where was Bonnie? She must have run ahead to the carriage. Jess felt too tired to run. If only someone would help her. A kindly old black face swam before her. Sam! He'd come all that way to help her.

A fluttering of lashes announced Jessica's return to consciousness. She opened her eyes to see a frantic Roxy beside her, wringing out a cool rag to replace the warmed one on her brow.

"Roxy," she whispered.

"I'm here, honey," Roxy answered, and sat on the bed to change the cloth.

"Oh, Roxy." Jess began to cry. "It's all so awful."

"There, there, honey," Roxy consoled her. "Tell me what happened." A stunned Roxy sat and listened to the tale Jess unfolded. "That no-good bastard!" she cried at the story's end.

"No! Please, don't call him that!" Jess cried.

"You don't still care for him, do you?"

"Y-yes, I do, Roxy." She watched her friend's expression. "But don't worry. I'm not fool enough to see him again." She was quiet for a moment or two before she drew a shuddered breath and changed the subject. "Is Papa in town? Th-that's why I came here."

"I don't know, honey. I'll send Sam lookin' for him. In the meantime you better get some rest. We'll talk more later."

As Jess closed her eyes, Roxy watched her a moment before going to find Sam. She paced about her small parlor awaiting his return and blaming herself for Jessie's misfortune. "If only I'd followed my instincts! I should have known he was too wild, too set in his ways to care for her properly, but to use her like that! Damn him!" She poured herself a drink and settled in a rocking chair. "And that Margo Harrison, of all people! Bill should have taken a switch to her years ago instead of pamperin' her like he did. What a mess, and poor innocent Jess right in the middle."

Within a quarter hour after his departure, Sam returned and informed Roxy that Jeff wasn't in town. Zeke had said that more of Jeff's order had come in at Riverton and he'd gone there to pick it up in Zeke's buckboard. Roxy thought it was just as well. Jess needed the rest and the better she looked when Jeff saw her, the better the chances he wouldn't try to kill Steve Kincaid. She was sure that in a fight there would be no doubt that Steve could beat Jeff, and he'd hurt Jess enough without taking her father.

It was dusk before Jess woke and discovered that her father was in Riverton. She wanted to go there at once, but Roxy, after some sound arguments, convinced her to stay until morning. She was feverish and tired. It made no sense to go. Sam could take her in the wagon then and they would probably meet him halfway.

Jess took some broth and drifted back to sleep as Roxy prepared to go out front and greet some of her customers. Saturday night was always the busiest and began early. Drifting cowboys and regular hands cleaned up and looked forward to a night of drinking, gambling, and, if things went well, a pretty gal to see to their more personal needs.

The whole town would grow boisterous before the night was through. Roxy shared that thought with Steve as he rode into town. His first stop would be her place. She seemed to know everything that happened in Lander as it occurred. She'd know if Jess was there or had been.

Roxy saw him walk in and search about for her. My God! What happened to him? His eye was black and his lip puffed and split. A patch decorated his cheek and he looked pale and drawn. She didn't know how she was going to play this out, yet she knew he'd expect her to see him and seek him out as usual.

"Well! What happened to you? You look like you wrestled a steer and lost!" She forced a laugh.

"It's not important." He brushed her question off. "Roxy, have you seen Jess?" He looked worried, nearly frantic.

"Jess? I reckon she's at her ranch." She turned to the bar and signaled for a drink for them both. Avoiding a direct answer, she rambled on. "Jeff was here this mornin' and was headin' for Riverton. I thought she'd be home while he went since she wasn't with him. Have you checked Windy Creek?"

He downed his drink. "She isn't there."

Roxy watched him for a second. He looked tired and defeated. She almost wanted to tell him, to ease his mind, but an image of a pale, bruised Jess changed her mind. She was angry enough then to let him suffer a bit longer before she laid the full wrath of her temper upon him.

He pushed his glass back on the bar. "Thanks for the drink." He started to leave.

"Where you goin'?" She expected him to stay a while. She hadn't had a chance to berate him.

"I have to find her, Roxy. She might need me." Before Roxy could stop him he was out the door. She was confused. He didn't act like a man who cared for someone else. He looked haunted and . . . and like a man in love! Yet Jess had said he'd chosen Margo. Something wasn't right here.

Steve walked up one side of the street and down the other. He walked in order to think and yet he found he couldn't. Pictures of Jess ran through his mind and he barely was aware of passing someone now and then.

Several shots rang out as rambunctious cowboys fired at the moon. "Damn fools!" Steve muttered. "Someday they're going to kill someone!" He stopped at a darkened storefront and rested against a rail. If she wasn't with Jeff or at Windy Creek, where could she be? The only person she was close to except those at the K-D was . . . Roxy! She had to be covering for Jess! There was no one else. He crossed the street and headed again to her saloon. This time he was determined to get answers.

His entrance was more dramatic this time. He spied Roxy going toward her rooms in the back and he moved quickly to catch her. Grabbing her arm, he spun her about.

"Where is she, Roxy? I know you know. You're the only one she would have come to if Jeff was gone."

The place had quieted. Roxy glanced about and pulled her arm free. "You're makin' quite a spectacle of yourself! Calm down and let's get a drink." She smiled to the onlookers and they resumed their own conversations. They moved to the bar and ordered. "Do you want to sit down?" Roxy motioned to a corner table.

"Don't stall, Roxy. You know where she is and I'm not leaving until you tell me." Controlled anger blazed in his hazel eyes, giving them a golden appearance, like a cat, as he joined her at the table.

"Very well, Steve. I'll tell you what I know." She related the same story he'd heard from his friends. She watched him hunched over his drink, miserable and visibly upset. "Now as to where she is, I'll tell you, right after I hear your side."

As Steve filled in the missing pieces, several more shots rang out on the street close to the saloon. Jess stirred at the sound and woke. She was terribly thirsty and felt the weight of the blankets as being suffocatingly heavy. There was something she was supposed to do, she thought as she quenched her thirst from a pitcher near the bed.

Jess eased her feet to the floor and sat still while her head cleared. She was supposed to find her father, she recalled. She had stopped and rested at Roxy's instead. Well, she could go now. She was sore, but she felt better. She walked to the door and looked up and down the hall. She thought Roxy would again try to stop her if she found her out, so she crept to the alley entrance and stepped outside.

The night air was cold and a light wind blew the nightgown Roxy had given her about her legs. She hadn't thought to look for her clothes. Her feverish brain could only handle one thought at a time, and it was to find her father. She moved to the light of the main street and peered around the corner. A dozen horses were tied a few feet from her. She glanced about nervously and saw no one near who would stop her.

Barefooted, she moved to the nearest mount and struggled aboard. The white flannel gown rode up about her thighs and chilled her quickly. She held her legs firmly to the warm flanks of the horse and moved to the darker side of the street. As she slowly rode out of town the shooting started again. Her body ached and she tried to ease it when she felt a burning pain in her side. Something warm and wet began to run down over her hip.

Not stopping, she placed her hand on the fiery spot and pressed. She looked down at her hand to see if she could find the cause of her new pain. In the dim light she saw the black sticky moisture in her palm. Her mind refused to believe the fact that she had taken a wild bullet in the ribs. Drying her hand on her gown, she continued her ride north to Riverton, and her father.

"That's quite a story, Steve. If I hadn't heard it firsthand I would have suspected it came from a dime novel, from the woman scorned to the heroine."

"Margo wasn't scorned, only in her mind." He poured another drink. "I've kept my part, Roxy. Where is she?"

"She's in my apartment."

His anger swelled. "You mean to tell me all the while we've been sitting here she's been only a few feet away?"

"Take it easy! She's asleep and doesn't need to be roused at this hour. I'll take you to her, but you have to let her rest." She led him to her private door and unlocked it. "She has a fever from the shock. She might even have a concussion." As she opened the bedroom door, she motioned for Steve to be quiet. They entered and moved to the bed. It was empty!

"What kind of a game are you playing?"

"I swear to you she was here!" Roxy was frantic. "The parlor!" Roxy searched it and every other room. She finally slumped to the sofa. "Where could she be? The poor child," she sobbed.

"Don't cry, Roxy. She can't have gone far, not as ill as she is." He went to the door. "I'll head north. She might have tried to follow Jeff."

Chapter 12

C old! So cold! Jess shivered. She was more tired than she ever remembered being in her life, and so cold. The trickling moisture at her side had slowed to almost nothing as her horse took its own lead. She left the road at some point after leaving Lander. She had tried to keep to it, but her fatigue and lack of strength couldn't keep the horse from choosing its own path. She didn't know how far she had come or where she was going.

Her weary mind saw the last sliver of the moon slide behind the distant mountains. She was drawn to them and the horse sensed her turning, changing its course once more. With each step she was being taken deeper and deeper into the wilderness, and farther from Riverton. A fog filled her mind so deeply, she didn't even hurt anymore. Numbness crept through her and the gentle rocking of the horse eased her into sleep.

Jess wasn't aware of slipping until she came up hard on the rocky ground. Whimpering, she knew she had fallen from the horse. Driven by something deep inside, she tried to reach out for the dangling reins just beyond her. Pulling herself to her knees, she began to crawl. Stones cut her palms and knees as she inched forward. ''Here, boy,'' she pleaded. Within inches of grasping her goal, she cried out as a sharp stone cut her palm. The horse shied and moved away. *"No!"*

Falling face-down in the dirt, Jess sobbed. Her heart was broken, her body had been pushed to the limit and lay battered and bleeding in the wilderness. It was the end of her journey. She could not go on.

Her side ached badly and she rolled to her back. Above her was a black velvet sky heavily littered with diamonds. As she lay there, on the cold, hard ground, a feeling of warmth flowed through her. Her trembling eased and she breathed deeply and evenly. She was slipping into oblivion and she was giving up the struggle. She watched as the black sky lowered and began to wrap itself about her. She was floating there among the diamonds. Each offered warmth and light, but stayed just beyond her reach. Then, one by one, they blinked out and total darkness engulfed her.

Little Sparrow stopped her stroll in the tall grasses and quietly knelt. The doe antelope stood vigil near her fawn. The beautiful animal had not seen the girl nearby. With tail and ears twitching, she picked up the human scent and, with some invisible signal, alerted her offspring to flee.

Bubbling laughter, like the sound of a quickly running brook, broke the natural silence. Little Sparrow was very happy this morning, more than on most mornings. The sun was warming the earth she walked upon. There were many chores she should be doing, but her husband was chief of the Absaroke, and he had given her this time to play. The camp had not yet begun to prepare for their move to Mirror Mountain. It would be at least six weeks before the Bird People would undertake their annual pilgrimage to the west end of their land.

These were always happy weeks, these of spring. Food was plentiful as herds moved from the plains to the high country and passed near their camp. The crafts of winter would soon be viewed by all at the tobacco-planting ceremony. Yes, it was a happy time, especially for her. She was wed to White Antelope in her sixteenth summer and a boy-child had come last spring. She was proud of Sparrow Hawk, her son, and proud to be the wife of a great chief. Indeed, life was good.

A butterfly flew across her path and, childlike, she gave chase. Lithe and graceful as the breeze, she moved about the meadowland, laughing and thanking the great God for such a day. Suddenly she froze. Something lay ahead of her on the ground. She could barely see the white form through the grasses, but she knew it did not fit the landscape.

Cautiously she investigated. A woman! A white woman! Little Sparrow placed her fingers on the woman's throat to see if she lived and sighed in relief. Not taking time to inspect her further, Little Sparrow jumped to her feet and ran off, like the wild things, fast and agile.

Strong brown hands slid beneath Jess and lifted her from the ground. She was set on a bed of furs in the back of a wagon.

''She has been badly hurt,'' spoke the deep voice of White Antelope to his wife. ''But not here. The marks are several days old. Only the bullet wound is new.'' He ordered Little Sparrow to the wagon and leaped aboard his spotted stallion.

They were silent in their short journey to the camp. Little Sparrow wished to ask her husband if the woman would survive and what he thought had happened, but she knew he would not like the chatter. They would talk later, in the privacy of their tent. It would not do for a chief to explain too many things to a woman in public. Her people had learned much from the white man and great changes had occurred, but the old ways remained the same between men and women.

* * *

Fire! She could see it coming from all around her and feel its heat. Flames! They danced around her and flicked at her legs like a whip. Closer and closer it came and she heard laughter. Steve! He was outside the circle of flame on a giant black steed. He was dressed all in black and, in contrast, a pale blonde Margo was in his arms. They began to ride away and she screamed for him. The fire burned into her side and she screamed again. "Steve! Help me, Steve!"

Cold water, icy and clear, gurgling and spilling around them. Kincaid's woman, in his arms and loving him. Wild emotions flooded through her. She was a fiery-haired savage and he a barbarian chief. He loved her as she whispered his name. A bitter brew was set to her lips and the dreams faded.

"She has been calling so for two full days and nights," Little Sparrow told her husband. She watched the concern on his face as he thought. He looked into the fire at the center of the tent for an answer.

Little Sparrow admired his long black shiny hair and his finely chiseled profile as the flame cast lights and shadows upon his bronzed skin. Wide, full brows arched over ebony eyes. Strong bones set high on his long face. His nose was straight and not too full. His lips were set firmly as he pondered, but they were soft and caressing when they loved. He would know what to do, she thought.

He rose and looked upon the white woman. "I will send for Hawk."

Little Sparrow smiled to herself as he left the tent. It was a wise decision.

Little Sparrow was summoned from the tent of her husband. The woman had awakened. She wanted to stay and listen to White Antelope and Hawk, but she was needed. She had found the woman and was responsible for her.

The tent was dark and quiet as Little Sparrow moved gracefully to the blankets where the woman lay. She looked down on her face, ashen save for the bruises, and smiled gently. Clear green eyes, too long fever-glazed, looked questioningly at her.

"I am Little Sparrow. I am wife to Chief White Antelope. We are the Absaroke, but we are called the Crow by your people."

"M-my name is Jessica." She tried to rise but a burning pain shot through her side and she moaned, dropping back to the bed.

"Lie still! Your wound is not yet healed. You must be still or it will open." Little Sparrow pressed concerned hands to her shoulders and made her stay. "The bullet has been removed but the wound has fever in it. You are weak and must build your strength."

There were so many questions Jess wanted to ask, yet she felt so tired. She would close her eyes for a moment, she thought, then seek her answers.

A small, satisfied smile touched Little Sparrow's lips as she watched Jessica succumb to sleep. She knew White Antelope and Hawk had silently entered and was pleased to hear her husband announce that the woman would stay.

The days turned to weeks and Jess made a slow, yet steady recovery. She looked forward to the time spent with Little Sparrow. Discovering it was she who had found her and tended her during the worst of the ordeal, Jess found a bond growing between herself and the other woman. They were not white and Indian, just two women. Jess was intrigued by Little Sparrow's speech. Her English was very good and Jess was delighted to hear there was a school on the reservation which her new friend had attended for eight years.

"My husband was also made to go." She smiled. "His father was then chief and he wanted White Antelope to be able to read and write the white man's language to keep safe our people." Laughter filled the air like tiny bells. "He hated it but he went,

though only long enough to learn what he needed."
Little Sparrow sat cross-legged beside Jess. "He was
ten summers when we came to the reservation and
already a brave warrior. It took him a long time to
accept it. Now he sees the way his people are happy
and well, and he is content. He even has some
braves who go to work for your army as scouts, and
a great friend who is a white man." She paused. "It
is good we can live in peace. It is good for my son
to know the ways of peace."

Jessica was surprised when Little Sparrow brought
Sparrowhawk to see her. He was a beautiful child
of nearly one, and maternal pride glowed from the
face of her friend as he crawled about and tried to
stand. Jess thought Little Sparrow too young to be
wed, let alone be a mother, yet her wisdom was apparent each time she spoke. She had wisely told Jess
to send a message to her father the day before when
she noticed the worry on her face.

"You did not think we would not help you, did
you?" Little Sparrow questioned seriously.

"I did not think at all!" Jess cried. "He must be
frantic and, I'm ashamed to say, I did not think to
contact him."

"You have been very ill," Little Sparrow soothed.
"You will write the message and I will see it sent."
And it was immediately seen to because she had a
reply with the setting sun.

Jess smiled at her friend as she read her short note.
"He is happy I am safe and knows I will be treated
well in your camp. He'll come to take me home
when I am ready to travel."

"Now you have nothing to worry about. You can
get better and learn the ways of my people as I learn
more of yours."

A cloud came over Jessica's bright mood. She had
asked her father not to tell Steve where she was and
he promised not to. He said he didn't understand,
yet he would honor her request until he could speak
to her.

"Are you in pain?" Little Sparrow noticed the drawn brow and trembling lips.

"No." Jess sighed heavily. "No, at least not the pain of the body."

"When a woman sighs like that, it is the pain of the heart, yes?"

"Yes, and I will tell you about it . . . someday, when I can speak of it myself." Tears escaped her eyes and slid down her cheek. When she regained control of her emotions, she looked to find Little Sparrow gone. She had been left to the privacy of her own thoughts.

By the middle of the second week she'd been at the Absaroke camp, Jess wanted to leave the confines of her tent. Little Sparrow agreed it was time and brought her a dress to wear. Fingering the exquisite article, Jess exclaimed, "I can't take this!"

"You do not like it?" Little Sparrow questioned hesitantly.

"Like it! It's the most beautiful dress I've ever seen! But . . . but it is too great a dress to borrow. If I harmed it . . ." Jessica's hands were gently touching the soft garment as Little Sparrow laughed in delight.

"It is not to use, it is for you to keep. I made it for you." She was pleased her gift was well-received and she beamed.

"Oh, Little Sparrow!" Jess hugged her friend. "It's the most wonderful gift I've ever had, and I thank you."

"Come." Little Sparrow stepped back. Her heart was full of happiness for the appreciation of the gift. "I will help you put it on."

Dressed as a Crow woman, Jess laughed as she looked down at herself in pure delight. "It's wonderful! Beautiful! I feel so free!" She smiled, childlike, at Little Sparrow. "I feel like a little girl playing dress-up."

The soft suede material hung in a tunic-like shirt

to just below her knees. Split on both sides to her thighs for easy movement, the dress was exotic. Thin leather strips crisscrossed up the open neck to secure it. The muted earth tones of the cloth were enhanced with beads of glass in natural colors from deep red to amber running down the long sleeves and dress front. Leather fringe hung from under each sleeve and about the bottom. To complete the image, a leather band was tied about her brow.

"I will soon have moccasins for you. Until they are done, you will have to go barefoot."

"How can I thank you?" Jess cried softly. "I feel like a princess!"

"Let us go outside. I will be proud to show the camp my friend Jessica." Little Sparrow offered her hand and they lifted the tent flap for Jessica's debut.

White Antelope watched his wife and the white woman come toward him. He was pleased she was nearly well and wore the dress his wife had made for her. He almost smiled at the pride she seemed to take in it. Hawk was right, she was an unusual woman.

"You are better," he stated instead of asking. "Will you stay among my people?"

Jess smiled shyly. She knew it was the closest thing to an invitation she would get from him. "Yes, I would like to stay a while." She felt Little Sparrow gently squeeze her hand for reassurance. "Your people have saved my life and . . . and your wife is my friend." They exchanged smiles. "I would like to stay and learn and repay them somehow."

The chief stood tall and proud as he listened to Jess speak. He watched her long chestnut hair catch the colors of the sun as it blew gently in the breeze. It was tied with the leather thong and it hung to her waist. His eyes sparkled in merriment for a second before he shielded his enjoyment of their guest and grew stern again.

"That is good." He looked at his wife and spoke

a short, cryptic line. "We shall call her Valley Woman." With that, he walked off.

Jessica turned to Little Sparrow. "Valley Woman? What does that mean?"

Little Sparrow thought a minute and kept looking at Jess. Her eyes began to sparkle as she understood her husband's choice. "Yes! It is a good name!" She laughed.

Confused and curious, Jess begged to know why.

"There is a place we go through each year. It is a deep canyon called Wind River." They began to walk slowly about the camp. "Its beauty is well-known even to your people yet it is a lonely place." Jess listened intently. "The colors of this valley are reds and browns and golds, and in the spring, there is new green scattered everywhere." Jess still did not understand. "You are the colors of the valley! Your hair and eyes, and you are beautiful and alone. It is a good name, Valley Woman."

Jess thought about the explanation and accepted Little Sparrow's words. "Valley Woman," she whispered. She pictured the majestic mountains she so loved and herself below them. "Yes." She smiled. "It is a good name."

The days passed quickly for Jess. The sun touched her gently and a golden tan graced her body as she and Little Sparrow swam each day in the river not far from camp. She learned to set a fire and cook over it. She was taught to clean fish and small game. She laughed and learned with a natural grace, and her friendship with Little Sparrow grew. They spoke of White Antelope and Sparrow Hawk, of Windy Creek and St. Louis. They shared feelings and thoughts about being a woman. They spoke of many things, but not about Steve. Jessica's hurt was too new, too raw to examine. Thoughts of him only surfaced in dreams where she had no control. Her traitorous body responded to him in sleep even if she denied her feelings for him while she was awake.

Little Sparrow was wise enough not to delve into the reason for the shadows in her friend's eyes. She knew of the one she pined for. She had heard his name called often when Jess was delirious, but she would only speak of him when she was ready. Even a visit from her father did not bring the words. He had come to take her home, yet he had left alone. Jessica was not ready to face the man who haunted her.

The sun felt warm and lazy on Jessica's skin as she lay on the bank of the river. She felt no shame in lying naked with the other women after the first few times. Her fingers traced the scar ridge on her rib cage and she winced only when she pressed it.

"Does it still pain you?" Little Sparrow asked her as she rubbed her little son dry.

"Only sometimes if I bump it or press at it with something." Jess stretched and eased herself down the bank and into the water. She swirled about and laughed. "I love this spot. It's so peaceful, so private." She looked at the trees sweeping gracefully about the slowly flowing waters. Tall grasses grew to it in places and huge boulders washed down a millennium before had made a natural dam, where the water was cool and deep in the hottest of summers.

A feeling of unease came over Jess unexpectedly. She looked about the trees and searched for the cause of the feeling she'd had several times in the last few days.

"Little Sparrow, have you ever caught anyone watching you here?"

Sensing Jessica's discomfort, Little Sparrow smiled. "You are becoming one of us, I think. You have sensed the presence of another who is near." She indicated a spot on the other side of the river. Jess looked up the rise of a hill to a cluster of trees at its top. She scanned the place and finally stiffened.

Down on his haunches beside a tree, a brave watched her. His bare chest was wide and deeply bronzed, his shoulders large and well-muscled. She could not see his face in the shadows, but his body caused a stirring deep within her.

"S-someone is there!" she rasped.

"So, you see him. He must want you to know he is there. Hawk can be nearly invisible if he wishes. He has watched you all week and only now has made himself seen." Handing her son to another, Little Sparrow entered the water and swam to Jessica. She watched her and silently laughed.

"All week! Then he has seen me . . ." Jess felt the heat of a blush suffuse her.

"Yes." Little Sparrow laughed aloud. "Hawk has seen you many times, many ways."

"Hawk? You have spoken of him before. Who is he?" Jess continued to watch him until he rose, stood tall, then turned and walked away.

"He is like a brother to White Antelope and very honored in our camp. He comes and goes like the wind." They swam to the shore and Little Sparrow chuckled as Jess declined to lie in the sun to dry, but dressed quickly instead.

"He doesn't live here, then?"

"No, he lives . . ." Little Sparrow looked about as if searching for words. "He lives in many places." With a desire to ease her friend's haunted dreams, she teased Jess. "You like our Hawk?"

"I don't even know him! How should I know if I l-like him?"

"I think you do not dislike him." Little Sparrow's eyes sparkled with merriment. "Remember, Jessica, Valley Woman is beautiful and alone and the hawk is always in search of prey."

Chapter 13

Excitement rippled through the camp in the following days. The braves hunted in preparation of the ceremony that would herald the coming summer, and the women hustled about gathering sufficient fuel and foods. Finishing touches were put to fine crafts and hours were spent grooming and seeing to the numerous horses in the huge herd owned by the tribe.

Jess took to following Little Sparrow in her chores and helping at every turn so that soon double the work was done in half the time. They managed to swim each afternoon, but not before Jess thoroughly scanned the surrounding landscape, much to Little Sparrow's delight. Jess wouldn't admit it, but she was disappointed she hadn't seen the dark, mysterious brave.

Two days before the week-long gala was to begin, Little Sparrow and Jess strolled about the lush grasses of the plains a short distance from camp. They gathered wildflowers and wove them into garlands to set upon their heads. Laughing and playing like children, they lay in the grass and looked skyward.

"I should be going home soon." Jess rolled to her stomach and played with a flower.

"Do you wish it?"

"Not really. I'd like to stay forever." She rested

her cheek on her arm. "I love it here with you and your people. They are so wise and gentle, and I love them."

Little Sparrow sat up and wrapped her arms about her knees. "You could stay."

With a deep sigh, Jess wondered and wished aloud. "No, I must go back. I have things I must face sooner or later and it . . . it won't get any easier." Wishing not to dwell on the sadder parts of her past, Jess hummed a soft tune to avoid further words.

"He is not in camp," Little Sparrow offered to break the somber mood.

"Who?" Jess rolled back over and shielded her eyes from the sun and her too-wise friend.

"The one who you have searched for these past days."

Jess couldn't deny what she was saying. She had looked for him. She knew that if she saw him, despite the fact she had never seen his face, she would know him. His hair was no darker or lighter than the hair of any other brave. There were no marks or scars on his bronze chest or powerful arms that could differentiate him, yet she would know. She would sense the draw, the magnetism that seemed to be pulling them together.

"Will he be here for the ceremony?"

Hearing the unspoken plea in Jessie's voice, Little Sparrow answered quickly. "Yes, he will come. White Antelope told me to make ready his tent and prepare his food while he stays."

Jess sat up quickly. She made a snap decision with no thoughts of the consequences. "Little Sparrow, let me serve him!" Watching her friend's thoughtful expression, she pressed her edge. "You can teach me what to do. It could save you from having to serve two men, and . . ." She thought of Steve, of the hurt he'd caused her and the need he'd awakened in her. "Please, I need to be with this brave!" She couldn't explain but Little Sparrow understood.

"Are you sure you are ready to do this? You spoke of facing something, someone. Do you not wish to do so before . . . before seeking someone else?"

Jess felt a bit nervous at the ease with which Little Sparrow could read her feelings, and she was right, yet Jess knew she had to go ahead with this plan.

"I . . . I'm only going to serve him!" she exclaimed.

"I think not, Jessica," was all Little Sparrow would say before she rose to her feet. Jess joined her as she began to walk back to the camp.

"You're right, my friend. I do need to know if I love another, or if he has merely taught me too well about desire and passion. This will be my test."

"And what of Hawk? What if he wants you to stay with him and you can't, or you wish to stay and he does not want you? Will there not be new hurts? It is a big gamble."

"Yes, it is, yet I know I must and will take it." For several strides there was silence. Jessica was making the biggest decision of her life and she prayed it was the right one.

The Indian woman stopped and faced Jess. She looked into her eyes and read the loneliness there. She could see the scars on her heart and sighed. "I will teach you, Valley Woman." She smiled sadly. "But I will also pray you are wiser than you now appear to be."

"Tonight he will come."

Jess heard the words but continued her chore with a barely noticeable pause. Little Sparrow didn't add to her statement, she merely waited for a response.

"I'm a little nervous." Jess tossed her head to flip her one long braid back behind her shoulder. "I'm not sure what to do, I mean to expect."

"Since you have learned well how our women serve I can only think you wonder if Hawk will make love to you." Little Sparrow's manner did not change, only a tiny grin appeared.

Jess, however, had become quite nonplussed. A deep blush flowed upward until her face was a bright red. "Oh! I—"

"I am too blunt?" Little Sparrow watched Jess and began to laugh. "No one would think you are not Crow, Valley Woman, if they saw your face now."

The jest broke the tension within Jess and she joined in the laughter. As their composure returned, Little Sparrow began to speak of Hawk. "He has come here many times, Jessica, yet he has never taken a woman. They have served him, and many wanted him, but always there were two blankets."

"Two blankets? I don't understand."

"If a brave wants to lie with a woman who shares his tent, he will put one blanket on the other. If not, there will be two blankets on the ground. This way there is no shame of being turned away, no misunderstanding. When you go to his tent to prepare for the night, you will know."

A huge fire burned in the center of the camp. Old women tended large boiling pots and turned venison on spits over glowing embers. Little Sparrow and Jessica waited until the food was pronounced done. A large bowl was filled with thick rabbit stew for Little Sparrow, and a platter of succulent venison was given to Jess along with crispy, crusted bread.

As they approached White Antelope's tent, Little Sparrow reminded Jess one last time about protocol. "Remember, keep your eyes cast down. If Hawk sees you are looking at him, he will think you are very brazen, and he will ignore you. Our men like to think they have chosen." She smiled. "And we let them think it." At the tent flap she added, "Just stay behind me and watch what I do."

Jess felt butterflies in her stomach as she entered the warm, dim tent. She followed Little Sparrow around behind the men, making sure she kept her head well bent. They spoke in the Indian tongue and Jess strained to hear the husky timbre of Hawk's voice but he spoke little and spent his time eating. She wanted to look at him, if only his back, but she recalled Little Sparrow's warning.

Kneeling and waiting quietly, Jessica fought back a giggle when her stomach grumbled, seeming to echo within the small confines. Little Sparrow gave her a poke and it made matters worse. She was just about to burst into laughter when the men rose and left the tent.

"Oh, Jessica!" Little Sparrow laughed. "I thought you were going to disgrace yourself!"

Jess dropped back onto a pile of furs and held her sides in mirthful abandon. "I . . . I couldn't b-believe it!" Her empty stomach complained again and new peals of laughter burst forth from them both.

"Please, Jessica! Eat!" Little Sparrow shoved a chunk of venison at her. "I do not think I can stand much more!"

Calm returned as they moved closer to the fire and began to dine. Chewing on a piece of meat, Jess thought about Hawk and how close he had been.

"What happens now, Little Sparrow?"

"White Antelope and Hawk will join the other men for many hours. They will examine and trade many horses. Each one will be magnificently outfitted with beads and feathers, with special blankets and silver ornaments. They will smoke and share stories. We will eat, then prepare some things for tomorrow. When our work is done, we will go to our tents and wait."

Jess did not like waiting. It was her nature to be active, not to sit idle. The night was warm and the air in the tent became close. She grew restless as she relived the late evening.

She had held her breath as she moved to the place of honor set aside for Hawk. She looked back to see Little Sparrow wave. Gathering her courage, she lifted the flap and entered. Her eyes were pressed tightly closed as she stood within. Part of her wanted him to choose her and part was frightened he would.

Taking a deep breath, Jess opened her eyes to meet her fate. One blanket! She fell to her knees and trembled. She knew she could separate the blankets and there would be nothing said, but she would not. It was necessary for her to discover if Steve was the only man who could awaken the passionate woman inside her. Hawk had made her feel, perhaps Hawk could answer the aching questions within herself. Sliding off her dress, she slipped beneath the blanket to wait.

Nerves and the low fire's heat kept Jessie from falling asleep. The noise from the camp was still quite loud and her restlessness intensified. She couldn't lie there and wait any longer. She would go to the river and swim a short while. She was sure she would return before he did.

Wrapping a blanket about herself, she ventured toward the cool, inviting water. The night air was clear and refreshing. Dropping the cover to the ground, Jess twisted her braid about her head and tucked it into itself. She eased into the night-darkened water and felt the tension flow from her body. This was what she needed to calm her. Firm strokes took her across the deep water and back several times before she relaxed. She swam to the bank and felt for the bottom. As her foot touched, a quiver ran through her.

He was there, in the dark! She could feel him waiting for her. Had he been to the tent? Had he seen the blankets still together? Would he come to her here and now? Before she could fathom what he would do, he was gone. She knew it as surely as if she could see him go.

Drawn to him, she stepped from the river and wrapped herself in the blanket. She let her braid drop down her damp back and move toward him. He was there, waiting. She could feel his presence, waiting, wanting, and she did not pause.

Inside the tent it was cooler now, and the fire was nearly out. It was darker than before, and she could only see the vague outline of him as he reclined on a soft pile of furs he'd laid in preparation. His wide bare back was toward her and she was glad to have the privacy to drop the blanket and move to him.

Drawing back his cover, Jessie lay down. Her heart was rapidly drumming and her breathing felt hampered. She turned her face to the dying fire and waited. In moments he stirred and turned to her. Her eyes closed as he traced her hairline and fingered the heavy braid.

Jess felt frozen with fear and anticipation until he placed a large, yet tender hand on her bare shoulder. His hand trembled as it slid down her arm to her hip, and she knew he wanted her. She tried to imagine his face and caught her breath as Steve's face appeared. She squeezed her eyes so tightly that tiny lights flashed before her and his image faded.

Hawk's hand slipped beneath the blanket and moved about her waist. Instead of exploring her, he pulled her tightly back against him. She felt the warmth of his chest against her back and his breath in her hair as he eased his other arm beneath her. For moments, he did not move, he merely held her wrapped in his arms. She felt a stirring deep within her and her body began to respond to his embrace. He slid his hands slowly up to her breasts and placed long fingers about them. She shuddered with the sweet agony racing to the core of her womanhood as he gently squeezed her erect nipples. He could do it, she thought. He could make her forget. She expelled a deep sigh.

Yes, he could make her forget. But did he have the right? And, more importantly, should she let him? His hands were strong yet gentle as he began to explore her body. She could feel his warm breath against her neck and his solid chest pressed to her back.

There was warmth and security in his touch. This

savage was reaching for her soul as he pressed the evidence of his desire against her bottom. His hand slid to her hip, pulling her firmly back to his arousal. She began to tremble as a result of the heat and power of him. God forgive her, but she wanted this man! Recognizing her own inevitable surrender, she sighed deeply.

"Why, woman, sigh?" a deep throaty whisper asked against her hair.

Jess nestled her head back against his shoulder. "I . . . I thought . . ."

"Answer," he breathed huskily when she paused.

Baring her soul, Jess replied honestly, "I thought only one man could make me feel this way."

"Only one man can, Jess," a clear voice growled.

"No!" she shrieked, her body stiffening. It was another bad dream! This was *Hawk*, not . . .

He knew when she was ready to bolt and he acted before she could. Pulling her to lie flat on her back, he threw his leg over hers and pressed a hand over her mouth a split second before she could scream at him. He looked down into violent, frightened eyes. She kept shaking her head in disbelief. He could read the questions—how? why? But there was too much to explain. It would take hours to clear it all up, and he had already waited a month. He couldn't wait a minute longer.

Fever raged through his blood as she began to fight in earnest. Her free arm began to pummel his back as he replaced his hand with his lips against hers. He tried to assault her mouth with his tongue but she clenched her teeth and refused him admittance. Wrapping her braid about her hand, he pulled hard and steady until she gasped, and he quickly took advantage.

Jess tried to bite him but he pulled her hair harder. Tears slid from her eyes as she felt his hardness press against her thigh. She tried to remain angry and cold. She tried to fight the primitive surges of pas-

sion pulsing through her, but it was too late. Hawk
had aroused her and Steve would reap the reward.

Little Sparrow had warned her about the predator
hawk, and she had not heeded the warning. Now,
she would pay for her foolishness, for she knew she
still loved him. Her body had called out to him when
she thought him a stranger. She was a fool because
she knew he could still hurt her, but it didn't seem
to matter at the moment. God help me, she thought,
as she continued to struggle.

Feeling her efforts to fight what he knew she
wanted, he changed from forceful lust to passionate
seduction. With care, he knew he could make her
surrender. Her rage would turn to a fury of another
kind if he handled her the right way. He tried to
nibble at her lips, but her head thrashed.

"You lying, no good—" she gasped.

Steve's fingers held her jaw and he took her
mouth, claiming her. His tongue penetrated her
mouth victoriously. He heard her groan and felt
her arch her hips to throw him from her, but all
she succeeded in doing was escalating his need for
her. Keeping his mouth on hers to silence her, his
hand slipped between them to find her breast. She
moaned into his mouth and he felt a deep surge of
satisfaction. Despite her fury and her struggles, her
body was responding. He pressed his knee between her legs and exposed her to more intimate
exploration. She was ready for him, and her stubborn denial would not stop him.

Jessie felt him fumbling with the laces on his buckskins, and a surge of panic engulfed her. "Don't do
this!" she groaned fiercely, sinking her nails into his
shoulders as she tried to shove him away. He had
stirred her body, but she could not surrender.

Steve wanted to take his time with her, to drive
away the ghosts with his hands and his mouth, but
he needed her too badly. Sensing within her the urgency she denied, he moved between her thighs and
held himself above her. He watched her in the dim

light as he pressed against her. With eyes tightly
shut, she slid her tongue over her lips and swallowed hard. He stayed poised above her, touching,
but not entering her.

"Jess," he rasped. "Look at me." She refused,
and he lowered his mouth to her breast, circling the
tip with his tongue. She stiffened. He bit gently and
she gasped. He inched upward to her neck and the
sensitive area behind her ear, whispering to her what
he was going to do, what she wanted done.

"You cannot deny me, Jess. Your mind fights
but your body cries out for mine. You want me in
you. You want my hardness to plunder you, take
you. You wish to tear at my eyes with anger and my
back with lust." He heard a weak denial. "Yes," he
growled. "Jessica Langley is dead. Jessie Morgan is
gone, but she'll return. Valley Woman is here, beneath me. They are all you, Jess, and you are all
mine."

"Damn you!" she groaned. He was right and she
hated him for it.

"Tell me you want me, Jess," he demanded.
When she refused to reply again, he rose from
her. The cool air came between them and she
ached. "Tell me, or I'll leave you. I won't force
you. We can't start over that way. Tell me!"

The battle raged in her. Her body screamed that
she wanted him. Her mind recalled the lies and de-
ceit, but she could have died and never held him
again. In her dreams she wanted him, called to him,
and now he was here. She looked up at him at last
as he leaned over her, braced on arms that wanted
to hold her, not hold himself away. Her eyes glistened like emeralds from unshed tears.

"You are Kincaid. You are the savage, Hawk. You
are the devil on earth . . ." A small sob escaped her.
". . . and damn you to hell, I want you."

"Ah, Jess." He sighed deeply before he lowered
his lips to hers. She raised her hands to his shoulders, kneading the taut flesh. As he eased into her

warmth, she saw his eyes close tightly and his lips tremble. She was suddenly the conqueror instead of the vanquished as he moved slowly. She saw the agony of desire and need as he pushed deeper and faster, and in her heart she knew she still loved him.

Holding him to her, she met his thrusts. One hand stroked his powerful back while the other slid down to massage the tightened muscles of his buttocks. Before she could join him, he stiffened and she could feel his scalding seed fill her.

Relaxing against her, his breathing shallow, he whispered against her cheek, "I . . . I'm sorry, Jess. I tried to hold on but . . . but it's been so long."

She brushed the hair from his damp brow. "Shh. It's all right." She held him gently, lovingly. She felt his breathing become deep and slow, and she knew he slept in her arms. She wanted to question him and answer him, yet there was suddenly no urgency. She pulled the blanket over their naked bodies, kissed his damp neck, and nestled into the furs to sleep.

In the land between sleep and wakefulness, Jess could feel hands teasing, tempting her body to life. She thought it another dream come to haunt her and she rolled to her stomach. She heard a chuckle from far off and ignored it. A moan of pleasure escaped her as firm hands stroked her back, her bottom, and thighs. The movement stopped and Jess felt bereft and abandoned, until her heavy braid was lifted from her shoulder and unbound. Long fingers combed lazily through her hair, and sensuously traced her hairline and kneaded her neck.

"Turn over." She heard and responded. She didn't want to struggle awake from the dream. It was amorous and carnal. She was a puppet being driven to spiraling heights. The voice instructed and she obeyed. Every nerve tingled as she writhed about on her bed of furs. She wanted to cry out her lover's name and she was startled fully awake when she did.

A devilish glint sparkled in Steve's heavy-lidded eyes and a smile twisted one side of his mouth. This was no dream, she realized too late, reaching for him. He pushed her hands away before she could touch him.

"No, lie still. This time is for you." But Jess had been driven to some euphoric place of pure sensation and she wanted Steve there beside her, in her, around her, so when the time came for them to join, they shared the sweet agony of desire and the sensuality of surrender and satisfaction.

Chapter 14

Steve slept fitfully. Each time he drifted off, he thought Jessie would leave him, so he lay awake most of the night holding her in his arms. He recalled the night he had left Roxy's and of his unsuccessful ride to Riverton. He had expected to catch up with Jessica within minutes of leaving Lander, but when the minutes turned to hours and he rode into Riverton, he was frantic. Finding Jeff had been easy enough. It was still early and he was in the second saloon Steve checked, sipping at a beer.

Without so much as a greeting, he asked him where Jess was. Jeff was truly surprised that she had left the K-D, let alone set off by herself to find him. He left the saloon, matching Steve's long strides as he was filled in on the events that touched his daughter's life in the last forty-eight hours.

Together they scoured Riverton, but to no avail. At first light they began a slow, systematic search of the road to Lander, zigzagging over the terrain in hopes of finding her or her trail. After checking in with Roxy upon their arrival in town, they each headed home in case she managed to return to Windy Creek or the K-D, but she was nowhere to be found.

Fear coursed through Steve as one possibility after another led to dead ends. For two days Chad and Jeff rode south and west, while he began a northerly search. Each sweep saw them return to the K-D alone, more frustrated and fearful.

The women spoke in whispers as they watched him change before their eyes. Lack of proper food and sleep, and too much whiskey, quickly left its mark. Dark circles formed about his haunted eyes and a two-day growth of stubble darkened his face.

He had just returned again to find Jeff and Chad in the parlor. There was no need to tell of his failure or theirs. He'd poured himself a large drink and dropped wearily into a chair. Stretching his legs out before him, he slumped and stared into the fire. There were no words to express his despair as he thought of Jessica and seeing her again.

Jeff and Chad saw a man of strength crumbling and didn't know how to prevent it. That he was in love with her, there was no doubt, yet he would still deny it.

Now Jessie stirred in his arms and he pressed a gentle kiss on her brow, drawing her closer to him. He knew a great peace in holding her, the same peace that had filled him when White Antelope's messenger arrived.

Fatigue forgotten, he had ridden immediately to the Crow camp. As he stood looking down at the restless, pale woman-child who had invaded his mind from the first, he felt a desire to cry. Her hair was matted from the hours of tossing feverishly, her cheeks were bruised and pallid. Little Sparrow was changing her bandage and fury raged through him when he saw her wound.

He had wanted to stay with her then, but White Antelope wisely drew him away, and the plan to leave Jess in the village came from Little Sparrow. She told him of Jessie's ramblings of love and hate. Steve schooled his face to remain impassive, but the hurt was there along with a gentle caring. Little Sparrow said to give Jess time, and he had, but he couldn't stay away. And so, he waited and watched.

Jessica's interest in Hawk disturbed him until he

realized she was responding to him, despite the fact she swore hatred. He grew confident that if he could get close to her, she would forget the lies Margo had told and they could pick up where they had left off. Though postponed, their wedding could go on as planned and she would finally be his.

Dawn was near to breaking when Steve finally fell asleep. Jess woke slowly as the weight of his arm across her ribs caused her wound to ache. Her eyes opened to see the curling black hairs on his golden chest. She could feel his breath in her hair and feel the steady rhythm of his heartbeat.

It had been so easy for him to slip back into her life. All the recriminations, the damnations, flew in the brief moment of his first caress. His lips burned away the mistrust, his hands promised a loving future, but the cool light of day restored the doubts.

Jessica carefully slipped from his arms and donned her dress. Pushing her hair back from her brow, she left the tent without looking back. The morning was chilled yet a promise of warmth was in the low-lying sun. Fires were being rekindled as the camp came to life. Jess saw Little Sparrow emerge from her tent and go toward a small pile of firewood. Moving quickly, she met her there. Little Sparrow looked into Jessica's eyes and waited.

"You knew," Jess stated flatly.

"Yes, I knew," Little Sparrow replied.

"I thought we were friends. How could you?"

"Because we are friends, I helped Hawk and you." Seeing the look of incredulity, she explained, "You love him. I learned this when you were ill. You do not wish it, but you do love him."

"No! I . . . I can't love him!" Jess cried. "Not after what happened."

"You have not heard his side. You have judged him by the words of one who is jealous and sees you as a threat. Valley Woman would not run from what she wanted. She would be proud of her man

Hawk. She would bask in her love for him and follow him. Can Jessica do less?" Little Sparrow smiled wisely. "Go to him, my friend. Listen to what he has to say and judge him with your heart." She left Jessie standing there to ponder her words.

Steve awoke with a start. She was gone, damn her! He rose quickly and grabbed his pants. Muttering curses to himself for letting his guard down, he was nearly ready to run from the tent when she pushed back the flap and entered. Her arms were full of firewood and she cast him a wary glance before dumping her burden beside the fire.

He watched her add tiny twigs and dry leaves to the embers. She leaned down and blew gently yet firmly. White smoke began to rise and she sat back on her heels until it caught. Satisfied it was burning sufficiently, Jess gathered two small pails and rose again.

Steve did not try to stop her as she left. He knew she would return. Feeling the need to face her with a clear head, he gathered his saddlebags and went to the river to wash and shave. Upon his return he stood just inside the tent and watched Jess boiling a pot of water and stirring a second pot of stew. She did not speak as she dropped ground coffee into the water and set it aside to brew. He followed her lead and sat silently on the furs, waiting. He did not know what she was up to and the excitement of the chase welled in him.

Still silent, Jess served Steve food and coffee. Following that, she took her own and sat across the fire from him to eat. She did not look at him or speak. If she had, she would have seen the amusement in his eyes at her stubbornness. Finishing, she gathered her utensils and set them in an empty bucket. She reached for his and gasped as he grabbed her wrist and pulled her across his lap.

"Let go of me!" She pushed against his chest, with no effect.

"Shut up!" he growled, pressing his lips against her throat.

"Stop! I . . . I don't want you to touch me!" There was an urgent demand in her voice and he loosened his hold to look at her.

"I think I like you better silent." He grinned and lowered his lips to hers. Before he could touch their soft sweetness, she turned away.

"We have to talk, Steve." She struggled against him.

Reluctantly he agreed and set her free. "Yes, as much as I hate to stop what I had in mind, you're right. We do have to talk." He rose and raked his fingers through his still-damp hair. "God, Jess! How did everything get so messed up? One minute I'm riding home to you and the next I'm running all over the territory trying to find you." He knelt and grabbed her arms to draw her to her knees before him. Shaking her, he yelled, "I should give you a good spanking for running off the way you did!"

With eyes wide with anger and fright, she pummeled his chest. "How dare you blame me! If you hadn't sent Margo to the K-D, none of this would have happened!"

"Christ! I didn't send the witch!" He pulled Jessie tightly to him and wrapped his arms about her firmly. "Ah, Jess," he sighed as she began to weep. "I swear, I never sent Margo. In fact, I warned her to stay away from both of us." He ran his hand down her hair to soothe her.

"B-but she knew about . . . she t-told me about . . . your back," she sobbed, relaxing her fists to lay her palms on his bare chest.

Steve rested his chin on her head and exhaled deeply. "She walked in on me in Riverton when I was shaving. Before I could throw her out, she saw it." Placing a finger beneath her chin, he pushed her head back so she would look at him. "I swear, Jess, there's no one but you, nor has there been since I first saw you. You were so scared, yet so proud and indignant. You were like a kitten, purring and soft one minute, and clawing and hissing the next.''

Looking into his eyes, she spoke from her heart. ''I . . . I want to believe you, Steve, but I'm afraid you'll—''

''Afraid! My God, honey! I told you I'd never hurt you!'' He placed his hands on her cheeks, his thumbs tracing her lips. ''You must believe that!''

Jessie watched his face. He was so anxious for her to believe him. It was as if his fate, his future happiness, lay in her reply. She could read it in his eyes. Still, she could not answer.

Steve was getting desperate. ''Jess, for heaven's sake! I want you! I want to marry you! Surely you must know that.''

''I believe you want me, Steve,'' she whispered, ''and I think you even care for me in your own way, but—'' Steve pulled her into his arms and kissed her before she could deny him.

''Jessie, Jessie,'' he murmured, thinking she was giving in. ''I'll make you happy, I swear it. As my woman you'll want for nothing. When you're mine—''

''No!'' Jess pushed him away and scurried to her feet. ''You . . . you make me sound like a . . . a thing, a possession!'' Steve reached for her and she slapped his hand away. ''Hear me, Steve, and hear me well! I will not be owned by you or any man! If there is one thing I've learned, it's that I can stand on my own two feet. If I share my life with you, I will because I want to do so!'' She wanted him to say three little words, and she would have gone to him under any circumstances, but he only spoke of wanting and having, not of loving. To protect herself from possible heartache, she set down the ground rules.

''You have taught me well that I . . . I need you.'' Pacing the area she missed Steve's self-assured grin. ''And you say you want me.'' She turned to face him and saw the answer in his half-closed eyes filled with desire. "Very well." She watched his mouth lift in a crooked grin. "We can use each other, but I won't marry you." His smile froze and he stood to tower over her.

"What the hell do you mean, use each other?"

"I won't marry you and give you that kind of power over me," she asserted. "This way, if either of us wishes to walk away, we can." She turned her back to him. Oh, God, how she loved him! If only he would love her in return. It hurt so badly to turn from him when all she wanted was to be in his arms. She hadn't known what her outburst would bring, but she gasped when he finally replied.

"Okay, if that's how you want it, that's how it will be," he rasped. He watched her stiffen. If he played his cards right, she would yet concede to wed him. He was gambling on the quality of woman she was. He didn't think she could barter her body for pleasure when she hadn't been able to do so for her father's ranch. Even loving him, she couldn't cheapen that love or herself, and he knew that no matter how it came about, he wanted this spitfire for his own.

"Damn you!" she screamed, darting under his arm and out of the tent. She ran for the main camp as fast as she could. Ducking behind first one tent, then another, she reached the corral.

She had never ridden bareback, but she was desperate. She climbed through the fence, moving carefully toward a small roan. Sliding her fingers into its mane and pleading softly, she led it to the fence to help her mount. Scaling the wall like a ladder, she edged the horse close enough, then let out a scream as a hand clamped about her waist, hauling her over the fence.

"Let me go! Let me go!" She pounded at her captor.

Steve chuckled and set her free, only to swing her still kicking and screaming over his shoulder. He swatted her bottom hard and laughed. "White Antelope says I should beat you so you will behave, but I have a better way to calm you down." He took long, purposeful strides back through the camp, smiling at Little Sparrow and White Antelope as he passed their tent.

"Little Sparrow! Help me!" Jess cried. She watched White Antelope lead his wife away with a slight smile on his usually firm mouth before her friend could aid her.

"Quiet!" Steve swatted her again. "No one will help you. I am Hawk, and you are Hawk's woman!"

Grumbling to herself, Jess stilled and rode on her precarious perch to his tent. She kept looking at the ground to avoid the amused eyes that fell on her. These were her friends, yet in this case they would not interfere.

Steve set her down outside the tent and shoved her inside. She spun on him like a virago and would have furiously assailed him if he hadn't thrown her down upon his bed and straddled her before she could react to his brutish behavior.

Steve's amusement increased as she worked herself into a frenzy, and it fueled her anger. It was a silent duel of punches and blocks, of grunts and squeals, until Jess, in pure exhaustion, slumped. She was panting heavily from her efforts, and new rage filled her when she saw him grinning, but she was too tired to continue the battle.

Steve looked upon her gently. She was like a cornered wild creature, ready to fight to the death for its freedom while hopelessly trapped. Her green eyes flashed and her hands clenched into fists.

"I hate you!" she said at last.

"No, Jess. You're only angry because I called your bluff." His hand brushed back her wild hair and she flinched at his touch. "You might as well face it here and now, you are my woman. No one will ever have you but me."

Jessie realized she was powerless to fight him. He had her beaten at every turn. That he was used to having his own way, she had no doubt, but he would find that having her would be bittersweet indeed.

"All right, Steve." She sighed, her eyes awash with unshed tears. "I will be your woman. You can have me and take me at your will." His hands, caressing her neck, slowly moved to her breast. She clenched her teeth and summoned images of Margo. It helped to steel her against the onslaught of his caress.

Steve sensed what she was doing. He had played the game too often and too well not to understand. Patiently he touched her through her clothing, slowly untying the leather laces at her throat and separating her dress to her waist. He watched her eyes close as his fingers brushed the sensitive peaks, and her lips part when he pushed her dress from her shoulders and bared her to her hips. Her hands clutched at the rich rugs beneath her and her hair spread wildly about her. She was like a pagan princess in the golden light of the fire and he ached for this tempest like no other.

Jessie was lost. She could deny him no longer. Her mind screamed at her surrender but her body rejoiced. He had won this battle; still she prayed to win the war as she placed her hands on his arms and he drew her to him.

Elated that he had broken through her defenses, Steve refused to free her of her need. He touched and promised with his hands and lips. He brought her to the brink of fulfillment only to stop and start again.

"Please!" she cried as he shed his pants, yet he would not take her. Instead, he lay on his back beside her and whispered huskily to her.

"No, Jess. You please me." He reached across her and grabbed her about the waist. Before she knew what he meant to do, she was astride him. He held her hips tightly down and she felt him deep inside her. Slowly he moved until she knew what to do.

"Ride, my savage beauty. You wanted to be a user, so use me."

"No! Not like this!" Jess sobbed. "You make it sound so wrong, so cheap!" She tried to pull away but his hands clamped her to him.

"I'll play your stud, Jess. Gladly." He kept moving until he knew she didn't need to be held any longer.

As Jess reached her peak of satisfaction, she threw back her head and cried his name. He joined her in mere seconds and shuddered as she settled against his chest. She quivered in his arms and he felt a tear drop against his skin.

He wanted to tell her he was sorry and, at the same time, demand she admit she was his, but he remained silent. He merely held her gently and let her cry.

Jessica's tears flowed unchecked. He had proved that she was his possession once again, and she could not let it go on. She would either have to marry him and hope he would come to love her, or stay away from him completely. She could not play the whore, no matter how deeply she loved him, nor could she turn from him if he touched her.

Steve rolled to his side and set her softly from him. He grabbed a blanket and wrapped it about her. Kissing her brow, he whispered, "Sleep," and watched as she shuddered and closed her eyes.

It was going wrong, he thought as he galloped across the plains. He had dressed and ridden out to think, but all his thoughts were of Jessica. He couldn't understand her. She said she loved him yet she refused to marry him. He promised her anything she wanted and still she refused. What the hell did she want from him? "Love," came a whisper from within. No! his mind cried. Love made strong men weak, and he would not fall into its trap. He wanted his freedom at the same time he wanted Jessie. He wouldn't be shackled by loving her or any woman, but neither would he let her go.

He decided at length that they could not settle it here. They would go home. He could handle her better there, where others could help convince her that marriage to him was the right thing to do.

Jess sat before Steve atop his huge midnight-black steed as they left the Crow camp, and she thought of how she came to be riding home. Steve returned to the tent after some absence and ordered her to gather her things. She thought he was moving her to another tent. She hastened to collect her few possessions and followed him to White Antelope's abode. It was only when he stuffed her things into his saddlebags and threw them over his saddle that she realized they were leaving. If they hadn't been the center of attention, she would have vented her fury.

She cried at her good-byes to the people who had been so good to her. It was especially difficult to say farewell to Little Sparrow. They had touched souls and shared so much in so short a time. Jess promised to return as often as possible and extended an invitation for Little Sparrow to come to Windy Creek when she could.

Even White Antelope seemed moved by her going. His aloof nature buckled long enough for him to wish her well. "Be happy, Valley Woman," he said, and Jess wondered if she ever would be.

She was dismayed to find she was to ride with Steve. She would have preferred her own horse or even to be allowed to go on foot. She wriggled about in front of him until he clamped his hands about her waist and threatened to toss her across his horse like the baggage she was.

"I don't know why I couldn't have a horse of my own," she said pointedly.

"Horses are very valuable to White Antelope's

people," he informed her. "Besides, you're lucky you're not wanted for horse-stealing as it is!"

She straightened angrily. "What are you talking about?"

"Technically, you're a horse thief!" He grinned at the back of her head.

"I am not! Why, I never—"

"What about the horse you took from the K-D when you left?" he reminded her.

"That was not stealing!" She struck her most indignant pose. "I only borrowed him."

Steve chuckled. "I fail to see the difference, but what about the one you took from Lander? And the one you tried to take from the Crow?"

"Well, I . . . I needed them badly," she stammered, and blushed enough for him to see her neck growing pink beneath her hair.

"And if you needed money, would you 'borrow' it from a bank?" he teased.

"Of course not!" she retorted.

"From now on, when you need something, you better come to me. It will help keep you out of trouble. I can't afford to keep paying off irate horse-owners!"

Jess grew quiet as she mused over what he said. Go to him! Marry him! Need him! All roads seemed to lead to Steve Kincaid. With a deep sigh, Jess leaned back against him. She was suddenly tired of fighting. For the time being, she would relent. Future plans would just have to wait for the future.

Chapter 15

J eff was able to identify his daughter nearly a half mile off. Her hair color was unique to her and its long strands blowing in the wind announced her homecoming like a banner announced knights of old. That she was with Steve was a good sign. He must have been right. Jeff had wanted to bring Jessica home when he'd visited her, but Steve had convinced him to let her stay. He hadn't been clear on his motives yet Jeff sensed trouble between them. Maybe Steve had managed to tame his daughter at last.

Jeff wasn't surprised at the natural spunk Jess had exhibited in coming west on her own. After all, as she said, she was his child. Nonetheless, her fighting spirit and stubborn resiliency after what happened at the K-D revealed a hidden strength he had to admire.

Steve rode up to the porch and set Jessie there. He dismounted and walked up to her father in silence.

"Well, daughter, you look none the worse for your adventures." He smiled as he hugged her.

"Papa, I'm so glad to see you. The Crow were wonderful to me, but all good things end, as they say." She wanted to be free of Steve's presence so she found an excuse, the only one she could think of. "Excuse me, Papa, but I really should change."

Without a glance toward her nemesis, she went inside. She really hated to leave the Crow camp, she thought, but once Steve interfered, there was no sense hiding away. Her peace was shattered.

Jeff followed her in and asked Steve to join them. "Everything okay?" he inquired.

"I'm not sure." Steve straddled a chair. "You have a most stubborn girl, Jeff. She's gotten it into her head not to marry me."

"She did seem a bit skittish." He offered coffee but Steve declined. "Tell me, Steve." He rubbed his chin, a bit embarrassed about what he was to ask. "Have you and Jess . . . well, have you—"

"Yes, Jeff, we have," Steve replied quickly to get him off the hook. He didn't know how Jeff would take it. He could only hope he'd understand.

"I see." He paused to assimilate his feelings. "I take it you still want to marry her?"

"You're damned right!" Steve bellowed. "But she's decided I want to own her! Can you believe such nonsense?"

"Take it easy, boy. I know that you're upset because she's fightin' what you want, but maybe you ought to try and figure out why."

Steve rose and walked to the open door. He braced a hand on the frame and looked out. "I've tried. I've offered her anything she wants and she still insists she remain free."

"Maybe . . ." Jeff paused and watched Steve turn to him hopefully. "It seems you have two choices when you deal with a wild filly. You can beat it into submission or you can gentle it with patient handling. Since I won't let you beat her—" He smiled. "—I suggest you give her time and try to use a gentle hand."

Steve looked perplexed. "You mean court her?"

"Yup! That's what I mean. If she sees you caring about her as a person, maybe she'll come around."

"What if she doesn't?" Steve asked, not sure he

could be patient enough to follow a courting ritual too long.

"If she doesn't in a reasonable amount of time, we'll have to think about the beating." Jeff chuckled.

Jess had pressed her ear to her bedroom door when she heard Steve shouting. She couldn't make out what he was so angry about, but she could guess it had to do with her refusal. She moved away and sat on her bed as she finished buttoning her shirt.

Why did she feel she had to antagonize this man? He was a pillar of the community, an integral part of the most powerful association in the West, and a successful man by his own achievements. Why did she feel she had to be the one to bring him to his knees? Love, she decided. If he couldn't love her then she'd fight him at every turn.

Perhaps she was wrong, her gentler side argued. Perhaps she should follow her heart as Little Sparrow had suggested. Maybe if she was meek and relented, he would love her. No! If he didn't love her as she was, it wouldn't work.

Damn him! Why, of all the women in Wyoming, had he chosen her? "Fool!" echoed in her thoughts. If he had not chosen her, would she ever know of loving? If he hadn't taken her so artfully, so thoughtfully, would she have discovered the passionate woman she was? Oh, yes, he was a great tutor in the field of lovemaking, but a bumbling ass in knowing how to love!

Taking a deep breath, Jess decided it was no time to think. There would be plenty of time for that in her lonely bed. She had to act. Tentatively, she went to the door and turned the knob. Peeking out, she saw the room was empty. She guessed Steve had left and her father's entrance alone confirmed it.

Jeff noticed Jessica's rather anxious state and wisely chose a neutral subject. "How's your side? Does it trouble you?"

"No, Papa. It's quite all right. Little Sparrow was an excellent nurse. There'll only be a small scar."

"Steve's trying to . . ." Jeff paused. He wanted to avoid Steve in their conversation but now that he'd brought him up, he'd best continue as naturally as possible. ". . . to talk to the sheriff about putting a stop to that senseless shooting in town."

"It was an accident. No one meant to hurt me, Papa." Jess poured out coffee for herself and her father and then sat with him at the table.

"Accident or not, somebody could get killed." He watched her nod her head pensively. He knew she was thinking about Steve and he decided to clear the air. "Honey, you've only been out here a few months, but we . . . we seem to be able to talk about things."

"Pa, I can only assume you want an explanation as to why I've decided not to marry Steve. He did tell you, didn't he?"

"Yeah, he told me." Jeff didn't expound on any other part of the conversation.

"I don't know if I can make you understand. You being a man, you might think I'm as crazy as he does, but I'll try." Jess took a sip from her cup and sat back in her chair. "Steve has offered me a home, his name, anything I want. He's made it clear that he wants me." She looked at her hands, now clenched in her lap. "Papa, he doesn't love me." She gave a ragged sigh.

Jeff recalled how Steve had behaved when they thought Jess was lost forever. He watched a tormented man, torn apart by something much stronger than life itself. "I think you're wrong, Jessica. I think he loves you very much."

"He's never told me!" Jess cried in an anguished voice. "I can't marry him just because everyone *thinks* he loves me." Jess leaned across the table and took her father's hand. "Papa, you loved Mother, but when she couldn't return that love, you couldn't hold her here. Don't you see? I love Steve and until he admits his love for me, it's not enough!''

"Look, honey, I'm no expert at love . . ." He looked rather sadly into space. ". . . but maybe you should grab at whatever happiness you can, while you can. Your mother left, but I will always have the memories of the good times."

"No, Papa. If I marry him and he never comes to love me, it will be like dying. I couldn't bear it." Jess left the table and began to prepare dinner.

Jeff watched her as she made biscuits and felt a deeper understanding of his girl. She was strong yet gentle. She was proud and determined. She knew her own mind and would follow her own way. He thought he could talk to Steve, tell him what she had said, but he knew it should be worked out between them. Connie had mentioned Steve's attitude days ago. Maybe he'd talk to her and see if they should interfere or mind their own business.

"I'm going to do some more work on the barn," he told Jess as he left the house. He'd be seeing Connie the next evening for dinner and they could talk it out then.

"If one more person praises the almighty Kincaid, I'll scream!" Jess yelled at the empty cabin. Her father had gone to dinner at the K-D. He'd been seeing Red lately and Jess smiled at his boyish charm when he'd spoken of Connie. It was "Connie thinks . . ." and "Connie says . . ." all day before he told Jess he'd been asked to dine with her.

Not being hungry and not wanting to eat alone anyway, Jess tried to sit and write to her cousin Bonnie, but all her thoughts revolved around the events of the day. It seemed there was an organized scheme to tear down her resistance. First it had been Sarah and Red. They'd come early in the day to see her and she had been delighted until Red had asked her when the wedding would take place. Trying to be as calm as possible, Jess explained to her friends about her decision.

"You're jokin'!" Red exclaimed. "Why, he's the best catch in the territory!"

Sarah, a bit more sensitive to Jessica's dilemma, had shushed Red, then gently inquired if Jess was sure.

Of course she was sure! She knew her own mind, didn't she? By the time they left, she felt like a recalcitrant child. Damn! It was so clear to her! Why couldn't they understand? But how could they? They married men who loved them. There had never been all these doubts.

Then there was Chad. He'd ridden over to help Jeff with raising some beams for the barn. He made some ribald comment about Steve seeming more relaxed since he found Jess again, and how he'd probably always be that way after the wedding.

"There's not going to be a wedding!" Jess yelled, and stomped off. She thought she might go visit Roxy, but the thought of one more person offering her advice kept her away.

The only saving grace about the day was that nearly all those involved had been faced at one time and the sun was setting. They had all crossed her path—all but the cause of all her problems. As if she conjured him up with her thoughts, Jess turned to the opening door to face him.

"Steve," she breathed. Gaining her composure she demanded, "What are you doing here?"

"Is that any way to greet me?" He smiled. His eyes were heavy-lidded and Jess drew her arms across her breast as if to cover herself. It seemed he was looking through her clothes.

"I didn't expect to see you again so soon, that's all," she said coolly.

"May I sit down?"

"Yes, yes, of course." Jess didn't know what to expect from him but it wasn't polite cordiality. She was a little off-guard with it. A Steve who was demanding and arrogant, she could handle. She wasn't sure if this new approach was a game and it unnerved her. She stood plucking at her skirt as he sat.

"Please, Jessica. Won't you sit with me?" He gestured to another chair. "I'd like to talk to you, if you don't mind."

Jess took a chair, sitting on the edge. She kept watching Steve, waiting for a move that didn't seem to be coming.

"I've been thinking about what you said, the things you've tried to tell me." He grasped a fisted hand in his other and propped his chin on both. "I'll be honest, Jess, I still don't understand it but I respect you and your right to change your mind."

Jess was more wary than ever. Could this be the same self-assured man who had manipulated her and her life?

"Are . . . are you saying that you don't want to marry me either?"

"No, honey, I'm not saying that. I'm still going to marry you but I've decided to give you time to come to grips with the idea." He smiled warmly.

"Well, how very thoughtful you are." She looked sweetly at him and watched him accept the praise as his due. "In other words, you think I'll get over this foolishness." If he had been as clever as he thought, he would have seen her hands clench into tight fists and her body stiffen with her words.

"I figure you're just upset because it's all happened so fast. You want the frills of courting like any other woman and I'm a reasonable man."

It was getting more difficult to remain seated. Jess was beginning to go from low boil to full rage. "So you've decided to court me?" He grinned and nodded his head. Jess rose and walked around behind her chair, gripping the back. "You pompous ass!" She saw his brow draw down in puzzlement. "I've never known such a fool!"

Throwing up his hands in dismay, he yelled, "Now what have I done?"

"Get out!" she screamed. "Get out and stay away from me!" She spun about to flee to her room but came up short as Steve grabbed her arm and swung her to face him.

"I'll go, but first I'll give you something to think about." He pulled her tightly against him. Muscular arms wrapped about her and large strong hands slid down her to grip her hips and hold her closely to him. With her arms held captive between their bodies, she couldn't push him away as he lowered his mouth to hers. Throwing back her head, she succeeded in stopping the kiss only to have his lips caress her neck. Her struggles ceased as he entwined a hand in her hair and pulled her mouth to his.

His kiss started as a punishing assault on her sensitive lips but it gave way to passion and yearning. Jess could feel the evidence of his desire pressed against her stomach and she felt her will beginning to crumble. He felt her responding, and when he knew he could easily carry her to her bed with no objections, he stepped back. Her eyes were glazed and green fire leaped from their depths. Her lips trembled and her breath had grown rapid.

"Good night, Jess." His voice was gravelly and deep as he released her and walked away.

She stood bereft and abandoned. Her body swayed as she regained her perspective and she wanted to scream out to him to return.

"You ignorant ass! You stupid fool! You blithering idiot!" She wasn't sure if she was shouting at Steve or herself.

Deciding the easiest route to forgetfulness lay in hard work, Jess spent hours working a thriving garden and helping her father in any chore she could. She struggled with siding for the barn and hauled planks for stalls and lofts. She dug furrows for irrigation and carried gallons of water to fill them. Chickens had been added to the ranch for eggs and meat, along with a pair of piglets, and Jess tended them all.

Jeff had admonished her on numerous occasions to let up, but she was driven. Every evening would find her exhausted after dinner and she gratefully would seek her bed to fall into oblivion, too tired even to dream.

She'd maintained her furious pace for just over two weeks when Sarah visited one afternoon. Pushing her large straw hat back from her brow and wiping her hands on her apron, Jess walked up to her friend with a smile and a wave.

"Sarah! It's so good to see you. I was just about to take a break."

"How are you, Jess?" Sarah looked around her. "I swear, everytime I come here I marvel at what you and Jeff are doing."

"It's getting there." Jess laughed. "Come on in the house. It's ten degrees cooler in there."

As Jess and Sarah went inside, Jess offered her whatever she would like to drink.

"I'll just have some water. It's warmer than I thought and I'm parched."

"I made some lemonade this morning. How about some?" Sarah gave a delighted nod and slipped off her jacket. Jess poured out two glasses and sat with her friend to visit.

Sarah took a big sip and sighed. "Ah, that's good." She suddenly grew more serious and looked at Jess. "How are you really, Jess?"

"I assume you mean can I live without Steve Kincaid and the answer is yes!" Jess noticed Sarah's genuine concern. "Oh, Sarah! I'm sorry. It's just that he makes me so furious I take it out on others."

Sarah's eyes softened. "So you still love him." It was a simple statement. There was no need to question.

"Of course I still love him," Jess sighed heavily. "But that doesn't change anything. It won't work the way it is."

"I didn't ride over here today just to see you," Sarah stated. "I came to see if you were as distraught as Steve. Maybe I better explain." Sarah was aware of Jessica's raised brow. "For the last two weeks he's been pacing about, growling at everyone, and Red and I are at our wits' end. Jess, I've never seen him in such a state. Why, he's a bear!" She smiled at the grin on Jessie's face. "He loves you, Jess."

"N-no, Sarah, you're wrong. He's just a spoiled boy sulking because he hasn't gotten his way."

"*You're* wrong, Jess! I've known Steve a long time. I've seen him lose his father, lose cattle and crops, and I've watched him when big deals fell through, but I've never seen him like this. He's always been able to handle everything. That is, until he met up with you."

"Don't you think I want him to love me? Don't you know how badly I wish we were married?" Jess rose and paced the room, struggling with Sarah's words. "If I thought he truly cared, I'd go to him on my hands and knees."

Sarah ran to her and clutched her hands. "Go to him. See what you're doing to each other. Then you'll know how much he loves you, despite what he doesn't say."

A message was sent with Sarah inviting Steve to join Jess and her father for dinner the following night. Sarah assured her that Steve was truly distraught and desperately in love. Not sure if either was true, she relented to see him, but only with her father present.

Rising early, Jess started to prepare her meal. She had Jeff slaughter a plump chicken and she sat pulling pin feathers shortly after dawn. Bread was rising and a pie had been made before noon. By early evening the table was set with fine china and newly polished silver. The aroma of roasting fowl filled the small house as she set a pan of potatoes and carrots on to cook. Realizing it was time to ready herself, she smiled when Jeff entered, shaking the last of his bathwater from his hair.

"My, but aren't you getting all dressed up. It will be so nice dining with such a handsome gentleman."

"It's a good thing Steve is handsome," he mused sheepishly, " 'cause I won't be here."

"Papa! You knew I'd asked Steve tonight only because you would be here!" Jess twisted her hands together.

"Well, honey, Connie asked me over tonight because . . . because we could spend some time alone without Steve. His presence has put a damper on things lately."

"How could you?" She threw up her hands. "You planned this! Both of you!"

"Now Jess . . ."

"Don't 'Now Jess' me! I don't believe it! A conspiracy to say the least." Angrily she pushed a long strand of hair from her cheek.

"You better get ready," Jeff advised. "Your guest will be here soon."

Jess fumed and went to her room. Of all the nerve! They were supposed to be her friends—and her own father too! Well, the damage was done. She had invited Steve to dinner and dinner he'd have—but that's all!

Chapter 16

⁓⦿⦿⁓

J ess chose to wear a pale pink gown. It was always a favorite of hers for afternoons in St. Louis, and now she wore it for its demure styling. A high collar of white lace circled her throat and highlighted her healthy-looking suntanned skin. Elbow-length full sleeves were trimmed in matching lace and a band of it circled her waist and entwined in the large bustle.

With her hair drawn up in a severe chignon, Jess entered the main room. Jeff was extremely proud of the way she looked.

"I thought you would be gone by now," Jess said, smiling at him.

"I wanted to see you before I left." He went to her and held out his hands. She placed hers in his. "If you want, I'll stay home," he offered.

Jess shook her head. "No, Papa. It will be all right. Go, and give Red a kiss for me." Her eyes twinkled.

"Yeah. Well, I guess I'll see you later." Jeff patted her hand. "Everything will be okay, honey." He kissed her cheek, picked up his hat, and left.

Jess wondered if everything really would be okay. This was no fairy tale with a "they lived happily ever after." This was real. Perhaps all the trouble was of her own making. Maybe she was hoping for a Prince Charming to sweep her off her feet with declarations of undying love. She had shared passions she was sure few women had experienced. Could she settle for less now? The thought of giving herself to anyone else caused her to shiver.

"Are you cold, my love, or did you sense my presence?" Steve asked as she spun about, startled.

"Don't you ever knock?" she asked, annoyed. In an instant she noticed the crisp white of his shirt and the narrow string tie beneath his collar. He wore black pants and shiny black boots. He tossed his Stetson on a hook near the door and his hair looked inky-black in the dim light of the cabin. At any other time, she would have admired the lazy grace of his tall frame and the way his clothing seemed perfectly fitted to his muscular body.

"Jessie! You know the highlights of my life have been coming through closed doors to you unannounced!" He grinned.

Clenching her teeth, Jess drew deep breaths to regain her composure. "It doesn't matter. You're here and . . . and dinner is nearly ready." She held her head high and turned to check the meal.

"I see a setting for three. Who else are you expecting?"

"The third was for Papa, but he's gone to dine with Red," she replied haughtily.

"Yeah, I just saw him on the trail. It must have been a surprise for you."

"Yes, it was." She kept her back to him and maintained a cool, clipped conversational tone.

Steve came up silently behind her and laid his hands on her shoulders. She flinched and would have pulled away but the stove blocked her retreat.

"You wouldn't have asked me if you had known, would you?" he whispered against her hair.

Jess closed her eyes and trembled. "No. No, I wouldn't have."

"Why, honey? Don't you trust me?" He pressed a kiss behind her ear. "Or is it yourself you don't trust?"

"You were invited to dinner and nothing else!"

She gripped the pot handle to stop her shaking. "Will you please sit down."

Steve chuckled and took a seat at the table. He chose the side between the other two, forcing Jess to sit at his right or his left instead of across from him. Bringing the food to the table, she noticed immediately. She thought about pulling one setting opposite, but decided a childish display would only serve to amuse him. When everything was served, she seated herself and began to fill her plate.

The mouthwatering aroma of the roasting bird had whetted her appetite earlier, and now it merely served to remind her she had to face the meal with him, alone, with no one to help the conversation. He attempted to draw her into polite chatting about the people and places they both knew, but she would have none of it. Her replies were all terse and allowed no room for expounding.

"You're a good cook, Jess." He pointed to her plate offhandedly. "You should try to eat something."

Setting her cutlery down on her plate, she pushed it away, hardly touched. "I'm not hungry." She placed her hands in her lap and cast her eyes downward. She sat that way until Steve finished his meal. The moment he was done, she rose and poured his coffee. He leaned back in his chair and pulled at the thin tie at his throat, releasing it and the top couple of buttons on his shirt.

"What are you doing?" she demanded, slamming the half-empty coffeepot on the table.

"Relaxing after an excellent meal," he replied innocently.

"Well, don't! You're not staying!" She gathered the dirty dishes and set them in a basin. "You were asked here to eat and you have, so you may leave!" Jessica's fury was not just from his leisurely attitude. She had expected to see a man miserably in need of her. From what Sarah had said, she expected him to be less sure of himself. What she hadn't noticed were the tiny lines about his mouth and his eyes. Perhaps if she had she would have been more tolerant.

Steve jumped to his feet and grabbed her arm. "What the hell's wrong with you?" Jessie's hand shook and she dropped a plate. The fine china hit the floor and shattered. She yanked her arm free and bent to retrieve a piece of the plate.

"You'll cut yourself!" Steve warned, pulling her away.

Tears formed in her eyes. "You . . . you broke it. It was my m-mother's," she sobbed. She began to pound his chest with clenched fists. "You broke it!" she cried.

Steve gathered her tightly in his arms, trapping hers. "Honey, don't." He gently ran his hand over her back. He'd seen her furious, laughing, teasing, and passionate, but he'd never seen her sobbing so brokenheartedly. "Shh, Jess," he whispered. "Don't cry."

As great sobs shuddered through her, he gently lifted her up. Her head lay against his shoulder as he carried her to a chair. He set her down and grabbed a towel. Soaking it in cool water, he squeezed it and returned to her. Slowly, he bathed her face and wiped away her tears. He dropped to his haunches and took her clenched hands in his.

"I'm sorry, Jess." His voice was low and tender. "It was an accident. I didn't mean to—"

"I know." Her voice quivered as she interrupted. "It's not that, it's just that I . . . I've never done this . . . acted like this before."

"I understand, honey. I really do." He stood and paced about the room until he stood behind her. "You overreact, and snap at friends for little or no reason. You sleep only when exhausted and you pick at your food." He raked his fingers through his hair. "You see, I understand because I've lived in the same hell for the last two weeks."

Jessie turned in her chair to look at him, and saw

a different man. Gone was the arrogance and the lordly demeanor. In their place were doubts, frustrations, and desperation. Sarah was right. He did care for her in his own way.

"Jess, I—"

"No!" She stood and pressed her fingers to his lips. "Don't say anything, just hold me," she breathed. It had to come his own way in his own time, not forced by tears and hysterics.

"Oh, God." He sighed deeply, holding her to him. "Jessie, Jessie, you're driving me crazy." He pressed kisses to her face and neck. "I want you so very much."

She placed her hands on his face and made him look at her. There was so much she could say. "I . . . I want you, too."

He looked at her so tenderly that tears welled in her eyes. He brushed a finger across her cheek and felt the cool drop between his fingers. He looked at her questioningly. Jess smiled lovingly and drew his head down to hers. It was the first time Steve was tentative and hesitant when they kissed. She let her tongue tease at his lower lip, touching, telling him of her desire, conveying her wish to be his.

He moaned, responding at last to her demands. He murmured her name between short, desperate kisses. Jessie's senses reeled as she felt him pull the pins from her hair and entwine his hands in the thick mass. Her hands went to his chest, seeking the buttons of his shirt, when she felt his hands close over hers. Breathing rapidly, Steve stopped her and held her at arm's length.

"I can't believe I'm saying this," he groaned, "but we have to stop." Jess, still trapped in the throes of desire, pleadingly called his name. "No, honey. Not this time. We'll go into town tomorrow and get married. Then . . ." He kissed her quivering lips. "Then it will be worth the wait. I promise you."

"Of all the times to be gallant," she mused, "you've chosen the worst." Her eyes cleared and she laughed. "Someday I'll have to tell our children how very strong and brave their father was—once."

"And I'll tell them about the witch, Valley Woman, who fought me all the time she led me to the altar." They kissed again, but it was a sealing, a joining that didn't need further words or actions. "I better go," he growled, "or your gallant suitor will forget all his pious declarations." He kissed her brow and whispered, "Until tomorrow."

Jess went to the door and watched him ride away. She would join him at the K-D tomorrow. She drew a deep breath of the cool evening air. Stars glistened and a full moon smiled down on her.

"Mrs. Steven Kincaid! Jessica Kincaid!" Liking the sound, she spun around to see to the dishes.

Having just finished washing her hair, Jess stood on the porch in her camisole and petticoat, vigorously toweling it dry. The stiff breeze blew her slip against her legs and she shivered. She watched her father working on a downed slat on the corral. He'd been late coming home the night before and, although she had still been awake in her room, she decided to speak with him the next morning. When she woke up, he had already left the house. She prepared water and washed her hair, hoping he would come in, but he hadn't. Smiling to herself, she thought he might already know about Steve and herself.

A rider approached from the north and anticipation welled up in Jessica. It was Steve! Forgetting her half-dressed state she tossed the towel aside and ran down the steps to greet him. He jumped from his horse and ran toward her. Clamping his hands on her waist, he swung her high in the air. Her hands gripped his shoulders below her and damp curls fell forward to whip at him. Laughing, he stopped his turn and slowly let her fall against him. Sliding her down the length of him until her feet finally touched the ground, he lowered his lips to hers.

They were not aware of their audience as Jeff leaned on the fence and smiled, shaking his head. If he lived to be a hundred, he would never understand women! Just when he figured out he knew what Jess was up to, she changed everything. Connie must have been right. She said they would work it out since they were destined for each other, and he guessed they had.

"You're early." Jess nestled her cheek against his chest. "I didn't think you would be here yet."

"Is that why you're running around half-naked?" He kissed her hair.

"Um." She placed her lips to his neck and murmured, "If I'd known you were coming . . ." Her hand moved provocatively down his chest to his belt and playfully traced it across his belly. ". . . I might have worn less."

A rumbling growl came from his throat. "You'll pay for this," he promised, and she snuggled closer. "Witch!" He laughed. "Go get dressed or I won't be responsible for the consequences." Jess backed away and looked at him through her lashes. "Go!" He swatted at her bottom to accent his words.

Jess ran to the house and turned at the door. She stretched out a hand to Steve with a sultry smile. His darkening eyes took in the exquisite sight of her and his feet obeyed her beckoning. As he reached the porch she ran inside, laughing. Steve entered and looked about to find the room empty and immediately spun to capture her behind the door.

"Did you think I would fall for that trick again?" He grinned as he stalked her.

Shaking her head she giggled as he inched closer, forcing her into the corner. She squealed when he grabbed her and tossed her over his shoulder.

"You would tempt me when I have hours to face before I can satisfy myself on you, wench, when I am ready to burst my seams with wanting you? Then

you must pay!'' he roared playfully, running his
hand over her bottom while heading for her room.

"Steve! Don't! What if Papa comes in?" She wiggled desperately.

"He wouldn't dare!" Steve threatened. "Not if he
wishes to ever see his grandchildren!" In several
long strides he stood beside her bed and tossed her
there. Humor fled and desire took its place. Looking
down at her he saw her hair tumbling over the side
to the floor. Her mouth silently beckoned to his. Her
breasts pushed against the white lace of her camisole and he felt the surge of pure passion in his
groin.

"Jess, please," he begged. "You must get ready.
I can't bear to see you there, so beautiful, so . . .
Please!"

Looking at the aching misery in his eyes, Jess
knew the power of being a woman. She sat up, taking pity on him, and heard a deep whoosh from him
as she got to her feet.

"Would you like to wait outside?" she asked at
the sound.

He shook his head and reached to caress a long
curl. "I'd like to watch you, if I may. It would be
novel to see you dressing instead of undressing." A
crooked grin lifted one side of his mouth.

Taking the haughtiest pose she could while standing barefoot in her undergarments, she retorted,
"Are you complaining, my lord?" She flicked her
finger down his shirtfront.

"You saucy wench! You play the temptress well
when you know you are safe from ravishment. What
will you do when I have you shackled to my bed to
do my bidding?"

Tossing her head, she grinned. "Why, my very
best!"

His laughter filled the room. "Ah, Jess. I've waited
a lifetime for a woman like you, and at last you will
be mine!"

A nibbling doubt threatened Jessica's bliss for a

moment, but she dismissed it. It was a gamble. Her whole future was being bet on a single hand, but she would not fold.

"Did you tell Papa?" Jess asked as she sat and pulled on her silk stockings. Her petticoats were pulled to her thighs while she arranged her garters. She put her skirts down and gave him a scolding look. "Steve!"

"What? Oh, uh . . . yes . . . no! No, I didn't. I thought you would want to." He sat nervously as far from her as he could in the confines of the small room.

"Well, we can tell him together." She smiled as she stepped into her gown of soft yellow. A high-standing collar went around the back of the neck but plunged to the valley of her breasts in a deep vee. Short sleeves gave way to lace so wide it fell below her elbows in soft folds. The full skirt gathered at the waist and a deeper yellow band circled it. She turned her back to Steve and requested his services in fastening her.

Steve came up behind her and pushed her drying tresses aside. He began to hook her up and couldn't resist placing a kiss on her exposed neck. "Beautiful," he whispered against her soft skin. And beautiful she was, standing there with her long, deeply waved coppery curls falling forward. Her eyes were nearly closed and her tongue daintily touched the corner of her parted lips.

Heavy footsteps in the other room brought them out of their reverie and back to the reality of the day.

"Hurry up, slowpoke." Jess wiggled for emphasis.

"Hold still!" he warned with a laugh.

Slipping on her shoes as he completed his chore, she was nearly ready except for her hair. She brushed at it vigorously and Steve could stand no more.

"I better go out and sit with your father. Your every movement is driving me to distraction."

Jess smiled at her reflection as he left the room, running a finger nervously under his collar. That he was anxious to wed her, and more so to bed her, there was no doubt, she thought.

Several minutes passed before Jess joined her father and Steve. Her hair was pulled up from the sides and held back with long yellow ribbons. She looked at her father and a soft flush touched her cheeks at what he must be thinking, but he merely smiled affectionately. Steve held out a hand and she placed hers into it.

"So, you two have finally decided to stop all your running around and settle down." Jeff shook his head happily. "It's about time, too."

"We're going into town in a little while to tie the knot." Steve smiled down at Jessie. "I think I can safely say we'd like you to be there."

Jeff sat and looked at the perfectly matched pair and pride welled in him. "Wouldn't miss it."

Steve sat and pulled Jess to his knee when she would have chosen a chair of her own. "After chasing you halfway around the territory, I'm not letting you go now, not until I have my ring on your finger." She wriggled about and kept her eyes averted from her father's. "Hold still! I don't think Jeff would object to a firm hand being applied to you from his future son-in-law." Jess slipped her arm about his shoulder and stilled with a shy smile as Steve's hand slid to her hip. He turned his attention to Jeff once more when she was settled. "Getting back to our discussion, do you agree?"

"Well, I guess with my hand leaving—" He grinned at his daughter. "—it's fair, but I still feel I should settle some of the account myself." Jeff scratched his chin. "I've never been one for takin' charity."

Jess was lost. She looked from one to the other, trying to understand the flow of conversation.

"It's not charity, Jeff. Call it a settlement, if you

like," Steve explained. "It's done in the tribes regularly, a compensation for your loss."

"Will somebody please tell me what's going on?" Jessie finally demanded, her curiosity well-piqued.

"Steve wants to wipe out my debt to him." Scratching an ear, he wished he'd led up to his announcement more slowly as he watched Jessie's face. She'd drawn a breath and held it, mulling over his words.

Steve sensed her change before she spoke. "What do you mean wipe it out?" She looked seriously at Steve. "You can't mean you expect us not to honor the loan?"

"That's exactly what I mean." He smiled tentatively and tried to make her understand. "The Crow do it, so do a lot of Europeans. When a man chooses a woman, he pays her people horses or money, something. The family is losing a pair of hands and is compensated. Jeff's losing you and I'm marking the loan paid."

Jessie jumped to her feet and faced first one, then the other. "And you accept this?" she asked her father.

"I understand the offer and I'm sure it was meant as a gesture from one family member to another. We will be one family when you get married." Jeff knew she was ready to explode in anger. Steve should have waited until after they were wed to make his generous offer, realizing the extent of her damnable pride.

"No!" She looked at Steve. "We'll pay the loan!"

Steve moved to stand before her. "Honey, there's no need." He sighed. "Jeff's proved himself a fine rancher. He only needed a stake."

"And because of me, you gave it to him?"

Laying his hands on her shoulders, he tried to pull her close but she held back. "I would have lent Jeff the money regardless, if he'd asked," he gently informed her. "You motivated him, not me."

"Would you have made him repay you if I wasn't

here?'' He hesitated and she demanded, "Would you?''

He thought of lying to her then decided on the truth. "Yes, Jessie. I would have, but—''

She pushed his hands away and moved back. "But nothing! Did you think you could buy me? Is that why you're being so generous? I'm not for sale, Mr. Kincaid!'' She half-ran to stand at her father's side.

Steve stood helplessly watching her anger build. "For God's sake, Jess. Now isn't the time to argue about this. We'll forget about the loan for now and go get married. We'll settle the whole thing later.'' He could cut out his tongue for having started this. He should have realized her pride would twist his offer.

"I should have known better than to believe you . . . you cared for me! You only wanted a new possession! Someone to satisfy your ego and your lust! There won't be a wedding, Mr. Kincaid! Not today, not ever!''

Steve slammed his fist down on the table. "Damn you, Jess! I'm tired of your games! Either you come with me right now, or we forget it!'' He watched her raise her chin in defiance. "Jeff, talk to her,'' he pleaded.

"She's not a child, Steve. I can't make her do what she's set against no matter how I feel.''

"Don't you want her to marry me?'' he asked, hoping to sway him.

"What I want isn't important. It's her life.''

Steve offered a hand to Jess in supplication. "Jess?''

"Good-bye, Mr. Kincaid,'' she replied with finality.

Steve drew himself to full height. "Jeff. Miss Morgan.'' He nodded to each in turn and, with long strides, he left.

"Oh, Papa,'' Jess sobbed. "I thought . . .''

Jeff took her in his arms and let her cry. "I know, honey.'' He patted her back gently. "I know.''

Chapter 17

A hot June sun beat down on Jessie as she pulled weeds that seemed to grow overnight each time there was the smallest rain. Her back ached as she crawled between the rows and yanked at the unwanted growth. She sat back on her heels and rubbed her arm across her forehead. A deep sigh escaped her as she arched her back and rubbed at the small of it. Thoughts of a crystal-clear, sparkling stream ran through her mind but she refused to heed its beckoning. She had not returned there since . . . there was no sense thinking about it. It only brought the pain and anger back.

To change the direction of her thoughts, Jess looked about the yard. New chicks were peeping about their mothers' legs and she chuckled at the clumsy antics they displayed. A pen had been built for the piglets and they were well on their way to becoming fat and succulent. The house had grown along with the livestock. A small new wing had been added, containing a room for her father and a large pantry.

Jeff spent his days working on the barn. He'd taken time away from it only to dig a big root cellar and to install a pump in the kitchen area to supplement the well and facilitate household chores. Jess could hear him hammering as she looked about. A movement caught her eye and brought her to her feet. She shielded her eyes and tried to identify the rider. She had been visited by Sarah on several occasions, and even Red rode out once, but this rider was a man.

With her heart pounding, she held her breath until she made out the intruder. It was Chad and she felt her fear subside. It had been nearly a month since her confrontation with Steve. Everytime she saw someone riding from the direction of the K-D, she feared it was him. Why she was so afraid, she didn't know. She knew he was a powerful man, and although he had never made a move to hurt her, the fears could not be banished.

Chad rode into the yard and reined in. He waved to Jessie with a smile and walked toward her, extending his hands. "Good mornin', Jess."

"Chad, how are you?" She wiped her hands on her apron and placed them in his. "It's been a while." Her smile was nervous. "How's Sarah?"

"She's fine." He watched Jessie look wistfully beyond him and he shook his head. He knew he should stay out of Steve's affairs but he'd botched things so many times, he couldn't make matters worse. "Jess, I . . . I don't know everything that's happened between you and Steve, but . . . well, can't you two stop bickering and settle things?"

Jess pulled her hands from his and turned away toward the house without answering. Chad followed, hoping for a reply. As she came to the porch, she sat on the step and pulled off her hat, tossing it to the side while Chad joined her.

"I don't know, Chad. We . . . we seem to be able to do only two things well together, argue and . . ." Her voice drifted off and a warming blush flooded her face.

"Yeah," he interrupted diplomatically, "but can't you work it out?"

"I think we're beyond that." She turned toward him, letting her anger surface. "He's so damned stubborn and . . . and arrogant! Why that egotistical, narrow-minded oaf thinks he can . . . can own me!" There was no doubt that her anger was gathering fuel.

"Whoa!" Chad laughed. "You sound just like him!" At her frown, he chuckled. "He used some similar terms as I recall. Something about a spoiled brat and a prideful, stubborn hoyden."

"Why, that—" Jess jumped to her feet.

"Take it easy, Jess." Chad grabbed her arm. "Turnabout is only fair." Seeing the wisdom of his words, Jess mumbled an apology and resumed her seat. "If you ask me, you both need a thrashing." He grinned and Jess smiled.

"I think you're right." They sat silent a moment. "How is he, Chad?" she asked at last.

Chad pushed his hat back with his thumb and laid his arms across his knees. "Not too good."

"He's not sick, is he?" Jessica's anxiety brought a crooked grin to Chad's lips and a raised eyebrow.

"Do you care?" he asked curiously.

"Of course I care! Why, I . . ." Jess caught herself in time and stubbornly clamped her teeth together.

Chad shook his head in disgust. "You both agree on one thing that's right—you're both stubborn! You love him. He loves you, but neither will give in. I can't figure either of you out." Jess started to protest but Chad stopped her. "Here you are, working yourself to exhaustion. Steve, he's either making everyone's life miserable yelling or jumping down on all of us or he's half-drunk, grumbling to the walls!"

Jessica's lip quivered at the thoughts Chad's words conjured. "Stop! I don't want to hear any more." Several unwanted tears began to trace her cheeks.

"Well, I said my piece." Chad kicked at the dirt at his feet. "I didn't come here to lecture you anyway. I came to see Jeff." He got up and hesitated. "I'm sorry, Jess. I didn't mean—"

"It's all right, Chad." She exhaled deeply. "Papa is in the barn."

"Yeah, I heard him when I rode up. Look, Jess, I really am sorry. Sarah told me to mind my own business and I guess she was right, as usual."

Jess gave him a weak smile and rose to return to the garden. Chad watched her go and whispered a few expletives at his foolish interference as he walked with long strides to see Jeff.

"What did Chad want?" Jess asked as she sat over a small lunch of biscuits and cold ham. "He didn't stay long."

Jeff wiped his mouth and took a large swallow of hot coffee. He looked at her and replied, "Steve wants to see me."

Jess froze and stared at him. "What for?"

"He didn't say. He just said Steve wants me to ride to the K-D this afternoon."

"Don't go!" Jess cried, suddenly wanting to keep a distance between them.

"Jess, don't be silly. I have to go," he admonished. "We're still neighbors and I happen to owe him over five hundred dollars, or had you forgotten that?"

"I'm sorry, Papa. I don't know why I said that." She slumped over her coffee mug, ashamed of her outburst. "And I haven't forgotten anything. How could I? It's all my fault."

Jeff watched her and was sorry he'd shouted. "It's not your fault, honey. Windy Creek wouldn't be anything if I hadn't borrowed that money. I only regret I didn't do it years ago. You gave me a reason to stop wallowing in the past and do something. How can I be angry with you for that?" He smiled and Jess returned it weakly. "Besides," he added cheerfully, "if all that's happened hadn't, I'd have never gotten to know Connie."

Jess laughed more naturally at last, and thought about Red and her father. It seemed to be the one good thing to come out of the mess she'd made.

They seemed fated to find each other and she was glad she had been the catalyst.

She began to clean up and stopped to address her father. "Papa, I know how you feel about the money Mother left me, but please, take it to Steve."

"Jess, you know what I said about it. It's yours and I don't want it," he sternly replied.

She knelt beside him. "Listen to me. Nothing can come of . . . of Steve and me as long as there's this loan over our heads. I still love that stubborn fool and maybe, if we start clean, it can work out. If you don't take the money, we may never know," she pleaded. "There's only two hundred dollars, but it will convince him I'm anxious to see an end to this. Please, Papa."

Jeff mulled over her words. This could be a way to reconcile their differences. "Okay, honey. We'll pay him that money, but only if you take it to him and tell him it's from you." He searched her face. "And why you want him to have it."

Trying to decide what course to take, Jess finally agreed. She would make the first move and give them hope. It wouldn't be easy to swallow her pride enough to go to him, but she would. After talking with Chad, she knew something had to be done before they destroyed each other.

He knew there was something he was supposed to do this afternoon, but he couldn't recall what it was. He had such a hangover that morning, he could barely remember talking to Chad. Why he'd spent another night at Roxy's, he didn't know. It didn't help him forget, it only gave him a different kind of headache, one that pounded each time he moved his head. Grimacing at the bad taste in his mouth, he thought about Roxy's girl, Cara. She'd done her best to help him forget Jess, but no matter how she applied herself, he ended up pushing her away in disgust, not with her but with himself.

Night after night of trying to drown his frustrations only heightened his need for the fiery-haired witch with the emerald eyes. The only thing he'd done right in the last two weeks was to send for Jeff and end the stand-off. Jeff! Yes, that's why he'd spoken to Chad. He'd arranged to see Morgan and work out some kind of solution to his dilemma. He knew he couldn't keep his distance much longer. The ache in his groin demanded her body and the agony in his heart demanded the rest of her. He admitted not to love, but to obsession. She had fought her way into his life and life without her would be hell.

Steve dunked his head in a basin of cold water and worked some of the pain and tension from his temples. He needed lots of coffee and something to eat. He'd better clean up, he told himself, and get ready to see Jeff with his proposal.

Red set food and coffee for Steve on the table and left to spend the afternoon with Sarah. They had to finish some curtains Sarah had begun and work on a gown Red had suddenly decided she needed.

Having finished his repast and taking a third cup of coffee with him, Steve went to the library and worked on some ledgers he'd let go. His headache was better and he was anxious to meet with Jeff. The tedious bookkeeping helped pass the time and refined his mental skills. A knock at the front door brought him to his feet. That would be Morgan and, if everything went well, he would have Jessie as his bride before much longer.

One would be hard-pressed to decide who was the more surprised. Jessie knew she would be seeing him, yet she gasped as he flung open the door. Expecting to see Red first, she flinched then began to stare as her heart beat loudly in her ears. Could he hear it? Did he know how badly she wanted to throw herself into his arms?

If she was surprised, Steve was dumbfounded!

The welcoming smile for Jeff froze on his face and he stared incredulously. The vision before him nearly tore him apart. Jess, her hair tied at her neck and blowing gently. Jess, her eyes betraying her love for him. Jess, her body swaying at his nearness.

He was the first to break the silence. "Jessie," he said softly, struggling to remain composed on the surface. "I was expecting Jeff. This is a . . . a pleasant surprise. Come in." He stepped back and gestured for her to enter.

Still speechless, Jessie went inside. He directed her to the library with his hand and she thought of the night almost three months before when she'd entered under duress and came out engaged to this complicated man. She chose the same chair she'd occupied that night, as did he. He offered her something to drink and she declined. Simultaneously they began.

"I wanted to talk—"

"I was going to talk—"

They looked at each other and laughed nervously. "Go ahead," Steve insisted. Jess began to explain why she had come. At first, she skirted the issue and he was able to half listen and half watch her. Her cheeks were flushed and her lips quivered from time to time. He knew she was hard-pressed to express her apology and . . .

"So, if you'll take this money, we'll get the rest to you within a few months. Then this mess will be behind us." She lowered her head shyly and missed the knitting of his brows and clenching of his fists. So, she hadn't come to see it his way. She was still worried about that damned debt.

Steve stood and went to the fireplace. He braced his hands on the mantel and gazed into the cold, black hearth. "Jessie, the money your father owes me is nothing. I've spent that much in an hour at the poker tables. It isn't necessary to repay it." He continued to keep his eyes from her and gauged her silence. "If it's a matter of pride, answer me this—

does pride warm your bed? Can you share your life with it?''

Jessie sat silently struggling with his words. She knew he was right. Pride was a hollow thing when you stood alone. Trying to vocalize her thoughts she said, "It's . . . it's not pride. It's just that . . . can't you understand? I won't be bought.''

Steve spun around and towered over her. His anger was controlled but she was so beautiful, so desirable, he found his good intentions to talk crumbling. "I don't want to buy you, damn it! If you have to, think of it as a merger.'' He began to rub his forehead to ease the returning headache.

Turning in her chair, Jess took his hand and looked pleadingly at him. "If I let you do this, everyone will think I came to you as a fortune hunter, that I sold myself to you.'' She pulled his hand against her cheek and tears dripped slowly from her lashes. "I'd be no better than a whore,'' she murmured.

"Does that mean you were a tramp because you were so easy to bed?'' he demanded ruthlessly, trying to make her see another side to her argument.

Jess looked up in disbelief. "N-no,'' she breathed. "I . . . I loved you. You know you were the first, the only . . .'' She watched his eyes darkening and she was suddenly afraid. They were here and alone. She was at his mercy. He read her thoughts as her eyes darted about the room seeking escape. "I shouldn't have come.'' She eased herself from the chair and backed away from him, snapping the last of his control.

"Jessica, come here!'' He saw her flinch and freeze. "You've made it this far, and it's only a short distance to my bed. Don't stop now.''

She let out a startled gasp and started to run. Before she could reach the door, he gripped her arm and pulled her to him. Jess fought desperately as she could, but he blocked her raking nails and battering fists. There were no words, only the grunts and groans of a struggle. Steve quickly tired of her refusal to have him and grabbed a handful of her hair to still her. With her head pulled back and her body arched painfully over his arm, she quieted. The cords in his neck strained as he tried to seek her lips and she begged him to stop.

"I'm sorry, Jessie," he groaned, taking advantage of her unbalanced state to sweep her into his arms. Reaching the stairs he took them two at a time and thought of his previous decision to let her have her way. He would have told Jeff and might have convinced her. If only she hadn't started her tirade. Whore? He'd show her the difference between making love and whoring!

Shouldering his way into his room, he laid her across the bed, his body holding her there. He suffered a stab of conscience but his flaming need for her became paramount to any regrets he might suffer later. Trapping her flaying arms with one of his, he began to pull at the buttons of her shirt until he managed to free them all, along with the ribbons on her shift.

Jessie wanted to scream at him as he pushed her shirt and camisole straps off her shoulder and bared a breast, but he pressed his lips to hers, forcing them apart until his tongue could seek the warm sweetness of her mouth. She would have bitten him as he traced the secret hollows if he had not squeezed her breast hard enough to deter her.

"Don't try anything like that again, Jess," he threatened. "You wouldn't like what happens to whores who struggle." He knew he was being cruel, yet somehow he felt driven to hurt her, to break her spirit. That it was part of what attracted him to her made no difference.

"Please, d-don't do this," she sobbed. He grabbed the hem of her skirt and yanked it up over her hips, ignoring her plea. "I'll never forgive you," she swore.

"It's too late, Jess. I have to have you," he

groaned, unfastening his belt and pants. Beyond reasoning, he thought if it must be rape, then so be it.

She tried to push away from him as he knelt between her thighs but he gripped her hips and pulled her to him. She was not ready for his entry and his first thrust caused her to cry out. Her fists pounded at his back in a furious assault.

Steve drove into her fiercely, wanting her, needing her. He'd take her hate if she had only hate to give, but he wouldn't live without her. He felt every muscle, every nerve tighten to aching as he stiffened against her in blessed release. Breathing heavily, he lay over her. She'd stopped struggling at his final thrust, wholly defeated. She could feel the damp heat of his body pressed to hers and she bit her lip to try to stop its quivering. Great tears welled from her eyes and she felt him rise on an elbow.

"I'm . . . I'm sorry, Jessie. I swear I didn't mean for this to happen." Steve saw the tears and felt like a bastard. "I needed you so badly. I . . . God, Jess! Talk to me! Yell, scream! I have it coming, but damn it, don't just lie there!" His guilt choked him. If she'd only do something, say something to break her silence! Ashamed, he could no longer face her. He rolled from her and fastened his pants, waiting.

Slowly, Jess pushed down her skirt and rose. She swayed a bit then regained her balance, straightened her clothes, and walked trancelike out of the room. Steve followed her down the stairs and into the library. She picked up her reticule and opened it. Pulling out a small wad of notes, she turned to face him. Her eyes were glazed with pain and humiliation, and her voice, when she finally spoke, was a low throaty whisper. "Mr. Kincaid."

Steve put out his hands to her. He wanted to hold her, tell her again how sorry he was. He wanted to protect her, even from himself. Instead, he stiffened when she pressed the money into his hand.

"You can apply this to our loan or . . . or consider

it payment for . . . for your services," she stammered, and fled the room.

He looked at the money and threw it on the floor before following her. He caught her at the door and turned her about. She stared at his chest and he kissed her brow.

"Jessie, please don't go. I'm so sorry. I never meant to hurt you and I swear I'll never hurt you again. Jess?" he begged.

At that moment Chad entered from the kitchen and called out Steve's name. He stopped abruptly as he quickly surveyed a teary, pale Jessie and the frantic helpless look on the face of his friend as he stepped away from her. He sensed a tragedy before him and he was incapable of setting it right.

Jess took this opportunity to turn and run. She ran across the porch and down the steps to her horse. As she pulled the reins hard about, she heard Steve calling her name. It died on the wind, unheeded, as she rode farther away.

How she managed to stay on her horse until she reached Windy Creek, she didn't know. As she rode into the yard her father saw her slumped shoulders and ran to her side to catch her as she slipped from the saddle.

"Jess! Are you all right? My God!" he cried, seeing her pale face. He gathered her into his arms and carried her to her room. Placing her on the bed, he ran for water. Pouring it into a basin, he quickly soaked the rags and wrung them, then turned to administer to his daughter.

Jess stared at the ceiling as he wiped away the tears and smudges. He bathed her hands and sat beside her. Good Lord! She was so ghostlike he trembled.

"Honey, what happened?" He took her cold, limp hand in his. "Did . . . did Steve hurt you?" He felt her shudder.

"N-no," she stammered. "I'm . . . I'm all right.

Just let me sleep.'' She closed her eyes and he started to rise. ''Sit with me, Papa. Please,'' she half-whimpered.

He wanted to find Steve and beat him into telling him what had happened. That he was the cause of her state Jeff was sure, but he couldn't leave her. She needed him at last. Here was something he could do for her as her father. He'd stay. He'd hold his fury in check and wait until she could or would tell him what had upset her so deeply.

Chapter 18

⁓⁓⁓⁓⁓⁓

The night was long and tortuous for Jeff. His daughter's restless tossing went on until past midnight. Finally, exhaustion overtook her and she slept. Jeff moved a chair near the bed and tried to sleep. Fatigue gnawed at him, but so too did the questions. There were no visible signs of violence, yet he knew someone had hurt his girl.

He heard her stir and went to her side. He looked down to see her struggling in her sleep. Her hands clutched at the blanket he had covered her with, and her body twitched as her lips muttered broken sounds. A shudder rippled through her and she stilled. Jeff watched her eyes flutter, then open.

Seeing him standing over her in concern, Jessie gave her father a weak smile. "Morning, Papa."

He sat on the bed beside her and brushed strands of hair from over her eyes. "Are you okay?" he questioned seriously.

"Yes." Her smile faded. "I'm okay."

"Honey, I don't want to pry, but . . . for God's sake, what happened to you yesterday?"

Jess wasn't sure how much she could tell him. She had no doubt but that he would try to kill Steve if he knew everything. The hurt was great, and not only to her body; her soul felt as though it had been torn from her. She looked at the rugged hands holding hers and felt like a child who had to admit a wrong, only this time the wrong had been done to her.

"Steve . . . Mr. Kincaid . . . he didn't want to talk." In essence that was true. "We fought again, but like never before." Again, true. She let her eyes seek his. "I've never been so . . . so upset, so humiliated." A lone tear slid down her cheek. "I never want to see him again, Papa. Never!"

Jeff knew that the story still lay untold. Yet he also knew it could be worse if she told it. In time, perhaps, it would unfold. Until then, he would wait and watch.

"Do you want to rest more, child?"

She shook her head and sat up. "I'll get up. I . . . I'd like to wash and then I'll start breakfast." Jeff said he'd start the fire and get some water as she swung her legs over the edge of the bed. He paused and kept his back to her, still seeking answers.

"Jessie, what about the money? Did he take it?"

"Yes, Papa. He took it."

Never in her life did she remember being so tired. She fell across her bed, still dressed, removing only her shoes from her sore feet. She would be getting up in a few hours and she badly needed sleep, yet her mind refused to stop replaying the last six weeks over and over. Maybe if she relived it one more time event by event, she could put the wretched nightmares to rest.

She remembered that first morning vividly. After her father brought her water, she stripped off everything and began to scrub viciously at her body, but no amount of cleansing could remove the bruises on her pale skin or her heart. As she bathed away the residue of Steve's callous assault, tears flowed freely. It was then she vowed to rid herself of their obligation to Steve. It was the only thing left that kept them tied and somehow she'd get the money to pay him off!

Donning a fresh shift, Jess tried to think what she

could do to earn the balance of the loan. There was a miserable moment when she realized she didn't know how to do anything but keep house and tend to the chores of a small ranch. No one would need that kind of help. Nothing in St. Louis had trained her for employment either. Why, the most tedious task she ever had was hostessing an occasional party with her mother. Her mind clamped on to that thought and she smiled. Yes. It could work. She'd ride to Lander that very day.

"You're out of your mind!" Roxy cried, stunned by Jessie's suggestion. "Don't you know what goes on here? The girls . . . the men . . ."

"Of course I know, Roxy! I'm not stupid, but my job would be different. I wouldn't . . . I couldn't do that!" Jess continued pacing, throwing up her hands in exasperation. "I'd just serve drinks and smile and walk around like . . . like a party hostess."

"Good God! This ain't no fancy ballroom! This is a saloon and a . . . damn it, Jess! You can't!" Roxy poured herself a brandy and took a stiff swallow. "What does your father think about this plan of yours?" she demanded.

Sitting on the edge of the sofa, Jess plucked at her skirt. "I haven't told him yet. I wanted to talk to you first, to arrange everything."

"He won't stand for it!" Roxy watched her young friend. "At least tell me why you want to do this," she asked more gently.

Jess lowered her eyes and stared at the blue carpet at her feet. "I . . . we . . . Pa and I owe Steve Kincaid money and . . . and I want to pay it off as soon as I can." Her eyes pleading, Jess slipped to her knees before Roxy. "I need this job, Roxy. Please."

Roxy laid her hand gently on Jessica's head then cupped her chin. She knew of the trouble between Steve and Jess. She knew the wedding was off, but the details had escaped everyone. That Jess was hurt by whatever happened was obvious. She had erected a shell to protect her still-vulnerable heart, but Roxy could see through it. She looked searchingly into the depths of anxious green eyes and half-smiled. "I suppose it could give the place a touch of class." Her smile widened. "And word would soon get around about the beautiful lady who was untouchable. It could be real good for business."

Jess closed her eyes and dropped her head to Roxy's knee in relief. "Thank you, Roxy."

"Don't thank me yet, honey. You don't get the job until you talk to Jeff and convince him. I can't see him too excited about this plan of yours."

And Roxy had been right. Jeff was angry and adamantly opposed at first. Then, after much discussion, he at least compromised. He agreed with Jessica's desire to earn enough money to pay off Kincaid. He knew it had become an obsession with her since her last visit to see him, but he thought it best if he hired out instead of her.

"You can't! Don't you see, Papa? If you go off to work, Windy Creek will revert back to what it was. All that we have done will have been in vain!"

There was sense to what she said, but Roxy's! There had to be another way. Much to his chagrin, there wasn't. No matter how they thought it out, there seemed no alternative. Jess would work for Roxy—only if she allowed either Jeff or Sam to escort her home every evening and if she spent no more than four nights a week there. Roxy agreed to these terms and they settled on twenty dollars a month as wages plus whatever tips she made.

Jess rolled off the bed and unfastened her gown, throwing it over a chair to be tended to in the morning. She was always the most tired after this fourth night and her neat habits became lax in direct proportion to her schedule. She washed her face and hands and sat at her small vanity, pulling pins from her hair. She stared at her image and picked up her thoughts.

The first few weeks had been exciting for Jess and her nervousness was well-hidden behind the mysterious image she evoked. An aura of gentility laced with subtle sexuality and a cool veneer that suggested she was unreachable blended to earn her the title of the Snow Duchess.

She smiled to herself as she remembered the first night she entered the saloon with Roxy. Heads turned and an electric silence fell on the room. Even Roxy's girls were duly impressed with the new addition. She was escorted to favored customers for introductions and left to chat with several of Lander's businessmen. Told not to linger long with any one person, Jess moved cautiously about the room, seeing to drinks and occasionally chatting.

Toward the end of the night, a young cowboy with too much drink in him tried to make advances on an unsuspecting Jess. She tried to convince him she wasn't available and he grew nasty. Did she think she was too good for him, too special? Jess was near to panicking when a giant of a man intervened. It was Jake, Roxy's guard, who came to her rescue. She was terribly grateful and relieved that someone would be watching, but she found she really didn't have to worry. After her first week, the clients quickly informed all newcomers that the Duchess was off limits!

From that time on she became special. She was invited to sit with trail-weary cowboys who treated her like the special lady they dreamed about but would never have. They held her in awe. Her beauty and grace were admired yet deeply respected. Her tinkling laughter brought smiles to the patrons and she shared a small part of herself with them, but maintained the mystery. She sat at tables with those who wished to dine with a lady and listened to lonely men tell her about their secret loves and things their trail mates might laugh at or tease them over.

Roxy was more than pleased. Word was spreading about the Duchess and her till could attest to her success. She decided to bring in a piano player who could play decently and Jess found herself dancing with a few brave gentlemen. To hold a soft, scented lady dressed in silks and satins in their arms was the highlight of their working lives and the best thing that could happen to Jess. She found out that the men would press a silver dollar in her hand from time to time just for the privilege of dancing with her. Each one brought her closer to her goal.

Everything was perfect that first month, Jess thought. She had earned her twenty dollars and thirty-two more by the end of the four weeks. If things continued at that pace, she would be free of Steve Kincaid by Thanksgiving.

Pulling her brush through her long tresses, Jess dwelled on Steve. Steve! If only she could keep him out of Roxy's. He'd been there every night for the past two weeks. It was unnerving seeing him standing at the bar for hours at a time just watching her. Occasionally he'd greet her with a curt nod, sometimes he'd rake his eyes over her and smile an all-knowing smile or silently toast her with a drink. There was no move she could make, no word she could speak, that didn't have his undivided attention.

Her nerves were near breaking when she would ride home and see him trailing her. He never came near enough to challenge her chaperone, he merely followed her to the new arch announcing Windy Creek, tipped his hat, and galloped north. Several times a diabolical laugh shattered the night's silence and sent chills down her spine as he rode away.

But tonight had been different, she recalled. Late in the evening he made his way to the table she shared with one of his own hands. "Would you care to dance?" His deep voice echoed through to her traitorous heart.

"N-no, thank you," she mumbled, not even looking at him.

Long, firm fingers wrapped about her arm and drew her up. The young cowhand she was with ignored the possessive glare of his boss and was about to protest in defense of her.

Trying to avoid trouble, Jess waved him off. "It's all right. I'll dance with Mr. Kincaid." Ironically enough, she was wearing the same dress of soft ivory she'd worn at the K-D when she thought him to be a mere cowboy. God! How could she ever have thought him a mere anything? Raw power emanated from him and his aristocratic bearing and lordly demeanor boldly announced him a leader among men.

Her heart was beating rapidly as he slid one arm about her waist and pulled her too close to him. She could feel his hip pressing against her stomach and a warm flush betrayed her cool, haughty display. He gripped her other hand in his and half-pulled her about the tiny dance floor. Jess could feel his breath against her temple and she trembled. She hated him! She couldn't bear his touch—could she?

"You look beautiful, Miss Morgan." He leaned back and let his eyes caress the fullness of her breasts as they rose and fell at the deep curve of her neckline. He grinned as he spied the rapidly beating pulse in her throat, and noticed she refused to reply.

Anyone watching would think they were ideally matched. He all in black with dark brooding eyes, and she in creamy white, a deep fire burning in hers and a saucy tilt to her chin. His devil to her angel. His strength to her femininity. Perhaps the Duchess had found her duke. Yet, if one looked closer, their physical compatibility belied the sparks that flew between them.

"Do you receive so many compliments that you find it easy to ignore one, Jess?" he asked in a cold, bored voice that belied his need to crush her in his arms. Why he'd touched her here, in a crowded saloon, he didn't know. He wanted her all to himself, with no one to interfere on behalf of the Duchess.

"No, Mr. Kincaid. I only ignore one when it means nothing," she countered. She felt him tense and knew she had scored a hit through his armor, then she steeled herself for the counter blow. But when it came, she was aghast.

"When does Roxy figure you'll be ready to move upstairs?" He knew she was enraged by the way she stumbled over his foot. Jessie pushed away and drew back her hand to slap him across the face. The resounding crack startled her and she clamped a hand to her mouth in horror of the act, but he wasn't finished.

Ignoring the now silent room, Steve spoke harshly. "Haven't you learned yet not to upset the clients? You're here for their pleasure." The last word was like venom, stinging her, burning deep, and Jess drew back her hand to hit him again.

Jake made to intervene but Roxy held him back with a slowly widening grin. "Let them go. Believe me, this is a fight that's just between them, and I want it left that way."

Before Jess could land her second blow, Steve gripped her wrist. "I asked for the first one," he growled, "but I'll not let you hit me again, not without cause, like this." He pulled her into his arms and ground his lips against hers. She stood paralyzed with surprise until his hands began to wander over her shoulders and down her back. For a split second she leaned into his hungry embrace, then sensed his victory. It was too much! She had to stop him. Before she became too enmeshed in his spiraling assault on her senses, she stomped her slipper heel hard on his instep.

Steve jumped back on one foot and rubbed at his injured extremity as Jess fled across the room to Roxy's private door. "Damn you, Jess!" he roared. "This isn't over!" He watched her stop and look back at him. She was chewing at her lip and her eyes expressed her fear. "Beware the Hawk, Jess!" He grinned. Deep, rumbling laughter filled the room as the door slammed behind her.

Murmurs began to spread through the room. Conjectures as to the status of the Duchess and Kincaid.

Were they lovers? Was he the reason for her aloof and untouchable demeanor? Had there been a lovers' quarrel? He certainly was pleased with himself now, despite the fact the Duchess had run off. They might never know the answers but the questions would help pass their night.

Now Jess closed her eyes and felt the same terror she'd felt with her back to the door at Roxy's. She remembered being unable to go back out until Roxy came and told her Steve had gone. The rest of the night had been a blur until she tried to sleep, then the whole of it returned to haunt her.

Sliding beneath her quilt, she forced herself to plan the day rapidly approaching. Many of the vegetables were ready to prepare for the coming fall and winter. Jeff had finished the barn and was harvesting hay. She kept up her household chores during the days at Roxy's but she never had enough energy to see to the garden until she was home a full day. Yes, she had a lot to do to keep her busy and to help her mind stay occupied so thoughts of a black-clad devil would have no room.

Her intentions of rising early were always good, Jeff thought as he crept from the house, and she usually did. But this morning he knew she needed rest. He'd been awake when Sam had brought her home the night before and he'd sensed in her a tense anger, despite the weary smile. Something had upset her again.

He reached the barn and hitched the horse to the wagon, wondering if Steve's appearance every night the last few weeks was the cause. He had talked to Roxy and was assured that Steve made no overt moves toward Jessie. He seemed content just to watch her.

Jeff threw the scythe into the wagon and grabbed his work gloves. It was just past dawn and already the day was growing warm. It would be another hot one, he thought as he hoisted himself onto the seat and gathered the reins. A short distance from the house, he pulled at a kerchief and flipped it open. Taking one of the cold biscuits he'd wrapped for his breakfast, he wondered if Steve and Jess ever thought about love and hate, and how they both closely rode the same track.

It was hot, Jess thought, kicking off the blanket, too hot to be early morning. She smiled as she thought of her father letting her sleep and she realized she was glad he had. She needed it and now she could face the next three days with enough stamina to catch up. She swung her feet to the floor and had to grip the bed. A light-headed feeling caught her off-guard. "Phew! I must have been more tired than I thought," she murmured aloud. Quickly the dizziness passed and she got to her feet. She was famished and decided to dress after she ate something.

Cold biscuits and preserves sat on the table and she grinned. Her father was so thoughtful. Fresh coffee sat at the back of the stove and everything was ready at the table. She poured out her beverage and sat down to devour two of the still-soft rolls piled high with the fruity jam. She was finishing her coffee when a wave of nausea rose in her throat. "My God!" she gasped. "I'm going to be sick!"

Dashing to a basin near the pump, Jess retched until she was quite empty. Perspiration dotted her brow and she trembled at the violent upheaval. At first she surmised she was falling ill from pushing herself too hard these days, but it was passing as quickly as it came. Then she realized it was because she had wolfed down her food too quickly. Testing the theory, she prepared another biscuit and sat nibbling at it over more coffee. Sure enough, her stomach settled and accepted the gentler offering. She had to remember to be more compassionate to her body or she really would get sick.

* * *

Careful to get the rest and food she needed, Jess nearly forgot the incident of her illness when she experienced it again several days later. This time, she was unable to even smell the morning coffee before she was racing for a basin. Again, as the day progressed, she felt revived and managed a sizable lunch and a hearty dinner. She'd heard that nerves did strange things and she could certainly attest to that. Why, she'd never had a sick day in her life until she met up with Steve Kincaid and he shattered her peaceful existence.

She didn't tell her father about her irritable stomach. Luckily he'd been outside both times the nausea had hit her. She didn't want to worry him or have him insist she quit Roxy's, so she decided that if it ever happened again, she'd try to keep it a secret.

Chapter 19

J essie felt as though she had run the gauntlet but survived. Her bouts of illness ceased as suddenly as they began and her normal good health returned. She mused over that fact with something akin to awe. That her morning visits to the basin slowed and stopped in direct proportion to the length of time since she'd seen Steve was in no way surprising to her. After all, they'd begun the morning after they'd danced at Roxy's.

Why he stopped coming to the saloon each night, Jess didn't know. At first she watched and waited, relaxing only as the night neared its end. After a few weeks, she gave up thinking about it and considered it a reprieve she would merely enjoy. That he would return to taunt her, she had no doubt. He was not a man to give up easily on something he wanted, and she knew he still wanted her.

Sighing deeply, Jess continued to knead the bread she was preparing. She managed to keep her father from finding out about her attack of nerves but several times it meant pretending to be asleep until he left for the morning. She hated the deception and she was glad it was over at last, like the summer just past.

The warmth of the days gave way to cool nights as autumn entered its infancy, though the days were still warm. The heat from the oven blended with that of the air and she brushed the moisture from her brow with a sleeve.

A ruckus in the barn brought Jessie out of her reverie. It sounded like someone banging on a metal basin or pails being knocked over. Jeff had ridden to the farthest edge of the ranch to survey the fence line. Perhaps, she thought, an animal had entered the barn and was rummaging around. Occasionally a coyote or a cougar came close to the ranch, and she figured she'd better investigate. A new foal was still stalled and could be an easy target for a predator.

Picking up her father's rifle, she checked to see if it was loaded and left to seek the intruder. There was no evidence of anyone in the yard and Jessie was relieved. There was always the possibility some drifter was about, and she felt better facing a wild animal of nature than one of man.

She noticed the doors were slightly ajar as she neared the barn and shook her head. If her father had remembered to close them, she wouldn't be facing this unknown raider. She slowly drew the door further open and was greeted with an eerie quiet from within the structure. Whatever was foraging stopped as it sensed her presence. Careful to avoid a direct confrontation with a cornered animal or an attack from above, she eased inside. Cautiously she inched forward into the dim interior, listening for the telltale sign of life.

A horse whinnied in the farthest stall and she moved toward it. Without warning, something shot past her head and banged against the wall behind her. She spun about in terror and screamed as a burlap sack descended over her from behind. Total darkness encompassed her. The sack reached to her hips and strong arms clamped about her middle to keep it in place. Panic rose in her as she felt the heat of his breath against her neck and she struggled furiously, dropping the rifle in her bid for freedom.

The heat was growing unbearable and Jessie could

hardly breathe when she felt herself turned about to face her captor. She tried to dig at his arms and chest blindly, but her efforts were blocked by tightening arms about her that hampered her restricted breathing further. With one last surge to try and escape, she kicked out at her assailant and heard a muffled oath at the success of her blow.

In an instant she was standing free, but before she could run, she thought she heard a murmured apology just before a blow to her chin brought blackness.

It had to be done; there was no other way, Steve told himself, heading for the high country. He couldn't let things go on the way they had. Jessie was driving him crazy with her cool bravado and, except for that one time at Roxy's when he danced with her, he'd been living in a hell of his own making. But no more. It occurred to him that very night that he had to get away. He had to find solace in the land. Then the idea started to take shape.

Steve wasn't sure how Jeff would react the day he rode to Windy Creek. It had been six weeks since he'd seen Jessie but he knew she wouldn't be at the ranch. He wanted to see Jeff without her knowing. He thought he could convince him of the importance of his scheme if given a chance and, between them, he could succeed.

The first few minutes of their encounter were stilted. Each man was feeling out the other. They had known each other a long time yet neither felt the comfort of familiarity at this meeting. After the normal exchange of greetings, Steve began while leaning against a post as Jeff worked at chopping wood.

"I'm going away for a while to a cabin I have in the mountains." He was anxious to get it over with. "I want Jessie to come with me."

Jeff lowered his ax to the ground. He walked to the well and ladled out a large drink. Having his fill, he rubbed his hand across his jaw and turned to face

Steve. "Do you really think that after what's happened between you two I'm going to allow it?" Jeff glared at the tall, dark man. "Your staying away from her the last six weeks is the only smart thing you've done since she got here." He started to walk away, deeming their conversation over, but Steve had just begun.

"I wasn't staying away from her, Jeff. I was preparing the cabin and hauling provisions up there for us."

Returning to his chore, Jeff began to rhythmically swing his ax, seeming to ignore his visitor until Steve clasped the ax handle in mid-stroke and yanked it from Jeff's hands. "Listen to me, Morgan!" he demanded. Jeff's face reddened with anger, but before he could reply Steve dropped the ax and lowered his voice. "I . . . I care a great deal for your daughter and I want her for my wife." He saw Jeff rub his neck, trying to absorb his words. "I think she still loves me but things have gotten out of hand and . . . and I think if she and I could go someplace, just the two of us, we could work it out. If given a chance to talk to her, I'm gambling she'll shelve that fierce pride of hers and accept what's good for her."

"She won't go with you, Steve. I know her and she'll refuse to even see you, let alone give you a chance to talk with her about this." Jeff turned toward the house. "Come on, let's go inside." He smiled. "And I promise to hear you out."

"You've spent a lot of time working this out, haven't you?" Jeff asked after Steve outlined his plan.

"I had to." Steve grinned. "Your daughter is too good at catching me unawares. I can't afford to give her an edge or I end up riding it. You once told me that if she wasn't reasonable, we could think about beating her. Somehow, I think we should have considered besting her instead."

"I don't understand," Jeff replied, his brow knitted.

"Jessie is quick-witted and too damned independent. It's worse now than ever since she's been at

Roxy's. In order to best her in an argument, I need surprise on my side and I can't give her a chance to run away."

"I still don't—"

"When I told you I wanted to take her to the high country with me, I meant I wanted your permission to kidnap her." He had summed up the whole conversation in one brash sentence.

Jeff stared in surprise and Steve waited. Slowly, understanding swept through him. It was Steve's turn to be bewildered as Jeff burst into rumbling laughter. "Well, I'll be damned!" he said as he wiped his eyes. "And you call *her* stubborn!"

"It's the only way I can see it happening, Jeff," Steve pleaded. "She won't listen to reason and I think she needs a firm hand. I—"

"Hold it!" Jeff grinned. "I'm on your side, my boy. I was just picturing my lovely daughter's reaction when she finds out what you have in store for her."

Looking down on the head nestled on his shoulder, Steve had to chuckle. Jeff was right, she was lovely. Her lashes lay on her cheeks and her lips were slightly parted. Her hair hung wildly about her face in disarray. She had fought like any wild thing for her freedom and he felt remorse at having to strike her, but she was almost more than he could handle. Carefully, he traced a finger over the darkening bruise on her chin. Well, at least she was quiet and he could savor her gently. Soon enough she'd become a lioness again and he'd need all his strength and wit to tame her.

He knew they wouldn't reach the cabin until the next day and that soon she would regain consciousness so he decided to stop and make his stand with Jess. Dismounting, he gathered her in his arms and carried her to a tree. The air was growing cooler and after propping her against a tree, he tucked a blanket snugly about her.

Trying to figure out how to approach her when

she woke, he decided he'd better just let it happen. He sat across from her and waited. A gentle breeze tousled her hair and an errant sunbeam filtered through the pines to shroud her in a golden haze. She was in contrast to the land as she lay soft and gentle on its rocky surface.

Granite outcroppings, hard and cold, littered the tall grass-covered hills now brown in the late summer. Steve knew the grasses would grow more sparsely as they neared their destination, soon to be taken over with thick moss and ferns. He gazed over the rugged valley to the west and spied a herd of grazing sheep not far below. It would not be long before the coming snows would camouflage their movements through these mountains.

His eyes returned to Jess at the sound of a low moan. He was startled to see her standing, struggling to keep her balance. Twisting about in a furious attempt to save her from a terrible blow, he was too late. For a fraction of time that felt like an eternity he saw her fall, her head connecting with a partially exposed chunk of granite.

"Jess!" he called to the hills and whispering pines before he clamped her still, pale form in his arms. She was alive but blood oozed from a long cut at her hairline above her ear.

Carefully, he settled her on the ground and rushed to gather his canteen and a spare shirt from his saddlebags. Frantically ripping at the shirt he returned to her side, soaked the rag, and bathed the trickling blood from her cheek and hair. When he was sure the wound was superficial, he drew her gently into his arms. Bracing himself against the tree, he held her across his lap, her head on his chest. Drawing the blanket over them both, he leaned his head back and closed his eyes, whispering her name and awaiting her awakening.

The air was fresh and cool against her skin and she thought she'd better get up. She had bread to bake today and was glad it was cool. The blanket felt good against her cheek but her pillow felt hard and coarse. She tried to nestle into it and rediscover its softness, only to find herself falling. Before she could free her arms to brace herself, her head hit something and there was nothing.

The void was clearing. Someone was calling to Jess. Jess? Who was that, she wondered. Her head was heavy and would have dropped if something firm had not supported it. She felt safe where she was now, as though in the arms of a protector. As she opened her eyes, she blinked at the light until she could see clearly. She was puzzled by a curious woven pattern of red and blue before her that seemed to be alive. She could feel it breathe and the heart of the thing kept a steady beat beneath her cheek. She tried to move but whatever held her tightened its grip until she moaned. Then her shackles became tender arms. A strong, calloused hand touched her face and gently brushed back her hair. When she looked up she saw a face, ruggedly handsome with coal-black hair hanging over a tanned forehead. Concerned hazel eyes, almost green in the forest light, searched her face. She gave him a shy smile and he seemed perplexed by her action. Thinking she played a game meant to drive him mad, he groaned and called her name.

"Is . . . is Jessie a . . . a friend of yours?" she asked softly.

Steve's brows arched and he sat searching her eyes for recognition but he saw only honest questioning. He was suddenly struck with the awesome realization that she didn't know him or herself! Fear was replaced by shock which in turn was replaced by a kind of gratitude. This was his chance. This was more than he could hope for.

"You're my Jessie." He smiled. "Don't you remember?" She shook her head as she tried to think. "You hit your head when you fell."

Pressing her fingers to her temple, she winced.

She didn't doubt his words but the bruise she felt added credence to what he said. "I . . . I don't remember. Oh, God! I don't remember anything!" She clutched at his shirt, tears beginning to fall.

"It's okay, honey." His arms gently encircled her and he drew her to him. "I'm sure it's only temporary from the fall. Shh, don't cry."

Jess quieted in the security of Steve's arms. She was so trusting he almost felt guilty at taking advantage of the unique situation, but not quite. He was prepared to perform to the very best of his acting ability.

"We better go back and see a doctor." He spoke gently.

"Go back where?" Jess sat up on his lap and looked questioningly into his eyes.

"Why, home, of course, honey." His expression saddened. "I had hoped our honeymoon would be special but it will have to wait until you're better."

"We . . . we're married?" She grew worried. "I . . . I should remember that, shouldn't I?"

"Not necessarily, my love." His fingers brushed her cheek. "You can't recall your name and you've certainly had that longer than you've been Mrs. Kincaid."

Jess played with the name and a spark of recognition flashed in her brain. "Mrs. Steve Kincaid. Jessica Kincaid." Yes, she remembered that! "I . . . your name is Steve. I remember that." She struggled to recall more but it wouldn't come.

"Don't try to force it, darling. You'll remember." Steve set her from him and rose. He reached for her hands and she shyly placed hers in them. Drawing her to her feet, he slipped a hand beneath her hair to her neck, and slowly drew her to him. He pressed a gentle, loving kiss on her trembling lips. "We better go back," he mumbled against her brow.

"Must we?" she asked shyly. "I feel fine, really."

Steve stepped back and grinned. "Are you sure?" Jess nodded her head and gave an impish grin of her own. "You're awfully anxious to go and I'll bet you don't remember where, do you?" He laughed.

"No, I don't." She grew serious. "But since you are my husband, I must trust you or . . . or I wouldn't have married you." Another picture briefly flashed in her mind as he scooped her up and carried her to his horse. Instead of trying to call back the flashing image, Jess relaxed and looped her arms about his neck. "Where are we going?"

"If you're sure you want to, we'll go on to the cabin. We won't get there until tomorrow, but I have a camp ready for us not too far ahead." He set her down beside his steed and gathered the blanket and canteen. Securing everything, he swung himself up into the saddle and reached down to circle her waist and draw her up before him. Jessie shivered as she sensed another time, another place, and he mistook her actions. "Are you cold?" Before she could reply, he drew her tightly against his chest and settled his arms snugly about her. "Better?"

Twisting her head, Jessie smiled and nodded. The sun-darkened skin crinkled at his eyes. They were dark brown! "Your eyes . . . I thought them nearly green! I know they were! What makes them change?"

Steve's laughter, deep and rumbling, caused his horse to prance. "You'll see, my love. You'll see."

After several hours of riding in and out of broken forests and over rugged ridges into lush upland meadows, Jess felt tired and wanted to stretch her weary body. Steve knew by her fidgeting that she was anxious to get to camp, as was he, but for different reasons.

"It won't be long now, honey." He pointed over her shoulder to a cliff rising above them. Deep shadows etched the base and he told her of the caves dotting its lower side. "There's a small spring that bubbles up near camp. The water's warm and has an almost lemony taste, but it's good water. You can bathe in it if you like."

Thinking of the soothing warmth over her aching muscles, she murmured, "Sounds wonderful."

There had been many things she wanted to know and earlier in their journey Steve told her about their ranch and the people there. He avoided mentioning Lander or St. Louis for fear he would stimulate her latent memories. When she asked about her family he told her of her father and how happy he was they were wed. Everything he told her, except for their wedding, was true, but he only told her the pleasant things and skirted questions he deemed dangerous with noncommittal replies.

"How long have we known each other?"

"Long enough for me to know I wanted to make you mine."

"Did we have a large wedding?"

"No, we both wanted a quiet one with just your father there."

As they neared the small, snug cave that would house them for the night, Jess grew nervous, like any bride on her wedding night. She didn't know how far their courtship had gone and yet she felt curious. Steve dismounted and led the horse up to a flat rise at the mouth of the granite hole, and tethered it. He reached up his strong hands and placed them about Jessie's waist. With her hands on his shoulders, she was lowered to the mossy ground. A warming blush suffused her cheeks and he chuckled.

"Don't be frightened, Jessie. Though it pains me that you don't remember, this will not be our first time together."

Gulping down her anxiety, she tentatively laid her hand on his chest. "You mean we've . . . we've had our . . . our wedding night?"

"Yes, my love." He grinned devilishly. "Many times."

Since he had told her they were newly married, that could only mean they—"Oh!" She drew her cool hands to her hot cheeks, and looked into his twinkling dark eyes. "Oh, my!"

Steve drew her into the circle of his arms and pressed his lips to her temple. "We're good together, honey." He ran his hands down her back and kneaded the flesh on her bottom. "We make love perfectly and I have faith that your body will remember what your mind cannot."

Jess felt a familiar ache between her thighs that confirmed what he was saying. They had been lovers and she had gone to him before. She could do no less as his wife. Sliding her hands up his chest, she slipped her slender arms about his neck. She leaned her head back and looked up at him. Running the tip of her tongue over her lips, she saw the naked desire in his eyes and felt the tensing of his body. "Help me remember," she said softly.

His lips met hers with an urgent demand for total possession. It had been so long. The weeks of waiting, the agony of wanting this complicated woman of extremes. He wanted to lay with her that very minute and slake his desires, but not this time. The last time he had taken her in cruel lust. He wanted perfection for this union. She thought she was his bride and he wanted her loving and giving. He had planned their lovemaking in the cabin and he would wait.

Reluctantly he wrenched his lips from hers. "Oh, God! Honey! I want you so." His ragged breathing was echoed by her own. "But I want it to be special." He held her to arm's length and tried to smile but it more resembled a grimace. "We'll wait."

Jessie didn't appreciate his self-control but she sensed it would be worth the wait. If he could rein the savage passions she instinctively knew he possessed, she knew his decision would not falter. That she could convince him otherwise, she had no doubt, but she would follow his lead and restrain her curiosity and her own newly discovered desires.

Chapter 20

⟪❦⟫

The cabin sat on the edge of a small clearing with its back against a solid granite wall that hung over the small log structure. Jessie questioned its safety and Steve proclaimed it very safe. He told her it helped keep snow from the roof and was a natural haven for the horses. It also served as a dry storage for firewood that was stacked in huge quantities behind the cabin. A stone chimney rose toward the front of the cabin to accommodate the rock formation.

Shutters covered the two windows and she wondered if the house ever saw the sunlight, nestled as it was in the shadows. It was late afternoon and already the area was in dusky light, the sun having dropped behind the ridge nearly an hour before. It was getting cold as she was lifted from the horse and began walking about the rocky yard. She thought of the warm bath she had turned down the evening before and now very much wanted to submerge in the tepid waters.

Steve watched her look about with her arms crossed to hug warmth to her body. He grinned at the memories of holding her throughout the night. He sensed her curiosity and silent yearnings and, through great effort, restrained his own. It wasn't until morning that he realized he might have gambled and lost. She could have awakened with her memory intact and he'd have lost the chance to prove to her that they belonged together. Thankfully, she didn't, and he impatiently anticipated this night as would a starving man a banquet.

Walking up behind her as she looked over the exquisite rainbow-colored valley, he slipped his hands around her waist and drew her back against him.

"Beautiful, isn't it?" His voice was deep and resonant.

"Um," she murmured, leaning against him. "It looks like an artist began at the top of that mountain with the golds of a summer sun and slid down to the deep purple and green of twilight into the valley. It's more beautiful than I could imagine. There seems to be no words glorious enough to describe it fittingly."

They stood and silently watched the dark hues inch ever upward until the mountain was gold-crowned and purple-robed.

"We better go in and get a fire going." Steve turned her in his arms. "Night comes cold and fast up here." She nodded agreement and they went toward the cabin. He pushed open the heavy door, then gathered her in his arms and carried her into the darkness. Setting her down, he moved by memory to the fireplace already set with logs and struck a match. In moments the warm golden flames leaped skyward and brought a cozy glow to the room.

Jessie looked about and smiled. There was only the one room, with the huge stone hearth taking up most of one wall to her left. An oven was built into one side and a large black hook with a kettle hung near it. Beside it, toward the front of the cabin, was a table and two chairs of scrubbed wood. A well-stocked pantry and cooking area was to her right at the entrance. An old braided rug covered the wood floor before the hearth, and a door, leading to the tiny corral and woodshed, was located at the far left corner. The pantry shelves, built from floor to ceiling, acted as the foot of the built-in bunk. Piled high with quilts, she could see snowy-white pillows propped against the wall. Several hooks graced the back wall over a cedar chest and served as the only closet.

"I have to take care of the horse." Steve looked down at her smiling face all honey-gold in the firelight. "Why don't you see about cooking up something for us to eat." Jess nodded and he feathered a kiss to the corner of her mouth before going.

The smell of frying bacon filled the cabin when Steve returned. Jessie was kneeling at the hearth, checking a pan of biscuits, and he stood quietly watching her. She must have rolled up her sleeves and set to work the moment he left since she was well into her preparations and he had only been gone about twenty minutes.

She looked up and watched him secure the door and move toward her. His hair was damp from a washing and she thought of the rain barrel where she had gotten water for her baking.

"You didn't wash in that barrel outside, did you?" He saw her brows knit and her white teeth chew at her lip. "That was the only water I could find to cook with, and if you've ruined it, what can I use?"

He grinned crookedly and offered her his hand. "Come on, woman. I'll show you something."

Jessie followed him out the back door and felt like she'd entered a grotto. The horse was quietly munching what looked like fresh-cut hay as it stood snugly quartered against the elements. A barnlike door covered the distance from the corner of the house to the stone wall and, except for the dark coolness, it could have been a part of the cabin.

Beyond the stall was a slender break in the smooth wall. From a crack high above trickled a steady stream of clear water. A hunk of granite jutted out below it and created a small falls over its side into a barrel. From it ran a duct to the trough, the excess from which spilled over the corner into a channel that led outside against the stone face.

"Did you do all this?" Jessie took in the water system and the mammoth supply of wood and numerous bales of hay. At his nod, she looked about again. "It must have taken you weeks!"

"You might say I was driven." He chuckled. "Inspired by an elfin queen." He drew her into his arms and held her against him. "Do you think you'll be comfortable here for a while?"

"Mmm hmm." She nodded vigorously. "You've thought of everything."

"Not everything." He grew serious, thinking of her imperfect memory and that his blissful world could end as easily as it had begun. A smile slowly replaced his frown at the questioning rise of her brow. He smoothed a finger across her forehead and slid it down her chin, tilting it up for a kiss. It was a gentle and undemanding one, and she leaned against him, letting her hands slide over his chest and about his middle.

Steve liked this warm and acquiescent Jessica. "Honey, why . . ." He kissed her cheek. ". . . don't we . . ." He kissed her ear. ". . . go in and . . ." His mouth nibbled at her neck. ". . . get something to eat. I'm starving." He laughed.

Jess pushed at him and squealed. "Why, you . . . !" Seeing the humor she joined his merriment and took his hand. "Come on and I'll see to your hunger." She led the way inside and coquettishly glanced over her shoulder. "All of them."

He swatted at her bottom and she half-skipped to the hearth and removed their repast. Serving it up, she joined him at the table. "How long will we stay here?" she asked.

"Depends," he replied before he bit into a flaky roll. "Maybe a few weeks, maybe all winter."

"Can we be gone that long?" she asked incredulously.

"One good thing about a large ranch is having

lots of people you can depend on to see to the chores." He reached for her hand. "We'll go when you want to go." He smiled. "Okay?" At her affirmative nod he resumed eating. "It should start snowing soon." He looked at her. "You'll be beautiful in the snow." He began to think of her and the fluffy down quilts they would be sharing on the cold nights ahead.

Jess watched his changing thoughts in his eyes. They darkened perceptibly and she sensed the reason. A becoming flush fanned across her cheeks and she wished she could remember the times they had spent together.

"Are you tired?" he asked softly, a hint of seduction in his deep voice.

"No," she breathed, nervously stalling for time.

"Good." He grinned. "I have a long evening planned and I want you awake and alert for all of it." He stood and moved behind her. "I promise you, Jess, you'll have enough memories in the morning to fill the void and last a lifetime."

He had indeed thought of every comfort, Jess thought as she dropped down into the makeshift tub. Steve had rolled a large empty barrel into the room to sit before the fire. He left the cabin and returned in moments with two buckets of steaming water. By the third trip he had filled it halfway.

"Your bath, my lady," he said with a bow.

Thrilled with the prospect of a warm bath when she thought to have a warm wash at best, Jess cried out her delight and began to remove her clothes. He begrudgingly left the cabin with a towel of his own to make do elsewhere. Having to climb on a chair to enter the barrel, she wiggled down into the tepid water until it welled up to her shoulders. The slightly sulphuric taint was quickly ignored amidst the luxury of warm water. It was hard to lather the soap but Jess felt wonderfully clean and relaxed when Steve returned.

His shirt was thrown over his shoulder and he was busily drying his dripping hair until he caught sight of her. With her hair piled high in riotous curls and her bare shoulders just visible over the top rim, she was as regal as her namesake, a duchess indeed.

Jessie watched him enter and felt a thrill of desire ripple through her as their eyes met and locked. Invisible bonds drew him to her side.

"Stand up," his throaty voice ordered, and she rose from the veil of water to stand hip-deep, unafraid and unashamed of her nakedness. This was the moment she'd simultaneously awaited with all the instincts of a woman and feared, not remembering.

Steve placed his hands about her waist and lifted her free of her tub. He set her on the rug before the fire and slowly shook out a soft piece of flannel to dry her with. He drew it about her shoulders like a cape and stopped short of wrapping her long enough to scan her lovely body. The torture was intense as he moved a chair nearer the flames and pulled her to his lap. Exquisite agony coursed through his veins as she freed her arms, clutching the blanket across her breasts and causing it to slide to her hips at her back. One slender arm snaked about his bare, warm shoulder and her fingers entwined in the thick wet strands of ebony on his neck.

He sat entranced by her searching kisses to his chin and throat until she released her cover and pressed her naked breasts to his chest. With a groan of ecstasy, he let his hands move over her bare back from her neck to the rounding of her hips while their mouths touched in a fiercely demanding kiss. Steve stood, never releasing her, and carried her to his bed.

Carefully laying her on the downy quilt, Steve sat at her side. His eyes caressed her as his hands pulled away the last of her covering. There would be no arguments and no intrusions to dampen the fine madness in his blood. At last, they would come together as lovers.

"Don't," he rasped as she tried to cover herself with her hands. "God, Jess, don't stop me from looking at you, touching you, ever again."

Jessie's lips trembled as she felt primevil urges as old as Eve wipe away her fears. This was her beginning, her feminine softness to his steel masculinity, her strength that was his weakness. She lifted her arms to him. "Come to me. Make me your woman for all times."

Primitive drums pounded in his ears as he saw her all golden and demanding. He stood and shed his pants, the proof of his great need boldly evident. The breath hissed between his clenched teeth as she lithely rose to her knees and pulled him to her.

"Touch me, teach me anew," she purred against his chest. Her hands drove him crazy with wanting and she gasped when he pushed her down and began his assault on her senses. In moments she was begging him to ease the terribly delicious ache deep between her thighs. There was no need to tutor the body to remember the bliss they had shared. It knew the euphoric levels she would attain as their erotic play became burning passion. Writhing in the agony of unreleased desire, Jess clutched at his arms, drawing him over her, pleading with him to ease her hunger.

"Yes, my love." Breathing heavily, he moved to lay between her thighs. "I'll give you pleasure, but . . ." He stopped just short of entry. ". . . the price may well be your soul."

Jess was frightened by his enigmatic words as she looked up at the dark-haired man above her, the flickering lights casting eerie shadows across his face. She felt she was about to make a pact with the very devil! Before she could shy away in fear, he thrust deeply into her. Doubts flew as he moved deep and slow, driving her higher, bringing a groan from deep in her throat as she experienced the ultimate climax. Within moments he stiffened and she felt the scalding essence of him fill her as he cried out her name.

She fell into a quiet sleep and did not wake as he lifted her to place her beneath the quilts. He moved to the fire and placed another large log within its flames. He thought of the words he had uttered to her just before his entry. He had asked for her soul. The words had come on their own, yet he knew it was the least he wanted from her. He suddenly realized that he needed her love, her every thought to be a part of him. She was an obsession with him and he refused to think of her being anywhere but in his arms.

The chill of the cabin reached him and he returned to bed. Settling into the softness of it, he saw her stir, seeking the warmth of him. Taking her into his arms, he kissed her brow.

"You are my woman, Jess, for all time. There will be no other for you but me." Jess moaned softly and grew restless for a moment before relaxing at his side. It was as though she resisted his dominance and possessiveness even in her sleep. A crooked grin lifted one corner of his mouth as she quieted. "I'll win, honey. I always do."

The morning was well advanced when Jess stirred. She could feel Steve pressed against her back and his legs entwined with hers. His breath was slow and even, and she knew he still slept. She smiled to herself as she thought of the future with her strong, handsome husband who would also be her passionate lover and, hopefully, her friend.

The words that frightened her the night before gnawed at her peace and she wondered at the demands they made on her. Perhaps he meant his love was such that he wanted all of her. That he had branded her as his own to her depths, she was sure. He need not worry she would leave him. She loved him and nothing could drive her away. That those thoughts would return to haunt her, she didn't know. For now, she would shelve her doubts and become the aggressor in their love play.

Steve could feel the gentle thrusting of her bottom against his groin. She was trying to wake him and he playfully pretended sleep. Grumbling, he turned to his other side and heard her mumble something. He fought down a smile as she wiggled about until she was snuggled against his back. She perched on an elbow, one hand playing with his hair while the other settled on his hip.

It was growing more difficult to feign slumber as she let her hand move up to his chest and slowly down to his stomach. He could sense that her growing desire to touch him was at war with her nervous shyness. He stayed still, anxious to see which side would win. It wasn't long before the thrill of her long fingers sensitively brushing against the growing strength of his shaft declared the victor. Her desires were fanned and he could feel her breath becoming more rapid.

Enrapt in a sensuous world of her own making, Jess jumped as Steve growled at her, "Damn it, woman! Will there be no rest for me from your hungers?" He twisted about and grabbed her at her waist, drawing her over him. The humorous glitter in his dark eyes and the crooked grin on his lips brought a chuckle from her.

"You beast! You've been lying there enjoying my exploration all along, haven't you?" She beat at his chest in mock anger until he gripped her wrists in one hand and slid the other beneath her hair to caress her neck.

"Witch!" He drew her lips to his own. They shared a kiss, not the hard, lusty kiss of full passion but one of discovery and sensual awakening. She began to squirm as he played a silent melody down her spine. "You would tease me when you have the advantage? You would tempt me when I am flat on my back and helpless?''

''Arrogant male! What makes you think I want you? Oh, you'll do while we're here but when we get home . . .'' She hunched her shoulders, pretending indifference, and would have thrown her leg over him to rise if he hadn't gripped her waist savagely.

''Where do you think you're going?'' He bit at her fingertips.

''In case you haven't noticed, it's morning and time to be up.'' She sat astride his middle and pulled a quilt about herself.

Steve yanked the cover away and grinned devilishly. ''And in case you haven't noticed, I'm already up.''

The days drifted into weeks and their world revolved around loving and laughing. It was a time of simple pleasures, like romping in the first snowfall and playing in the misty springs. Every day drew them closer together and Steve thanked God she still did not remember the hurts and recriminations. They were happy in their snug haven, safe and secure in the pleasures they shared.

Marveling at the possessive passion he felt strengthen with each passing day, Steve found what he had searched for in her arms. The restless wondering was laid to rest. He cared deeply for his woman. Who knows, he thought, he might even come to love her someday. Perhaps in his dotage, he chuckled to himself.

Where Steve knew total satisfaction in their haven, Jessie was plagued at quiet times with her unknown past. When he was off hunting or busy with chores, she would find herself staring into the fire pondering a mental picture that had flashed across her mind. She did not dwell on these invasions into her happy world, but she did try and silently sort them out.

The dream of an Indian camp and one called Hawk unnerved her most. She was in pain in the dream and she woke clutching the small jagged scar on her side. She hadn't told Steve about them because of her feelings for the other man. She had hated and loved him at the same time, and even though he looked like Steve, she was worried he was not. She prayed the dream was just that. Somehow she felt there was something in her forgotten past that was trying to break into her idyllic life and wreak havoc with it. Part of her yearned to remember but another part was afraid. She loved Steve. If there was someone once who she loved and lost, it could happen again and she didn't want to lose this time.

Chapter 21

The wind howled about the cabin, rattling the shutters and spiraling down the chimney to drive the flames into a savage dance. Jess, huddled beneath the quilts, watched Steve clean his rifle near the warm fire. She marveled at his bare chest and seeming indifference to the cold that nibbled at her toes until she took refuge in the bunk. Stew was bubbling on the hearth for dinner, prepared in the warmer part of the day.

"Aren't you cold?" Jessie inquired from her haven.

Turning his head to watch her nestled under a pile of soft blankets, he grinned. "All I have to do to keep warm is think of you." He stood, laid his rifle aside, and strode toward her. He stretched out on top of the quilts and nuzzled her neck. "That always heats my blood. Unfortunately, it also takes my mind off everything but making love to you."

Jess lifted her arms from the covers and wrapped them about him. With his head pressed to her breasts, she stroked his hair and kissed his brow. "We do seem to spend a lot of time here."

"Can you think of a better way to stay warm?" At the negative shake of her head, he slid his hand beneath the blankets and began to caress her breasts boldly through her shirt. "Um, I think I'm

229

suddenly cold. I better get in there with you and warm up.''

Giggling, Jess moved over and patted the spot beside her. Unfastening his pants, he watched her lips part in anticipation. ''Vixen!'' Just as he began to remove his breeches, Steve grew taut and alert.

''What's wrong? What is it?'' Jess asked as Steve redid his clothes and moved to the door, grabbing his rifle en route. Listening intently, he eased open a shutter and peered into the dark. Jessie scurried from the bed and ran to stand behind him. ''Steve, what's happening?''

''Quiet!'' he ordered, and Jess would have demanded an answer if a thunderous knock hadn't startled her and drawn a muffled scream. With gun ready, Steve moved to the door and threw it open. A burst of cold air and flurrying snow mushroomed into the room and Jess gasped at a bearlike creature that came lumbering in.

''Damn you, Steve!'' roared the giant. ''What the hell took you so long?'' Gnarled hands pushed a beaver hat off his head and burly arms clamped about Steve's body for a robust embrace.

''McKinley! You old goat! Hell, I thought you were an old grizzly roaming about!'' Steve returned the hug. ''I damned near was ready to put a bullet in that thick hide of yours!''

''Why, you son of a . . .'' The old man drew up and held his tongue when he spotted Jessie clasping her hands to her chest. ''Well, what ya got here?''

Steve secured the door and set the rifle aside. ''McKinley, I'd like you to meet my wife, Jessica.'' He slipped his arm about her shoulders and pulled her against his side. ''Honey, this is Simon McKinley, the best trapper in the territory.''

Jess reached out her hand and was surprised that so large a man could be so gentle as he took it. ''I'm pleased to meet you, Mr. McKinley.''

''The pleasure's mine, little lady, and call me Mac.

All my friends do.'' He looked her over and smiled through his full gray-white beard. ''Ya got yourself a real looker, Steve. Yup, a right fine lady.''

With a smile, Jess offered their guest coffee laced with brandy and a hearty dish of stew. Accepting both, Mac unloaded his gear and shed his sheepskin coat. Jess listened to Steve and Mac talk about what had transpired in the year or so since they had seen each other. After serving them both, she drew a shawl about her and sat before the fire with a mug of her own. Half-listening, she looked into the flames and felt its heat. The heat on her face from an oven, bread baking and a noise in the barn . . .

''Jess!'' Steve called for the third time.

Shaking herself from her reverie, Jessie rose to see to her husband. ''I'm sorry. I must have dozed.'' She placed her hand on his shoulder. ''What did you want?''

Mac noticed the uneasy stirring of Steve as he watched his beautiful wife in her trancelike state. He was nervous about something but the woman was quite at ease as she came to his side. That she loved him was evident, and Mac felt they looked well-suited, but he sensed there was something not quite right.

''Mac will be spending the night,'' Steve told her, and Jess smiled and nodded. ''He's heading to his camp in the morning.''

Mac mopped up the last of his stew with a biscuit and sat staring at Jessie. ''You sure I ain't met ya before, lass?'' He noticed Steve stiffen and was surprised at how quickly he answered for his wife.

''You couldn't have met her, Mac. She's not from around here.'' Jess stared at Steve in amazement. He'd always implied she was born and raised at Windy Creek, and now he was either lying to Mc-Kinley or he'd omitted certain facts from her—but why?

Noticing her surprised look at Steve's words, Mac mused further. ''Well, if I ain't never met her, I knew someone like her. Same hair. Same sweet smile. Funny, I don't usually forget a face. I see too few ta forget 'em.''

Nervously, Steve laughed. "You must be getting old, you crazy Scot! You're mixing up your memories!" He turned to Jess. "You better get some blankets for our guest. He'll want to leave early in the morning."

They retired a short while later. Mac lay comfortably before the fire and dozed. He could hear his hosts murmuring from their bed. Whispered words drifted to him and he knew they were discussing what had been said earlier. The young lass was angry and confused, and Steve was trying to placate her.

Something was wrong all right, but Mac was damned if he knew what. There were two things he was sure of—Steve wanted him gone, and fast; and he knew this girl, or someone just like her. He struggled to recall, to no avail. He'd remember, sooner or later. His memory would clear and he'd remember.

October came to a close. Heavy snow kept Jessica indoors and she spent hours reliving the weeks since McKinley's brief visit. They had had their first argument the following morning, or at least the first she could remember. Steve relented enough to tell her about St. Louis. She was trapped in the mountains with him and would be until spring no matter what happened, yet happen something did.

"Why didn't you tell me? You have no right to hide my past from me! My God, I have a right to know who I am!" she yelled.

"You didn't need to know!" Steve shouted. "I told you everything you had to know about. That didn't seem to matter."

"No! You only told me what you wanted me to know. What are you still hiding, Steve? Why won't you answer me?'' Clenching her fists, she stomped her foot in fury.

Evading her questions, he gripped her arms. "Haven't you been happy here with me? Has your forgotten past made any difference when we're together?'' He pulled her resisting form into his arms. "Until Mac came you never questioned me. You didn't think of anything but us and our loving. There were no ghosts to haunt you when we lay together. It didn't matter then!''

Jessie pushed him away. "You're wrong!'' Steve arched a brow in wonder. "There have been ghosts! Dreams have haunted me all along!'' She turned from him and twisted her hands. "I . . . I think I love someone else.''

If Jess could have seen Steve's face at that moment she would have cried out in alarm. Towering fury filled him and he wanted to beat the name of her lover from her.

"I don't remember him clearly, but I know his name.''

Steve came up behind her and placed his hands high on her neck. "Who is he?'' he growled. His thoughts were murderous.

Swallowing her sudden fear, she swayed a moment then took a deep breath. "His name is Hawk.'' She felt the rumbling laughter before she heard it. Spinning to see him throw back his head in uncontrolled mirth, her own anger seethed that he could not care enough to be jealous. "How dare you!'' She pounded at his chest with her fists.

Steve grabbed a handful of her hair and cast his darkening eyes on her. "I dare because I am Hawk!''

She needed time to think, to sort things out! What was he saying? God, she thought, rubbing the headache that threatened, why couldn't she remember? Her eyes were squeezed shut when he lifted her clear of the floor and she screamed as he deposited her on the bed. "No!" she yelled, fighting his hold on her.

"Yes!" he countered, settling his large frame over her.

Jessie cried out for him to stop. He'd always been so gentle. He never . . . ! A mournful cry tore from her throat and she became brittle, like ice. She heard him swear and felt the cool air as he rolled from her. There was silence, except for the thundering of her heartbeat in her head.

Sitting on the edge of the bed with his back to her, Steve raked his fingers through his hair and clutched his head. "You remember." He didn't ask, he merely stated what he knew to be a fact.

Bile rose in her throat and she felt the screaming of muscles held so tightly they burned. She couldn't speak! She couldn't move! The only motion was the violent thoughts in her mind. It was all there! Every memory, every moment they shared. She saw the past as clearly as sunlight passing through a crystal. He had tricked her! He had lied! She thought of the many nights, the times they had loved, exploring each other intimately until there were no secrets, or so she thought! My God! How he had played her for a fool!

Steve looked at her at last. She stared at the ceiling and he waited for the recriminations. Her silence was tearing at him. He knew all along it could happen, but the ideal weeks made him let down his guard and hope it would go on just one more day. As he sat in the purgatory of his own making, he wanted to demand her forgiveness, to go on as they had, but one look at her convinced him it was not the time to insist on anything. Slowly, hesitant to leave her, he rose and donned his boots and heavy coat. At the door he turned to watch her for a sign, any sign that she would talk to him, but she continued to stare mutely into nothingness and he grabbed his hat, stomping out the door.

* * *

Jess didn't know how long she lay there before forcing life back into her limbs. Steve returned to find her staring silently at the fire. She was determined that she would not fight him, yet she also knew she would never forgive him. He had used her for his baser needs with no thought to the damage to her heart and soul. All she wanted now was to survive, to go home and to try to forget the nightmare he had induced.

He did not try to speak with her that day, and made his bed before the hearth that night. Jess feared retiring until he threw some blankets on the floor and she knew he would not force her.

Morning was met with eyes burning from too little sleep. Each time she'd drifted off, she felt bereft of the warm, strong body she had snuggled against these past weeks. He had used her and molded her to his needs. She felt that she no longer had ownership of her own body, and she hated him for it.

They moved through the following day joylessly. All the mundane chores were accomplished with no more enthusiasm than needed. It was Jessie who at last broke the silent barrier. Steve was in his makeshift bed for the fourth night when she spoke at last.

"You told me we would return home when I wanted to," she stated coldly. "I wish to leave tomorrow." Jess winced at the sound of a wild growl that reached her moments before his hands fell on her shoulders.

"We're not going anywhere, not until you cease this stubbornness and agree to marry me!" His eyes were in the shadows but she could see the tight muscles in his neck, and she could feel the iron strength of his fingers as they bit into her skin, marking her in his fury.

"Never!" she spat at him. "I'd die before I'd ever let you touch me again!"

Driven by fury and his need for this woman, he tore the covers from her, ignored her thrashing arms and legs, and forced his knees between her tightly clamped thighs. "Then you better will yourself to die this instant," he retorted through clenched teeth as he pushed into her. He knew he hurt her. He heard her cries and swore at himself for his lack of control that made him no better than an animal. He stopped his movement yet remained imbedded in her depths. "I won't let you go, Jess. You're mine, and if I have to keep you here until hell freezes over, I will."

He began to move again, slowly, sensuously. He could feel her moisten, aroused despite her wish to remain cold. "I hate you!" she moaned.

"Only with your mind, my love. Your body is mine to do with as I please." He began to move faster, deeper. "And I please to seduce it at every turn and in every way possible until you wed me or carry my child."

His words were like cold water. Jessie fought desperately to free herself but he clamped his hands about her waist and held her tightly until he filled her with his seed.

"Bastard!" she swore as he moved away from her and drew the blanket over them both.

So the pattern was set, a pattern of struggle and hatred. Steve was driven by a need to possess her totally, and Jess by the need to destroy him. She dwelled in a land of alert fear. He was good at his word and continued to press her at every turn. She tried to fight savagely at one time and lie cold and unfeeling at others, yet he always managed to convince her traitorous body to obey him. The only motivation to remain sane came from her drive to escape him, to somehow beat him in this macabre game.

It came to him at a pristine stream as he bent to scoop up a pail of water. The clear blue sky was reflected there and a burnished leaf floated through the image. Jennifer Morgan! By God, Mac thought, that's who she reminded him of! He remembered the young woman who married a friend of his, a woman who came west from St. Louis. Steve's woman was from there. Could she be Morgan's daughter? Seems he recalled Morgan's wife left him. Maybe she went back and maybe there had been another child.

Deciding he didn't wish to wait to discover if what he suspected was true, he set out before noon. It would take him two days to reach the cabin now that the snows were regular and accumulating at a rapid pace. There was more precipitation than normal for the middle of November and McKinley wondered if the passes were closed yet, not that he planned to leave his mountain home until late spring, and only then to head for the July rendezvous on the Green.

What drove him to the girl, he didn't know. Some instinct told him she needed him and, the closer he got, the deeper the feeling persisted. Alert to every sign, Mac knew Steve had left the cabin about an hour before his arrival. He had gone alone and on foot, probably to seek game.

Unsure of his reception, McKinley called from a short distance away. He was just ready to call again when the door eased open. As beautiful as she had been by firelight, she was more so in the weak winter sun.

"Oh, Mac!" Jessie cried, and ran through the knee-deep snow that circled the cabin's yard, hurling herself into his arms. "Thank God!"

"What's wrong, lass?" He held her from him and examined her teary face. Dark circles were apparent at close range and she was tense and terribly upset. "Is it Steve?"

Brushing her hair back behind her ears, she shook her head. "No, he's fine." Reminded of her nemesis, she looked about nervously. "Come inside," she said, retracing her steps.

Shedding his coat and gloves, Mac took a mug of

steaming coffee and knew he had been right to come. Something *was* wrong—but nothing prepared him for the story Jess related. He knew Steve to be headstrong and determined, even a bit arrogant, but kidnapping! Good Lord! It was like the old days, when he was much younger, and even then it had only been a squaw, never a white woman! Never in his sixty-seven years had he known anyone who would steal a woman, prey on her lost memory, and force her to . . . God only knew what!

"Can you help me, Mac?" Jess begged. "I have to get away!"

Scratching at his bearded chin, Mac wasn't sure if he should get involved. Kincaid was a mighty power in the territory. But what he was doing was wrong. He looked at Jessica and saw the pleading in her constantly moving fingers and tear-glazed eyes.

"He doesn't know about the babe, does he?" he asked gently.

"Baby! I'm not—" Jess clutched at her stomach. Her time was long past! Why hadn't she realized? How could she have ignored the signs of a thickening waist and fuller breasts? She couldn't remember having her monthly flow since before her illness. She stumbled to a chair, trying to come to terms with the fact that she was four months pregnant. "How . . . how did you know when even I didn't?"

"I may be old, lass, but I'm not blind! It ain't hard ta see the changes in ya, if ya stand back and look." He placed a kindly hand over hers. "You're Morgan's daughter, ain't ya?"

"Why, yes! Do you know my father?"

"Aye, I know him. Knew yer ma, too." He smiled at her widening eyes. "I remembered the other day. I was with yer pa when yer ma birthed the boy. Jeff and me knew he'd never make it." He grew very thoughtful for a few moments. "This

ain't no place ta have babies." He stood to his full
towering height and offered her his hand. "We better hurry if we're goin' ta leave 'fore Steve gets
back."

"Oh!" Jess threw her arms about his neck.
"Thank you!" she cried.

"There, there, lass. No need ta cry." He patted
her back. "Steve ain't doin' right keepin' ya here.
He'll be mad as hell when he finds ya gone, but I
don't figure he'll think ya can get out yerself so he'll
waste a lot of time lookin' around here. By then,
we'll be on the way home, and he'll be trapped here
till spring."

"What about you?" Jess looked intently at her
new friend.

"Don't ya go worryin' 'bout me. I know these
mountains well enough ta get back up when no man
thinks it's possible." He gave her a gentle push.
"Now, get dressed as warm as ya can and I'll get us
some more provisions."

Jess didn't even look back as she and McKinley
headed away from the cabin. A light snow was falling, with a promise to grow more heavy. It would
help to cover their tracks and should lead Steve to
believe she left alone. She left a note stating simply, *I'm going home.* As much as she hated him, she
didn't want him to think she had met with foul
play. If he was to suffer, it had to be for the truth.

It took nearly five days to reach the hills a half day
west of Windy Creek. Mac knew all the caves and
niches where they could find shelter and managed
a rather comfortable journey back for her. Expecting
to move trancelike over the terrain, Jess was fascinated by what she saw. The icy touch of winter
transformed every drop of water to crystal splendor
and every object to primevil beauty. Snow-ladened
boughs gracefully curtsied before the travelers. The
gentle sun brought a blush to the snow as it moved
across the sky to settle for the night. Jess thought of

pink lace and diamonds as they entered the last of
their refuges.

Mac told her she would be home this time tomorrow. She felt she'd known him all her life. He told
her of his Indian wife of thirty years and the seven
years he'd been alone since her death. He had a son
somewhere in the Oregon Territory who was married and he proudly proclaimed he had at least three
grandchildren. He seemed bent on cheering her with
tales of his life.

He had an intuitive quality about him, Jess recognized. He always knew when she needed to rest
or if she was hungry. He sensed when she needed
to think quietly or when she needed to laugh and
forget. He told her that if he'd had a daughter, he
would have wished for one as brave and strong as
she. Brave? Strong? Jess felt neither description fit
her. If Mac wasn't so astute to her needs, she would
have crumpled more than once. She felt heart-
broken and had yet to come to grips with her pregnancy.

It wasn't going to be easy to have a child and raise
him without a husband, but she would do it. Nothing would harm her child. Her child! She gently
curved her arms about her stomach and cradled the
unborn innocent. Her child! At last, she could say
it. She had loved his father, but he was conceived
in violence. He? Yes, it would be a son. Kincaid
would have it no other way.

Smoke was rising from the ranch house, and they
reined to a stop. "Well, lassie, there's yer home."
He gestured across the frosted landscape to the nestled group of buildings that comprised Windy Creek.

"How can I thank you, Mac?" Tears glistened on
her lashes as she reached for his hand.

"Be happy, child." He saw her smile fade. "Ya
might not believe me but I think ya've not seen the
last of Kincaid, and I don't think ya wish it. Yer
heart's broken but it'll mend if ya let it. You and he
have created the greatest miracle. He lies in yer

womb and he'll grow ta be all ya wish for him. Don't deny him his father because of stubborn pride." He leaned toward her and kissed her wet cheek. "He won't be able ta get out of the mountains 'fore spring. That'll give ya time ta think, and maybe forgive."

Unable to convince him to ride to the ranch with her, Jess bid him a farewell and watched him ride westward. She wondered if she would ever see him again, this man who had been her companion, her confidante, and the mirror to her inner soul. Sighing, Jess drew about and headed home.

Chapter 22

The sound of a horse's hooves striking the frozen ground brought Jeff to the door. A rider approached but he could not identify the bundled visitor. Dark was rushing over the land to embrace the night and it wasn't until his guest was just a few yards away that he recognized her.

"Jessie!" He helped her dismount and pulled her into his arms. "My God! How did you get here?"

"Papa!" Jess permitted a tear to fall, and it was her undoing. She could not stop the torrent that followed, and clung to her father for support. Slowly, her trembling ceased and she allowed him to lead her toward the house.

"What's goin' on out here?" Red came through the door, drying her hands on an apron. Seeing the wrapped bundle lift its head to the light, she clutched her middle. "Saints be praised! It's Jess!" Running out into the cold night, Red opened her arms to envelop the young woman. "I don't know how ya got here, lass, but I think we best get ya in the house 'fore we all freeze ta death!"

Walking between Red and her father, Jess was ushered to the warm confines of the cabin. Jeff hustled to stoke up the fire and set a kettle on to brew while Red helped Jess out of her extra layers of clothing and into a soft, warm robe. When she was settled at the table with a minimum of chatter and a mug of cocoa, Red and Jeff joined her and sat silently waiting for her to tell them why she had returned and how she had accomplished it. Anxiously, Jeff stumbled over some words at last.

"Jess, I . . . why . . . how did you get here?"

Jessica looked at her father. Those words—he'd asked that before. He didn't ask where she had been. Somehow, he knew, but if he knew, then he must have—God! Jessie paled at the realization. "You!"

"Honey, what's wrong?" Jeff rose and tried to touch her shoulder but she spun away.

"Don't!" she screamed. "Papa, how could you? You let him take me away! You helped him . . ." She stared coldly, not wanting to believe what she was discovering.

There was no defense for himself, and Jeff stood silent. It was Red who came to his aid. "Lass, you know how I feel about ya. Ya know I want the best for ya and the lad. Your pa only did what he thought best for ya both." She reached Jessie's side and forced her to face her. "You were too stubborn ta admit your love for each other so he . . . he did what he thought best."

Jessie stood with her eyes closed and tried to assimilate everything. Out of love for her, her father helped Steve take her to the mountains. Because he was her father, she found she could forgive him. He had not lied or tried to deceive her. She realized she was angry with her father for his interference in her life, but not for what had happened. Steve was still the culprit and she'd never forgive him!

Looking at her father, Jess breathed a deep sigh. "I'm sorry, I shouldn't have shouted. Papa, I . . . I've been through quite an ordeal and . . . and realizing you had something to . . . to do with it, well, it was hard for me to . . . oh, Papa!" Jess ran to him and flung herself into his arms.

"Don't cry, baby." He brushed her hair back. "It's me who should be sayin' I'm sorry. I just thought . . .

I hoped you two could work it out, but it's over now. You never have to think of him again."

Jessie's tearful trembling gave way to broken laughter, then deep sobs. "Oh, God! Over? It'll never be over!" Jess pulled back and looked at her father's worried face. He thought perhaps her mind had snapped until she spoke vehemently. "I'm pregnant!"

Not sure whether to furiously rage or understandingly sympathize, Jeff stared dumbfounded. He looked from Jess to Red and back without saying a word. Mistaking his silence for contempt, Jessie's shoulders drooped, and she lowered her head in shame.

"If you want me to go, Papa, I will. I'm sure Aunt Clara would take me in." Jess rattled on about her uncertain future. "Of course, I could tell her I was widowed. She need not know the child is a . . . a bastard."

"Jessica!" her father roared. "Don't you ever call my grandchild that!" He took her in his arms and led her to a chair. Cradling her spent form, Jeff rocked her gently. "You must not think of leaving, honey. You'll stay right here with Connie and me. We'll take care of you and the baby."

"Connie?" Jessica sat up and looked at Red. "Oh! I . . . I didn't think! I'm sorry!" She became more flustered as her thoughts took the wrong turn. "I didn't know you were—"

"Married," Connie supplied with a grin.

Terribly pleased with the turn of events, Jess hugged her father. "I'm so happy for you both. I knew, or at least I hoped it would work out this way." Jess vacated her chair and embraced her new stepmother. "Red, how can I thank you for making him so happy?"

"No need, lass. I assure you, I get as good as I give. Now, you must be tired. Are you hungry?" At the shake of her head, Red stepped toward Jessie's old room. "Then I better see ta your room. You need ta get proper rest. That wee one'll be growin' and takin' all you can give 'im.''

Left with her father, Jess grew nervous. She fidgeted with her cup and kept her eyes on it.

Clearing his throat, Jeff tried to console her. "Honey, don't worry. Everything will be all right. You'll see.''

"Don't patronize me, Papa. I'm an unwed mother! My child will be a bast . . . fatherless. You and Red can't protect me from what people will say." She began to pace the small room. "It's not fair to put either of you through this. It would be better if I really do leave.''

"Stop it!" Jeff jumped out of his chair and stood before her, placing his hands on her cheeks. "You are my daughter and no one will ever hurt you again, not as long as I draw breath! I've failed you once but no more. Windy Creek is as much yours as mine and it will go to the child you carry. Don't ever let me hear you say you want to walk away from it. Do you understand?''

Jess nodded and slipped her arms about his waist. "Yes, Papa," she sighed, content to ignore the future for the time being. Disengaging her arms, she smiled weakly. "I think I'll go to bed now.''

As she reached the bedroom door, Jeff asked her one final question. "Jessie, is there a chance for you and Steve with the baby coming?''

Without turning she replied. "No, Papa. Steve doesn't know about the baby and I don't want him to know. Promise me you won't tell anyone until I do.''

"But Jess, he's the father and he's responsible! He should at least—''

"Promise me!''

After a moment's hesitation, Jeff agreed. "All right, honey. I promise.''

"Thank you, Papa." She looked over her shoulder at him. "I'll handle it—" She paused. "—when the time comes.''

* * *

"You son of a b—ugh!" Steve hit the floor after a solid blow to his jaw had knocked the wind from him.

"Look, lad," Mac offered his hand to help Steve rise. "I don't want ta hurt ya and I don't want ta fight with ya either, but I—umph!" Mac grunted as Steve's fist landed squarely in his middle.

"You had no right to help her get away!" Steve swung, missed, and was the target again of several quick punches which made him stagger backward until he came up against the table. Losing his balance, he crashed through the wooden structure.

"Had enough?" Mac questioned coolly. "Or do I have ta beat ya inta listenin'?"

Waving his hand to signal defeat, Steve rose on shaky legs and rubbed his face. "Enough!" He glowered. He was still furious but he allowed his rage to smolder. He had to hear Mac out, and then, maybe, he'd kill him.

Grabbing a jug of brandy and two mugs, Mac kicked aside the broken table pieces and took a chair. He poured out stiff drinks for each of them and gestured for Steve to sit, thrusting a cup of spirits at him.

"Ya have a right ta be angry and—"

"Angry!" Steve yelled. "Do you know what it's been like these last few days? Christ! I thought . . ." Steve braced his head in his hands and reflected on the hellish nightmare.

He'd returned after sunset to find the cabin cold and empty. Terror raced through him as he yelled for Jessie. At first he thought she was hurt somewhere, then he considered her doing harm to herself. Gnawing fear was laced with agony as he tore about trying to find her. Then he saw the note. She had left him, damn her!

Using a lantern, he'd tried to find her trail but to no avail. The darkness and new snow hid her path. Giving up until the break of day, he lay awake throughout the night. She had chosen to risk her life in the unknown and frigid wilderness rather than stay with him, and he knew he had driven her out there. It had gone wrong from the beginning. He'd bullied and demanded his way, never considering her needs, always taking, never giving.

His frantic search lasted three days and he covered as many square miles of rocky terrain as he could. At one point he fell to his knees in the snow, digging frantically at a small mound with his bare hands only to find the carcass of a young mule deer.

It wasn't until McKinley came blundering through the snow to the cabin that he grasped reality. In a blaze of temper, he didn't wait for McKinley to explain. All Mac got out was that he had seen Jessie safely home to Windy Creek when Steve erupted violently. Now, in better control, he would listen.

McKinley knew the pain Steve was enduring. Even though he had been wrong in taking the girl, it was for the right reasons. Steve cared deeply for her. Mac had warned Jessie about pride and it seemed Steve needed the same warning, but this wasn't the time. His young friend looked beaten. Dark shadows outlined his eyes and a shaggy beard covered his face. He was tired and had spent all his energies in trying to find his woman.

"I'm sorry it's been rough on ya, boy, but it was worse on her. Ya had no right ta take her away like ya did."

"You don't know what the hell you're talking about, Mac. I had every right. She was going to be my wife until she got some harebrained idea I wanted to buy her!"

"Ya treated her badly," Mac said simply.

"She had everything she could want!" Steve glared defensively.

"She didn't have a choice. Ya were her master and she was no better than any of your property." Mac couldn't tell if Steve was mulling over what he was saying or wallowing in self-disgust as he turned away with a groan. "It was the only way she could give as good as she got, by running away."

Steve jumped to his feet. "Well, she isn't going to get away with this!" He began to gather some supplies.

"What do ya think you're doin'?" Mac asked irately.

"I'm going after her!"

"No, Steve, you're not."

Steve spun toward the old man and glared. "Don't try and stop me. We've been friends a long time, but so help me, I'll kill you if you try to stop me!"

"I promised her time ta sort things out." Mac began to plead Jessie's case. "Give her that time. Besides, ya won't do her no good gettin' yerself killed or lost out there." Mac chuckled as he thought about the babe. "Though right now she might thank ya for it." He grew serious again. "You're angry now, raging about like a bull elk in rut, but it's better this way. I won't lead ya out and, even though you're good, ya probably wouldn't make it on your own."

Discouraged, Steve threw his gear aside. "All right, Mac. I'll play it your way, but come spring I'm going and if I have to bind and gag her to have her back, I will, and not you or anyone else will stand in my way!"

"I just can't go." Jess pouted self-indulgently. "I can't face Sarah and Chad. Not like this!" She gestured to her rounding shape. "They'll know!"

Red chuckled. "Of course they'll know, but you won't be able to hide it any longer anyway. Lord, Jess, you're pregnant and it can't be undone." Trying to further the cause she and Jeff were working on she added an aside. " 'Course, if you and Steve could work things out and get married, you wouldn't have no cause to be ashamed."

"Red!" Jess spun to face her. "I've told you and Papa a dozen times, I won't marry that insufferable,

self-serving louse!" Feeling righteous, Jessie grew
bitter. "Besides, he was so adept at using me, one
has to wonder how many other whelps he has in
the territory. One more might not matter."

Before thinking, Red drew back her hand and
slapped Jess on the cheek. "Don't you ever talk such
trash again!" Red scolded. "You sit here feelin' sorry
for yerself but ya won't listen or seek help! Ya have
no right ta sulk about. Yer a woman and yer havin'
a babe, and ya ain't the first ta not be havin' a husband and carryin'!" Seeing the tears fill Jessie's eyes
as her hand covered the print of Red's hand, she
felt remorse but knew pity wasn't what Jess needed.
"I ain't sorry I hit ya, ya had it comin'. Now, get ta
yer room and wash yer face. Put on a pretty dress
and get ready. When yer pa comes in we're goin' ta
the K-D for dinner!"

Jess felt like a recalcitrant child. Red was right.
She had just two choices. She could marry Steve or
raise the child alone, but she couldn't waste away
with thoughts of what might have been. No wishes
for changed yesterdays would come true, there was
only today and, with the help of God and luck, to-
morrows. Drawing a deep breath, Jess gave Red an
embarrassed grin and summed up her feelings and
an apology in two words. "Yes, Mama."

Red opened her arms and Jess fell into them. Jeff
found his two girls embracing with laughter and
tears. "What the devil's goin' on in here?" he asked,
surprised.

"Why, you big ox—" Red smiled lovingly. "—it's
Christmas and we're goin' to a party." She looked
anxiously at Jessie. "Ain't that right, lass?"

Gently Jess replied, "Yes, Red. That's right."

Hearing that Jessie was home, Sarah decided it
might be best to have their dinner in the large house
where the small group could be extra-comfortable.
She and Chad had taken to staying there in Steve's
absence and it was easier to plan from their tempo-

rary abode. Sarah thought about what Chad told her. She found it incredible that Steve would force Jessie to go away with him. Men! Sometimes she wondered if they ever considered women as people. Steve certainly hadn't considered Jessie's reputation or feelings by hauling her off like so much chattel. Chad hadn't seen her, but Jeff told him she was fine. "Fine" covered a lot of ground.

Checking the goose one more time, Sarah removed her apron and went to the parlor to find Chad placing a package under the tree. She smiled as he picked up one for him and gave it a shake.

"If you guess what it is, I'll take it back," Sarah teased. Her husband sat back on his heels and she thought he looked like a little boy caught in the cookie jar. His hair fell over his brow and an impish grin twisted below his finely groomed mustache.

"I was only rearranging things." His cheeks grew pink.

Sarah bent down beside him and ruffled his hair. "I already had it all arranged, thank you, so keep your hands off the gifts."

Chad grabbed her about the waist and pulled her across his thighs. Sarah squealed that he was going to mess up her dress, and he merely held her tighter. "Too bad we have company coming. I see one present I'd like to unwrap this minute." He looked lovingly at her flushed face.

"You're a rogue, Chad Duncan." She smiled seductively. "And Christmas isn't until tomorrow." She ran her hand over his chest.

"I'm worse than a child." He kissed the bare skin at her shoulder. "I can't wait until tomorrow." His lips trailed up her neck to nibble her ear and he sighed as her slender arms wound about his neck. Their lips met and the glorious wonder of their love wrapped them in an exquisite cloak of passion.

The door opened and the gusty, cold wind whipped around the three guests to scurry across the floor and embrace the lovers. In embarrassed

haste, Sarah and Chad separated and rose to their
feet.

Laughing merrily, Red confronted them. "We
knocked, but ya were too busy ta hear us, I guess.
Excuse us for walkin' in on ya, but it's too cold out
there ta wait . . ." She paused for effect ". . . and
gettin' too warm in here, I'm thinkin'."

Still bundled in her coat, Jess stood back, afraid,
unsure of her reception, but as soon as Sarah saw
her, she couldn't resist the extended arms of her
friend.

"I should be angry with you, you know." Sarah
drew back but continued to hold Jessie's hands.
"You've been home over a month and I have to hear
it from Chad."

"I . . . well, I . . ." Jess stammered, and Red res-
cued her again.

"Is that what you and Chad were discussin' just
now?"

"Oh, Red. You know men! They seem to take what
they want when they want it!" Sarah realized her
blunder the moment her words were out and she felt
Jessie stiffen. "Jessie! I'm sorry. I didn't mean—"

"It's all right, Sarah. I know you meant no harm."
A weak smile on her pale face only exacerbated Sarah's sorrow at her retort to Red.

"Are we going to stand here all night or move in
by that nice roaring fire?" Jeff prodded.

Chad shook hands with Jeff and then offered to
take everyone's coat. Jessie was reluctant to give hers
up and only a stern look from her father made her
relinquish her wrap. Sure that the Duncans would
notice immediately, she was surprised and relieved
that they didn't. Replacing her coat with a shawl she
had taken to wearing to hide her womanly shape,
Jess entered the parlor and took a chair near the heat.

Staring at the beautiful Christmas tree, Jessie listened to the party around her. Jeff and Chad went
off to prepare spiked hot cider and Red followed

Sarah into the kitchen to check on dinner. A single tear of loneliness slid down her cheek, for she was the odd man out. It would always be like this from now on and she knew she had to accept it. The only companion, the only one she could share with, lay within her body. Soon she would have someone for herself, someone to love and cherish.

Sarah moved quietly to the side of Jessica's chair. She had watched the once-vibrant beauty sitting absolutely still. Her hair was drawn back into a loose bun on her neck and she wore a dark blue gown with a very prim lace trim about her neck. With long, fitted sleeves, the dress made Jessie look like a slender child.

"Jessie, are you all right?" Sarah asked gently. She knelt beside the chair and set her hand on Jessie's arm.

Seeing the genuine concern on Sarah's face, Jessie tried to smile, but the travesty was heart-wrenching. "Y-yes, Sarah. I'm all right." Deciding it was time to tell her friend of her condition and avoid the embarrassment of detection, she turned about in the chair to face her. "I want to tell you something, Sarah. If you want me to leave when I'm finished, I will." Jess lowered her head. Without raising her eyes she related the story. "And it was only due to Mr. McKinley that I was able to get away."

Sarah was dumbfounded. "I can't believe he'd do that!"

"I assure you, Sarah, he did," Jess murmured, her hands clasped in her lap.

"Oh, I believe you. It's just . . . well, I've never known Steve to care enough to chase any woman, let alone risk so much to kidnap one! He must love you very much," Sarah offered kindly.

"He doesn't love me at all!" Jessie shot back. "If he did, he wouldn't treat me like . . . like a whore!"

"If he didn't love you, he would have taken what he wanted and walked away." Sarah watched Jessie turn crimson. "I'm sorry to be so blunt, but I think you're overlooking the obvious. Maybe you're the one afraid to commit yourself." Startled, Sarah stared as the laughter bubbled out of Jessie.

"Oh, Sarah, that's choice! I'm so committed it's pathetic!" Tears rolled from her eyes and she began to cry softly. "I'm going to have his child."

Sarah's eyes widened and her jaw dropped open in astonishment. Jess felt it best if she left rather than face the shame of being ostracized. She rose and tried to brush past Sarah only to find herself held fast.

"My dear friend, what has he done to you?"

Hearing the sympathy devoid of pity, Jessie fell into Sarah's arms. "You . . . you don't hate me?" she asked between sobs.

"Hate you? Never!" Sarah stood back. "But I'm a little angry and hurt that you thought so little of our friendship you feared my knowing."

"It wasn't that, Sarah. It's just not easy to admit to anyone. I'm afraid and ashamed."

"Well, don't be." A rich-timbred voice filled the room. Jess gasped as Chad strode purposefully to her side. "I'm sorry, but I've been eavesdropping." Seeing the reddening on her cheeks, he placed his hand beneath her chin. "We're your friends, honey, and we don't cast stones." He smiled gently. "But I'd like to drop a few boulders on another friend of mine."

Frantically Jessie clutched his arms. "He mustn't know! Promise me you won't tell him! I . . . I need to handle this my way!"

"Okay, honey." He turned to his wife and pulled her to his side. "We'll let you work this out, but if you need us, you promise to let us know?" With a weak smile of relief, Jessie nodded. "Good! then let's eat!"

"I'm not really hungry, Chad." She spoke softly, anxiety taking away the empty feeling of no dinner.

"That's too bad." He turned her toward the dining room and pushed her forward carefully. "Because you're eating. If not for you, then for the little one.''

Jess and Sarah giggled at the paternal Chad and allowed him to steer everyone into the dining room to enjoy their Christmas feast.

Chapter 23

Growing more restless as the afternoon progressed, Jess stood before the large, black stove and rubbed the dull ache in her back. Her father and Red had gone to the K-D but she'd begged off. Her swollen form was not conducive to either sitting on a horse or bouncing in the carriage. Rubbing her hands and holding them to the radiating heat, she thought about the last few months. She kept her secret well. The only ones who knew about her condition were the Duncans and Roxy.

Jeff went to town in early January and somehow let it slip that Jessie was home. The very next day, an exuberant Roxy came riding out to see her, the heavy snow no deterrent. At first she was surprised, then angry, but within minutes she was clucking like a mother hen.

"How can I cast stones?" She blustered at Jessie's embarrassment and predicament before asking about a layette and ushering Jess to her room to see each and every item she and Red had already made.

The stove's heat became oppressive as sudden thoughts of Steve invaded her mind. Opening the door, she took her shawl from a peg and wrapped it about herself securely. She stepped to the porch and breathed deeply of the frosty air to clear her head. Another tightening in her abdomen brought her up straight. It passed quickly, and she wondered if her time was near. These little aches had begun in the early morning but she had brushed them aside. Anyone as awkward and enlarged as she was bound to have some aches and pains, so they were dismissed.

Looking about the landscape, Jessie smiled her appreciation of the wonder and beauty of it all. The mantle of white covered everything and presented a virginal side of nature. The newest snow had been cleared from the steps and the weak winter sun managed to dry them. Easing herself carefully down, she sat and tried to find a comfortable spot. Settling at last, a line from Shakespeare's *Julius Caesar* that she had seen in St. Louis ages ago skipped across her mind. "Beware the Ides of March," echoed again and again. Jessie chuckled then as she realized it was the fifteenth! She had checked the calendar that morning as she mentally calculated when her babe could arrive. It could be anytime. Red didn't want to leave her that morning, but Jess had insisted. Just because she was due didn't mean the world should skid to a halt to wait.

Pressing her hands to her hard stomach, she gently massaged the stretched skin. "You're quiet today, my love." She looked down and lightly cradled her burden. "Are you resting for your journey into the world?" As if in reply, a deep cramp gripped her. With the easing she giggled. "You took my wind that time!" Jess awkwardly got to her feet and took the steps in a rather ungainly manner. She had a sudden urge to bake cookies and was mentally listing the ingredients as she entered the house to seek its cozy warmth.

Amassing what she needed, Jess began to blend the batter and let out a moan as the cramp returned, a bit stronger than the last. "Not now, child! Not now!" She clutched the table edge until her knuckles whitened. She began to breathe deeply until the pain passed. Brushing the tears from her eyes, she returned to her task, mumbling a prayer that Red and her father would return soon, for she was certain her time had indeed come.

There was a rhythm to her progress. With each batch of cookies sent to the oven, a wrenching tightness would grip her, each wave seeming more intense than the previous one. Sweat rolled off her brow and down between her breasts. It was happening too fast, she thought. He was coming too soon. There was no one to help.

Panting as the latest pain subsided, Jess sat at the table trying to think of what to do. She hadn't realized until now how little she knew and how ignorant she was. She'd been left in the dark about childbirth and could only go on instinct. She would need linen; she needed to prepare her bed. Slowly, she moved to her room and set out the extra sheeting she would need. She was wracked by a new pain halfway between the bed and the door and it was all she could do to remain on her feet.

"Damn you, Kincaid!" she screamed as a warm wetness trickled down her legs and she looked dumbfounded at the small puddle. She thought of wiping it up but the smell of burning cookies convinced her that was the first order of business.

Making it to the stove, she removed the tray as the tightening began anew. Cookies scattered over the floor as she dropped the tray and gripped her stomach.

"Oh! Oh, God!" she cried, and inched toward her bed. Collapsing upon it, she began to whimper. She was alone and afraid. He was coming too fast! It had only been a few hours since her first real pain. Could the earlier discomfort have been a sign? She wished fervently that she had mentioned it to Red.

Her strength dissipated with each new contraction and she dozed fitfully until a new one tore through her. "Dear God, please let someone come!" she cried.

As if in answer to her prayer, a knock rattled the door. Jessie tried to push herself to her elbows but was unable to attain even that. Afraid her caller would leave, she screamed out. At the sound of a banging door and hurried footsteps, she fell back to her pillows with a thankful sigh. A muffled curse reached her and she opened her eyes to see a worried Chad. He knelt beside her and she gripped his hand.

"He's coming, Chad!" she cried hoarsely, Her simple statement brought a nervous shudder through him.

Brushing back her sweat-dampened hair, he winced when a new spasm gave terrible strength to the grip she had on his hand. "Easy, honey. Take it easy. I'll . . . I'll go get help."

"No!" she moaned. "Don't . . . don't leave me," she begged.

Chad didn't know what to do. This dilemma was more than he could handle. She was having a baby and he knew he couldn't help her, yet he couldn't leave her either. "You need a woman with you, honey. Damned if I know what to do!" He ran his fingers through his hair. He'd only stopped on his way to town to see if she needed anything. He certainly didn't expect to play midwife!

"There isn't time." Jessie's breathing grew more rapid. "You . . . you must have . . . ugh!" She moaned and he paled. "You must have delivered foals and . . . and calves." Chad nodded and she pressed on. "You can do it, Chad." She arched her back and held her breath in pain. Falling back to the mattress with teary eyes, she pleaded, "You have to!"

He knew she was right. If no one else arrived, he would have to. Taking a deep breath to give him the courage, he disengaged Jessica's hand and set to helping her. Gently, he removed her shoes and clothes until she lay in her damp shift. Covering her with a light blanket, he gathered towels and

warm water. Slowly, carefully, he rinsed her body
down between pains and coaxed her to relax. Between them, their limited knowledge would have
to suffice and he fervently prayed it was enough.

Should it take this long? Was she in more pain
than she could stand? Damn, but he wished he
knew the answers! Maybe the child was stuck! Did
they get stuck? Hell, he didn't know! All he could
do was soothe her during the lulls and gently calm
her in her agony, and pray someone else would
come.

It went on for what seemed ages, but was in reality only a couple of hours. Jessie moaned and
whimpered, Chad groaned in sympathy, and neither heard the chattering of voices at the still-open
door.

"I'm sure that's Chad's horse."

"Where are they?"

"Why's the door hangin' open?"

Conjectures and questions flew until, upon entering, Red and Jeff took in the scattered cookies and
heard the soft coaxing in Chad's voice coming from
Jessie's room.

"It's okay, Jess. Everything's going to be okay."

Red threw aside her shawl and bundles, and hurried to Jessie's room, crying out as she went. "It's
the baby! He's comin'!"

Jeff stood transfixed for a moment, then went into
action. The door was secured and wood quickly
added to the stove to reheat the rooms. He set to
making coffee. When all else failed, he always made
coffee. It gave his trembling hands a task they badly
needed. At the sound of shuffling feet, Jeff turned
to face a very pale and distraught Chad.

He looked exhausted and as taut as a banjo string.
There was a glaze over his eyes as if he'd experienced an unbelievable event. "Boil water," he
mumbled, and staggered to a chair.

"Is . . . is she all right?" Jeff asked, afraid of the
worst.

"Huh? Oh, yeah. Yeah, she's fine." Chad dropped his head into his hands. "God! I hope I never have to go through that again!"

Jeff grew fearful. "The baby?"

"Not for a while. Red said it would be a while yet." Chad grimaced. "I . . . she . . . we thought it was going to happen anytime. Christ! How can they stand it? So much pain!" He shook his head. "I swear, I'll never let that happen to Sarah!"

Jeff went to the cupboard and pulled out a bottle of whiskey. He grabbed two glasses and plunked them on the table. "I know, boy." He half-grinned. "I know."

"Next pain, you push," Red directed. "It's gonna hurt like hell but it should be the last one." She watched Jess start to stiffen. From what she could figure, Jessie had been in hard labor over seven hours, and about fifteen from the start, but she was doing wonderfully well, more so than the two drunks sleeping it off in the front room. Well, maybe it was best they were out of the way. She chuckled at Chad and Jeff when they were in their cups. They acted like nervous fathers and looked about as bad.

"Scream, honey. If it helps, let it out." She wiped her sweaty brow on her sleeve. "You're doin' fine, now push!"

Jess endured her labor in silence, but the excruciating agony tearing through her was at its peak. Gathering all her reserves, she gave a mighty push and let loose with one long piercing scream.

"Ah, Jessie. You did it!" Red cried. Working silently for a moment to tie off the cord and check the child and mother, she let the tears flow.

"Is . . . is he all right?" Jess whispered. "Red?"

A tiny squeak echoed in the now-quiet room. A gurgle, followed by a strong wail, filled the silence. "Yes, darlin'," Red crooned. "Come meet your mama." Handing the snug bundle to Jessie, Red smiled through her tears. "You've a fine, healthy son, Jessie. God bless ya both."

The babe was laid on the crook of her arm and she looked upon her child. His little face was deep red and his eyes were clenched shut. A restless fist brushed his mouth. Soft downy black hair covered his tiny head and Jess found herself placing a loving kiss upon it.

"He's beautiful." Jessie sighed.

"Aye, and he's perfect. He has the right amount of everything." Red grinned, watching the baby sense the warmth of his mother's arms as something familiar in a big, new world, and fall asleep. "I'll take him, lass. You need some rest." Before she could reach the child, Jess had slipped into much-needed slumber, a contented smile on her weary face.

"How . . . how is she?" Jeff sprang to his feet the moment Red opened the bedroom door. He saw her bundle but needed to know about his daughter first.

"The lass is sleepin' and a fine job she did, too." Red was tired, yet she wouldn't miss this moment for anything. "You have a fine, strappin' grandson, Jeff." Tears filled her eyes as she watched her husband and their young friend fold back the blanket to see him. Their hands looked huge next to the tightly clenched little fists and so brown and ruddy near the pale pink skin of the newest member of the family.

"Well, I'll be! I'm a grandpa!" Jeff smiled proudly.

"Ain't he something!" Chad remarked in awe. "Kind of looks like his pa." He looked a bit nervously at the Morgans. "Doesn't he?"

Jeff looked at the thick black hair and the stubborn little chin, evident already. The babe began to fuss, looking for food. His patience was short and in moments he let out a hearty howl.

Jeff turned to Chad and laughed. "He's just like him!"

"Wait until I tell Sarah!" Chad chuckled. "Holy cow! Sarah! I better get going or she'll chew my rump for being gone so long!" He gathered his hat and headed for the door. "She'll swear I was at Roxy's all this time!" He grinned.

Red watched the somewhat bedraggled young man leave with a shake of her head and a chuckle. Letting her eyes fall on her squalling bundle, her eyes softened. "I better get you some sugar-water and we'll let your mama sleep a while." Handing the child to Jeff while she prepared his first meal, she offered a silent prayer of thanks for his safe arrival.

Jeff took the child and felt great pride well up in him for his daughter and her child. Her child! It suddenly was nineteen years earlier and he was looking upon the face of his child. He felt he was immortal for a time as he thought of the generations to come from his loins. "We did a good job after all, Jennifer," he whispered. Red came near with a cup and a soft cloth with which to feed the babe and she placed her hand on Jeff's shoulder. He looked at her and smiled lovingly. "Do you think you'll mind sleepin' with an old grandfather?"

"Oh, I think I can handle it." She smiled back and pressed a kiss to his brow. "But not until I feed this lad."

The sounds of morning reached Jess and she stirred. She felt strangely light and free as her hands slid down over her flattened stomach. A smile played at her lips as she thought about her son. Looking about the room, she wondered where he was. She was about to rise and seek him out when Red peeked in, saw her awake, and entered with a satisfied grin.

"So you're awake. Yer son has been fussin' over an hour for his breakfast and I need ta get ya washed up 'fore him and his grandpa can come in."

They carried on light conversation as Jess was
bathed and dressed in a clean gown, and settled back
in bed. She was amazed how quickly she felt tired
with so little effort.

"Don't worry none, honey. You'll get yer strength
back right fast. You'll have ta if ya want ta keep up
with the lad." Red smiled. She walked to the door
and pulled it open. "Okay, Grandpa, bring in 'is
lordship."

Jessie smiled radiantly at the sight of her father
and her son. The exquisite wonder of the newborn
in the arms of her graying father filled her with tre-
mendous awe and pride. She lifted her own arms to
seek the small child. Jeff carefully deposited his burden where he knew the child would find all the love
he could want in his lifetime.

Gently drawing back the blanket, Jessica looked
upon her son. His little face was wrinkled in preparation for fussing as his tiny fist brushed his seeking mouth.

"So, you're hungry." She smiled shyly and
opened her gown to accomplish her first act of
motherhood. As the child found the source of
nourishment he was seeking, Jessie gasped. "My
goodness! He's . . . he's certainly a strong lad!"

Red laughed lovingly at the beautiful picture before her. A tiny pink infant pressed to the creamy
ivory skin of his mother's breast.

"I . . . I never had a child of me own, lass." Red
sniffled. "But I feel like yer me own."

Tears glistened in Jessica's eyes as Jeff slid his arm
about his wife. "We're all family, my love, and nobody will ever say any different."

Nodding, Red regained her festive air and sat beside Jess. "Didn't take him long ta figure out where
the food is, did it?"

Shaking her head with a giggle, Jessie traced the
tiny cheek. "He most surely knows what he wants
already. He's just like his . . ." Stiffening slightly at

what she was about to say, Jess felt the heat of a blush suffuse her face.

Red took her hand and patted it. "He is the father, Jess. You can't deny it, nor can ya pretend he was no part of this." She laid her hand on the baby's legs.

"You're right, Red." Jessie chewed at her lower lip for a brief moment. Then, with a deep sigh, she smiled at her son. "You're just like your father." She spoke softly, saddened that the man she loved, would always love, could not be standing there, admiring his own son as a father should.

"What'll you name him, honey?" Jeff asked, hoping to change the darker mood that was settling in.

Jessie's lip quivered and her brow knit. "Hmm, let me think." Her thoughts traversed time to a day in the mountains with Steve. He spoke of his parents with love and admiration that day. Matt and Lucy Kincaid shared much and together created an empire and bestowed all their love on each other and their son. Since this was a child that descended from that love, it seemed appropriate he bear the name of his sire's sire, since he'd never have the family name.

Jess moved her now-sleeping son and his bowed lips continued to suckle. He stirred as she refastened her gown and his eyes fluttered as he settled snugly back into her arms.

"I'll call him Jeffrey Matthew Morgan," she announced, pressing a kiss to his brow, "after his grandfathers."

"Red, why don't you take Matt to his cradle," Jeff asked and sat next to Jess as Red gathered the child, smiled understandingly to her husband, and left the room, cooing to the baby lovingly.

Jeff took his daughter's hand and patted it. "You have a fine son and I thank you for his name, but having two Jeffs will only be confusin', so let's make it Matthew Jeffrey. I know Matt would be as pleased as I am."

A tear fell from Jessie's eyes. "I love you, Papa."

"And I love you, Jess." He rose and drew the quilt to her shoulders. "Now, you get some rest."

"You sure did a fine job, honey." Roxy settled on the step next to Jessie. "He's a real doll, that one. I bet you have a hard time keepin' Sarah away, huh?" Jess nodded with a grin. "I swear—" Roxy smiled. "—he's the prettiest babe I ever saw, 'cept for my Becky, of course." She chuckled.

Jess smiled brightly and agreed. "Yes, he is beautiful, isn't he?" She looked over the still-bleak landscape. "And he's so good. All he does is smile and gurgle." She reflected on her son and stared down at her hands. "I love him so much, Roxy."

Roxy pushed at the bun at her neck. She had shed the brassy facade of the saloon and altered her appearance to one of sedate respectability since first laying eyes on the new arrival. She had taken to spending less time at the saloon and more at her newest enterprise, one that took everyone, especially herself, by surprise.

It began with the death of a widow in town. She had had two small sons and no one to take them in upon her death. Driven by a need to protect these children, Roxy bought an empty warehouse building, hired a reliable housekeeper, and proceeded to convert all of it into an orphanage. Only a select few knew where the money came from and Roxy was deeply pleased that her best friend greatly approved. Her main worry now was Jessie, and her future happiness.

"What ya gonna do now, honey?" Roxy asked with sincere interest.

"Do? What do you mean, do?" Jess fidgeted with her skirt. "I'm going to raise my son, that's what!"

Roxy half-turned and clutched at Jessie's hands.

"Look, honey, I'm kind of responsible for what's happened with you and Steve, so—"

"You!" Jess laughed. "Oh, Roxy. Between you and Chad and Papa, I have more people defending me than Richmond did from Sherman." She faced her friend. "Look, I'm a big girl. Whatever happened with . . . with Steve and me, well, it was between him and me. No one is at fault."

"But I—"

"No one!" Jess emphasized.

"Okay, so I'm not responsible, but I am your friend and, as that, I want to know how you're gonna support your boy."

"It's too soon for me to return to work yet, Roxy. It's only been a month and I . . . I don't think I have the stamina."

"Hell! I ain't talkin' about your comin' back to the saloon! I'm talkin' about the future! You can't keep stayin' here no matter what Red and your pa say. It ain't fair to Red."

That same thought plagued Jessie of late. Windy Creek was not her home anymore. Red deserved to rule it as her domain, not share it. "You're right, Roxy. I do need to make plans, but I don't know what to do."

"You could still work for me." Roxy smiled. "At the home, if you want." She examined Jessie's thoughtful face. "You could have room and board as part of your wages." Trying to enhance her proposition, she added, "There's five kids there now, you know."

"Ah, Roxy, I don't know if I should." Jess stood and walked several paces into the yard only to turn back to her friend. "What will people say, an unwed mother raising children?"

"Look, honey, these kids don't have any folks. Do you think they care about your problems when they'd have someone to love them?"

Chewing at her lip, Jess thought for a moment.

"All right, Roxy! You've got yourself a new employee!"

Roxy hugged her. "Good!" She felt she might yet help the lovely woman and atone for her own past sins at the same time. "You can start whenever you're ready."

Chapter 24

"I think this is my favorite part of the day."
Jess sighed as she sat before the stove mending clothes the children seemed to wear out daily.

"Mine, too," said Hilda, "especially once they're all asleep." She rocked gently and looked down at Matt. "He's sure growin' like a weed."

Jessica stopped sewing and smiled at the older woman. Hilda was tall and huskily built but she was as gentle as a spring breeze. She adored the children, being childless herself for years. Born of German immigrants, Hilda had married a man her parents thought to be a dedicated farmer, but she soon realized he was a dreamer, never content to stay in one place when unexplored lands lay over the hill. She followed him as he followed his rainbow, searching for the impossible dream. His wanderlust led them from Pennsylvania to California and finally to Wyoming where he died in a timber accident. All she had for her fifty-two years were the memories of four scattered graves of her children and a strong desire to mother every stray that came her way.

"Yes, it's hard to believe he's almost two months old. So much has happened in the last few weeks, I forget how much time is passing."

"That's good. You don't worry when you're bone-tired and busy." Hilda chuckled, for bone-tired they were.

Roxy supplied all the tangible things they needed, but doing all the laundry, cooking, and cleaning for five children, one infant, and two adults was a full-time job. They'd finished tilling a garden that afternoon and were ready to plant. Jess hoped some of the townspeople would come to their aid, but no one had lent them a hand so far except Sam and Chad, and, of course, her dear father. Not a morning went by in the two weeks she had been there that one or the other hadn't shown up with a hammer and saw or an ax to help them out.

The one-time warehouse had shed its abandoned, run-down appearance for one of a strong, secure home. It had taken yards of fabric to curtain the newly installed windows and days to take care of the installation of three wood stoves, a new staircase with a solid banister, and the numerous walls needed to divide the large storage area into usable rooms. Chad made a lift for hauling wood to the second floor and Sam had seen to a fenced area for the younger children, complete with a teeter-totter and a rope swing from the oak tree within its confines. Between the three men a huge stack of firewood filled a large old outbuilding and a small curing shed had been added. Two milk cows along with several chickens and a pig came from her father while Chad added three beef cattle to round out their livestock. With the garden, the little community would be nearly self-sufficient. Whatever else they needed, Roxy would see to it. Be it shoes for the children or flour for bread, she was there.

More than anything, Jess was thankful to Roxy for this chance. She had been right. Jess needed a greater purpose, a means of self-support and self-respect. It was obvious to Jessica that it would not be easy, but she was too busy to let it bother her greatly.

Jeff and Red had objected to her decision. However, after seeing her determination, there was no argument strong enough to dissuade her, and she packed up the personal items she and her son would need and bid farewell to Windy Creek. It hadn't been as difficult as she expected, nor had it been as easy as she would have wished to enter Lander.

As the daughter of a local rancher, she had been graciously accepted within the social circles, but as an unwed mother, polite courtesies were replaced with cool tolerance at best. After her first trip for supplies, Jess vowed she would never leave the home again. Hilda quietly came to her defense with a firm scolding of the offenders, but Jess refused to go back into town.

"I think you're right, Hilda. I can't say I lie awake nights wondering about my son's future or about . . ." Jess hesitated to continue for fear of old memories surfacing.

"About that stubborn fool of a man you're in love with?" Hilda finished.

"I don't love him!" Jessie replied, too fast to satisfy her companion.

"Oh, you can fool yourself, Jess, but you can't fool me. I've seen you look at the boy here with tears in your eyes and I've watched you stare off at the mountains longing for him. He is in those mountains, isn't he?"

"I . . . I'm only thinking that it's nearly spring and he'll . . . he'll be getting home soon." Jess dumped the mended shirt on the pile yet to do beside her and stood. She twisted her hands as she paced about the small parlor.

"You're a liar, girl." Hilda spoke gently. "Worst of all, you're lying to yourself, and that makes you a hypocrite of the worst kind."

Jessie faced her in angry defiance and saw the sincere concern on Hilda's face. A frown turned to a grin and both women began to laugh.

"Where did you get so clever, Hilda?" Jess asked at last.

"You can't live over fifty years and not pick up a thing or two."

"Well, just so you don't think poorly of me." Jess sobered. "You're right. I do love the stubborn fool but I swear I'll never—"

"Don't make promises you can't keep, Jess."

"But—"

"But nothing. If he comes for you, you'll go." Hilda lifted Matt from her lap and handed him to Jess. She looked down on his slumbering face. "You'll go and follow him to hell if that's where he takes you." Hilda squeezed Jessie's arm. "But you won't be the first foolish woman to do so." She smiled sadly. "That I can assure you."

Hilda bid her good night and left the parlor for her own room at the top of the stairs. Jessie checked the stove, turned down the lamps, and followed Hilda's example.

Moving to the rear of the first floor, Jessie entered her room just off the kitchen. The austere contents reminded her of a jail cell; it was, she mused, her own self-made prison. She really should fix it up a bit. Maybe if she had time tomorrow she would put some effort into it. But she was too tired to worry about it tonight.

Jess brought the teapot to the table, poured out two cups, and settled wearily into her chair across from Sarah.

"You look awfully tired, Jess," Sarah said after carefully searching her friend's face. She had lost the honey color of the summer sun and her hair was pulled severely back into a knot at her neck. Long strands escaped and lay limply about her shoulders. Dark smudges shadowed eyes that had lost their luster in the struggle of hard and lonely living.

"Oh, it's not so bad." Jess examined her reddened hands that belied her statement.

"But Jess, you're so beautiful. You shouldn't be working like a drudge! You should be dressed in fine clothes and . . . well, you ought to go out more!"

"Just what do you expect me to do, Sarah, set up a sign saying 'Eligible woman on the premises seeking escort'? Slightly used but still serviceable!" Jess said sarcastically.

Sarah sighed and sat back in her chair. "I'm sorry. I didn't mean to pry. It's just that I care about you and Matt. I don't want to see you spending your life trying to atone for some sin you think you've committed."

"It's not like that, Sarah!"

"Isn't it? Isn't it really, Jess?" Sarah asked. "You've blamed yourself from the start for what's happened between you and Steve." Jessie's lips quivered but Sarah wouldn't relent. "For God's sake, Jess! Steve has always been the most determined man I've ever known. You didn't stand a chance against him. He's a master, you're a novice. If anyone has to take the blame for this, it's him!"

Tears filled Jessie's eyes and she let them fall to her folded hands. "Don't you understand, Sarah? It's not a question of where the blame lies. It's where society places it. No matter who is responsible, I'm the one branded harlot. It may not be fair, but it is a fact."

"And here I am adding to your burden." Sarah laughed harshly at herself. "Forgive me, Jess."

A weak smile broke on Jessie's face. "Of course I forgive you. After all—" She gave a nervous shrug. "—I can ill afford to lose the few friends I have."

Just as they embraced with tears and smiles, a screeching flurry of fury with flying pigtails ran into the kitchen.

"Missy Jess! Missy Jess! Billy and Davey won't let me on the swing!"

Jess knelt solemnly before the smudged cherubic five-year-old Ellen, who had mysteriously appeared the second week after the orphanage opened. Wiping away her tears with the corner of her apron, Jess held out her arms and the child flew into them.

"So, they won't let you, huh? Well, you go tell those boys that they either let you share the swing or there will be no pie for them after dinner. Okay?"

Ellen nodded her blonde head vigorously and grinned as Jess stood and scooted Ellen toward the back door. Before Ellen departed, she spun about with a self-satisfied expression and grew quite haughty in her stance. "Damn men!" she stated, and fled with a giggle.

Jess turned to Sarah in surprise. "I think Roxy's been talking too much to that child!" She began to chuckle and Sarah burst into laughter.

An hour later Sarah was preparing to leave. "What are you going to do when he comes home?" she finally asked. The question had hung between them all afternoon.

"I don't really know, Sarah. I've thought about going back to St. Louis, but I'd sorely miss this place. Wyoming has gotten into my blood. I don't think I could bear not to see the mountains again. And there's Pa. I suppose I'll have to wait and see what the mighty Kincaid has planned. He may not even want to see me . . ." Her voice drifted off sadly. "And I don't know if I want to see him either."

Sarah read between the lines. "My God! You still love him!" She'd thought all the love had turned into its nearest emotion—pure hatred—but instead, it had grown deeper. And now there was the bond of the child.

"Don't be so surprised," Jess said drily. "It's been known to happen to foolish women."

Sarah set her hand on Jessie's arm. "When he learns of his son he'll—"

"No! He mustn't know! I . . . I couldn't bear it if he wanted me only because of his son or . . . or worse yet, if he wanted only Matt and not . . ." She began to weep.

"He's bound to find out, honey, but he won't hear

it from me or Chad. I promise you that," Sarah said consolingly as she looked at the sleeping son of her two best friends, and pledged silently to try somehow to unite this family.

Sarah sat curled up in a chair before the fireplace. Dinner had been quiet as she mulled over the day spent with Jessie, and Chad wisely refrained from any questions. He knew his wife would share her thoughts when she was ready.

Throwing another log on the fire, Chad sat on the floor at Sarah's feet and waited. Unconsciously, she placed her hand on his shoulder and let her fingers play with the hair that curled over his collar.

"We can't tell Steve about Matthew," she finally mumbled.

"What?" He turned to look at her thoughtfully.

"I promised Jess we wouldn't tell him."

"So what's the problem? I promised at Christmas and, even though I think it's silly, I won't break my word."

Sarah looked at her husband and tried to communicate her feelings. "I know it's silly. He'll find out soon enough but Jessie's afraid he'll want his son and not her." After a moment of silence, she added, "She still loves him, honey."

"What kind of rubbish is she thinking? My God, the man's insanely jealous and desperately in love for the first time in his life, and she thinks he doesn't want her!" Chad shook his head. "He chases her all over the countryside, drags her off like a captive bride, and she thinks he doesn't care! I think they're both crazy!" Chad started to laugh. "God! What a match, the mad baron and his witch!"

"Chad! What a terrible thing to call her!" Sarah protested.

"Her!" Chad pulled his wife down to the floor beside him. "Just like a woman!" he growled. "I can tear apart my best friend and she agrees, but let me call her friend anything unfavorable and she turns on me!'' He began to nip playfully at her ear.

"Stop it this minute, Chad Duncan!'' She struggled. "This is very serious!'' He tried to kiss her but she pushed him away. "Not now!'' Sarah squealed. At her husband's hurt little-boy pout, she relented somewhat. "Hear me out . . .'' She smiled provocatively. ". . . and maybe later.''

"All right,'' Chad agreed, and sat up. "I suppose I better listen or I'll never get you to see it my way tonight.'' He pulled her into his lap.

"No matter what we think about how they feel, I promised her we would keep her secret, and keep it we will.''

"Okay, but I still think he has the right to know. Besides, it won't be a secret long. Enough people know they were . . . well, close, and it isn't hard to figure who Matthew's father is.''

"I know that!'' Sarah retorted, then grew pensive.

"What do you have cooking in that wicked little mind of yours?'' Chad watched her chew her lip in thought. "Sarah?'' He knew she was planning something.

"I was just thinking how nice it would be if Steve and Jess could get together. They'd be such a beautiful family and you know how wonderful it would be for Steve to have his son and . . . and wife at the K-D.''

"Jess won't marry him, remember? We are dealing with two very proud, very stubborn people.''

"Oh, Chad! So you'll help me!'' Sarah hugged him.

"I never said that!'' He pulled away, perplexed by her reasoning.

"You said 'we.' '' She had jumped on the word and turned it to her advantage.

"Ah, hell! All right, honey, what's your plan?'' He was resigned to helping whether he wanted to or not, for he really had no choice in the end.

Smiling widely, Sarah expounded on her idea. "What's the easiest way to get Steve to do something?" Before he could reply she answered her own question. "Tell him not to!"

Chad mulled over her words and a grin started to form. "Well, I'll be! You're right! I've never met a more perverse man. When you tell him he can't—he does!" Chad pulled Sarah into his arms. "And what about Jessica? How do we manipulate her?"

"We won't have to if Steve is smart enough to keep her this time. Remember, Chad, she loves him."

As if that was supposed to be the answer to all their problems. Chad just nodded his head. He wasn't sure if Sarah's plan would work, but it was the best chance they had.

McKinley stood some distance off and smiled as he saw the smoke from the cabin. Steve had kept his word and not tried to leave in the dead of winter, but Mac continued to check at irregular times just in case. What he would have done if Steve departed, he didn't know, and he was pleased he didn't have to find out. That he would be leaving soon was evident in the pile of gear growing near the door. Oh, well, perhaps it was time for him and the lass to meet, over their child.

Moving on, Mac grinned to himself as he gave some thought to Jessica Morgan. She was a fine lass and she should have her wee one by now. It would be a boy, he was sure. It would be poetic justice though if he had a daughter, Mac mused. Thunderous laughter echoed through the canyon when he released his humorous opinion of such a situation. Kincaid defending a lass instead of pursuing one would be choice.

"I might just meander down that way sometime," he said aloud. "Might be real interestin' ta see if the little lady will put up with that arrogant, overbearin' pup!"

* * *

Steve scratched at the heavy beard that covered his face, then slid his fingers through hair that hung nearly to his shoulders. It would feel good to bathe and shave off his extra growth, he thought. He'd allowed himself to grow slovenly as he whiled away the many days until he could get home.

The passing months had been a time of many transitions for him. The fury of discovering Jessie had fled led to a time of intense anger and bitterness directed mostly at McKinley. As days became weeks, melancholy took hold. Hours were spent remembering every word, each kiss they shared. That was the most difficult time, for he ached for her and cursed her alternately. He realized the only way he could mentally survive the winter was to replace his memories with hard work and physical fatigue.

He drove himself then. He hunted for furs but the senseless slaughter appalled him. He had no use for the money the furs would bring nor the meat that would be left to rot. Instead, he walked and climbed and scoured every trail that was passable. He toyed with the idea of trying to leave his mountain prison and was preparing for the rigorous attempt when he happened upon a small herd of sheep. He sat and watched them cautiously pick their way across a hillside when a rumbling sound caught his attention.

His eyes were drawn to what looked like a boiling white dust cloud advancing toward the sheep and catching them as they stood frozen with fear. In a moment they were gone, caught in the frenzy of the awesome avalanche. Before he could react, it was over. The rumbling stopped. Only small airborne flurries blew up along the edges and filled the small canyon below. What had been a lovely, serene landscape now lay scarred and despoiled by its own violence.

Mac was right. He could have just as easily been snuffed out if he'd risked traveling through these treacherous guardians of the West. But his entrapment was coming to an end, and he wouldn't have to wait much longer. Spring was in the air. He could smell it in the grasses pushing through the melting snow. He could see it in the occasional newborn animal he found bedded in some private spot. He could feel it in the warming breezes. But more than all that, he could sense it like a buck senses the time to find a mate.

It was time to return to the K-D and find out if he had lost Jessie forever. The thought of spending his life without her was a very bleak one indeed. A shiver ran through him as he imagined her gone from the dream he spun of late. He had created a euphoric world where Jessie was sharing his home, his world, and his bed. She had to be there. She had to want him as desperately as he wanted her.

Damn her! She was the most stubborn female he had ever met, he thought, wanting more than ever to leave his prison for the warmth of her arms. She had disrupted his life from the start. She'd driven him mad with fury and desire. Why, she'd . . . He began to chuckle. What an ass he had been! Why, it had been his own desires that had made him seek her out! He'd been the one to choose her. She never ran after him, only away until he taught her about love and lust! All the time he'd blamed her, it was his own foolishness that caused him all this anguish.

If only he would have . . . ah, hell! What difference would it make now, he thought. He might have already lost his chance for true happiness, but maybe it wasn't too late. Perhaps he could find her and humble himself enough to win her.

Throwing the last of his supplies into a pile, Steve smiled weakly. This would be the last night he would spend here. He went to the opened door and braced his hands on the overhead frame. He'd told her once and only once that he loved her. In the heat of passion it had been what she wanted to hear, yet she had fallen asleep before he uttered the words. The time for him had come to analyze his rash, unheard statement. Perhaps it was the truth. Maybe, just maybe, he couldn't recognize love for a woman, never having loved one before.

His love had gone to his parents in his youth. He had transferred it to the K-D and the land as he reached manhood. Then, she came into his life. He never meant for emotions to enter into their relationship, but they had. Everything seemed to pale unless she was there to share it. Was that what love was all about?

"Tomorrow, Jessie," he said to the mountains. "Tomorrow I'm coming home." He closed his eyes and offered a prayer. "Be there. Dear God, please let her be there."

Chapter 25

It was near midnight when Steve rode into the yard at the K-D. The house was dark and barely visible in the moonless night. Dismounting near the barn, he led his steed within its walls. A lone lantern burned to light his way. He could hear a muffled snoring in the tack room and grinned wearily at the thought of young Willy curled snugly in his cot. As quietly as possible, Steve unsaddled his horse, rubbed it down, and led him to a stall without disturbing the lad.

Leaving most of his gear stashed in the barn, Steve lifted his saddlebags over his shoulder and strode to the back of the house. If he wanted a bath at this hour, it would have to be in the kitchen. He wasn't about to haul the tub and water up to his room in the middle of the night. Finding the stove banked down he added a few logs and soon chased the chill from the room. He lit a lamp and rummaged for something to eat, certain that Red must have left something about. Locating some cookies, he downed an even dozen while drawing the tub from the corner, placing it near the fire, and pumping buckets of cold well water.

A hot bath was preferable but he didn't want to spend the whole night heating water. He was tired from his arduous journey home. What had taken two days in the fall with Jessie had taken five to return.

Spring left the streams swollen with runoff and the ground was marshy in some areas and still snow-covered in others. Each mile brought its own problems and he was able to allow himself to relax only when he left the mountains behind him.

Steve was rifling through the contents of a cupboard in search of soap when he heard an ear-shattering scream that brought him about with a crash of cookware.

"Christ, Sarah!" he growled out. "You scared the hell out of me with that banshee cry!"

"Steve!" she cried, and ran to embrace him. Pulling up short, she wrinkled her nose and grimaced. "My God! Haven't you bathed all winter?" He began to laugh at her expression of distaste and she swatted at him. "Why didn't you let us know you were coming—or at least have the decency to come home in the daylight? I thought you were a bear or . . . or some kind of wild creature!"

"What the hell's goin' on out—Steve! You son of a . . ." Chad grinned at his friend as he entered the kitchen, fastening his pants. "I should have known all that ruckus could be nothing less than the master returning home."

"Shall I get you something to eat?" Sarah asked as the two men shook hands in greeting.

"Not unless you're prepared to watch me shed some of this filth." He grinned through his beard as he pulled off his heavy coat and began to unbutton his shirt.

"Well, if you're not hungry," she said, "I'll go back to bed. You coming, Chad?"

"No, you go ahead, honey. I'll sit with Steve a spell," he replied, straddling a chair.

"Okay." She turned to Steve and smiled. "I'm glad you're home safe, Steve. Real glad."

"I'm glad to be home." He rubbed the back of his neck. "It's been a damned long winter."

Sarah looked at Chad and winked. "Then I'll say good-night."

After a moment, Steve stepped into the tub. "The only one I didn't manage to wake tonight was Red." He eased into the water. "Damn, but this is cold!" He sucked air through his clenched teeth and settled into the cool water.

"You didn't wake her because she isn't here." He saw Steve's raised brow and related the romantic saga of Red and Jeff. "So, he gained a wife and you lost a housekeeper."

Steve rubbed soap up his arm and across his chest, mulling over Chad's words. So Red had married Jeff. He rather suspected they would wed, but where then was Jessie? He couldn't imagine the three of them in that small house. She might have gone back to St. Louis after all. There was only one way to find out and that was to ask.

"I'm real happy for them. About time they had someone for themselves." He dipped his head into the water and spent a few minutes alternately washing and rinsing his hair. Chad handed him scissors upon request and Steve chopped away most of the growth on his face while they spoke about the ranch and what the winter at the K-D had been like. Rising out of the water, Steve donned a robe Chad had fetched for him and took a cup of hot tea he offered him. He grimaced at the taste until Chad produced a whiskey bottle and splashed a generous amount into their cups.

"Um, that's better." Steve sighed as he sat near the stove to try and get some warmth back into his body. As he absorbed the heat from the stove and the whiskey, he relaxed and grew more tired. He lowered his guard and began to think about Jessie.

Chad sat quietly watching and waiting. He wasn't about to offer any information. If his stubborn friend could remain silent about his woman, so could he. He grinned into his drink when Steve began to fish for answers.

"I guess it was a tough winter for Jeff with two women in the house."

"No, not really. It had its moments—" Chad thought of Matt's birth. "—but all in all it ended up okay."

"I take it they're all happy, the two of them, I mean." He kept staring at the cup in his hands.

"Yeah, they are." Chad could see the anxiety building on Steve's face. He knew he wanted him to give out the information he was so ineptly seeking without a direct question, but Chad held his tongue, trying to force Steve to admit his concern and interest. Finally, unable to delay any longer, Steve asked.

"Where is she, Chad?"

"I wondered how long it would take you to get around to her." Chad grinned. He could see that Steve was in no mood for games. "She's at Roxy's new place. She working real hard at—"

"Damn!" Steve pounded the table with a clenched fist. "I thought she might have gone back East, but Roxy's!"

"Now wait a minute, Steve," Chad demanded. "It's not like you're thinking."

"Oh, I know exactly what it's like!" He rose and paced the kitchen. "She may have been a virgin when I first took her but she learned fast, real fast!"

"Hold it, Steve. I can't let you slander her that way. She never asked you to use her the way you did and she's made the best of a bad situation." Chad was defending Jessie, knowing all the facts, but he'd forgotten that Steve was in the dark about too many things.

"Oh, don't worry, I won't bother to mention her again. I spent all winter worried about her but she's like a cat. She landed on her feet and played me the fool at the last." He headed for the stairs. "I'm going to bed," he announced, to close their conversation.

"Steve, wait! You don't understand!" Chad grabbed his arm to stop him.

"I understand plenty." He pulled his arm free. "Good night, Chad."

Filling his cup with more whiskey, Chad sat and pondered the whole mess. What right did Steve have to be angry with Jess? Why was he so upset about her working herself sick at the . . . of course! Steve hadn't let him explain so he didn't know. He thought she was at the saloon! He wasn't aware of Roxy's other place. He was jealous! Insanely and unequivocally jealous! Chuckling to himself, Chad banked the stove, turned down the lamp, and went upstairs.

Sarah would be waiting to find out what happened. They could both enjoy this misunderstanding together. He'd let Steve stew tonight and clear it all up in the morning.

Steve's bed could attest to the fact that the night had been a restless one. Blankets were strewn about and his pillows were wadded and punched into balls. He had fallen asleep only mere hours before dawn and woke with gravelly eyes and a dull headache to find a steaming pitcher of water on his dresser. He smiled wearily at Sarah's thoughtfulness and threw his legs over the edge of the bed. He sat and stared at the floor, wishing he had stayed in his mountain retreat. There, at least, he could fabricate his homecoming into something worth looking forward to. As he sat in his room, the reality was hard to take.

Thoughts of Jessie, warm and willing, dissolved into a red haze when he imagined her in the arms of some saddle tramp or dusty cowboy. He groaned and forced himself to his feet. Pulling on his pants, he walked barefoot to the mirror and ran his hand over his chin. Gazing at his image he looked into his dark eyes. God help him, but he still wanted her. Gripping the dresser's edge he breathed deeply to quell the urges welling up within him. He had been man enough to tackle the mountains and survive.

He'd ridden the plains, crossed burning deserts, and forded raging rivers. That he stood there could attest to the odds he had beaten. He couldn't, he wouldn't let this green-eyed vixen be his downfall. He wouldn't give her the satisfaction of seeing him crawl to her, not after what she had become.

Lathering his face, he set his mind to focus on shaving and nothing else. If he could discipline himself to go from one chore to another, maybe he could forget her in time. Maybe.

"So he thinks she's in the brothel, does he?" Red chuckled. "Well, I hope that thought is giving him a lot of pain. Would serve him right for thinkin' such a thing about our Jess! We should set him straight in no uncertain terms."

"Yes, we should, but you know Steve. Once he gets something in his head it isn't easy to turn him around." Sarah went to the work counter and started another batch of bread for the hands.

Red joined her to help. "Imagine what he'd say if he knew what she was really doin'?"

"First, he'd be too cocky to handle, thinking he still had control over her." Sarah strutted about. "Then—" She clutched at her heart in mock dread. "—he'd race off to save her from a fate worse than death, just to have her come here and cook and clean for him!" They laughed.

"Ya know, I think her working so hard really would upset him though. She's doing too much for her own good, and her just gettin' back on her feet. Roxy came out ta see us yesterday and told us that she's near exhaustion but she won't quit." Red took a sip of coffee. "Jeff wanted ta haul her home but I told him that it's her life. She's as stubborn as Steve in a lot of ways."

"Maybe we should tell him, Red. Perhaps he can stop her before she kills herself caring for all those children. We don't have to reveal Roxy's secret about owning the place and, even if we did, I know Steve wouldn't let her down. It's a great thing she's doing with that orphanage."

"A man could starve to death around here with you two and your talking!" Steve roared playfully as he entered the kitchen.

"Steve!" Red cried, and ran to embrace her one-time charge. "When you take off for a while, you take off! Six months! A body could worry themselves ta death over you, if ya weren't such a rogue!"

"How are ya, me darlin'?" Steve imitated her brogue. He stepped back and shook his head. "I hear you've been unfaithful to me. I go off on a little trip and come home to find you all married. You've broken my heart, Red." He grinned and asked, "Are you happy?"

"You have no heart," she teased, "and aye, I'm very happy. Jeff's a good man and I love him dearly, but don't ya go tellin' him I said so." She shook her finger at him. "I'll only deny it. I wouldn't be able ta live with him if he gets too sure of himself!" She looked over the handsome young man and thought he looked older. And, despite the smiles, something was troubling him.

"Morning, Sarah," he called over Red's shoulder. "Could you do me a favor and give me a haircut? I feel like if I go much longer, I'll have to go to White Antelope's camp or don a dress to accommodate my locks, and I'm not inclined to do either at the moment," he joked good-naturedly.

Sarah was confused. Chad had told her about their conversation the night before. He was angry and troubled then, and his bed attested to a restless night. Something wasn't right but she couldn't figure out what it was.

"Sure, Steve. Sit down and have some coffee. I'll be right with you."

Climbing into bed that night, Steve smiled into the darkness. He spent the day making up for some of his absence and catching up on what had transpired. His spirits were high as he sped through the day, anxiously awaiting the next. Chad tried to talk to him but Steve managed to avoid him each time. He had decided what to do. It had come to him that morning.

Not one to eavesdrop, he drew up short at the bottom of the stairs when he heard Sarah and Red talking about himself and Jess. A bit perplexed at what they were saying, he neared the door but stayed out of sight. At first, he was lost, not hearing their earlier conversation, but as they progressed, he realized that Jessie was not working in the saloon, but in some orphanage of Roxy's! How and why it had all come about, he didn't know but he did know Jessie was alone, and had been alone since leaving him. Although he was deeply concerned about her welfare, he was strangely content that she had chosen no other man. It marked her as his in his mind and meant they might well pick up where they had left off. Surely she wasn't still angry about the events of the fall. If anything, the memories should have her missing him as badly as he missed her.

"Not tonight, my sweet Jessica, but soon, very soon."

She was exhausted when she fell into bed and was immediately asleep. Her nights had been dreamless for a long time and she assumed it was fatigue that swept them away, but the same was not true this night.

She was in the cabin and could hear the winds embracing the small house as they swirled about the mountain face. Nestled beneath a pile of soft quilts, she looked at the outline advancing toward her in the semidarkness. Flames leaped high behind him and added to the mystery. As he knelt beside her, she pulled her arms free of the blankets and set her hands to his strong, warm chest. Her senses reeled and she felt the heat of him course down her arms to race to her female parts. She moaned as he laid his lips on her bare flesh and nibbled at her neck and ear. Her fingers entwined in his ebony hair and she called out to him. She needed him, wanted him, and loved him desperately.

"Soon, very soon," he breathed huskily against her hair.

Jerking herself awake, Jess sat up. She gulped great mouthfuls of air, trying to calm herself. She heard him! He spoke in her dream but it was real! Slowly, she left her bed and went to check on her son. He slept quietly, blissfully unaware of his mother's fears. She lovingly covered the little arm thrown clear of the blankets, then left the room.

Walking quietly on bare feet to the back door, she opened it and stepped out into the night. There was no moon and the stars competed for dominance in the dark sky. The air was cool but not uncomfortably so.

He was home. She didn't know how she knew, but she did. She could sense it. There was an energy in the air that only Steve Kincaid could generate. It flowed over the miles between them and touched her, caressed her, as if he was there beside her.

"So, you made it back," she whispered to the night. "And my troubles begin in earnest." Would he come or stay away? Could she bear it either way? "Damn you, Kincaid! If it wasn't for you, I'd be content now!" she said angrily. "I'd be free of haunted dreams and a tormented heart! I never would have . . ." Her voice trailed off at the sound of her son fussing. She spun about and entered their room.

Gathering Matthew into her arms, she crooned soothingly to him and he quieted. "God forgive me, my little darling. If not for Steve Kincaid, I'd not have you, and you are my life." She kissed his small brow.

She sat in a rocker and opened her nightgown to give her child the nourishment he sought. As he fed, she laid her head back and closed her eyes. "For

him, I thank you, Steve." She sighed. "And because of him, God help me, I still love you."

A thunderous pounding at the back door brought
Jessie quickly to it. Throwing it open, she sighed
with relief. "Sam! You scared me with that racket!"
She smiled and motioned him in. "Whatever brings
you out here so urgently?"

"Miss Roxy done sent me, Miss Jess." Sam
clutched his hat and worried the brim.

"Is something wrong? Does she need me?" Jessie
reached for her shawl on a peg near the door.

"No, Miss Jess. She ain't needin' ya and nothin's
wrong, but she got a message fo ya." He shuffled
about nervously.

"Well, what is it?" Jess grew anxious. "My father?"

Sam shook his head. "No, miss. It's Mista Kincaid."

Jess stiffened. "What about Mr. Kincaid?" she
asked breathlessly, feeling as though she had been
running a great distance.

"He's in town, Miss Jess. He's lookin' fo ya. Miss
Roxy, she done seen him and sent me ta tell ya. She
said that if'n ya wants ta go, she'd understand." He
inhaled deeply when he realized he'd relayed the
entire message and his errand was over.

"Thank you, Sam." Jessie went back to peeling
apples, needing a mundane chore to occupy her
mind for a moment. "Sam," she called as he made
for the door, "t-tell Roxy I thank her for the warning, but I'm not running, not yet." She looked at
the concern on the black man's face. "I mean it,
Sam. You tell her."

He nodded and left Jessie to her thoughts.

"Ow!" Jess cried as she nicked her finger with the
paring knife for the second time in ten minutes.

"What's wrong with you, girl? I've never seen you
so jumpy." Hilda looked at the cut and pronounced

it a minor one. She wrapped it with a small strip of cloth and shook her head. "You going to tell me what's gotten you so shook?"

Jessie's eyes filled and her lip quivered. "Steve's back, and . . . and he's looking for me." Jess looked away from Hilda.

"So what's the problem? You wanted him to come for you, didn't you?" She half-grinned.

"Well, yes and . . . and no. I'm afraid he might know about Matthew and he's after him."

"Balderdash!" Hilda retorted and Jess jerked about, startled by her vehemence. "If he wanted you enough to get you pregnant the first time, he'll want you enough to do it again."

"Hilda!" Jessie blushed. "How can you say such a thing?"

" 'Cause it's true, only you're too scared of your feelings to admit it, that's how!"

Jess released a quivering sigh. "Perhaps you're right. Maybe I am afraid of how I feel." She stuck the knife into an apple and set the fruit bowl aside. "You *are* right." She stood and turned to Hilda. "I know there's nothing he can do to me. He has no legal claim on me or Matthew, but somehow, that makes it worse. You see, I love him, but I won't be his chattel, and that's all he really wants—to own me, not to love me. I should have realized that sooner. It can't work for us. We both want different things from our relationship. I just have to forget how I feel and make a life for my son and me."

These thoughts carried with them a sense of calm. She sat back down to finish the apples, and the morning passed swiftly. Jess remained occupied with the children for a while then decided to exert herself on some heavy cleaning. She heated water and pushed all the kitchen furniture to one side of the room. Her energy was at its peak with her new-found knowledge of how she felt and where it was leading her.

"You're in for a good scrubbing," she said to the

floor. "I need to vent and you're where I'll do it."
Grabbing a brush, she began to apply herself. Down
on her knees, she began to make small circles of soap
across the floor. It became an arduous task as the
day heated up. Perspiration rolled off her brow and
her hair became loose from its pins and hung in long
strands.

Sitting back on her heels halfway through, she
wiped her brow with her rolled-up sleeves. She
could feel the moisture between her breasts and
down the center of her back as she alternately
scrubbed and rubbed at the dull ache in her spine.
Her energy was spent and the chore still unfinished.
Resolved to continue, Jessie dipped the brush into
the bucket and began anew. She was so busy with
the tedious chore that she didn't hear the door open.

"Hello, Jessie."

Chapter 26

The deep baritone filled the room and turned Jessie's limbs to water. She dropped the brush and gripped her apron in her lap, closing her eyes and swaying. God! He has come, she thought. She opened her eyes to find him standing directly in front of her. She let herself look up, all the way up to the towering black-clad giant before her. He offered her his hand and she hesitated to take it.

"Take my hand, Jess," he ordered deeply, drawing her to her feet. He wanted to pull her into his arms, to kiss her and hold her, but he restrained himself. "How are you, honey?" He flashed her a devastating smile and her fears returned. With the fear came anger.

"Don't call me that!" she flared, pulling her hand from his. She took a deep breath and tried to calm herself. "I'm . . . I'm fine, and . . . and you?"

He peered from beneath half-closed lashes. "As well as can be expected." He was seducing her with every word, every action.

Steeling herself, she asked if he wanted coffee and he accepted, settling his tall frame into a chair.

Jessica fumbled with the pot and spilled some before finally getting the two cups poured. Her hands shook as she set the cups on the edge of the table and, somehow, she managed to knock one across Steve's lap.

"Oh!" She pressed her hands to her cheeks. "Oh, I'm . . . I'm sorry. I . . ." She grabbed a towel and began to brush at his thigh until his hand fell over hers. She froze and looked up to see him staring deeply into her eyes with his the dark color of desire.

"Come home with me, Jess." His voice was a husky whisper.

All the woman in her cried out yes! She wanted to go with him, to love him and share her life with him. It would be so easy to go. All she would have to do was say yes, to lean against him and let him know of her hunger and her love.

"I . . . I need to think. So much has happened." She pulled her hand from beneath his and stood. Stepping back, she said, "There's the . . . the children and . . . and there's Hilda. They need . . . I . . . please, Steve," she begged, "give me some time." It was all happening too fast. She just couldn't fall back into the same trap.

Steve moved to stand before her. He looked down on her pale face and nodded. "Okay, honey. I'll come back tomorrow." He placed his fingers beneath her chin and drew her face to within inches of his own. "If you promise to be here."

"I'll be here, Steve. Where else can I go?" She closed her eyes and felt a feathery kiss touch her lips. Her heart was pounding and she suddenly felt very much alive. After all those months of lassitude, she was reborn in a single moment.

Steve sensed her desires and the force between them. He could afford to be magnanimous, he thought. After all, she would be his again, and soon.

"Noon, tomorrow." His fingers gently tapped her chin. "Be ready." He was gone as quickly as he had come. Jess stood transfixed, unable to move or even to think beyond that gentle kiss.

"Must have been your man," Hilda announced as she entered from the yard.

"What? Oh, yes. Yes, that was Steve." Jess

walked to the opened portal and watched him ride off.

"He's a right good-looking hombre." Hilda chuckled. "No wonder you're between a rock and a hard place on what to do." She let Jess watch until she knew she could no longer see him. "You going?"

Jess sighed. "I don't know, Hilda. He's sure I will, but I just don't know."

"Well, if you ask me . . ." She looked on as Jess moved trancelike to a chair. ". . . but then, you're not asking me, are you, honey?"

Jessie didn't reply. She merely went back to her knees and continued to scrub the floor. She wasn't even aware that Hilda had left her. Her own thoughts blocked out everything.

All her convictions, all her fears and worries had flown in his presence. He hadn't mentioned love or marriage, he merely said "Come" and she nearly had. It was the shock of seeing him, she argued with herself. Nothing had prepared her for the sound of his voice, the touch of his hand. All the hurts blew away like dust in the wind, but calm had returned. She promised to be there the next day, but she hadn't promised to go with him.

Suddenly, she needed to talk to Roxy. She had some questions only Roxy could answer. She jumped to her feet. "Hilda, I have to go see Roxy. Could you watch Matthew while I'm gone? I won't be long."

"Sure, Jess." Hilda smiled. "You need to get away anyhow. Go get cleaned up and scat."

Jess nodded with a smile and went to change.

If Jessie had watched Steve a moment longer, she would have seen him turn about and ride back toward town. It seemed he thought only Roxy could clarify some of the doubts and questions he had.

He found Sam washing the huge mirror above the glasses, and bid him to tell Roxy he wanted to see her. Walking around behind the bar, Steve helped himself to a bottle, poured out a generous amount, and downed it in one swallow. He'd poured another when Roxy entered. With the glass halfway to his lips, he stopped to stare at the new Roxy.

"Well, what's happened to you?" He gestured at her conservative attire.

"I might say the same," Roxy replied. "I've never known you to down good whiskey like water."

"Yeah, well, I just saw Jessie and I didn't think much of what I saw." He gripped the bottle at its neck and moved to a table. Filling his glass again, he sat over it. "How long's she been there?" he asked.

"Only a few weeks." Roxy was pleased with his concern but she was inclined to let him stew. "Why?"

"She looked so damned tired," he mused. "Why'd she go there in the first place?"

"Where else should she have gone? St. Louis? Would you have preferred that?"

"Hell, no!" His temper flared.

"Then be happy she decided to help . . . to work there. She could have come here and worked for me."

"Cut the playacting, Roxy. I know that place is yours." He wasn't in the mood for polite conversation.

Roxy rubbed her hand across the back of her neck. "Okay, so you know." She looked at him pleadingly. "As a friend, I'm asking you not to let it go any further. This town will let me run this place because of what they think I am and that's okay, but they wouldn't tolerate me helping those kids." Her face looked sad. "They didn't let me raise my own."

Steve was touched by her sincerity and patted her hand in a gesture of compassion. "I think they'd be more understanding and appreciative than you think, Roxy. It's a fine thing you're doing. Nonetheless, I won't tell anyone if you don't want me to."

"Thanks, Steve." She released her held breath.
"It'll be better that way."

He nodded and sipped his drink. "Has she been
ill or something?" he asked, returning to the object
of his visit.

"She, ah . . . she was down for a while a few
months back, but she'll be okay." She could sense
how deeply troubled he was. "You want me to talk
to her, tell her to ease up?"

"That won't be necessary. I'm taking her out to
the K-D tomorrow. I'll see she's cared for there."

Roxy was surprised and didn't bother to conceal
it. "She told you she'd go?"

"Not exactly." He grinned and rubbed a thumb
across his chin. "But she did promise not to run
away again. That's some progress."

"Yeah, but it could mean she won't go with you
to the K-D either. She might just sit tight where she
is." Jess had obviously not told Steve about young
Matthew or he wouldn't be sitting here so coolly,
she thought.

"I don't think so."

"You're up to something, my friend. I can read
that look and it spells trouble for someone." Roxy
stood and smoothed down her skirt. "That someone
better not be Jessie," she warned. "A lot of people
close to her have put up with your games long
enough. Don't press your luck, Steve." She watched
his brow raise mockingly. "Consider that a friendly
warning, one you'd be wise to heed."

She would have pressed the point, but Sam called
to her and she went toward her private rooms. Before entering she turned to Steve. "Remember what
I said."

Roxy shook her head and chuckled when she went
into her parlor to greet her other guest. "Jessie,"
she said, smiling, "what can I do for you?" It
pleased Roxy that both factions had come to her to
talk. She felt very close to each of them and still

partially responsible for their problems. The fact that they were only a few yards apart from each other at the moment, yet miles apart in their thinking, also tickled her matchmaking instincts.

"It's about Steve." Jess rose and paced as Roxy settled herself upon the sofa. "He was out to see me this morning." She dropped to her knees beside Roxy. "He wants me to go and stay at the K-D."

"And you want to go?" Roxy asked.

"Yes! No! Oh!" Jess moaned. "I don't know, Roxy." She sat on the floor and cradled her head in her arms. "What am I going to do? Part of me is afraid to go, afraid it's a passing thing with him." She looked up with tears brimming. "But part of me, the part that loves him so, wants to follow him anywhere."

Roxy brushed her fingers over Jessie's hair. "Does he know about Matthew?" Jessie shook her head sadly. "Then you can at least be sure it's you he wants."

Jess nodded. "Yes, he wants me, Roxy, only I keep thinking it's the chase he loves, not me." Jess drew up her knees and circled her arms about them. "When you loved Phillip, was it enough to just love him, no matter what he did or where you were? Would you do it again, Roxy?" Jess asked earnestly.

Roxy sat back and leaned her head on the back of the sofa. "Oh, Jess. How can I tell you what to do when I made such a mess of my life?"

"Please, Roxy." Jessie rose and sat beside her friend. "I need to have your help."

Setting her hands on her knees, Roxy sat up straight. "All right, honey, but remember, I can't promise you happiness or forecast doom for you. Whatever happens, it'll be what you make of it."

"I know," Jessie whispered.

"Well, in the beginning my love for him was part real and part adventure. I told you he was charming, very much like your Steve is." She winked and Jess blushed. "Phillip made me feel special when I was with him and scared when I wasn't, yet I'd have to say it was good. Maybe if he'd been a different kind of man, less of a dreamer, we could have had something together. I guess what I mean is you can't compare Phillip and Steve. They're not enough alike. Phillip was filled with wanderlust and Steve is a man of the land. Phillip lived for the moment, Steve for the future.''

Roxy took Jessie's hand in her own. "What you're really needing to know is if I regret it, aren't you?" Chewing at her lip, Jess nodded. "Again I have to give you two answers. Because of Becky, I don't regret a thing. When I wanted to quit, to give up living, she was there to see me through. If I've done nothing else in my life that's good, I've seen her to a proper life and I love her deeply. I'd never want to change that.''

Roxy brushed away an unwanted tear and stood. She walked about a moment, then stopped to brace her hands on the mantel. "But to be honest, I do have regrets, Jess. I wasted my youth loving someone who could never really love me back." She spun about. "Oh, don't get me wrong, he tried, but it wasn't in him to love just one woman for too long.''

Jess rose and walked to her side. "Is Steve capable of loving forever, Roxy? Can he commit to me in his heart?''

"I can't answer that, yet I believe he's more taken with you than he wants to be. Perhaps it will take a gamble, Jess.''

"If you were me, would you go?''

"I'm not you, honey, but I'll tell you this, when the time comes to decide, follow your instincts." She hugged her young friend. "It's a troublesome thing. I'm sorry I can't help you more than that.''

"It's okay, Roxy. I don't think there is an answer, anyway." A bleak smile touched Jessie's lips. She pulled away and sighed. "I better be getting back. Hilda's going to have her hands full." Jessie was at the door when Roxy called to her.

"Jessie! Phillip also gave me my memories." She watched Jess wrinkle her brow, not understanding. "I'll never be entirely alone again. I'll always have him when I close my eyes and summon him, but Steve can give you more than memories."

Roxy was telling her to take the chance in her own enigmatic way. "Thank you," Jess said softly, and left.

Weighing all her thoughts and options, Jess made it through the day and a restless night. Hilda found Jess and Matthew asleep in the rocker and shook her head.

"Child," she said to the beautiful sleeping woman, "go with your man and let yourself be happy."

"Hmm?" Jess woke and looked about, unsure of where she was or why until she saw Hilda with her hands on her hips. "Did you say something?"

"Yup!" She began to bustle about the kitchen. "I said you and your man should get together and make more beautiful babies like Matt!"

"Not again, Hilda!" Jess whispered harshly, and placed the sleeping infant in his cradle.

"I know, I know. You've decided you're not going with him. Well, forgive an old woman for butting in but you don't need this place. You need a man, a strong, good man like Steve Kincaid, who'll give you a home and babies and a firm hand on your bottom when you get uppity!"

"Hilda! That's enough!" Jess cried. "I've made my decision. These children need me and he doesn't!"

"Okay, I've said my piece," she replied, disgruntled. "So, I'll make breakfast and mind my own business!"

Jessie was overcome with regret at her sharp tongue. "I'm sorry, Hilda. I didn't mean to—"

"Forget it, honey." Hilda smiled. "You don't live

this long and not develop a thick hide. Now, go wash up and give me a hand.''

True to his word, Steve rode into the yard within ten minutes of noon. He waved to a busy Sam as he labored on a sawhorse teeter-totter while his young observers gave him instructions. Dismounting, he tied his horse and strode to the back door. A quick, firm knock brought Hilda to the threshold.

"Hello, Hilda. How are you?" he asked the woman.

"Better than you're gonna be, I reckon." She waved him in.

"What do you mean by that?" He took an offered chair in the kitchen.

"Not for me to say!" she huffed, and left him sitting there.

He was about to go after her when Jessie appeared from her room. She had taken care to look her best. She needed confidence in herself and thought a show of bravado would help.

"You look lovely, Jess," he said as he stood up and went toward her. Her hair was drawn up and wound about her head. She wore a gown of soft apricot. Long fitted sleeves and a demure square neck edged in ecru gave a pearly luster to her skin. He was reminded of a statue of a madonna he had once seen in a church in Santa Fe.

"Thank you. Would you like some coffee or . . . or some pie?" She turned from him to await his answer.

Grasping her wrist, he drew her against him. "No coffee. No pie," he breathed against her ear. "Only you, Jess." He pressed a kiss on her neck and let his hands circle her waist and travel over her back down to her hips. "God, you feel good," he groaned, and would have let his emotions get the best of him if Jess hadn't found the strength to pull away.

"Stop!" she cried, and clutched her middle.

"You're not going to . . . I can't let you do this."
Her chest rose and fell as she tried to regain her
composure. "We have to talk." Steve reached for
her again. "Don't touch me!" she yelled and jerked
away. "I . . . I can't think when you touch me!" she
admitted.

A smile pulled at the side of his mouth. He knew
what she was feeling and he enjoyed the power he
held over her body. "We can talk later. Go get your
things."

Jess shook her head. "Now! We'll talk now!" she
cried, and moaned when Matthew let out a startled
wail. Without hesitation she ran to his bed and
pulled him into her arms, gently shushing him.
"Shh, darling. It's okay." She patted his bottom.
"Don't cry, I'm here."

Steve followed her and watched as she held the
infant. Again the madonna, he thought, but this time
with child. And what a beautiful madonna she was.
His savage desires waned as he watched her.

"What's his name?" he asked standing behind
her.

Jess felt a shiver run through her. Father and son
together yet not together. What should she do?
Should she hand him his son and tell him or . . .

"M-Mark. We call him Mark." She allowed her
fears to dictate.

Placing his hand near the smaller one, Steve caressed the pudgy fingers. "I wonder how someone
could have a child and then leave him. Is he or-
phaned or abandoned?"

"Oh, he's . . . he wasn't abandoned!" Half-truths
were coming easier.

"If I had a son like him, I'd—"

"Well, well! I thought I heard our Matthew crying." Hilda bustled in. She heard enough to know
what Jess was implying and she decided to intervene, so she contrived a way to let Steve know the
truth as subtly as possible. She disregarded Jessie's
scathing frown and looked directly at a confused

Steve. "You better feed that son of yours, Jessica. You know what a temper he has." Before Jess could say a word, she turned in a flurry of skirts and left, grinning.

Jess waited. She knew Steve was assimilating this new information and it wouldn't take him long to figure out that this was his son.

"Your son? Matthew?" He was putting the startling facts together. "My God, woman! Matthew Kincaid! My father's name!"

"No!" She turned on him like a tigress protecting her cub. "Matthew Morgan! My name!" she cried. "My name for my son!"

It was all clear to him now. Why she ran away! Her supposed illness! Her fears! She was a mother, the mother of his son!

Robust laughter filled the room and rebounded through the house. It wasn't until Hilda peeked in and bid Jess to feed Matt that Steve settled. She tried to get him to leave so she could nurse her son, but he refused and stood silently in awe as she opened her gown to their child.

"Matthew, my son." He spoke softly as he knelt beside her and lovingly touched the dark little head. His fingers brushed her breast and he looked deeply into Jessie's eyes. He finally realized that this woman had borne him a son of her own body. That she had carried him and labored to have him.

"Are you all right?" he asked a bit nervously. "I mean, having him, did it hurt you?"

Jess had to smile. He was as naive as she had been in the ways of babies. "Not too much," she said at last.

Steve was filled with pride at that moment for her and what she had done, and it welled forth in the repeating of his son's name. "Well, Matthew Kincaid, I'm a little late, but I'm your father."

"It's Matthew Jeffrey Morgan," she corrected abruptly.

"Do you deny that he's my son?" He stood over her, anger just beneath the surface.

"He's Matthew Morgan," is all she would say.

Bracing himself for a showdown, Steve planted his feet firmly, and threw up his hands. "Good Lord, woman! I'll give you credit for being unique. I'll admit you've done well for yourself and proved to be quite self-sufficient. You're stubborn, intelligent, proud, and determined, but by God, not even you could do this alone!" he roared.

"Damn you, Steve!" she said through clenched teeth. "Stop shouting! He's not used to it!"

"Well, he better get used to it because I'm sure he'll be hearing a lot of it at home, in his room, at the K-D when you and I take him there!" He stormed out before Jess could stop his words or argue with his statement.

Chapter 27

$\sim\!\!\curvearrowleft\!\!\mathcal{O}\!\!\mathcal{O}\!\!\curvearrowright\!\!\sim$

Steve strode past Hilda, grabbed his hat, and bumped into Sam at the door without even a nod of recognition. Yanking the reins free of the post, he threw himself up into the saddle and pulled about. Like a man possessed, he rode off.

"Damn her!" he mumbled, heading for the K-D at breakneck speed. He let the horse have its head and rode with a vengence. His mind refused to focus on the landscape streaking past in a blur. It concentrated instead on one fiery hellion who managed to disrupt his life like no other. Seeing her bestow all her love and tenderness on their son tore at his vitals and set his blood to boiling with desire to possess them both.

Sensing his rider's urgency, the horse covered the miles in record time. Within mere minutes, Steve thundered into the yard at the K-D. He was off the horse before it came to a stop and half-ran to the barn.

"Chad! Willy!" he called out and received no response.

"They ain't here, boss," one of the hands called from the back. "Chad's gone out to check on new calves and Willy's helpin' Miss Sarah with supplies."

"Thanks," he replied shortly. "Take care of my horse, will you?" He had set himself the chore of hitching a team to the buckboard. "If you see Chad, tell him I'll be back this afternoon, with Jessie." He led the team outside and climbed into the wagon. "And my son!" he called out as he left the yard.

He expected Jess to run and he had no time to spare. He'd thrown down the gauntlet and he knew she would accept the challenge in one of two ways. She would take their child and run, or follow him meekly—which would never do for her. It wasn't in her to do anything meekly, he thought.

Jess reacted as Steve predicted she would. After losing time finishing with Matthew, she laid him in his bed, checked his diaper, then proceeded to pull out her suitcase. Hilda found her tossing items helter-skelter into a carpetbag and muttering something about "that pompous ass" and "if he thinks I'll sit back and let him run my life."

Hilda knew the race was on and thought to stall Jessie as she closed one suitcase and pulled out another.

"The only way you can get out of town with Matthew is in a carriage, and you can't go traipsing about the countryside in that!" She pointed to Jessie's lovely dress.

"Damn! You're right!" She began to pull at the hooks of her dress. "I better change." She stripped away her finery, tossing it carelessly aside, and grabbed a plain brown shirt. As she finished with the buttons, she pulled a dark riding skirt from her pile of clothes. The faster she tried to move, the more tangled she became in its folds. "Help me, Hilda!" She gave a muffled cry. "Hurry!"

Hilda made to move when a hand restrained her. Startled, she turned to see Steve, a finger pressed to his lips for silence. Grinning broadly, she winked and left the room. She hadn't heard the carriage above Jessica's ramblings but she was glad he made it back in time.

"Hilda!" Jess grew more impatient and stilled

only when she felt hands untangling her hair from the skirt hooks. Freed at last, she pulled the fabric down to its rightful place and reached behind herself to fasten it. She spun about to continue packing and fell directly into the arms of her nemesis. She tried to pull away, but his arms of steel crushed her, trapping her in his embrace.

"Let me go!" she screamed, kicking and wiggling frantically to gain her freedom. Her yells startled Matthew and he began to cry, afraid of the harsh sounds coming from his mother. "Damn you! Let me go or . . . or I'll kill you!"

Tiring of her resistance and angry at her inability to know what was good for her, Steve entwined his fingers in her already disheveled hair and gripped hard. He yanked back her head and looked down on her furious, lovely face.

"Shut up!"

"Don't tell me to—"

His lips ground into hers, silencing her the only way he knew he could, or wanted to. The savage assault became the releasing of pent-up frustration and suppressed desires. His imprisoning arms began to touch, to explore the once-familiar body of his lover.

Caught off-guard, Jess didn't have time to think. She was fully engulfed in his body's demands. Her senses soared as she slid her arms about his neck and pressed her supple curves against his rock-hard frame. So intense was the mindless passion that neither heard Hilda as she picked up Matthew and left, closing the door softly and saying to herself, "About time."

Urgent hands pulled at buttons and fastenings until they both lay naked in each other's arms upon the small bed. This was not the coming together of lovers but a mindless frenzy of need and want. Never had Jessie experienced such a world of sensation, nor Steve such a burning need. They moved as one, each knowing what they wanted and how to please the other.

Jessie's tongue drew sensual patterns beneath his ear as she whimpered to him of wanting him and needing him within her. Steve, driven on by her whispered words, kneaded the flesh at her hips and nibbled the warm fullness of her breasts. There was no world beyond that room for either of them. No sound penetrated the breathless words and moans of ecstasy. No touch could be felt but that of a fervent caress. Their world was viewed through half-closed eyes that only saw the other.

His body glistened. He was in agony but he had to hold back. He had to! Jessie would hate him when this was done and she realized her part in it. Yet he had to bring her all the pleasure he could, to make her respond to him and remember. He couldn't wait much longer. He couldn't . . . Jessie cried out and arched her back to bring them closer.

"Oh, yes!" he groaned as his body pulsed in response to her plea. "God, yes, Jessie!"

He spoke her name and ice began to flow where scalding fire had preceded. She'd fallen from her own good graces. She slipped into the trap of her own desperation and paid full score. Her hands slid from his shoulders to lay limply at her sides. The shame of her own unleashed passion reflected in the tears that followed a path across her cheek to fall silently to her pillow.

He knew her thoughts. He could feel it in the slow withdrawal of her arms and the cringing of her body as he pressed satisfied kisses on her neck. He had to make his choice here and now. He could reason with her until she relented or force her to go with him somehow. That he had superior strength, there was no doubt, but that she was the more stubborn was equally true.

Steve rose to balance on his elbow and look down at her. He saw the tears but knew she'd cried before and learned to laugh and love again. He was hardened to them when he thought of her trying to leave.

"I didn't mean for this to happen, you have to believe that." His voice was still husky from the effects of rapture. "But I'm not sorry. It will make your homecoming less urgent. We can take our time," he promised in a throaty whisper.

Jess could feel him growing within her again. "I won't go." She shivered as the heat of him radiated itself to her. "You . . . you can't make me."

He pushed deeply into her and rotated his hips slowly. "I can, honey, just like I can make you want me." He continued to move seductively over her body until the fire was lit. He watched her clench her teeth and try to resist, only to surrender with a whimper. As her hands clutched at his arms in silent pleading, he knew she needed release and stopped his movement.

"Tell me you don't want me—" He swallowed hard. "—and I'll leave you forever." He was gambling she truly did want him despite the harsh words of pride. Slowly he began to coax her to answer with the motions of his body.

"Don't make me say it." Her voice quivered.

"Jess?" he insisted.

"Yes! Yes! Yes!" she cried. "I want you and I hate you and I'll never forgive you for doing this!"

He moved faster and deeper until they exploded again in mutual bliss. "I'll take your hatred, honey," he breathed, "if that's how I have to have you."

Jessie dozed off, exhausted and depleted of all her energy. She felt him rise from her and shivered from the loss of his warmth until a quilt was drawn over her body. She didn't see him standing beside her, watching tenderly. She didn't realize he moved quietly to dress so she could sleep.

Steve looked once more upon her and smiled sadly. "I may be selfish and stubborn, call me what you will, but I'll not let you go, Jessie. If I have to follow you to hell, I'll not let you go." He saw her stir, then settle again, and left the room.

Hilda noticed his rumpled hair, his shirt left hanging open and the heavy-lidded eyes and knew they had worked out at least part of their problems. She smiled when he walked over to the gurgling infant and placed his finger along his son's cheek.

"You have a stubborn mother, Matt." He smiled gently. "Did you know that?" In reply, Matthew gave his father a crooked grin.

"He knows," Hilda sighed, pressing a coffee mug into his hands. He raised an eyebrow at the first sip. It was generously laced with whiskey and he nodded his appreciation. "Thought you might be needin' that."

Steve watched his child a moment longer then sat down. He spread his feet and balanced his elbows on his knees. Raking back his hair, he rubbed at his neck wearily and finished his coffee.

Matt, lacking the attention of his dark, towering playmate, began to fuss. Hilda checked on him and picked him up. It was time for Steve to hold his son, she thought, and shuffled to him. "Here." Steve jerked upright. "I have things to do," she said gruffly. "You hold him."

"Me!" He drew back. "I . . . I don't know how to . . ." Before he could finish, Hilda deposited Matthew in Steve's arms.

"Relax." She smiled. "He won't hurt you and he's not made of glass. He won't break."

Steve leaned back and crossed his legs. He couldn't explain the feelings welling up in his chest. Paternal pride? Perhaps, or was it love? It wouldn't be hard to love this child of his loins, of that he was sure. The little face grinned again as if he recognized his new friend, and Steve was lost. He did indeed love this child, but what of the mother? So willful! So defiant! Why couldn't she lay in his arms and accept his love so trustingly? His love!

God, yes! he thought. "I do love her. I have from

the first time I saw her!'' he admitted to his son. It explained the drive to possess her, drove him to the depths of despair and the magnificent heights of exquisite pleasures.

Love was the reason he searched her out and died a thousand deaths when he saw her lying in White Antelope's camp. Love was why he was in agony when she fled from him in the mountains. That he had been so blind was unforgivable! If he had only recognized his feelings sooner, perhaps by now they would be wed and happy together.

''What a waste,'' he moaned softly. All this time of hating and arguing could have been filled with love and sharing. His ignorance cost him seeing the woman he loved filled with his child and the birth of his son. Raising his bundle, Steve placed a kiss on the dark little head and rose to place him back in his cradle.

''Hilda, would you get Matt ready to go?'' She nodded and wondered when he had had time to convince Jess. ''I'm going to wake Jessie. When we come out, whether she's willing or not, we'll be leaving.''

''Good luck,'' she called to him as he entered Jessie's room, sure that he'd need it.

Steve sat on the edge of the bed and leaned down to press a kiss on Jessie's pouted lips. She moaned and rolled to her side, facing him. The quilt lay just over the peaks of her breasts and he had to steel himself not to undress and rejoin her.

Setting his hands on her bare shoulder, he gently shook her awake. ''Jessie, it's time to get ready.'' He saw her eyes flutter and a smile pull at the corners of her mouth until she realized he was really there and not a dream.

Gripping the blanket tightly to her chest, Jess sat up quickly. ''Get out!'' she demanded.

Unruffled by her outburst, Steve spoke softly. He wanted to tell her of his love and hoped it would make a difference. "Jessie, I have something to tell you. I lo—"

"I said get out!" she screamed before he could finish.

"Honey." He gripped her shoulder. "Listen to me! I'm trying to tell you . . ." His temper was heating up despite his attempt to subdue it.

"I don't want to listen to you anymore!" She jerked away from his hands and dragged the quilt about herself. She climbed out of bed.

"Hold it!" He grabbed her at the door. "You're not getting out of my sight until we leave for the K-D, together!" His temper flared to nearly full bore. He would have to wait to tell her of his love until he could count on his own feelings and rely on her to listen.

"Huh! What audacity! What makes you think I'll go with you?" She tossed her head defiantly. "Just because . . . because we . . . I won't!"

Pressing her back against the wall and blocking her escape on either side with his arms, he scowled. "I'm getting sick and tired of your waspish tongue! I've a mind to give you a good spanking for acting like a spoiled brat!"

"You wouldn't dare!" She drew as haughty a pose as she could, standing eye level with his shoulder and wrapped in a cumbersome quilt.

"Ah, Jessie." He sighed. "Don't tempt me. I'd like nothing better than to prove to you again just how much I dare, but we don't have time nor do I have the inclination to give you pleasure when at the moment I'd like to beat you! Now, get dressed!"

"No! I won't! Do you hear me!" she shouted. "I won't!"

"Very well." Steve stepped back and raised his hands in exasperation. "If that's how you want it." He turned and picked up a blanket at his feet. Before she could enjoy her victory, it descended over her head, blocking out the light. Steve chuckled as she tried to flail about beneath her cover and clutch the quilt she was wrapped in at the same time.

"You asked for this, Jess," he announced as he threw her over his shoulder. He marched into the kitchen with Jess kicking out furiously. Hilda stood bewildered for a brief moment and then began to laugh.

"I see you've worked things out." She continued to chuckle.

"Yes." He grinned a little sheepishly, embarrassed by the squealing, wiggling bundle he carried. "I do seem to have everything well in hand." He patted Jessie's bottom. "Yet as you can see I'm unable to pick up the rest of my baggage." He gestured toward Matthew's cradle. "Would you mind helping me out?"

"Hilda!" came a muffled cry. "Hilda, don't you dare!" Jess ordered.

"Did you hear something?" She winked at Steve. "Must be mice!" She was delighted to be playing Cupid and pleased to help in this escapade. Clutching each end of the cradle, Hilda hoisted it, complete with its occupant, and carried it to the back porch.

Carefully, Matthew was deposited in the back of the wagon, his eyes crinkling in the light until Hilda draped a small blanket over the cradle.

"What about her things?" Hilda inquired.

Steve made sure Jessie was quiet to hear his reply. "I'd like to keep her just like this." He swatted her again. "Wrapped in nothing but a blanket." He felt her stiffen. "But I suppose she'll eventually need them," he conceded, and dumped his parcel into the wagon bed with a thump.

As soon as she was free of his arms, Jessie struggled out of her imprisoning wrapper and turned on him. Wisely, he ignored her and left to gather her things. Instead of attacking him, she turned on Hilda.

"How could you?" Jess cried, trying to cover herself.

"Because I know what it's like to be lonely, honey. You won't admit it, but he's right for you."

"Right for me!" Jess shouted back. "What gives you the right to decide what's right for me?" Tears began to fill Jessie's eyes at the apparent hopelessness of the situation. Everyone was on his side! "You don't know him! He's a rogue!" Jess sobbed. "He . . . he kidnapped me and . . . and he lied to me! He pretended to be a cowboy and . . . and he wouldn't let me pay back the loan!"

To Hilda she wasn't making much sense as she rattled on. "You are overwrought, Jess." She waved away her broken statements. "I'm sure you'll see I'm right when you calm down."

"I'm not overwrought!" Jess struggled to her knees and hobbled to the open end of the wagon. Freeing her feet, she slipped over the edge and gathered an armful of quilt. She began to back away from Hilda.

Steve came out of the house with two cases in his hands and a box under his arm. He transferred everything to one side and came up behind Jess. Without breaking stride, he walked past her, wrapped his free arm about her waist, and hauled her back to the wagon as she yelled the most vile names she could think of.

He threw her belongings aboard and dumped her beside them with no more than a shake of his head. He took Hilda's hand and kissed her cheek.

"Thanks for everything, Hilda." Catching sight of Jessie struggling to her knees again, he climbed into the seat and took the reins. Tipping his hat, he flashed a brilliant smile and started the wagon with a quick jerk.

Jessie let out a scream and tumbled over as they left. Hilda chuckled at the display of shapely legs entangled in the pile of blankets visible as the buckboard left the yard. Shaking her head, she went inside, wondering how this saga would end.

* * *

Steve kept the wagon heading homeward at an even pace. He looked back at Jessie often and had to laugh as she lost more ground than she gained trying to cover herself. Feeling sorry for his rough treatment of her, he pulled off the road and drew under some newly bedecked trees. He wrapped the reins about the brake stick and jumped to the ground.

Coming up behind the wagon, he had to restrain himself from laughing. She wouldn't appreciate the humor when she was at her lowest. Sitting on the floor with her bare legs tucked beneath her and her hair in a state of total disorder, she was crying as she rubbed at a raw spot on her elbow.

Checking Matthew and finding him asleep, he held out his arms to her. "Come here, honey." He nearly grinned when she shook her head. Her lip quivered and she brushed at the flowing tears with the back of her hand.

"No," she moaned. "I can't."

His voice grew firm. "No more games, Jessica! Come here!"

"I c-can't!" she cried harder. "I'm stuck!"

Steve sighed and climbed aboard, sorry for his little outburst when he saw what a state of dishevelment she was in. He didn't say anything in the end. He merely sat beside her, disentangled her quilt from the broken floorboard, and helped her to her feet.

"Do you want to get dressed?" he asked, his finger beneath her chin.

"P-please," she said softly, not even trying to pull away from his touch.

Steve jumped to the ground and reached up for her. She leaned forward until his hands circled her waist and swung her down. He felt the need to protect her and, in her subdued state, he dared to hold her, not the embrace of a lover but the warm circle of deep caring. After a moment, he kissed the top of her head.

"You better get dressed," he breathed against her

hair. The Steve of old would have taken advantage of her pliant form and state of undress. The new Steve was in love, and that knowledge gave him the strength to step away. Perhaps now was the time to tell her about his love, to bare his soul and take his chances.

"Yes." She drew herself as straight and tall as bare feet would allow. She dragged out a suitcase and flipped it open. Rummaging, she found what she needed. Clutching the items close, she looked about, spied a spot for privacy near the trees and, like a princess dragging a train, she marched off.

"Watch out for—"

"Ouch!" she cried, and rubbed at her foot.

"—thistles." He chuckled.

Jess glared over her shoulder and disappeared into the brush. As he thought about telling her, he decided to hold off a bit longer. She was in quite a mood now, and she might use the information to turn the tables on him. Now that he knew how he felt, he was vulnerable. No, he thought, he'd keep it to himself a while longer.

Chapter 28

He helped her climb aboard and, when she was settled, reached in the back for his son. Handing him to his mother after giving him a brief smile, Steve joined her. To anyone passing, they presented a picture of the perfect family. Steve sat tall and proud, his hat pulled low on his brow to cast a shadow on his handsome face. His thigh pressed against Jessie's and he grinned each time she tried to pull it away, only to return with the rocking of the wagon.

With her composure restored, Jess chose to sit quietly for the remainder of their journey. She had brushed out her wild hair and drew it back into a ribbon to fall down her back. Her silken shirt and heather skirt made her feel that she was again in control of herself. Holding her son in her arms, her thoughts were of escaping the clutches of the man she once would have sold her soul to stand beside.

She glanced at him and noticed how contentedly he sat beside her. He was so sure of himself and her, so sure she would meekly move into the K-D and stay until . . . until what? He tired of her? Their son no longer needed her? God forbid. She shuddered. No, the best thing she could do was avoid the kind of humiliation and heartache he offered. She would play out the charade until she could contrive to leave. Perhaps she could find someone to help her, an ally who could get a message to her father. Surely he would see her to freedom.

There was a lump in her throat as the wagon moved past the hanging sign of Windy Creek. If not for Matthew, she would jump off and run to her land, her own family. Steve watched her stare longingly back at the gate and discovered he was angry that she had yet to admit his supremacy. He hastened the horses and she turned to stare ahead.

As the house came into view, Steve broke the silence. "When we get to the house, I won't have you behaving like a spoiled child, do you understand?" He slowed the team to nearly a stop.

"I understand," she replied, but refused to look at him.

"And I won't tolerate any outburst about you being here against your will. I know you are here by force and that's all that matters—unless you prefer me to haul you into the house over my shoulder like a captive slave so there will be no doubt to anyone."

"You wouldn't da—" She clamped her mouth shut. She knew better than to call his bluff. He *would* dare! She could see it in his raised brow and crooked grin.

"You're learning, honey." He smiled and let his eyes caress her. "Now, if I can just teach you to stop running away." A muscle ticked in his cheek as he felt the sensual tension between them flow into his loins, and the smile faded.

Jessie felt the attraction, too. She wanted to draw away, to scream for him to stop the magnetism, but she was frozen in a world of feeling without touching, of hearing within the silence.

They might have sat thus for hours if Matthew hadn't begun to fuss over the ever-tightening arms of his mother. Distracted at last from the spell, Jess took a deep breath and turned away.

Steve's laughter had a nervous edge as he snapped the reins to get them moving once more.

* * *

The house held so many memories for Jessica. In the few times she had gone through its doors, she had experienced the gamut, from blushing bride-to-be to a despondent pawn in a game of wits. Her very life had been threatened within its walls, yet, under different circumstances, she would have gladly returned.

They rode up to the front steps and Steve tossed the reins to an awaiting Willy.

"Howdy, Mr. Kincaid!" Willy's exuberance echoed in the excitement in his voice. "Miss Jessica." He whipped off his hat and gave her an awkward nod.

"Hello, Willy," Jess replied, a shy smile enhancing her beauty. Before she could talk to the boy, Steve instructed him to bring in her things and lifted her clear of the wagon. Instead of putting her down, he carried her and his son in his arms up the stairs.

"You don't have to carry us!" she growled at him. "I'm not going to try and run off right under your nose! Please, Steve!" she begged embarrassedly.

Steve ignored her plea and reached the door in several long strides, threw it open, and crossed the threshold. Before he could put them down, Sarah entered the parlor with a bowl of early spring flowers.

"So you're back." She glanced at him and turned away. A second later the picture of him standing there with Jessie and Matthew in his arms registered, and she spun around so quickly the vase flew from her hands and crashed against the wall. Without a flinch, she ran to her friend.

"Jessie!" she cried. "Oh, Jessie, you and Matt have come! I . . . I'm so glad to see you've settled your differences with Steve. It'll be wonderful having you here!"

Steve set Jess to the floor and stood behind her,

his hand resting possessively on the side of her neck. "We haven't exactly settled anything," Steve interrupted. "I guess you could say we've merely called a temporary truce."

"What he means is he dragged me here against my will and . . . ouch!"

"That's enough, Jessie." Steve's fingers tightened on her neck and he began to grow angry with her again. And she'd only been at the house a few minutes!

"It's not enough!" Jess shouted, and pulled free of his grip. Turning on him, she wanted to air her frustration and her fury at being manipulated in front of witnesses. Before she could inform Sarah of the details surrounding her presence, Chad bustled in.

"Jessica! Good to see you back at the K-D!" He looked down on the dark head in her arms. "And Matt. You're growing like a weed." He ushered Sarah and Jess into the parlor and watched them settle. "How'd he ever talk you into coming? Last time we talked you weren't budging!" Chad missed Sarah's warning look.

"That's enough!" came a roar from the foyer. Steve strode in and looked at the occupants, one by one. "It seems everyone in this territory knows all about Jess and me except me! It appears even my best friend knew about my son and saw fit to keep it from me!"

"Don't go getting your dander up, Steve." Chad smiled. "We promised her that we wouldn't—"

"Damn it! Jessie isn't your partner, nor does she run the K-D! This is my house on my land and she's my woman! Is that clear?"

"Very clear." Chad sobered. "Sarah and I will leave you then." He reached for his wife's hand. "Come on, honey." Sarah rose to go but couldn't resist turning to Jessie with a look of sympathy.

"No, don't go!" Jess cried out as they reached the door.

"Sorry, honey." Chad raised a shoulder with a shrug. "The boss—" He emphasized the word. "—has spoken."

The room grew tense as Jessie and Steve refused to look at one another. Jess felt that it was time to clear the air. She couldn't stay at the K-D if the result was constant bickering. She set Matthew on the sofa and propped pillows around him. She moved to face Steve at the bar.

"Steve." She placed her hand on his and felt him flinch. "This isn't going to work." He pulled away and downed a whiskey without answering. His silence didn't dissuade her and she went on. "I know you think this is how you want it and that that makes it right, but it isn't. You can't use people just for your own ends. You and Chad have been friends for years and now you're at each other's throats, and it's all because of me." She didn't know if he was listening until he made a dismissing comment.

"He'll come around."

"And what about the people you do business with, the townspeople? Will they come around to you and your whore?" she cried. "Will they accept me and your bastard?"

Steve drew back a hand to hit her and froze. Good Lord, he thought, what was he doing? He lowered his hand and started to leave. Stopping at the door, he turned to Jessica. "You're staying, Jess." He spoke wearily. "I'll hear no more of it except this one last thing. If you go or even try to leave, I'll be forced to contact a friend of mine in Philadelphia."

Jess stood bewildered until Steve played his trump card. "My friend's sister runs a school for young ladies there. Young ladies of good breeding." He could see that Jess still didn't understand. "He'll inform one Becky Santini that she will have to leave and send her back to her mother."

He watched the blood drain from Jessica's face.

"You wouldn't! You couldn't hurt her like that!"
She ran to him and clutched his arm. "You're not
God! You can't play with the lives of those about
you like this!" Tears began to spill from her glisten-
ing green eyes.

Steve ran a finger over her cheek and looked at
the tear that clung to it. "I'll do whatever it takes to
keep you here."

Dropping her arms to her sides, Jess let her head
fall forward in defeat. "Very well." She sighed. "I'll
stay." She drew a deep breath and looked up until
her eyes met his. "But I'm warning you, Mr. Kincaid—" She raised her chin defiantly. "—it won't be
pleasant." Gathering up her skirts, she spun about
and ran out of the parlor.

Steve would have followed her if Willy hadn't
chosen that propitious moment to enter with her
things. "Take them upstairs," he ordered. "To my
room!" The door slammed as he left.

Sarah watched Steve ride from the barn. His face
was blacker than any other time she had seen him
angry. "Phew! They must have had one terrible argument!" She spoke aloud to herself. "I better check
on Jessie."

She entered the house to find the ground floor
vacant. A shuffling from above told her where Jess
was and she ran up the stairs calling her name.

"In here, Sarah," Jessie called from the room she
had occupied during her last stay.

Sarah found her dragging the cradle into a corner.
Matthew was lying on the bed and she moved him
to his own without waking him.

"He's growing so fast." Sarah peered over Jessica's shoulder.

"Yes." Jess smiled down on her sleeping son.
"Oh, Sarah, what am I going to do?" She walked
to the window and drew back the curtains. "We
can't stay here, not hating each other the way we
do."

Sarah took a seat on the bed. "Do you hate him, Jess?" she asked. "Do you really?"

Jessie reflected on the question. "I should, shouldn't I? He's ruined my life. He's threatened my peace of mind and lied to me. He's done all sorts of things that anyone but the mighty Kincaid would have hung for and still . . ."

"And still you love him."

"Am I crazy? Is there something wrong with me that I should love such a man?" She threw herself across the bed and began to weep bitterly.

"Don't cry, Jessie." Sarah patted her shoulder. "We can't help who we love. It just happens and, if we're lucky, they love us back." Her words brought deeper sobs instead of the consolation she wished for. "He loves you, Jessie. I know he does."

Sitting up and brushing away the tears, Jessie looked at Sarah in disbelief. "How can you even think that? My God, Sarah, he couldn't love me and do the things he's done!"

Sarah chuckled, much to Jessie's chagrin. "Oh, Jess. You didn't know him before you came on the scene. Let me tell you, he's a different man since meeting you. The easygoing Steve has become a man possessed! He never took the time to worry about anyone or anything before. Oh, his friends maybe, but never a mere woman! He took nothing seriously. Life was a big game of chance. He'd commit to nothing but his ranch and took pleasure where it came."

"So what has all that to do with me?" Jess knew of Steve's escapades but felt he was still the rogue they professed him to be.

"He's like a madman now!" Sarah continued. "All we hear is Jess this and Jess that. He's either thundering around like a prairie storm or moping by himself. And his temper! He used to be always laughing and filled with mischief, but no more!"

"You make it sound like I'm ruining him instead of him me!"

"Let's just say you're not helping each other with your stubborn streaks. You can't make a bow if you're pulling both ends." Sarah could see it would take more than a lecture from her to help. "Okay, let's forget about it for now, but promise me you'll at least try to keep the peace, if not for Matthew, then for my sake. I . . . I'm not feeling all that well lately." She glanced at her hands and fidgeted.

Forgetting all her own problems, Jess grew anxious. "Oh, Sarah! I'm sorry! I didn't know you were ill!"

Sarah giggled. "Well, I'm not exactly ill." She looked about as if she was engaged in some dark intrigue. "Promise to keep a secret?" She leaned toward Jess when she gave a quick conspiratorial nod. "I'm going to have a baby." Her face was enchanting as she smiled.

Jessie squealed and hugged her. "Sarah! I'm so happy for you!" She grasped her hands and looked her over. "When?"

"December, I think. Would make a great Christmas present for Chad if I could keep it a secret, wouldn't it?" She laughed.

"He doesn't know?" Jess knew it would be the best news he could hear. Ever since Matthew was born, he talked of a child of his own.

"Not yet." Sarah smiled. "I'm saving it for a special occasion but I suppose I'll have to tell him soon. Seems I get ill in the morning and it's getting harder to keep it a secret."

Jessie opened her arms and flung them about Sarah again. "He'll be so happy! I know it!" She drew back to arm's length. "Is there anything I can do?"

"Well . . ." Sarah paused. ". . . you . . . you could try to make things right with you and Steve."

"Oh, Sarah," Jessie moaned. "You ask an awful lot of me." She got up and returned to the window.

She looked out and watched as Steve tried to control an unruly mount. Settling him at last, he sensed someone watching him and looked up to see Jessie in the window.

She knew she should draw back but was held fast by the look in his eyes. They promised her passion and she felt her body responding. Finally, he tipped his hat, and pulled his horse about.

"Damn!" she cried as she faced Sarah. "I can't promise you that, Sarah." She felt like a traitor and she noticed Sarah's elation begin to crumble. "But I will promise to give him every chance and not to start anything."

Sarah sighed. "I suppose that's something." She started to leave. "I better go. Jess, thank you. I know it won't be easy."

"I think that's an understatement if I ever heard one," Jess mumbled and smiled weakly, shaking her head with a sigh.

He rode hard and spent more energy working out a nearly broken mustang. He was about ready to ride into town and get roaring drunk when he saw Jessie at the window. Ashamed of himself for dealing such a low blow to her by using Roxy's daughter as a hold, he tried to figure out how he'd let her know he wouldn't follow through with his threat and still maintain his credibility. He also wanted her to know he wasn't going to force her to his bed. And then he saw her peering out from a guest room.

Her blatant display of defiance returned his good humor and he hoped he could keep it a while. Just knowing she was in his home gave him great peace of mind. If she could curb her acerbic tongue, he might be able to hold his temper, and let her know of his decisions. He entered the house and ran into Sarah as she was leaving. "Hi, honey." He smiled and kissed her on the forehead. "Jess all settled in?"

Sarah was speechless and just shook her head.

"Good." He went to the sink and washed his hands. Sarah still stood watching Steve in disbelief. He had been running hot and cold and she just couldn't figure him out. "Well, if there's nothing I can do for you," he said, smiling, "I think I'll go up and see if Jess is comfortable."

He wanted to laugh at the bewilderment Sarah exhibited as he left the room. Taking the stairs two at a time, he moved slowly when he reached the landing. Her door was open and he stood silently watching Jess as she folded clothing into the dresser. His eyes traveled over her hair and followed it down her back to her curvaceous hips.

This won't do, he thought. If he couldn't keep his appetites under control, he'd ruin everything. With that fact accepted, he summoned all of his willpower and relaxed against the frame of the door.

"Is everything all right with the room?" he asked, giving the impression of only partial interest in her reply as he lounged lazily.

Jess pivoted to face him and stood staring for long moments. He seemed to beckon her despite the detached aura he displayed. Swallowing back any retort for Sarah's sake, she presented a calm picture of her own.

"Yes, everything's fine for Matt and me in here." She wanted him to know she intended to stay there and waited for him to demand she move to his room. After all, he had had her things put there originally, and it was she who dragged everything to this room.

"Good!" His lithe form moved catlike to full height and he started to walk away. "Oh!" He returned. "Could you do me a favor? Sarah and Chad have moved back to their place, and . . ." He looked down at his boot toe. ". . . well, could you make up something for dinner?"

Betraying her nervousness, Jess stammered,

"D-dinner? Oh, of course. Yes! I'll . . . I'll make dinner!"

"Thanks, Jess," he called over his shoulder.

"Well, I never!" Jess flounced to the bed. "He expects me to be his cook and . . . and probably his housekeeper, too! He drags me out here to . . ." She took a deep breath and placed a hand to her brow. "I must be sick." She sighed. "He's behaving pleasantly and I'm reacting ungraciously. I promised Sarah to try, and I will. As long as he behaves, I will!"

Jess resumed her chore and berated herself for her real concern. He was being cordial but undemanding. It wasn't like him and she wasn't sure if there was some underlying scheme in the works. Then again, he could have tired of the game now that the chase was over and he had her and his son under his roof.

"Damn him!" she said. "Why didn't he try something? I can't hate him when he's so damned . . . oh!" She whirled about to throw her things in the drawer.

It wasn't going to be easy, he thought as he paced his room, yet he knew it was the only way he could keep her at the ranch. He'd set his mind to court her and court her he would. He'd go slowly and convince her that his intentions were honorable. He wanted marriage to that hellcat and nothing less would do.

They shared a quiet dinner, and he retired to the library as she cleaned up the kitchen. When she entered the library, remembering the two other times she had been there, and told him she was going to bed, he waved her off and returned to some papers he later couldn't remember reading.

Was there a flash of disappointment in her eyes? Had she expected him to vault over the desk and ravish her? It was what he wanted to do. Still, he refrained and was glad for the large piece of furni-

ture between them. He'd been tempted to act the
barbarian yet he sat apparently calm. He didn't
want to gamble one night of pleasure against a lifetime.

He could hear her pacing about in her room as he
followed suit, and smiled. At least she was as restless as he. Maybe it wouldn't take too long. At least
he fervently hoped not.

Chapter 29

In the month Jessie spent at the K-D, Steve's change of tactics seemed to make an impression on her. The wary glances and agitation gave way to a somewhat uneasy truce. Each day was one of facing the unknown for both of them. There were times of quiet sharing when Jessie would see to Matthew and Steve would look on, almost lovingly, she thought. Sometimes they would sit and talk over a meal as if no trouble had ever occurred between them. They would stay on neutral ground and discuss Windy Creek and her family, or the K-D and its occupants.

No matter how hard they tried, though, nothing stayed on an even keel for long. A near-collision in a doorway would set the sparks flying. A careless brush of a knee to a thigh beneath the table would produce a dark scowl and muffled oaths before one or the other would flee.

On the fringes of their self-imposed hell, onlookers shook their heads and wondered why. No one knew from day to day if Steve would exit the house in a tolerant frame of mind or in restrained fury. Bets were being taken on who would be the first to break. That it couldn't continue was obvious. The two were like capped volcanoes. Pressure was building. There were threatening rumbles and soon, very soon, one was bound to erupt.

* * *

Tempers grew shorter as the days grew longer and warmer. Steve's six months of celibacy in the mountains was nothing like the six weeks he'd shared his home with Jessie. Not one day passed that he wasn't driven to distraction by something she did. Was she intentionally driving him mad? he wondered. Did she know of the ache in his loins and purposefully add to it? Seeing her in her daily chores was bad enough, but seeing her dainty underthings drying on the line or hearing her humming in her room interrupted by a gut-rendering splash from her bath was carving his heart out and devouring his vitals.

It had been a particularly difficult morning. His night was filled with dreams of Jessie, in his home, in his arms and in his bed. He woke feeling the strain and took a quick ride to the stream for an icy bath. Feeling only marginally better, he returned to find her in the kitchen, stripped to her shift and pouring a pitcher of water over her head.

Not hearing him enter, she completed her task and squeezed the water from her long tresses. Wrapping a towel about her head, she nonchalantly rubbed out the excess water and began to walk, partially blinded with the towel and hair, to the stairs. Meeting the obstacle of a chest, Jess squealed and jumped back.

Using her arm to push back the snarled strands, Jess laughed nervously. "You . . . you scared me! I . . . I thought you were . . . were out."

Set the herculean task of keeping his distance, Steve snapped at her. "Watch where you're going, Jess. You might find you've run into more than you can handle!" Leaving her bewildered and nonplussed, he stomped off to his room.

Jess had brushed out the tangles in her wet hair and sat on the bed with her son, watching him kicking and grabbing at his toes. He gurgled and she laughed. She didn't know they were being observed until Steve walked boldly in and stood with his shoulder braced against the bedpost. He looked at his son and could not resist a crooked grin.

"He seems to be enjoying himself." His rich-timbred voice filled the room. He didn't trust himself to look at Jess. The vision of her sitting cross-legged on her bed, her hair hanging freely over her shoulders and clad like a Viking bride in a soft shift of ivory, was more than his shattered nerves could stand.

Jess released her breath and sat perplexed. A few hours before he had been a seething, raging bull, belligerent and infuriating. Now, he stood calmly sharing an intimate moment with her. There was no sense to it. Yet she supposed she should be getting used to it.

"May I hold him?" Steve asked, and lifted his child after her softly spoken yes.

Matthew looked so small in the powerful arms of his father. The pain in her chest from seeing the two of them together like this brought tears to her eyes. She watched Steve sit on the bed and lean his broad shoulders against the headboard, bringing his legs up to support Matthew's weight. They sat this way for a long while. It was again Steve who spoke, but this time his voice was subdued.

"Jessie? Why didn't you want me t-to know about our son?" He didn't look at her but played absently with a tiny hand.

Taken back by the heart-wrenching catch in his voice, Jess sat staring. How could she tell him? How could she let him know she feared he wouldn't want her? Unless she told him of her love, he wouldn't understand.

"I . . . I was afraid you . . . you'd take him," she whispered.

Steve drew his sleepy son to his chest and let him rest on it as he leaned his head back and closed his eyes. He could feel Matthew wiggle about until he found a comfortable spot, then he quieted and drifted into a peaceful sleep.

"If you were so afraid, why did you name him after my father?"

"It was my father who changed it." She rose and paced about nervously, wringing her hands. "I wanted to call him Jeffrey Ma—"

"Jeffrey Matthew," he offered.

"Y-yes. Papa said that he and Matt were friends and they would both be proud of his name." She turned to Steve. "How could I do less than honor his grandfathers? I couldn't blame them for the sins of their children!"

Steve was watching her through lowered lashes. He saw her pace and sensed the difficulty she was having; but more than that, he saw Jessica, the woman. Never had he seen anyone as beautiful, as desirable as she who stood before him. God, but he wanted her, loved her beyond anything. Even the child he held within his arms, the child he would die for, came second to the deep love he held for his mother.

"What sins, Jess?" He laid Matthew carefully on the bed. Slowly he moved to within inches of her. With infinite care, he raised his hand to set it on her neck. "Was it sinful to want each other so? Was it sinful to come together and create something as magnificent as our son?"

He pressed a kiss to her trembling lips and felt her sway against him. His arms slipped about her and he knew she wanted him to hold her.

"Let me love you, honey. Let me hold you and make love to you, the way we both want," he whispered against her hair. "I've never begged, Jessie—" His hands slid over her hips and drew her nearer. "—but I'm begging you now."

Her body was his, Jessie knew that. She could feel the beat of her heart rapidly pulsing in her throat and her blood flowed like quicksilver through her veins. That her mind drew back in fear of what cost loving him would be, she ignored it. She needed him so. Roxy had told her to take a chance and Hilda had admonished her to go with her man. Maybe it was time for her to take the gamble. She knew she couldn't go on living with him and not make love to him.

Drawing back to look into his face, Jessie lifted her hand to his cheek and touched it. He had tried, really tried to be gentle these past weeks. He must care! He must!

"He is magnificent, isn't he?" She let a smile play at her lips but it couldn't compare with the one in her eyes.

"He couldn't miss." Steve returned the smile. "Look at the beautiful, intelligent spitfire he has for a mother."

"And the handsome, stubborn rogue he has for a father." The smile faded and she rose up, offering her mouth to his.

"Does this mean you'll let me—"

"Steve! Jessie!" Chad came thundering into the room. "Did you hear about—" He looked at the two of them in each other's arms and the beaming smile froze. "Oh! Excuse me. I . . . I was so excited, I . . ." Matt began to wail, disturbed by the outburst.

Jessie gathered up her son and started to laugh. "Whatever has you so wound up?" she asked, knowing the reason.

"Yeah!" Steve added. "You bust in here like a wild man and now you clam up and leave us hanging." He looked at Jess and had the good graces to redden. "You've already exhibited your great sense of timing, you might as well spill it!"

"I'm going to have a baby!" He realized what he had said when Steve raised a brow. "I mean, I'm going to be a father! Sarah's going to have a baby!"

"Well, I'll be damned!" Steve roared and slapped his hand on Chad's back. "Imagine, you! A father!"

"That makes two of us!" Chad laughed.

"You got a point." He glanced at Jess. "And here

we were just talking about trying to make a sister
for Matt!''

"Oooh!" Jessie cried and started Matthew crying
again. "How could you?" She set her wailing child
in the cradle and moved to stand before the two
men, unmindful of her state of undress. "Get out!"
She pointed to the door. "Get out, both of you!"

Her mind was in a cloud of red fury. How could
he stand there and talk so nonchalantly about something as wonderful and private as them sharing love?

Steve made to reach for her. "Jessie, honey!
What—"

She slapped his hand away and pushed at his
chest to rid herself of his presence. "Get out, now!"

Chad departed without hesitation, and Steve followed with "But Jess . . ." just before the door
slammed. He turned to Chad instead. "What did I
say?" He was truly vexed.

"Beats me," Chad said consolingly. "Let's go
have a drink and see if we can figure it out."

"Yeah," Steve mumbled, and scratched his head.
"Yeah!"

"I should have known this would happen." Sarah
laughed at the roaring party going on outside. "I
think Chad's drunk a toast to his upcoming child
with every hand on the ranch, one at a time."

"He's happy." Jess placed her arm about Sarah
and they watched the merriment a few moments
longer.

"And what about you? You're fussing about like
a caged cat." Sarah had observed Jess in various
moods but this one was different.

Jessie flounced onto the bed and sat cross-legged,
her elbows perched on her knees and her chin
propped in her hands. "That bumbling ass is what's
the matter!"

"Who else!" Sarah threw up her hands. "Now
what did that diplomatic fool do?" She joined Jess
on the bed.

With a great deal of aplomb, Jess related the events of the afternoon. "And after playing me for a fool, he informs Chad that I've decided to sleep with him!"

"He didn't!" Sarah giggled at the picture of Steve with egg on his face.

"He damned well did!" Jessie frowned. "Imagine, just because I was touched by his endearments he thought I would fall into his bed!"

Sarah plucked at the bedspread and cast a wicked glance at Jess. "And were you going to?" She grinned.

"Well, I . . ." She started to giggle. "Yes, I was!" They both burst into laughter and spent an hour sharing their combined knowledge of men and their delicate egos.

"Have you figured her out yet?" Chad asked a somber Steve as he sat on the back porch steps over another drink.

"Hell, no!" he growled. "I don't think I'll ever figure her out! One minute she's all warm and willin' and the next she's a bitch!" He threw up his hands and splashed whiskey all over Chad.

"Take it easy! You don't have ta drown me 'cause you're mad at her!" He chuckled, well in his cups. He settled beside Steve and produced a bottle to refill their glasses. "Don't you know that a woman like her is special? Her moods are what keep you goin' back for more. You never know if she's goin' ta play the whore or the schoolmarm, and damned if you don't want 'em both!" He slapped Steve's back. "When you get it all figured out, there's no mystery and it's time to move on. So relax, and be glad you got her here."

"Yeah, great! She's here and I'm sitting in an ice-cold creek every damned day 'cause I can't get her to bed." Steve finished his drink and pushed the glass at Chad for more.

"Hmmm. You do seem to have a problem." Chad

rubbed his chin with his knuckles. "You tried force and that didn't work. You threatened her and that didn't work. Christ, you even tried sweet-talkin' her! 'Course, I blew that one.'' He blushed and chuckled.

"Yeah! You sure as hell did!" Steve jumped to his feet, fighting for balance. "I ought ta knock your head off for that!" He brought up his fists and stumbled backward until he lost his footing and sat with a thud.

Laughing, Chad extended his hand and pulled him to his feet. "Now don't go taking it out on me. Hell, who'll help ya work this out if not me?" They resumed their seats and had another round. "Did ya ever tell her ya loved her?" Chad asked after a few moments of concentration.

Steve tried to roll a cigarette and managed to put together a crumpled facsimile. As he lit it and nearly burned his fingers, he replied, "I tried to tell her but she wouldn't listen the first time, and you interrupted before I could today." Steve grabbed Chad's shirtfront. "I oughta—"

"We already did this, remember?" Chad butted in.

"Oh, yeah." Steve sighed.

"You do love her, don't ya?"

"Hell, yes, I love her! What do you think I'm going through all this hell for, a roll in the sack? Christ, Chad. You can be so thick sometimes."

"It's the company I keep." He chuckled at his own wit. He slapped his hands to his knees and turned to Steve. "My friend, what are we goin' ta do?"

"I don't know what Steve's going to do, but you're going home to sleep it off!" Sarah stood in the door, her hands on her hips.

"Aw, honey. I don't want to sleep." He grinned and tried to wink at his wife. "But I'll go quietly if you let me take you ta bed with me."

"Come on." She helped him to his feet. "I'll let

you try," she said tolerantly, knowing full well he'd pass out before she could get his boots off.

"God, you're a good wench." Chad leaned on her shoulder. "How'd I get so lucky?"

Sarah looked skyward and shook her head. "Lord only knows, Chad," she mumbled as she led him home.

Abandoned, Steve struggled with himself. Should he go up to his cold, lonely bed and spend a night tossing and turning, thinking about Jess in the next room, or should he take her, willing or not, and still the throbbing in his loins? He started to chuckle to himself. He hadn't gotten around to telling her his threats about Roxy were idle ones. She'd be too scared to leave no matter what he did!

Tossing his glass into the brush, he began his journey to her side. A few missed steps and some muffled curses kept him company as he drew up before her door. He tapped lightly and got no response. She was making it easy for him, he thought, and opened the door. The more angry he was, the easier it would be for him to argue with his conscience and win.

Jess was sitting up in bed. Her hair hung down her back and lay in soft burnished curls on her pale blue gown. The lamp was low and she looked like a little girl, but not so much so it deterred him. Her breasts rose and fell beneath the thin fabric.

"What do you want?" she asked impatiently. Steve tripped as he moved forward and she knew he was stinking drunk. She wanted to laugh at him and his stupor yet she managed to restrain herself. His clothes were dusty and awry, and the shadow of a beard darkened his face. His hair lay in unruly waves over his brow and the last thing he looked like was Steve Kincaid, leading citizen!

Steve drew up to full height and let his hands settle on his lean hips. "I want you." He weaved to stand beside the bed. He grabbed the quilt from her hands and yanked it back. She didn't say it, but he could read the dare in her eyes. "One of these days, Jess, I'm going to dare more than even you can imagine!"

"You're drunk!" she said between clenched teeth. She didn't want to wake Matthew and she glanced at the crib to be sure he wasn't disturbed.

Steve caught the action and it registered. He couldn't take her here. He'd have to get her to his room. Striking like lightning his hands shot out and grabbed her, one arm about her waist and a hand clamped over her mouth. He covered half the distance to the door before she realized what he intended and began to struggle.

Numbed with his consumption of spirits, he didn't feel the blows to his shins as he hauled her to his bedroom and tossed her carelessly upon the bed. As she spun about to berate him, his mind grew fuzzy. There was something he wanted to tell her but she kept yelling at him and he couldn't think clearly, so he yelled back.

"Take your clothes off!"

"Go to hell!" She tried to climb off the bed but he threw his arms about her hips and tossed her back.

"I'm no monk, Jess. I've had all the celibacy I can take. Either you take off that gown or I'll rip it off you." He tore at his own shirt and stood bare to the waist, unbuckling his belt.

"No! I won't make this easy for you! I won't stay here!"

This time he fell across her and pinned her to the bed. "You will stay and you will sleep in my bed!" He pressed his lips to hers in a savage assault, raping her mouth with his tongue as he fondled her through her gown.

Jess froze. He wouldn't succeed this time, she vowed. Slowly, his mouth lowered to her collar and followed his fumbling fingers down each button while it fell away. She gripped the bedding and squeezed her eyes shut. He pushed aside the fabric and rested his head between her breasts.

"Oh, Jessie, Jessie." He sighed.

She waited for him to continue, and when he didn't, she ventured to open an eye and peek at him. Soft rumbling snores began to reach her senses. He was asleep! He had drunk himself into a stupor! Carefully, she disengaged his arms and slid from beneath him. She stood looking down at his sprawled form. She expected to feel furious that he would try something like this but all she felt was a terrible loss and a deep sadness for what could have been.

"I love you, my darling." She gently touched his hand. "But I cannot play your whore. I cannot stay, no matter how much I love you. It would destroy me." She rebuttoned her gown and opened the door, looking back over her shoulder. "All you would have had to say was that you loved me," she whispered, and left.

Steve stirred and hugged a pillow to his chest. "I love you, Jessie," he moaned in his sleep.

She wouldn't take much, she thought as she stuffed more of Matthew's things in the pillowcase than her own. She would have to take a horse if she wanted to make the best time; a carriage would only slow her down and be easier to follow.

Looking at her sleeping son, so blissfully unaware of his uprooting, she tried to figure how she could hold him and ride, too. She tried to imagine something that would enable her to keep her hands free and still safeguard Matthew. Snapping her fingers, she knew a way!

Little Sparrow had gotten through her day of chores and tasks with no hindrance, and managed to carry her son whenever necessary. She had used a sling of sorts, and Jessie was sure she could fashion one sufficiently well to fit her needs.

Tearing a sheet from the bed, Jess ripped the fabric until she had a large triangle. She tied two points together, then tied the third to them. Slipping it over her head, she tested its strength and found it stable.

Gingerly, she lifted Matthew and settled him in the sling. He snuggled against her, never even fluttering his lashes. Jess sighed, picked up her impromptu bag, and left. She walked quietly down the stairs and out the back door.

Glancing about the quiet yard, she moved cautiously to the barn. There was no sound but that of the horses, and she looked about for one she could handle. Choosing a chestnut mare, she led it from the stall and found a bridle. She was able to get it on the horse but she wasn't sure she could manage a saddle. After what seemed an eternity, she completed her task, gathered up her son, and led the horse to a bale of hay to mount.

She flicked the reins and headed into the night. Knotting her shawl about Matthew, she began to head for Lander at an even pace. About a quarter mile from the house, she pulled the horse to a stop. Reviewing her options, Jess knew that no matter what she decided to do, Steve would come after his son. She had to do something he wouldn't expect. Where could they be safe from him? Where could she ensure their survival without notoriety?

A star fell across the blackness to disappear in the northern sky. That was the answer she was seeking. Some unseen hand was showing her the way.

Chapter 30

She could see the camp ahead of her and sighed. She had ridden all night and her body ached with fatigue. The smell of cooking reminded her of her empty stomach and she plodded on toward the shelter of the Crow camp as the sun reached a point just over the horizon.

Children ran after her as she rode into the circle of tents and women smiled shyly as they recognized Valley Woman. White Antelope came from his tent to investigate the commotion and was joined by Little Sparrow. Before he could show his surprise or welcome their friend, Little Sparrow ran to her side and smiled brightly.

"Jessica! You have come to see me!" She opened her arms to the bundle Jess removed from about her neck and pulled back the sheeting to look upon the infant. "Oh, Jessie! This is your child?"

Struggling off the horse, Jess rubbed at her neck and shoulders. "Yes, this is my son, Matthew." Wearily, she smiled and took the baby from his binding. He was wet and needed feeding but Jess took a moment to embrace her friend. "How are you, Little Sparrow? I've missed you and thought of you often."

"I am fine, but you look tired." She took Jessie's hand to lead her. "Come, I will have a place prepared for you while you share the abode of my husband.''

Jessie followed Little Sparrow and stopped in front of White Antelope. ''You are well?'' he asked, a smile of welcome playing at his mouth.

''Yes,'' Jess answered simply, ''but I must talk to you.''

White Antelope gave a terse nod and entered the tent with the two women following. They sat on furs about a fire and Little Sparrow asked Jess if she was hungry. Receiving an affirmative nod, she left to get her some food. White Antelope watched Jessie with Matthew for long silent moments, then spoke.

''You have a fine son, Valley Woman. He has the look of the Hawk.''

In his own way he let her know he was aware of the child's parentage. She looked at the dark curls on her son's head and agreed. ''Yes, he looks like his father.''

''Will my friend Hawk be coming for you again?''

''N-not this time, I hope.''

Little Sparrow returned with Sparrow Hawk. She handed Jess a bowl of stew and took Matthew. Sitting beside her husband, she listened to her friend while she played with the baby and her own child.

''White Antelope, I have a favor to ask of you. I have no right to ask, your people have done so much for me already.'' She paused to eat more of her food while White Antelope silently watched.

His outward appearance was one of cool indifference yet he was deeply intrigued. Something had happened between his friend Hawk and this woman. They had a son and should be together. He was filled with questions but it was not in character for him to show interest. He would listen to Valley Woman. What she did not tell him, she would tell Little Sparrow. If he was patient, he would soon know all. ''My people will help you, if we can.''

A tear slid down Jessie's cheek as she told White Antelope of her leaving Steve and needing some-

where to raise her son in peace. She told him it
would not be forever, only until she could go to St.
Louis without fear of him finding her.

White Antelope seemed stone-hearted when he
spoke. "It is not good for a woman to leave her
man."

"He is not my man." She sighed. "In our culture
what we have done is not accepted." She looked
down on her clasped hands and let the tears flow.
She was so tired. All she wanted was a place to rest.
She should have known he would see only the
man's side. She was so involved in her thoughts,
she did not see Little Sparrow place a hand on her
husband's arm pleadingly.

"We go to Mirror Mountain in four days," he announced after more consideration. "Valley Woman
and her son are welcome to go." Before Jess could
express her gratitude, White Antelope rose and left
the tent. She began to laugh through her tears as
Little Sparrow smiled at her.

"He is not so uncaring as you think," she said as
she set Matthew into Jessie's arms. "But he is a
man." That was supposed to explain everything and
make it acceptable.

At one time Jessie would have misunderstood, a
time before she met Steve Kincaid, but his intrusion
into her life made the statement simple and clear.
Despite the differences in their way of life, one fact
held true—it was a man's world. He was not pres-
sured by society to obey its rules. He could come
and go at will with no one wondering about his
moral code. He could drift into a town with no questions asked and see to his needs undisturbed. What
chance would a woman have if she tried the same
thing?

"I know he cares." Jess said quietly. She put Matthew to her breast and let him feed. "And I am
grateful."

They spent long minutes speaking of the past year.
Jessie found she could not yet spill out her heart to

Little Sparrow. It was too soon, the hurt too new, but she told her she would not go back. Not one to pry, Little Sparrow reserved comment and question to merely ask about Jessie's needs.

"I have very little with me. I'm afraid I only took what I would need immediately for Matthew. If I'm going with you to Mirror Mountain, I'll need to contact my father and have my things sent here." She didn't want to let anyone know where she was but she could see no other way and she relayed this wish to her friend.

"You mean even your father does not know you are here?"

"No, he doesn't. I found I couldn't go to him." Jess drew a deep breath and released it slowly, thinking of how he'd been swayed to accept Steve's latest decree that she and Matt live with him at the K-D. "I'm afraid he tends to agree with Steve too often, and I don't want to be found by him until I can sort out some things." She laughed nervously. "He's a little like White Antelope."

"Um, I see." Little Sparrow gave her a small smile. "Perhaps you should write him a note telling him you will be safe and I will see it delivered so that he does not know you are with us. I will also see that you get clothes and have a lodge for now."

"Thank you!" Jess cried. "I know you do not understand this thing between Steve and me, but you still help me. How can I ever repay you?"

"Just by being my friend, Valley Woman." She smiled when Jessie hugged her. "Strange," she mused. "You came to us the first time wounded and so it is again." Jessie sniffed and wiped at a lone tear in silent agreement.

Steve grunted when he tried to raise his head. "Oh, God!" He sat up and clutched his head to help stop the pounding. With any luck at all, he thought, he'd die in minutes. He could recall celebrating Chad's announcement and the party that followed but what took place after that was all foggy. He couldn't tell what was real and what was a dream.

He tried to replay his night with Jessie and surmised it had been a dream. The ache he felt for her was not satisfied. He would have to settle their differences soon, or go mad.

Getting to his feet, he knew he must have passed out before finishing undressing. He was still half-clad and wearing boots. Donning a fresh shirt after washing away some of the grogginess, he left his room. Pausing outside Jessie's door, he hesitated and listened. She must still be asleep, he thought, as no sound was coming from behind the door, and he moved on.

Entering the kitchen he could smell bacon frying and fought down the nausea rising in his throat.

"Morning!" Sarah spoke louder than necessary and chuckled at Steve's grimace. He raked his hair and pressed his fingers to his temple.

"Must you be so cheery?" he snapped, and took the cup of coffee she offered him without thanks.

"My, my." Sarah clicked her tongue. "Aren't we charming this morning? Must be something in the air. Chad has the same symptoms." She pretended concern. "Maybe I should call for the doctor."

"Don't be smug, honey," Chad called from the back door as he came in, water dripping from his hair after the dunking it took in the trough. "Being a witch doesn't become you."

"Oh!" Sarah laughed. "Last night I was a good wench, and now I'm a witch!"

"You're also loud!" Steve groaned. "Can't you scold us a bit more quietly?"

"Okay." She smiled sympathetically. "How about something to eat?" She was met with moans and head shakes. "Well, if you're not going to eat, I'll go hang out some laundry."

Neither man noticed when she picked up her basket and left. They were both living in a hell of their own making and couldn't bear to move or talk until heads and stomachs came into accord. After another cup of black coffee, Chad became more communicative. "We had a hell of a good time last night, didn't we?"

"Damned if I know." Steve grimaced sheepishly. "I don't remember much."

"Me neither." Chad rubbed at his head. "But it must have been or I wouldn't feel as rotten as I do."

"Yeah." Steve gave an ironic laugh. "How's Sarah feeling? She mad at you?"

"Naw, she ain't mad. Just a little disappointed I went overboard." He seemed a bit restless. "I guess it started out as a celebration but I got carried away."

Steve sat quietly nursing his hangover until Chad's next statement. "I think what I really mean is I got scared when I realized what it meant to have Sarah pregnant."

"Scared! What the hell are you afraid of?" Steve seemed genuinely perplexed. "It's Sarah that's having the baby, not you!"

"That's just it!" Chad closed his eyes and braced his head in his hands. "I keep thinking about Jessie when she had Matt."

Steve leaned back in his chair and stretched out his legs. He sat silently thinking and staring into the cup that he held balanced at his waist between both hands. "Tell me about it, Chad," he quietly requested without looking up.

Chad slowly related the events leading up to Matthew's arrival into the world. He told Steve of Jessie's awkward shape and even drew a smile when he told him about her bad temper at being restricted by her pregnancy. He spoke of her silent struggle in the end, and the pain and tears. There was pride in Steve's eyes when he heard the story of her strength, and pride and love for the woman who suffered so to give him a son.

Chad's narrative drew to a close and Steve leaned forward to set his elbows on the table. "And you don't think Sarah can handle it?"

"Oh, she'll handle it fine." He smiled. "But I don't know if I can go through it again!"

Steve laughed. "I think you'll be all right. I'll just make sure you have a good supply of whiskey to see you through."

"Ugh! Don't mention whiskey!" Chad grimaced and then checked his watch. "I wonder where Jess is. I haven't seen her all day."

"Still sleeping, I reckon." Steve was about to pour himself more coffee.

"Sleeping! It's past noon! Are you sure she's okay?"

"Past noon?" Steve slammed down the pot and cup, and raced from the room. Something had to be wrong and he had a terrible premonition he knew what it was.

Chad was right behind him as Steve ran up the stairs and threw open Jessie's door. It slammed back against the wall and Steve stood transfixed. She was gone! There was no need to look further. They could see by the clothing strewn about and the empty cradle that Jess had once again taken flight.

The dream was no dream, Steve thought, moving slowly into the room. Drawn by her things, he looked for a clue that could lead him to her. No dream! He had held her and God knew what else! He'd done it again! He'd driven her away, just as he'd been on the brink of having her. He was momentarily defeated as he sat on the edge of the bed.

Chad watched, not sure what to say. He felt helpless as he stood looking down on Steve's bent head. There was a sense of disaster emanating from the man that caused Chad to draw back. "Steve," he said, and got no response. "Steve! What are you going to do now?"

"Do? What can I do?" He looked past his partner. "I've done enough. I drove her away." His eyes glazed with what could have been tears.

Chad had to act quickly. His friend was growing more depressed, and he had to be spurred into action. "Yeah, you're right. Why bother with her? She's been nothing but trouble from the first." There was no reaction. "You'll have no trouble getting a new woman here in short order to replace her." He detected a stirring. "Why, how you lasted so long with such a contrary gal is beyond me." He could sense Steve's protective temper flaring and used his trump card. "Hell, you can't even be sure that Matt's yours. Why, she could have been with—"

"That's enough!" Steve jumped to his feet and grabbed Chad's shirtfront in one hand and drew back the other tightly fisted. Instead of fear of a thrashing on Chad's face, he looked upon a satisfied grin. He released his friend and rubbed his fist across his chin. "You took quite a chance with that ploy."

"I had faith you'd see the light before you knocked mine out." Chad chuckled at his own wit. "Now, what are you going to do?" He sat on the bed.

"Well, she obviously left sometime last night," Steve replied, sitting beside Chad. "Somebody would have reported seeing her if it was this morning. That gives her about a twelve-hour head start. Since it was dark, she couldn't have gotten far, not packing Matt. I figure she either headed for Windy Creek or back to Lander."

"Yeah, that's what I think, but, just in case, how about I ride into Riverton. She may be a hellcat, but she ain't stupid. She might figure you'll think exactly what you're thinkin'."

"You may be right." Steve slapped his hands to his knees and got up. "Well, my friend, we better go get her." They left the room and headed down the stairs. At the bottom, they strapped on their holsters and donned their hats.

"I'm goin' to tell Sarah where we're off to," Chad said.

"I'll see you tonight." Steve paused. "And if you find her, tie her good and tight, and haul her back. That's what I'm going to do!"

* * *

Steve rode home in desolate silence. There was no sign of Jessie or Matt at Windy Creek and his ride to Lander was as fruitless. Roxy and Hilda promised to let him know if they saw or heard from Jess and wished him good luck in his search. All he could hope for was that Chad had been right. She'd known what path he'd choose and had purposefully gone the other way.

He thought that when he found her—for find her he would—he might well strangle her or, at least, place his brand upon her, tie her to his bed, and keep her there under lock and key until she came to her senses! The chase had been exciting but he was tired of it now. He loved her and she loved him! Or did she? Had time and Matt's birth done something to change that? No! She had come into his arms of her own accord. It was something else.

"You drove her away!" some part of him scolded, and he knew it was true. His own possessiveness, his obstinate determination to have his own way had been the dividing force from the start. He wouldn't give up until he possessed her. Then, after tasting her forbidden fruit, he was filled with wanting her again and again, no matter what she said or did. Everything always had to be his way! She tried to tell him. She had pleaded with him about Windy Creek and the mortgage, and begged at the cabin for him to let her come to him through love, not threats, yet all he did was try and crush her damned pride until she admitted to only being his. At every turn he'd bullied and pulled at her until he finally pushed her away.

"I've been such a fool," he said to the night sky. "God, if ever you grant me forgiveness, hear me. I promise I'll find her and, when I do, the choice will be hers. I swear it!" Coming to an understanding with himself, Steve headed home.

* * *

"How could she just disappear?" Steve stomped about the library. "She couldn't know this country well enough to bypass Lander, could she? When I think of her out there . . ." Steve was plagued with thoughts of her and his son, struggling through the barren land to the south, trying to reach the rail line. "And you are sure nobody in Riverton remembers seeing her?"

"I'm sure. I checked everywhere and left word with the sheriff. I even swung through Hudson on my way back and came up empty-handed." Chad reached for Sarah's hand and kissed it absently. "Steve, you don't think Jeff is covering for her, do you?"

"I don't think so, Chad." Steve braced his hands on the mantel.

"Good, because I'm not."

"Jeff!" Steve strode toward him. "Have you seen her?"

He shook his head helplessly. "Not exactly." He pulled a folded paper from his vest. "But Connie found this in her room."

"How'd it get there?" Chad asked.

Grabbing the note, Steve scanned it and threw it aside. "This tells us nothing!" he shouted. "Not a damned thing about where she is!"

Sarah picked up the note and read the reassuring words Jess had written. She said she would be safe and not to worry. She and Matt would be taken care of and she would contact them when she could. "Who does she know that would take care of her and Matt?" Sarah had read the note looking for clues, not answers.

"Well . . ." Jeff poured himself a drink. "The only ones I know who would help, no questions asked, would be Jennifer's sister Clara, in St. Louis."

"Then you think there's a chance she'd head there?" Chad questioned.

"Yup, I do, and she's just stubborn enough to

make it.'' Jeff looked into the amber-filled glass. ''She made it here on her own, I reckon she could make it back.''

Steve digested his words and knew he could be right. She had tangled with him more than once and landed on her feet. She'd come out of the mountains in the dead of winter and survived. She'd made a place for herself and their son when other women might have given up. If any woman could make that trip alone and survive, it was his Jessica.

''Chad, when's the next stage to Green River?''

''Not until the day after tomorrow.''

''Very well, I'll take a horse in the morning. With any luck, I can catch her before a train heads east. Matt should slow her down and I have the advantage of knowing the country.''

Jeff placed a hand on Steve's shoulder. ''Find her, son. Find her and bring her home. We both owe her too much to let it end here.''

''I will, Jeff.'' He smiled hopefully. ''But not until I find a preacher who'll marry her, bound and gagged if need be, to me!''

At first light, Steve tossed his saddlebags and bedroll over his saddle and tied them down. He was ready for some hard riding and he planned to travel light and fast.

''Be careful,'' Sarah warned, and hugged him.

''Good luck.'' Chad shook his hand. ''And don't worry about anything here. I'll handle it.''

''Nothing, not even the K-D, matters if I don't find her and my son.''

Chad knew it was true and stepped back to place an arm around Sarah. They watched their best friend ride off to find his life, and a reason to live it.

Chapter 31

J ess had grown used to the bare back of her horse as she got through her second day of travel. Little Sparrow was true to her word and supplied her with clothing. Nothing as beautiful as the dress she had been given before, but serviceable items that allowed her the freedom to ride or walk comfortably.

With her hair in two long braids tied with leather thongs, Jess moved with the women and children behind the men in their trek. It was dusty and, at the best of times, tiring, but a sense of well-being invaded her and numbed the pain of heartbreak.

She was happy to be moving ever north and west with these people. There had been a moment when she thought she might not be allowed to accompany them. White Antelope was proud and a man of truth. Jess implored him not to tell Steve of her presence until she left and he agreed, but when she asked him not to say where she went from there, he adamantly refused to be a part of a lie or the deception. He did promise to think on it and had not given her his answer yet, but she was hopeful.

Checking Matthew as he hung in the folds of her makeshift sling, she smiled sadly and continued to plod onward, increasing the miles between herself and Steve, the man she loved more than life itself. She was glad for the rigors of the trip. They allowed

her to fall exhausted to her blankets at nights and to
seek the blissful oblivion of dreamless sleep.

She saw the stone pillars for a full day before they
came upon them and watched them grow into
mighty sentinels to the canyon beyond. Camped below them, the rising sun set them afire with the colors of reds and yellows in flame. Never had she
dreamed anything could be so formidable or so
beautiful as what they guarded.

As the Bird People moved into the canyon beyond
the awesome portal, Jess stood mesmerized by the
prehistoric vista spread ahead of her. Could anything be so primitive yet so breathtaking? The land
appeared to be barren at first glance, but a critical
eye soon found small animals and a profusion of
tiny flowers and plants nestled among the rocks.

Moving into the canyon, Jess felt as though she
had moved back in time to a period before man
walked the earth. The many shapes and colors of
the rock seemed to have grown from the earth, layer
upon layer, to stand in magnificent silence and mo-
mentary benevolence to those passing.

That night the camp took on a mystical aura.
Campfires danced and cast shadows across the towering cliffs. Sounds reverberated and came back to
haunt the darkness. The stars twinkled brilliantly
and Jess lay upon her bed and stared at them in
wonder. She was a grain of sand on an endless
beach. All her problems were nothing compared to
the greater magnitude of the space above her.

She recalled watching a colony of ants scurrying
over their limited world and wondered if some
greater force looked upon her in the same way.
Rather than cause her to feel insignificant, it brought
a sense of peace and belonging to her world. She
was one tiny part of the world; she could survive or
fail and the world would continue. But, she thought,
she would not fail. She would bury her love for
Steve and make a new life for herself and her son.

She turned to her side and felt a tear slip over her cheek.

Just when Jessie thought nothing could impress her more deeply in nature's realm, she was again proved wrong. Unprepared for the vista that greeted her at the top of a twisting pass, she stood facing Mirror Mountain.

Little Sparrow came up beside her and saw wonder in Jessie's face. Before them stood a range of mountains. In the center rose a magnificent peak, covered with white snow. Below the majestic ridge was a glassy lake of such brilliance that it reflected the image of the mountain back like a giant mirror.

"You see?" Little Sparrow asked in a hushed whisper. "Mirror Mountain."

"Yes." Jess breathed out slowly. "I see and I understand."

"And did you see your valley as we see it?"

"I think so." Jess recalled the soul-searching she had done within its walls and looked at Little Sparrow. The wisdom of understanding the impotence of man in nature's plan was clearly in her eyes.

"You are truly Valley Woman." Little Sparrow smiled. "The girl Jessica is no more."

The summer matured and with it Jess became more like the Crow. Her skin turned the coppery gold as she learned the ways of survival. What had been to her a delicate lily on a mountainside became a potato-like bulb that supplemented the meats the men brought in. There was a nutty food source in the cones of the many pines and firs. Roots and plants of all kinds added to the abundance.

Her deep auburn hair took on the color of burnished gold as she trekked over the landscape with Little Sparrow and the other women. Her lithe limbs knew strength and hard work and remained supple and slender. She moved gracefully over the hills and found great joy in the beauty around her.

The only intrusion from the outside world came in early autumn. A trio of trappers entered the village and spent the night. She was singled out by one and tried to keep her tongue as he made freely with his hands each time she drew near. Managing to avoid him at last, she sought her bed and saw to her son. The hour was late when she felt a hand upon her hip slowly tracing her contour.

"What are you—" she began, silenced as a hand clamped over her mouth.

"I knowed you were white, girlie, and could speak English," a voice whispered against her ear. "Now you be good and ol' Mike will take better care of ya than any buck."

Jessie was afraid to fight or scream. Matthew lay at her side and she feared for him, but she had to stop the assault. Remembering the knife Little Sparrow had given her a week before, she pretended acquiescence to his blundering hands as she slipped her own cautiously to her thigh and the wicked little blade strapped there.

Thinking she accepted his idea of coupling, Mike grew lax and began to fumble with his breeches. "That's a good girl," he whispered as she let her arm slide up his back. She didn't think she could kill him but she could dissuade him and defend herself.

Quickly, before she could change her mind, she let the blade come up against his throat. "Get off!" she ordered, and he stiffened in surprise. "Very slowly, move off of me."

With great care he shifted his weight and rolled from her. He laid on his back at her side and noticed the smallness of the weapon. Convinced he could disarm her, he rolled away quickly and got to his feet, clutching his pants and making a grab for the knife. With a startled yelp he glared down at the wicked slice across his arm.

"Why, you bloodthirsty little bitch!" He lunged at her.

Desperate and frenzied by her own actions, she pushed the knife forward and felt it pierce his skin and come up against a bone. He pulled away, jerking the knife from her hand in the process. He clutched the intruding weapon and drew it quickly from the hole in his shoulder.

He flipped the blade until it pointed at her. She was terrified by the hatred in his eyes and crawled backward until she was up against the side of the tent. She wanted to scream but her throat was dry and refused to respond. Firelight flashed off the steel as he drew back his good arm. She squeezed her eyes shut, sure this was the end and then she heard a scuffle.

Looking at the source, Jess was relieved. One of the trappers, the one who'd appeared to be in charge, had run into her tent, gripped Mike's wrist and shoved him to the ground.

"I told you not to make trouble, Mike!" he roared. "Now you get your carcass out of here before I tell White Antelope that you were after one of his squaws!"

"She ain't no squaw! She's white!" Mike defended himself.

"See to that wound!" the mountain man yelled. "You can worry about your other needs when we get to a town."

Jess watched Mike stagger off and turned to her rescuer. "Thank you." She extended a hand.

The large man took it gently. "You're welcome, miss. I'm sorry Mike got carried away. He has a problem where women are concerned."

"Well, I certainly appreciate your help." She took the knife he had retrieved and held it tightly.

"How are you called?" he inquired curiously.

"I'm . . . I'm Valley Woman." She moved away from the small fire, afraid she might be recognized.

"Then I'll say good-bye, Valley Woman." He smiled through his shaggy beard, granting her her choice of worlds. "We'll be leaving in a few hours and I doubt we'll meet again."

"Good-bye," Jess replied as he strode out of her tent, carrying her secret.

The trip had been tiring, and wearily Steve stretched out on the bed. His hotel room was of high quality yet he paid little attention to it other than as a place to sleep and acquire the food he'd need to sustain him.

His mood was as black as midnight as he looked at the stucco ceiling. He had to be up to catch the train in a few hours and should be getting some sleep but all he could do was lie there and think.

Jessie hadn't come to St. Louis. Her aunt and uncle were cordial and terribly concerned but they didn't know where she was. Bonnie, in absolute awe of Steve, sat starry-eyed during his visit silently nodding at what her parents said.

As he'd walked down the stairs, heading for the street, he stopped at the sound of his name from behind him.

"Mr. Kincaid!" Bonnie slipped out of the house and joined him on the walk. "Mr. Kincaid . . ." Hesitantly she gripped his arm. "I have to talk to you."

He knew it had taken a great effort on her part to overcome her shyness and speak up, so he smiled gently at her, not realizing how devastating that smile was. "What is it, Bonnie?"

Blushing, she stammered for a moment. "I . . . I wanted to talk to you about my c-cousin." She drew a deep breath and struggled to gain some composure. "She wrote me about you."

"Oh!" He raised an eyebrow in concern. How much had she told her young cousin?

"I wanted you to know how glad I am that you love her, too." He hadn't mentioned his feelings but Bonnie had read between the lines. "I know you're not here for her father. She told me about how much she loved you and hinted that, despite some small problems, you two would probably get married."

A crooked grin played at his lips. "We had some small problems," he repeated thoughtfully, "and she'd probably marry me." He took Bonnie's hands in his own and looked down on her from his much greater height. "There's no 'probably' about it, Bonnie. She *will* marry me, just as soon as I catch up with her."

He kissed her cheek and bid her farewell. He didn't want her to see the pain his useless excursion caused or the worry he was filled with for Jessica and his son. The only thing he could do was return to the K-D and believe that somehow, somewhere, she would turn up.

Within a week, the Crow would return to their winter camp. Jess watched the snow line, unchanged through the summer, begin to inch its way down the mountain walls as October left its infancy. She was playing with Matt on a pile of furs in White Antelope's tent and watching Sparrow Hawk wrestling a bear skin. Little Sparrow laughed as he tripped himself up and rolled to his back.

"Your father will not be pleased if you wrestle a dead bear and lose. You must have him tell you again how to hunt the mighty one." Sparrow Hawk nodded and ran to find his father, deeming the story must be told at once.

"He is such a fine boy, Little Sparrow. You must be very proud of him."

"I am as proud of my son as you are of yours." She observed the loving brush of a curl from Matt's brow. "He grows fast, this little one."

"Yes, and he'll be tall like his—" Jess grew silent and let Matthew sip from the cup of milk as he sat trying to decide whether to drink from it or play with it.

"Does it still pain you so to speak of him?" Jessie had avoided any mention of Steve if possible. Little

Sparrow could not help but notice the teary eyes and clenched fists Jessie exhibited when there was no choice but to speak of him.

"Yes, it still hurts terribly. I . . . I hoped I would get over him, go east and start over with him just a memory, but I find it gets harder to think of leaving and never seeing him again."

"If you love him so, why do you waste that love? Love like that does not come to many. I have been so blessed." Little Sparrow looked dreamily at the place she shared with her husband. "So have you and Hawk. Look at your son. He is Hawk! You'll never escape him."

"Don't you think I know that?" Jessie cried. "Don't you think I see him every day, not only in Matthew, but in my dreams?"

"I think you will always love Hawk but you are too proud to go to him."

Jess stared at Little Sparrow. She did not mean to hurt her or malign their friendship. She only wanted to make her see the truth. Her damnable pride was what stood between her and Steve. It always had! Maybe it was time to swallow some of it and see him. "Perhaps," she said, sighing, "when we return, I'll . . . I'll see him before I go."

It was a large concession for her to make and Little Sparrow smiled in satisfaction.

Her words would haunt her as they covered the miles back. Could she see him and walk away again? Could she stand before him and not throw herself into his arms? Could she watch him hold his son and then take him away? No! No! No! she cried to herself. It wouldn't work. She would have to choose between leaving without seeing him or staying with him. There could be no in-between, of that she was sure.

She helped Little Sparrow set up her winter home. They had not spoken of the war that raged within Jessie's heart but they knew the answer would need to come soon. Winter approached and her decision would need to come before the first snow if she stood any chance of getting to Green River and, ultimately, St. Louis. After Little Sparrow spent the past few days watching her friend, she knew the answer.

"You are leaving, and not seeing Hawk," she stated as a fact rather than a question.

Jess drew up in surprise. "How did you know?"

"I've seen the sadness in your eyes. I know your heart is torn. You are brave and have done many things most women would not do, but you cannot face Hawk, loving him as you do. You will not take the first step." She wasn't scolding, but Jess could see she wished it had gone the other way.

It had been like a dream, or more like a nightmare, Steve thought as he galloped home. When he awoke that morning he never suspected his world would turn around before the sun set. One day had been like another, with the agony of knowing nothing. Driven to work to exhaustion, the weeks passed and became months, with little notice of anything but the absence of Jessica. Now all that had ended with a note from Roxy.

He had been mending a fence behind the barn when Chad came running out, yelling, "Steve!" He stepped from behind his cover to see Chad waving a note and grinning from ear to ear. "Steve, read this!"

The letter was shoved into his hands. He scanned the paper, looked at Chad in disbelief, and read it again. "Roxy thinks she has a lead on Jessie and Matt." He stared at Chad and saw him shake his head happily. The news began to sink in and thaw the bitterness. Steve grabbed his friend's arms and started to grin. "She knows something. Roxy knows something!"

"Don't tell me!" Chad laughed. "Go find out what!"

"Yeah!" He took off his hat and slapped it against his dusty pant leg. Suddenly he was afraid to move. It could be another false trail, another dead end. He moved slowly toward the house and stopped. Turning to Chad, he said, "What if—"

"You won't find out standing here."

"Yeah." Steve rubbed his jaw and looked about absently. This could be what he'd prayed for, hoped for with every fiber of his being. "Yeah!" He grinned and took off at a run for the barn.

Chad watched him ride out and sent a prayer skyward that this time he would find the woman he loved.

The look on Roxy's face when he ran into the saloon convinced him she knew something concrete. She sat anxiously twisting her hands and jumped to her feet the moment she saw him.

"Oh, Steve!" she cried, and ran toward him, oblivious to the curious glances of the few patrons seated about. "I have some wonderful news about Jessie!" Tears flowed freely and she smiled through them.

"Where is she?" He grabbed Roxy's shoulders, catching her excitement.

"I don't know exactly, but you will."

He stepped back, confused. "What the hell does that mean?"

"Come on." She grabbed his arm and led him to a table, taking a bottle from the bar in passing. She pushed him into a chair and handed him the full, uncorked bottle. He shook his head no and she ordered him to take it. "Go on, you're gonna need it when I tell you what I have to say."

Steve took a mouthful, swallowed hard, and slammed the bottle on the table. "Get on with it, Roxy!"

She sat beside him and leaned her elbows on the table. "Last night—"

"Last night! You found out last night and waited until today to let me know?"

"Will you shut up and let me tell you!" Roxy snapped back. He impatiently shook his head and took another drink. "Last night, three trappers came in. They'd been to the rendezvous in July and headed back this way figuring on getting supplies and raising some hell before heading back into the mountains." Steve kept staring at the table, absorbing what she said. "One of them, a guy named Mike, picked out one of my girls and went off upstairs. To make a long story short, he spent the night. This morning his two friends came back to get him. While they waited one started talking about Mike and women. I overheard him saying something about a red-haired squaw that had stabbed him a few weeks back."

She paused and let Steve digest what she said. He sat stiffly and looked at her. His mind was whirling. "Did they say anything else?"

She nodded. "I started to talk to them, asking them about this squaw. One of them described her to me and, so help me, Steve, it sounded like our Jessie!"

"Did they mention the Crow or where this camp was?" he asked.

"I . . . I didn't think to ask." Roxy chewed at her lip. "I was so excited . . . I didn't ask!"

"It's okay, Roxy." He pushed back his chair and stood. "If it *is* Jess, I have a good idea where she is." He started to leave and Roxy ran after him, pulling him up short before the door.

"I just thought of something else. It may help. She used a different name, Steve. It was Valley Woman."

Roxy couldn't believe her eyes. Steve threw back his head and laughed riotously. "Steve?" She looked worried. "Steve, are you all right?"

Steve threw his arms around Roxy and spun her off the floor. "Roxy, you're an angel!" He laughed again and set a robust kiss upon her cheek. "Now I know it's my Jess!" He left with such urgency that when Roxy called out, asking how he knew, he didn't even hear her.

"The Crow," he said aloud as he neared Windy Creek. "She was with the Crow!" He started to laugh again, an alien sound from his lips all the time she was gone. He thought of her safely living with White Antelope's people and he smiled. He should have thought of it sooner himself. When she had disappeared the first time, she'd been with them. She would have felt safe returning to them again. When there had been no trace of her, he should have checked with White Antelope.

He rode through the gate to Windy Creek. He'd tell Jeff and Red and then ride home with his news. First thing in the morning he'd ride out to see his Indian friend. They would have returned from their summer camp and, if Jess planned anything, it would be from their winter lodgings. Smiling to himself, he knew that for the first time in months, he would sleep well that night.

Chapter 32

He felt like laughing aloud as he stood with White Antelope out on the open prairie. They were far enough from camp to avoid detection. He trailed a Crow brave out hunting earlier until he could send word to White Antelope to meet him. Toying with riding blatantly into camp, Steve decided to track Jess down in secret before making himself known.

"So, she's been with your people all this time?"

"Yes." White Antelope sat and chewed a blade of grass, thinking of the story his old friend had just relayed. "Your woman, she is different. She is brave and proud like my people yet she is still just a woman, stubborn and defiant. You should beat her, I think."

Steve lay down and put his hands beneath his head, looking skyward at the wispy white clouds playing tag against the blue. "It's the only thing I haven't tried," he mused.

"I think not." White Antelope looked across the blowing grasses at his friend's confused expression. "I know you, Hawk. I have shared my tent with you and you have shared your camp with me. When we were boys, did we not run away together to be great warriors? Did you not search with me for my brother when he was lost in the snowstorm, and grieve with me when we found him too late?"

Steve didn't know where the conversation was leading but he did remember. "Yes, we've shared many things, White Antelope." He sat up and bent one knee to lean on. "But what's that got to do with Jessie?"

"The one thing I know best about you, my friend, is that you do not know how to love. You have been alone too long."

"What do you suggest?" Steve hadn't denied the truth of White Antelope's statement.

"You will think of something." He rose quickly. "Do you wish to see her now?"

Steve joined him and pushed his hat firmly on his head. "As long as she doesn't see me."

Squatting down in the brush beside the river, Steve watched Jessie and several women come to get water and do some washing. He saw her place Matthew high on the bank and haul a basket to the water's edge, dumping the contents near a large flat rock.

A deep ache formed in his chest as he looked upon her, laughing and sharing chores with the other women. He wanted to rush to her side and hold her in his arms. He wanted to free her hair from its braids and revel in the luxury of it.

Matthew tumbled over and began to cry. Jessie ran to his side and laid in the grass beside him, rolling to her back and hauling him to sit on her stomach, playing away the tears. He heard the melodic tinkle of her laughter and saw tanned flesh tempting him as she romped with their son.

His desire was strong to make love to her but his desire to have her forever as his wife was stronger. He wanted to haul her to a church as soon as he could. A church! A wedding! Yes! It would work with some help from White Antelope.

He cautiously drew away and joined White Antelope at the base of the hill, well out of sight of the women. "My friend," he said, grinning broadly. "I have thought of something after all."

"Little Sparrow has told me you wish to leave us in four days." White Antelope sat stony-faced across from Jessie in the warm confines of his tent.

"Yes. I've decided I must go before the first snow." Jess was glad he didn't show any emotion. Right now she knew she would burst into tears if he did.

"You have done well here, Valley Woman." He nearly grinned at the surprise on her face at the compliment. "I have spoken with my other chiefs and we have decided to honor you. You will become one of the People."

Astonished that the proud Absaroke would so honor a lowly woman, Jess sat dumbfounded. "Me? A Crow?"

"Do not be surprised." He condescended to offer a small smile. "You have proven your worth as one of us."

With eyes tear-filled, she smiled. "Thank you, White Antelope. I . . . I'd be very honored and proud to be known as one of your people."

"Good. Then we will begin the ceremony." He clapped his hands and Little Sparrow entered. "You will go with Little Sparrow to your tent. There you will be left alone until morning. Son of Hawk will stay with us." Jess nodded her understanding. "Then you will be prepared and taken away from camp to a special place. You will stay there three days. When you return, you will be one of the People."

She had questions but she couldn't bring herself to ask them. Silently she got to her feet and followed a smiling Little Sparrow into the evening air. Her curiosity finally got the better of her. "What will I do alone for three days? I can't hunt and I don't know if I could bear the nights." She sighed.

"You have spent many nights alone." Little Sparrow giggled. "As for food, it will be provided along with all your other needs." They entered Jessie's tent and gathered Matthew's things.

"I'll miss him." Jess caressed the little blanket he used.

"It will only be for three days. He will do well with us and you do not have to worry. I will care for him as my own."

"I'm not worried." Jessie smiled. "I couldn't leave him in better hands."

They shared a hug. "Sleep well, Valley Woman," Little Sparrow said, her eyes twinkling as she left Jess alone for the night.

The sun was just making its appearance over the horizon when Little Sparrow and two other women entered the tent to wake Jess and begin their ritual. She was stripped down and allowed to bathe using large buckets of hot water. When she was dried and wrapped in a soft blanket, she was given the luxury of having her hair washed and brushed out to dry. There was little said but much shared laughter and shy glances until Jess sat alone once again before the fire with her morning fare.

Her interlude of silence was soon shattered as they returned, bearing clothing for her. A dress of soft white doeskin was shown to her and she squealed in delight.

"Oh! I've never seen anything so beautiful!" The dress was set with amber beads and long slender thongs hung down from each sleeve. Rather than having the usual lacing up the front, it had several ties from the waist to the chest, leaving a vee neckline to her breasts.

Leggings were not included with this dress, only soft moccasins that matched. Donning the lovely dress, Jess felt exquisite. It was slipped over her head and down her body to lay softly about her hips. There was a sensuous feel to the fabric as it laid against her bare skin and she let her hands slide down her sides with the feel of it beneath her fingers. A beaded band was tied about her forehead and she was ready.

"I feel like a bride," Jess joked, and drew a startled gasp from Little Sparrow that was quickly laughed off.

"You do look beautiful," she replied, then said something to the other women in their native tongue that made them all laugh together. Pulling up the tent flap, Little Sparrow smiled. "Come, Valley Woman. It is time."

Led to stand before White Antelope, Jess walked proudly and with exquisite grace. He nodded approval and she was taken to a great black steed. White Antelope himself lifted her to sit on its back before mounting his own great steed. Sitting as regally as a queen, Jessie rode behind him, taking only a moment to smile at Little Sparrow before setting off.

They rode for nearly an hour until Jess could make out a tent standing alone in the shelter of a hillside. Smoke rose from its peak and a large pile of wood sat beside it. It was midday and the breeze was already quite cool. Jess would welcome the warmth of her abode yet felt frightened by the solitude all about her. She didn't express her fears to White Antelope for she knew he wouldn't understand. She was being honored; could she do less than act honorably?

Without a word, White Antelope motioned for her to dismount. She slid from the back of the horse and saw him take her reins. Just before he rode off with both mounts, he smiled warmly for the first time since she had met him.

Jess watched him ride back to the camp. She stood until he was out of sight and continued to stare at the nothingness. The sound of the crackling fire drew her back to the trial set for her. Taking a deep breath of resignation, she turned to enter the tent.

There is a moment of blindness in going from light to dark and so it was for Jessica. She closed her eyes and gave them time to adjust. Testing them with the flutter of lashes, she faced the warmth of the fire and drew nearer to it, dropping to her knees and extending her hands to the heat.

She gazed into the dancing light and began to wonder why the elaborate preparations were necessary. She would be alone and would have to work hard to stay comfortable. The exquisite beauty of her attire would be wasted.

Some sound in the shadows made her spin about in fright. Like a vision conjured up during the lonely night, Steve lay on his side watching her. A soft exuberant laugh bubbled from deep in his throat at the disbelief on her face.

"You!" she cried out. "What are you doing here?"

Steve let his eyes travel over her like a visual caress. She was incapable of movement as she took in the magnificence of him. His bronzed chest and wide shoulders reflected the light. Buckskins rode low on his hips and hugged his thighs. Her eyes traveled upward to meet his and were locked in a seething declaration of passion.

Slowly, ever so slowly, he began to move, closer and closer until he was kneeling before her. The only sound was the deep cadence of their breathing. She could see his hand coming toward her but was as unable to stop him as she could stop the sun's path. His fingers touched her cheek in a gentle caress that set the world spinning. Each move seemed calculated to play on her desires and if she did not pull away soon, it would be too late.

Steve watched her half-parted lips quivering and saw the gentle flare of her nostrils as she was deeply affected by his touch. He sensed her need to flee and broke the spell with the magic words that would decide his fate.

"I love you, Jessie," he said in a throaty whisper.

She felt her body sway and tried to take in what he was saying. Her eyes glistened like wet emeralds and she could feel the heat of the fire at her side and the heat of him before her.

Steve didn't move as he waited for her to respond. His muscles screamed but he held them taut and watched her eyes dart about, unsure, afraid to believe her ears. "I love you," he said again, louder and stronger than before.

Her eyes met his and he saw a tear slide down her cheek. "I . . . you . . . you never said that before." She sighed. "I wanted you to. God, how I wanted you to, but . . ." She paused and he thought it might be too late.

"I've been a fool, Jessie, a terrible, thickheaded, stubborn fool! I thought that if I gave you my name and all that goes with it, that would be enough. I was afraid to love you, afraid it would make me weak, less of a man. So I selfishly convinced myself it just couldn't happen." His hands reached for her but he pulled back, clenching his fists at his side.

"You have every right to hate me. I've used you and forced you to come to me. I've played on your passions and manipulated events to have you." His eyes were pleading with her to understand him. "Jessie," he breathed. "Will you forgive a fool, a fool who loves you with all his heart?"

Silence engulfed them. He had bared his heart and left it open to her will. She could wrap it in the warmth of her love or tear it from his chest with her answer.

Jessie thought of how difficult it must be for him to admit he'd been wrong. The mighty Kincaid, the man with a heart of steel, knelt before her as a mortal, open to pain and heartache, sensitive for the first time in his life, humble and vulnerable. It was more than she could stand.

Her lips quivered with the magnitude of her love for this man, and she sat back on her heels to think. Oh, he was right! He *was* arrogant and possessive. He *was* selfish and stubborn. Yet weren't these traits part of what she'd fallen in love with? Could she have loved a lesser man? How could she tell him of her love and save his pride at the same time?

Watching him slump in what he thought was defeat, she knew. Adoration filled her eyes as he bent his head and his arms fell limply to his sides. Careful not to draw his attention too soon, Jess moved her hand to the ties of her dress, then softly called his name.

Raising his eyes, Steve couldn't believe the vision before him. Golden skin and auburn curls blended in an image of such beauty that his chest ached. As she undid each tie slowly, shrugged the velvety fabric from her shoulders and let it fall about her hips, the ache spread through his tensed body.

"Jessie," he whispered. "Ah, Jess!" he cried, lifting his arms to her. She moved into the shelter of them and he held her pressed to him so gently, almost afraid to move, afraid the warmth of her body next to his, the trembling arms that held him, would fade and drive him into a hell of his own making.

"I love you, Steve," she breathed against his chest. "I love you, Hawk." She slid her arms upward until they were free and laid her hands upon his face. Looking deeply into his eyes and touching his very soul, she sighed. "I love you."

Their lips touched and touched again. Each savoring the new reality of their love for one another. There was no urgency. They had a lifetime to live and love. They could go slowly, exploring and seeking out the very best each had to give because, at last, there would be a tomorrow.

Without breaking their kiss, Steve lowered her to the furs beside the fire. When she lay with her hair spread like living flame about her, he sat back and looked at her. The beaded band about her brow glistened in the reflective light like a halo, but no angel did he see. He saw a woman of flesh and blood who lay beside him. Her breasts rose and fell in anticipation of what was to come and he moaned as he lowered his lips to kiss each peak.

"I'll love you forever, Jessie," he sighed against them.

"Just love me now, my darling," she begged, and arched her back to press him closer.

No time before had the torture been so exquisite nor the passion so intensely experienced. Each touch, each kiss brought joy and greater heights to climb until their dampened bodies came together in rapture so intense the world ceased to exist.

The dying fire brought a chill and with it wakefulness. Without a word, they lay entwined and drifted into sleep, but now the elements dictated they rise and meet the needs of survival.

"I better get some wood," he mumbled against her temple, pressing tiny kisses there.

"Um." She snuggled closer. "I don't need a fire to keep warm." She wiggled her hip against him. "I have you."

"Any self-respecting squaw would have a roaring fire going and food cooking," he teased, and threw off the blankets he had drawn about them earlier.

"Oh!" she squealed, reaching for the cover he held just out of her grasp. "Oh! Don't! It's c-cold!"

His eyes began to caress her lovingly and his hands followed. The shivers of cold turned to ones of desire. With eyes half-closed, Jessie let her tongue slide slowly over her lips. The utterly sensual picture she evoked nearly drove him mad with renewed longing.

"If you keep looking like that—" His breathing grew more rapid. "—I guarantee we'll freeze or starve."

Just as he reached for her, she jumped to her feet. "You're right. I'll go get some wo—*oh!*" Before she could complete a step she found herself on her back with him astride her.

"Witch!" He grinned and kissed her neck. "Tease!" His lips moved to her breast. "Lover!" His body moved to cover hers. "Wife!" His breath caressed her ear as he moved between her thighs.

Jess suddenly tried to wiggle from his embrace. "Wife?" Had he gone mad? The grin across his face was sane enough, though somewhat tinged with more lust than amusement.

"Yes, wife. What do you think this shelter is?" He rolled to her side, robbing her of his warmth, and wrapped a fur about his shoulders.

"I'm becoming a member of the Crow people!" she retorted.

He looked like an ancient great chief as he sat and caressed her with his eyes. He began to chuckle, a deep resonant sound within the confines of the tent. "I suppose you could call it that." He seemed to be deep in thought as she drew a blanket about her chilled flesh. "Yes, indeed, it could be called that."

"What are you muttering about?" she demanded.

"Go get some wood." He leaned back and stretched out on the furs, unashamed of his nakedness.

Jess knew he would not tell her until she did as she was told. The wind had risen and with it the air chilled as Jess struggled with the fuel and her wrapping until safe inside the tent. She threw the wood on the embers and returned to Steve's side.

"What are you talking about?" she asked again.

Having closed his eyes, he lifted one to peek at her. "I am a Crow blood brother. This—" He gestured at their abode. "—is a Crow wedding hut. You, therefore, are now married to one of the Absaroke and hence, are one. White Antelope never lies, he just twisted the truth in this case."

Before she could think out his words, he grabbed her and pulled her across his chest. Holding her trapped in his arms, he looked up at her. "You are my wife, my love, according to the laws of this nation. When we leave, I'll take care of the laws of the territory." He grew serious for a moment. "You'll never be able to run from me again in either nation. You're mine until death do us—"

Her fingers silenced him. "Yes, my husband." She leaned to kiss the corner of his mouth. "Whatever you say, my darling." Her teeth nibbled at his lips. "I'm just an obedient wife who hears and obeys."

She could feel the laughter rumbling in his chest before she heard it. Clear, robust laughter, unfettered by fear, relieved of all doubts. His hand slid up her arm to sit about her throat, his thumbs tracing her jaw and playing with her chin.

"Ah, Jessie Kincaid," he said, smiling, "you are one special lady."

"I have to be," she replied flippantly. "I have to keep up with one very special man."

The laughter came from both of them and neither was aware of it turning from playful antics to passionate embraces until the fires were quenched once again.

As Steve held her in his arms, he spoke half to himself. "Thank God, I'll never have to spend another day without you."

Avon Romances—
the best in exceptional authors and unforgettable novels!

DEVIL'S MOON   Suzannah Davis
76127-0/$3.95 US/$4.95 Can

ROUGH AND TENDER   Selina MacPherson
76322-2/$3.95 US/$4.95 Can

CAPTIVE ROSE   Miriam Minger
76311-7/$3.95 US/$4.95 Can

RUGGED SPLENDOR   Robin Leigh
76318-4/$3.95 US/$4.95 Can

CHEROKEE NIGHTS   Genell Dellin
76014-2/$4.50 US/$5.50 Can

SCANDAL'S DARLING   Anne Caldwell
76110-6/$4.50 US/$5.50 Can

LAVENDER FLAME   Karen Stratford
76267-6/$4.50 US/$5.50 Can

FOOL FOR LOVE   DeLoras Scott
76342-7/$4.50 US/$5.50 Can

OUTLAW BRIDE   Katherine Compton
76411-3/$4.50 US/$5.50 Can

DEFIANT ANGEL   Stephanie Stevens
76449-0/$4.50 US/$5.50 Can

The WONDER of WOODIWISS

continues with the publication of
her newest novel in rack-size paperback—

SO WORTHY MY LOVE

☐ #76148-3
$5.95 U.S. ($6.95 Canada)

THE FLAME AND THE FLOWER ☐ #00525-5 $5.50 U.S. ($6.50 Canada)	**ASHES IN THE WIND** ☐ #76984-0 $5.50 U.S. ($6.50 Canada)
THE WOLF AND THE DOVE ☐ #00778-9 $5.50 U.S. ($6.50 Canada)	**A ROSE IN WINTER** ☐ #84400-1 $5.50 U.S. ($6.50 Canada)
SHANNA ☐ #38588-0 $5.50 U.S. ($6.50 Canada)	**COME LOVE A STRANGER** ☐ #89936-1 $5.50 U.S. ($6.50 Canada)

THE COMPLETE COLLECTION AVAILABLE FROM AVON BOOKS WHEREVER PAPERBACKS ARE SOLD

Buy these books at your local bookstore or use this coupon for ordering:

Mail to: Avon Books, Dept BP, Box 767, Rte 2, Dresden, TN 38225
Please send me the book(s) I have checked above.
☐ My check or money order—no cash or CODs please—for $_____ is enclosed
please add $1.00 to cover postage and handling for each book ordered to a maximum of
three dollars).
☐ Charge my VISA/MC Acct#_____ Exp Date_____
Phone No_____ I am ordering a minimum of two books (please add
postage and handling charge of $2.00 plus 50 cents per title after the first two books to a
maximum of six dollars). For faster service, call 1-800-762-0779. Residents of Tennessee,
please call 1-800-633-1607. Prices and numbers are subject to change without notice.
Please allow six to eight weeks for delivery.

Name_____

Address_____

City_____ State/Zip_____

WDW 0391

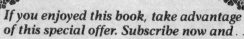